D0348875

To see the complete list of titles available from
Delores Fossen, please visit www.deloresfossen.com.

DELORES FOSSEN

WILD NIGHTS
IN
Texas

HQN

HQN

ISBN-13: 978-1-335-08129-2

Recycling programs for this product may not exist in your area.

Wild Nights in Texas
Copyright © 2020 by Delores Fossen

Hot Summer in Texas
Copyright © 2020 by Delores Fossen

This edition published by arrangement with Harlequin Books S.A.

For questions and comments about the quality of this book, please contact us at CustomerService@Harlequin.com.

HQN
22 Adelaide St. West, 40th Floor
Toronto, Ontario M5H 4E3, Canada
www.Harlequin.com

Printed in Spain

CONTENTS

WILD NIGHTS IN TEXAS

CHAPTER ONE

THE ROOSTER STARTED IT.

Sheriff Leyton Jameson saw it all go down from the window of his office at the Lone Star Ridge Police Department. Squawking and flapping its wings, the Rhode Island Red came out of the alley at lightning speed. A blur of feathers and spindly yellow legs, it arrowed off the sidewalk by the hardware store and into the street.

And right in front of the Jeep.

The driver swerved to avoid hitting the rooster. Barely. The brakes squealed before the Jeep slammed into the four-foot-high concrete cowboy boots sporting the name Hank's Hardware. Leyton heard the sound of crunching metal, followed by a spewing radiator.

Leyton set his coffee aside and hurried out of his office, through the now empty bullpen for the deputies, past reception and out onto Main Street. Even though he hadn't dawdled, he wasn't the first to make it to the wrecked Jeep. That honor belonged to Carter Bodell, the town's mortician, who was sporting a T-shirt that read I Will Bury You. Since that probably wasn't something an accident victim would want to see right off, Leyton muscled Carter aside and stepped in front of him.

Leyton immediately spotted the airbag. It had deployed like a tire-sized marshmallow and was now squished against the driver's face. A fog of the talcum powder that had come out with the airbag fluttered around the cab of the Jeep, falling onto the woman's black hair.

"Crap," the driver grumbled, batting away the bag and sending some of that powder right at Leyton. The motion caused the dozen or so thin silver bracelets she was wearing to jangle. Her earrings did some jangling, too. There was a trio of what appeared to be Goth fairies in her right earlobe.

He helped her with the batting, unhooking her seat belt, but Leyton stopped her when she tried to get out. "You need to stay put," he told her. "I'll call for an EMT to come and check you."

Leyton fired off a text to the dispatcher to get that started. Since the hospital was just a couple of blocks up the street, it wouldn't take them long to get there.

"Crap," she repeated, turning her head in his direction.

Their eyes met. Familiar dark blue eyes. And despite the fact the woman's face was covered in talc, the rest of her was familiar, too.

Hadley Dalton.

Leyton got the jolt he always did when he saw Hadley. Which wasn't very often. But it was sort of a gut-punch mixture of red-hot lust and cold, dark dread. The lust because, well, this crap-muttering woman would apparently always ring his manly bell. The dread was because there wasn't another woman on earth who could give him as much trouble as Hadley.

It'd been a while, years, since Leyton had seen Hadley, but he had heard that she'd come back for a visit about six weeks earlier. A short visit where their paths hadn't crossed. Considering how small Lone Star Ridge was, that likely meant she'd purposely avoided him. Judging from the scowl she gave him, she would have preferred for that avoidance to continue.

"It's Badly Hadley," Carter said, as if making an announcement to the entire town.

Hadley immediately shifted her scowl from Leyton to Carter. With good reason. *Badly Hadley* was the nickname Leyton knew she hated. She'd gotten dubbed with it when she and her two sisters were the stars of the reality show *Little Cowgirls*, which documented the triplets' lives. It was filmed right here in Lone Star Ridge, at her grandmother's ranch, and was on the air for a dozen years. A dozen years of TV viewers tuning in to see just how bad Badly Hadley could be.

Leyton knew for a fact that she could be very, very bad.

"Are you drunk?" Carter asked, because he, too, knew about the very, very bad. In a generic sort of way, that was. Unlike Leyton, whose knowledge of Hadley was a bit more…personal.

"No, I'm not drunk," she snarled. She blinked as if trying to focus and looked at Leyton. Her gaze slid from his face to the badge clipped to his belt. "I wrecked because I dodged a chicken."

"A rooster," Leyton corrected.

Though the rooster was now nowhere in sight. He made a mental note to find it so it didn't cause any other accidents. There were plenty of ranches and farms nearby that had poultry, but this was a first for one making its way into town.

Still scowling and groaning, Hadley turned in the seat and would have gotten out had Leyton not stopped her again. "Just wait until the EMTs get here."

"I'm fine," she insisted. "But I need to move this unicorn horn. It's poking my thigh."

Of all the things Leyton had thought she might say, that wasn't one of them. "Unicorn horn?" he questioned.

Hell. She probably had a concussion or was maybe in shock if she was hallucinating about something like that.

Hadley nodded as if she'd just explained everything to him, and she practically oozed off the seat. Leyton caught her in his arms. Good thing, too, because Hadley wobbled when she stood, and she looked down. Leyton followed her gaze, and that was when he saw that there was indeed a, well, unicorn horn.

It appeared to be a hat with a hard plastic horn jutting out from the rainbow-colored head. The horn was jammed and tangled into the laced-up side of Hadley's black jeans. She yanked it out, winced, and Leyton saw some blood. Not much, but it appeared to have broken the skin.

"It's something my grandmother wanted me to make," she said, her voice a little steadier now. "It was on the seat next to me when I wrecked."

Hadley was a costume designer in California, so that made sense. Well, sort of made sense. Her grandmother Em wasn't the most conventional person, but a unicorn hat seemed on the strange side even for her.

"You're bleeding," Carter blurted out the way a weatherman would warn of a tornado bearing down on him. There was volume, urgency and panic in his voice, and he hooked his arm around Hadley's waist.

Hadley gave Carter a look that could have frozen lava. "Carter Bodell, if you're going to shock me or have some kind of device on you to make farting noises, I'll knee you in the nuts," she snarled.

Unlike the unicorn horn, this particular comment hadn't come from left field. Carter was a prankster. One with the sense of humor of a third grader. He often had shocking or farting devices on him that went off when he shook hands with someone or slapped that person on the back.

"And if you try to feel me up again like you did in high school," Hadley added to the snarl, "I'll also knee you in the nuts."

Leyton wasn't sure if Carter had intended to do any feeling up, but that got the undertaker to back away from Hadley. She didn't give the same warning to Leyton, however, which was ironic, since he had indeed felt up Hadley many times. Not now, though.

Definitely not now.

Hopefully, not ever again. He needed an entanglement with Hadley about as much as he needed a unicorn horn in his thigh or a wreck-causing rooster on Main Street.

"Is she okay?" someone called out.

Ty Copperfield, the young, fresh-faced EMT, was running up the sidewalk toward them. Leyton knew him, of course. He knew everyone in town and vice versa, since Leyton had lived in Lone Star Ridge most of his life.

"I'm fine," Hadley grumbled, and she wiped some of the talc from her face.

With enough of the airbag powder gone, Leyton got a better look at her. No cuts or nicks as there sometimes were with an airbag deployment.

"Her leg's bleeding," Carter said, pointing in the direction of the wound.

"It's just a scratch," Hadley insisted, but that didn't stop Ty from stooping down and checking it for himself.

"You're right," Ty said a moment later. "Just a scratch, but you'll need to have it cleaned."

Ty waved a little penlight in front of her eyes and made a sound of approval. Then, as Leyton had done, he continued to check Hadley for other injuries. So did the "crowd" that was gathering on Main Street. But the crowd did it from a respectable distance.

Everyone who'd been in the shops and businesses was now outside, and the possibility of heatstroke from the sweltering July temps wouldn't stop them from milling around to find out what was happening. Leyton saw a lot of texting and calling going on, and soon it would be all over town that Hadley was back and had been involved in a wreck. There'd be embellishments to the gossip, no doubt. Gossip that might include him, since he still had an arm around Hadley.

Ty halted his once-over exam of Hadley and snagged her gaze. He grinned. "Hey! You're Badly Hadley. Man, I can't believe it's you. I used to see you on that TV show when I was a kid."

"Little Cowgirls," Carter supplied, as if being helpful. "Hadley used to be a star."

Talk about some ego slamming. *Used to be a star* was the same as saying a has-been, and Ty's *when I was a kid* remark sure hadn't helped. Hadley was just thirty-three, only a year younger than Leyton, but to the twenty-two-year-old Ty, she probably did seem oldish. Added to that, *Little Cowgirls* had been off the air for eighteen years now, so Ty had indeed been a kid when he'd watched the show.

"I need to go," Hadley muttered, and she stepped out of Leyton's grip so she could turn and look at the Jeep.

Hadley groaned, then cursed when her gaze skimmed over the airbag debris in the front seats, the bashed-in front end and the spewing radiator. The Jeep would have to be towed.

She certainly made an odd picture standing there in loose-fitting laced-up jeans, black tank top and bloodred flip-flops. Her long, straight hair was black—which he knew was dyed from her natural dark brown—and pulled back in a ponytail. Not fussy, but that only seemed to draw more attention to it. Just like the woman herself. Hadley might have been born and raised here, but she looked city. And very much out of place on a small-town Main Street where a rooster could cause a wreck.

"I need to go," she repeated, this time aiming her comment at Leyton. Ty resumed his exam and began checking Hadley's head. "I have to see Em."

It wasn't a surprise that she'd want to see her grandmother. Em had practically raised Hadley, her sisters and their brother since their own parents had been pretty much scum. But there was a high level of concern in Hadley's voice that made him think this was more than just a visit.

"Is Em okay?" Leyton asked. When Hadley didn't jump to answer, Leyton felt a knot form in his gut.

"I'm not sure," Hadley finally said.

And just like that, the knot tightened. Em had always been good to him. Unlike plenty of others in town. Em had never judged him, either, for being a "love child" instead of being born with the Jameson name.

Hadley batted away Ty, who was now examining her neck, and she grabbed her purse from the passenger seat of the Jeep. "Em called me late last night and insisted I come home," Hadley told Leyton.

She opened her mouth, no doubt to add to that explanation, but she must have realized she had Ty's and Carter's complete attention. The attention of the dozen or so other townsfolk, too.

"I'll call the rental company and report the accident," she continued, still gripping the unicorn hat in her left hand. "First, though, I need to see Em."

Leyton hesitated, nodded. He should probably insist

on taking her to the ER and getting her statement about the accident, but the gut knot won out. Those things could wait. "I'll drive you."

And just like that, their *uncomfortable* past washed over her expression. "I can walk."

Yeah, she could, since it was less than a half mile, but Leyton had no intention of letting her do that. "I'll drive you," he insisted, and he grabbed the large suitcase from the back seat of the Jeep.

Since he wasn't sure if she was steady on her feet, Leyton took hold of her arm and maneuvered Hadley and her suitcase around the crowd and across the street to the police station parking lot, where his cruiser was parked.

It occurred to him had this been her sisters, Sunny or McCall, more folks would have greeted her. There would have been more smiles, too, and "Welcome home!" would have been offered to the friendlier sisters. But Hadley always seemed to wear an implicit "back off" sign.

"I'll need to have the Jeep towed," Hadley muttered, glancing back over her shoulder at it before she got into the cruiser.

"I can help with that." He could also arrange for anything else in the Jeep to be brought out to her grandmother's ranch. For now, though, he wanted answers. So, he put her suitcase in the cruiser, got in and started the engine. "What do you think is wrong with Em?"

She shook her head, causing more of the talcum to fall and her ponytail to swish. "Like I said, she insisted I come. I asked her why, and she said she just had something important to tell me." Hadley cursed under her breath. "She also asked me to bring her the unicorn hat."

Leyton met Hadley's gaze before he pulled out of the parking lot. "Why the hat?"

Hadley made a frustrated sigh. "She said it was for a costume party at the preschool where she does story time. She sketched out a picture of what she wanted and asked me to make it for her. Apparently, she already has the actual costume but wanted the hat to finish off the look." *Look* went in air quotes.

Well, Em did do story time, but he couldn't imagine that the hat would be safe to have around kids. It did ease the gut knot some, however. Things couldn't be that bad for Em if she still planned on going to the preschool. Then again, maybe the hat was some kind of ploy. Exactly what kind of ploy, he didn't know, but it could have something to do with the rumors he'd heard that Hadley had recently been fired from her job. Maybe this was Em's way of giving Hadley busywork?

"I got stuck in a traffic jam in San Antonio," Hadley went on, "so I took out the unicorn cap from my luggage and did some work on it. Em wanted rhinestones added to the horn."

He heard the tension and worry in her voice and pushed for more info. "Do McCall and Sunny know if anything's wrong with Em?"

"No. I called them right away, and they said that Em seemed fine. McCall's in Dallas, closing down her office there, so I told her to stay put, that there was no need to worry."

He knew about McCall being in Dallas. Knew, too, that she was shutting down her counseling practice so she could move it to Lone Star Ridge. McCall was living at the ranch with Em, but that would change as well once she and her fiancé, Austin Jameson, got married. Since Austin was also his half brother, Leyton had stayed apprised of their plans.

"Sunny's on a book tour for the next couple of days," Hadley added. "I told her to stay put, too."

Again, Leyton knew about that. Sunny was an illustrator for a popular graphic novel series, *Slacker Quackers*, and she'd gone on a tour to promote the latest issue. In fact, he knew plenty about Sunny as well since she was engaged to another of his half brothers, Shaw.

"I hadn't texted Em my flight info because I didn't want her coming to the airport to pick me up," Hadley went on. "I didn't want her making that drive. So, I called her when I landed to tell her I was getting a rental car and would be here soon, but she didn't answer."

She took out her phone from her purse, and with the call on speaker, she tried again. The call went straight to voice mail. "Em hasn't answered any of my six calls or texts," Hadley added.

Hell. He hoped the woman hadn't fallen or something. Em was in her seventies, and while she seemed in good health, that didn't mean she hadn't had an accident.

Leyton pushed the accelerator, going well past the thirty-mph speed limit, and he pushed it even more when he took the turn on the road that led to the ranch.

Whenever he came here to Em's, he always got the same feeling. That time had somehow stopped. The house and the grounds hadn't changed since *Little Cowgirls* had been filmed here.

Maybe Hadley was also seeing that, because she dragged in a long breath, and he didn't think it was his imagination that she seemed even more unsteady than she had right after the wreck. Home usually held plenty of memories, and in Hadley's case, there were just as many bad as good ones here.

Hadley barreled out of his cruiser the moment Leyton

came to a stop, and he had to hurry to catch up with her. By the time he was on the porch, she already had the front door open—it was unlocked—and was rushing inside.

"Em?" she called out.

No answer.

"Em?" Hadley tried again.

Still nothing, but Leyton tried to tamp down any real concern. The ranch was a big place, and it was possible that Em was in the barn or outside in her garden.

Obviously, Hadley wasn't tamping down anything. Moving fast and leaving a trail of talcum in her wake, she raced through the maze of rooms and to the kitchen. Em wasn't there, either, so Hadley headed toward the woman's bedroom suite. And she stopped cold.

Because Leyton was behind her, it took a moment for him to see why she'd frozen. Another moment to figure out what was lying on the floor. Or rather what was *possibly* on the floor. It appeared to be a stretchy rainbow unicorn costume, and it was in the middle of the hall, as if someone had dropped it there.

Hadley picked up the costume, taking it with her into Em's room. Again, no sign of the woman, but her dresser drawers were wide open, and there were more clothes and shoes strewn around.

"Is this usual?" Leyton wanted to know, since this was the first time he'd been in this part of the house.

Hadley shook her head. "No. She's usually a neat freak." And still clutching the costume, she walked to the bed, her attention zooming in on something there.

A note.

"Is that Em's handwriting?" Leyton asked.

She nodded and picked it up. "'Hadley, I'm fine, but I had to go on a short trip to visit an old friend,'" she read aloud. "'Remember that secret box we buried when you were twelve?'"

"Box?" Leyton repeated, but he didn't wait for an answer. Looking over Hadley's shoulder, he read the last part of the note, his voice blending with Hadley's.

"'Well, it's time for you to dig it up,'" they read. "'Because there are some things about me that you need to know.'"

CHAPTER TWO

HADLEY REREAD HER grandmother's note several times, and she tried to steady herself with Em's *I'm fine*, but nothing about this felt anywhere near fine. Something was wrong.

"Do you know anything about this old friend she's visiting?" Leyton asked, and he sounded very much like the cop he was.

She shook her head. "I've never heard her mention any *old friends*." Hadley looked at Leyton. "You'd know as many of her friends as I would. Maybe more."

After all, Leyton had lived in Lone Star Ridge since he was a kid, when he moved in with his biological father, Marty Jameson, and his wife. Unlike Hadley, who'd left town when she turned eighteen, Leyton had stayed.

And he'd become the sheriff.

It didn't surprise her that he had gone the good-guy route, but the fact he'd done so well with that good-guy stuff, and without her, had always felt a little like salt in an old wound.

"What about this secret box?" Leyton pressed, tapping what Em had written.

Hadley drew in a long breath and took a quick mental trip down memory lane. "When I was a kid, I was feeling down about…something, and Em said we should make a time capsule of sorts. She wanted us to put things in the box that made me happy. Then anytime I needed to be cheered up, I could think about the box."

Hearing it all aloud, Hadley knew how silly it sounded. How caring, too. Em had loved her and had done this silly, caring thing to try to pull her out of a dark mood. It had worked. For a little while, anyway.

"I haven't thought of that box in years," Hadley admitted. But she certainly thought about it now. Thought about what she'd put in it, too, and she silently groaned.

"What's in the box that Em now wants you to know?" Leyton pressed.

Hadley tried to visualize everything that Em had added to the stash. "I don't have a clue. I remember she put in an old eight-track tape and a peach pit that she thought looked like Elvis."

She had to hand it to Leyton. He didn't give her a flat look or good belly laugh. That was because he knew that Em wasn't exactly conventional. But neither an eight track nor a peach pit explained the last line of that note.

Because there are some things about me that you need to know.

Well, unless there was something hidden among those items. That was possible, she supposed, but Hadley certainly hadn't picked up on any vibes that Em had been trying to hide anything.

"It's twenty-one years since that box went in the ground, and until now Em's never said a word about it." Hadley paused. "I have to dig up the box," she added, already heading out of Em's bedroom and toward the back door off the kitchen.

Of course, Leyton was right behind her, but he took out his phone and made a call. "Cait," he said to the person he'd called.

Cait Jameson, his half sister. Also his deputy sheriff.

"Ask around and see if anyone knows where Em is," Leyton told his sister. "She's not at her place, and the scene looks, well, disturbed."

Hadley couldn't hear Cait's response, but she figured the deputy would jump right on that. *Disturbed* was the right word. Something had gone on in Em's bedroom. There'd been clear signs of that frantic rush to either pack or find something. Maybe Em had done that.

Maybe someone else had.

But Hadley quickly pushed that last thought aside. It wouldn't help her to jump to a worst-case scenario even if the dread and worry were starting to pulse through her.

By the time they reached the barn, Leyton had finished his call, and he took the shovel from her after she plucked it from where it hung on the wall.

"Where's this box?" he asked, obviously planning on doing the digging himself.

Hadley didn't argue with him. The truth was she was still feeling a little light-headed. Maybe because of a combination of the wreck, all the stupid talcum powder she'd breathed in, the blistering heat and the fear that something had happened to her grandmother.

She led him to the large oak that still sported a swing, and then, with her back to the tree, Hadley started walking, pacing off the fifty steps that she and Em had taken twenty-one years ago.

It'd been much cooler that day. A drizzly March morning when her mother, Sunshine, had taken "Good Girl" McCall and "Funny" Sunny to the ice cream shop to film a scene for *Little Cowgirls*. Hadley had been grounded—again—so she hadn't been invited. She and Em had had the ranch to themselves that day.

A rarity.

Hadley had much preferred being at the ranch alone with Em to going somewhere with the cameraman and producer, who would record an ordinary outing and try to make it into something that would entertain viewers. That meant doing whatever it took to create an embarrassing or memorable situation.

On that specific outing, the writers had scripted that McCall drop her ice cream in her lap. Even if McCall hadn't gone along with it, Sunshine would have made sure it happened. Made sure there was drama and embellishment, too. Even though Hadley didn't know all the details about how things had played out, McCall had come home in tears that day.

There'd been lots of tears on lots of days, and her mother had been at the root of so many of them. So many. No happy mother-daughter relationships for Sunshine and the Little Cowgirls. Heck, not between Sunshine and Hadley's brother, Hayes, either. Hayes was just as jacked up as the rest of the Dalton sibling gene pool.

"You okay?" she heard Leyton ask.

Maybe he'd picked up on the fact that she was doing more than counting paces and was reliving a thing or two that shouldn't be relived. The past could be a mean, bitter bitch. So could her mother. That was the reason Hadley hadn't seen her in over a decade. It'd been longer than that for her father, who left after *Little Cowgirls* got canceled when Hadley was fifteen. Not only had he not returned, but he also hadn't bothered to contact any of his kids.

Hadley now thought of herself as a self-orphaned orphan. Still, the estrangement had its benefits. Along with not having to see or speak to her folks, she didn't have to worry about picking out Mother's and Father's Day cards.

Good thing, too, because it would have been pretty hard to find one that conveyed the sentiment of *You don't have a single parental bone in your entire bodies.*

"I was just thinking about greeting cards," she muttered.

Not exactly a lie, but Hadley didn't want to open a vein when she already had so much weighing on her mind. She needed to keep the emotional bloodletting to a minimum.

Hadley stopped at the fifty paces and glanced around, hoping this was the right spot. There'd been no trees or shrubs back then, her grandmother hadn't planted them yet, but there had been a large landscape boulder, and it was still there.

Next to it was a birdbath, and the base was a concrete statue of, well, *something.* A squat little creature with a winking eye and an extremely large butt. A *bare* butt, with dimpled cheeks. And its nose was missing. It'd been lopped off, maybe by design or Mother Nature.

"What is that thing?" Leyton asked, tipping his head to the noseless figure.

Hadley shook her head. "Your guess is as good as mine." Which applied to so many of Em's decorating choices.

"I think we buried it here," she said, pointing to the right of the birdbath. "It's a green metal fishing-tackle box."

Unlike twenty-one years ago, the ground wasn't soft today, but Leyton jammed the shovel into the grass and dirt in one strong, fluid motion. A reminder that he wasn't just a sheriff but that he also worked on his family's ranch. It was no doubt the reason he had all those muscles to flex and remind her that he was a well-built cowboy.

She watched as he hefted a shovel full of dirt and tossed it to the side before she went back in for another shovel.

"We didn't bury it deep," she added. "Maybe a foot down, so if you don't hit it soon—"

Hadley broke off when she heard the crack of metal against metal. She dropped to her knees for a better look. It was the tackle box, all right, but it was no longer green. It was now a rectangle of flaking rust. Leyton loosened it from the ground, and together they pulled it out.

She immediately went for the latch. It wasn't a lock, but the rust had fused it together, so Hadley couldn't open it. Leyton helped with that, too. He motioned for her to move back and struck the latch with the point of the shovel. It popped right open.

And they both groaned.

Because the white packing paper that Em had put on top of the contents was now a mess that resembled dirty clots of lard.

"The water leaked in," Leyton grumbled, causing Hadley's stomach to drop to her ankles. She hadn't been sure what they'd find in this box, but it'd been their best bet for figuring out what had happened to her grandmother. Well, if Em's note had been accurate.

Leyton put the shovel aside, took out his pocketknife and began to flick out the packing paper blobs. After he'd cleared the path, she saw the peach pit. It didn't look any more like Elvis now than it had way back then, but it was still intact. There was also a plastic sandwich bag that contained an index card with a handwritten recipe for Sweetie Pie, a chocolate pecan concoction.

Despite this situation, Hadley did indeed smile at the recipe. "It was my favorite. I wanted her to add it to the box."

Hadley took out the bag, flipping it over so she could see if Em had written anything on the back, but it was blank. No cryptic messages to decode anything that might be going on now.

Leyton took out the next sandwich bag. The water hadn't gotten to it, either, but the flower inside had definitely seen better days. It was dried and flat. He looked at her, his eyebrow lifted, to let her know he was waiting for an explanation. But Hadley didn't give him one.

"I don't remember what this is," she lied. She took the bag from him, put it behind her and reached for the next one.

But Leyton beat her to that, too, and, like the recipe, it was in pristine condition in the baggie. Not a drop of moisture had gotten on the picture.

Of Leyton.

It was a photo Hadley had taken of him by the corral when he'd come over to do some work for Em. He wasn't looking directly into the camera, but Hadley had still managed to catch him grinning in that cocky way that only a thirteen-year-old boy could grin.

Once again, Leyton's eyebrow came up, and once again, Hadley didn't want to explain it. She just snatched it from him, dropped it with the dried flower and pulled out the eight track. The water had definitely done some damage here, but the label was still easy enough to make out. It caused Leyton to groan.

"My father," Leyton grumbled in a "toenail fungus" tone.

It was indeed music from his father, Marty Jameson, who'd once been a country-music star. Well, sort of a star, anyway. He'd had some hits and successful tours. He'd also abandoned his family and slept around enough to produce many offspring. Three from his marriage, and many, many others born on the wrong side of the sheets. Leyton was one of those.

"Em loves his music," Hadley commented while she

looked on the back of the eight track and then down into what she could see of the actual tape. Nothing there, either. "Maybe one of the songs means something. Or the album title, *Running Ragged*. Any idea if your dad wrote a song for Em?"

"Not that I know of," Leyton said almost idly.

That was because, like hers, his attention was no longer on the eight track but on the envelope that had been beneath it. It, too, was in a bag, but it wasn't completely dry. The moisture had smeared the writing on the front, but she still had no trouble reading it.

For Hadley.

"I don't remember her putting this in there," Hadley said, taking it out. "But I left the box with Em when I went to the barn to get a shovel. Em could have slipped it in there then."

Hadley's hands were a little unsteady when she opened it and pulled out the single page of paper inside. Like the writing on the envelope, the ink was smeared here, too. In fact, there were huge ink blotches over most of the paper. It was anyone's guess as to what the first paragraphs said, but Hadley could make out the line below it.

"I had a life before here," Em had written. "I used to be somebody else."

Hadley's mind did a little mental stutter, and she read it again. And again.

"Somebody else?" Leyton asked. Obviously, he was also having a hard time figuring out what it meant.

Hadley continued to study the letter. Or rather the non-smudged parts she could make out, but she could only get a word here and there. *Love. Safe. Sorry.* She finally looked at Leyton to see if he had gotten more of it than she had, but he just shook his head.

"Maybe Em had a different name before she moved here," Leyton suggested.

She thought about that a moment. "It's possible, I guess." And it frustrated her to realize that she knew so little about a woman she loved. "Em moved here from East Texas after she met and married my grandfather. This was his family's ranch."

"And what about her family?" Leyton pressed.

Hadley tried to shuffle through the memories she had of Em, but she didn't come up with much. "She didn't really talk about her past, but I remember her saying her folks died when she was very young. I never met any of her relatives."

The sound of a car engine got their attention, and Hadley lifted her head to see the SUV pull to a stop in front of the house. Leyton's sister Cait got out. Like Leyton, she had a badge clipped to her belt, and she made a beeline toward them.

"Please tell me that's not where Em buried the dead skunk she found on the road when we were kids," Cait remarked.

"No," Hadley assured her. But she remembered the incident. Despite the horrible stench, Em had indeed buried the critter in a Dick's Sporting Goods shoebox.

"Thank God." Cait went to her and pulled her into a hug. "Heard you had a run-in with Rosco the rooster. You okay?"

Hadley nodded and tried not to go stiff from the hug, but she didn't quite manage it. It wasn't that she didn't like Cait; she did, but it always felt weird to be welcomed in a place where Badly Hadley had done so many unwelcoming things.

"Rosco?" Leyton asked, standing.

Cait let go of Hadley and turned back to her brother.

"Yep. It belongs to Delbert Watley. He'd brought it into town with him to do errands, and it jumped out of his truck window when he was parked behind the hardware store. I gave him a warning and told him if he didn't want to leave Rosco alone, then he should look into getting a rooster sitter."

Propping her hands on her hips, Cait tipped her head to the metal box. "I'm guessing that has something to do with Em…and with you?" she added to Leyton when she saw his picture in the plastic bag. Cait frowned. "And our worthless excuse for a father."

Hadley quickly scooped up the plastic bags and the eight track. No way did she want to explain Leyton's picture to his sister. Or to Leyton.

"This was a memory box that Em and Hadley buried," Leyton explained. "Any news about Em?"

"Maybe," Cait answered. "Late yesterday afternoon, Howie Hargrove and Hildie Stoddermeyer saw a black car with Louisiana plates. They think Em was in the passenger seat."

Howie was the mayor and Hildie owned the diner, so they were reliable when it came to this sort of thing. Still, Hadley had to shake her head. "I don't know of any family or friends that Em has in Louisiana."

And that caused Hadley's worry to soar.

Maybe Em had been kidnapped.

"Did Em look scared?" Hadley blurted out.

Cait shook her head. "Nope, but Howie and Hildie only got quick looks. The car was heading toward the interstate. Any idea where she'd be going?"

Hadley looked down at the items from the tackle box. Em had said there'd be answers in these things, and maybe there was. Maybe in the smeared portions of the letter. Or in some portion of the eight track. Since it'd been one of Em's favorites, it didn't feel right to toss the eight track to the ground and stomp on it so the plastic would crack and she could see inside. It might come to that, however.

"No idea," Hadley told Cait. "But I need to take a better look at these things. A better look at her room, too."

Cait and Leyton started walking with her when she headed toward the house. "Keep asking around town," Leyton instructed his sister. "Press to see if anyone remembers any of the numbers on the license plate of that black car."

"Will do," Cait said. "You want me to do something about the wrecked Jeep? I can go ahead and call for a tow truck."

Hadley hadn't forgotten about the Jeep, but it wasn't a high priority right now. "Leyton said he'd take care of that. But please ask around about Em."

Cait repeated her *Will do*, and she gave Hadley's hand a quick squeeze before she peeled off to go to her SUV.

With Leyton right behind her, Hadley carried the items from the tackle box inside and spread them out on the kitchen counter. She zoomed right in on the smeared letter, trying to make out the words. Beside her, Leyton appeared to be doing the same thing.

I had a life before here. I used to be somebody else.

Those were still the only clear sentences, so she moved on to the eight track, taking out a butter knife so she could pry open the plastic case.

"Why'd you put my picture in that box?" Leyton asked.

Hadley's hand slipped, and she almost stabbed herself with the knife. Huffing, Leyton took both it and the eight track from her. "Why?" he repeated.

"Because I was twelve." When she'd still believed that she could have something good.

Or rather *someone* good.

Someone with a hot face to go along with the goodness. And the hot face had been pretty important to her back then. All that dark brown hair and smoky gray eyes. Even that cocky grin had been on her list of reasons to lust after him. The DNA gods had sure been generous when it came to the Jameson brothers, and Leyton had gotten more than his fair share of hotness.

Once, they'd come very close to being lovers. A lifetime ago, when she was fifteen and he sixteen. Then teenage life as she'd known it had come to an end when one of their make-out sessions was secretly filmed by the camera crew. She and Leyton had been clothed, but there was full-body fondling with lots of tongue kissing. And sounds. Moans and grunts of pleasure. Whispered wants.

Hickeys.

Things that teenagers definitely hadn't wanted a camera to record.

Well, not most teenagers, anyway. She and Leyton hadn't been into the whole "let's get stupid and film ourselves so we can watch" thing.

All in all, the recording wasn't as revealing as it could have been. Other times when they'd made out, Leyton's hand had made it into her pants. And vice versa. On this particular night they could thank pollen and perhaps hay for alerting them before that happened. The cameraman's allergies had gotten the best of him, and the loud sneeze caused her and Leyton to fly apart and notice the camera aimed at them.

Hadley had begged her mother and the producer not to air it. But they did anyway. And when Leyton found out that it was all going to be on TV, he broke up with her. She couldn't blame him, not then, not now. As Marty Jameson's illegitimate son, Leyton always had to walk a line. The footage made him a "like father, like son" joke around town.

She put all of that aside to focus on the present. Specifically focus on the questioning look that Leyton was giving her. He was obviously waiting for her to explain the *Because I was twelve*, but that wasn't going to happen.

Thankfully, she got a change of subject when Leyton popped open the eight track. She saw the spool of tape with the recorded music and a little plastic wheel to feed the tape through the playing surface. What she didn't see was a note or message from Em.

"Anything about this that'll help us?" Leyton asked, tapping the pressed flower in the plastic bag. "Why is it in there?"

Because I was twelve would be the truthful answer, but like the picture, it would require too much explaining. Hadley just settled for shaking her head, and she started back toward Em's bedroom.

She felt another gut punch when she got a second look at the disorder there. Before today, Hadley couldn't remember ever seeing anything out of place in here, and it only confirmed that something was indeed wrong.

"This might sound a little like a Hardy Boys mystery, but maybe there's some kind of secret code in the recipe," Leyton said from the doorway. He had the baggie with the recipe card and was studying it.

Since that was as good a theory as any, Hadley went to him to take it and examine it again. While she did that, Leyton began to look around the room.

The ingredients for the recipe all looked legit. So did

the baking instructions. However, Hadley found herself trying to analyze each word, even the little smiley face that Em had put at the bottom of the index card. But Hadley doubted that meant anything other than Em was happy when she doodled it. Any real clues had to be in the letter.

"Can a crime lab analyze the letter?" she asked.

"Since there's no evidence of a crime, no. But I know of some private labs that can do it."

She glanced up at him to say they should get right on that, but Hadley saw what he was holding. Or rather what he was reading. It was a trashy tabloid, *Tattle Tale*, and it had her picture on the cover with the headline Badly Hadley Strikes Again.

"Where'd you find that?" she blurted out.

"On the nightstand next to Em's bed. It was open to the story about tit-gate," he said, skimming the page.

Considering that Leyton didn't hesitate over the stupid tit-gate headline, that meant he likely knew all about the wardrobe malfunction of a costume that Hadley had designed for an aging pop-star legend, Myla Livingston. Myla hadn't reacted well to the incident, which was a serious understatement, and then she'd done her best to smear Hadley's business. It turned out that Myla's "best" was plenty good enough, because Hadley had been fired from her contracts.

All of them.

And other than a very low budget movie that would never see any real distribution, she didn't have any future prospects of work. As much as that stung, and it stung bad, Hadley had to push that bad down deep inside her and focus on figuring out what was going on with her grandmother.

Leyton flipped through the tabloid and came to a page

where the top corner had been folded down. Hadley went to him, hoping that maybe Em had written something on the page. But no. It was just an ad of a hot guy in snug boxer briefs that framed his superior junk.

"I don't think that's a clue to her whereabouts," Leyton commented.

Hadley made a sound of agreement and kept looking, not at the hot guy's junk, but around the rest of the room. There was a notepad on the nightstand, and Em had written *Waterstone Productions* with a phone number.

Her stomach sank a little.

"'Waterstone Productions'?" Leyton read aloud when he looked over her shoulder. "That's the company that wants to do a reunion special for *Little Cowgirls.*"

"You know about that?" Hadley asked.

"Em and Sunny mentioned it. Apparently, some guy's been calling them and trying to convince them to do it. Sunny and McCall aren't interested."

Neither was Hadley. In fact, she had no intention of going down that road again. Especially when she had to find out what had happened to Em.

Considering the best way to approach this, she took out her phone and composed a text.

I've been in a car accident.

Hadley showed the text to Leyton before she sent it to Em. And Hadley waited, already second-guessing herself. She didn't want Em to worry about her, but she didn't want her own worry to continue, either.

Even though she'd been hoping for a text response, the sound of her phone ringing was even better. She nearly pulled a muscle hitting the answer button when she saw

Em's name on the screen. The relief washed over her. But so did the questions.

"Are you all right?" Em blurted out at the same moment Hadley asked her the same.

"I'm fine," Hadley assured her. "It was little more than a fender bender." Okay, that was a lie, but she hadn't been hurt. "Where are you?"

"I'm fine, too," Em said, even though that didn't answer Hadley's question. "Did you dig up the box?"

"I did. Where are you—"

"Did you read the letter and look at the eight track?" Em interrupted.

Hadley gave a frustrated huff. She didn't want to talk about this. She wanted to know where her grandmother was and why she'd left. "The letter has a lot of water damage, so I couldn't make out what it said. What did you mean that you had another life?"

"I mean I used to be someone else. But that's not important right now," Em continued, rolling right over Hadley's repeated *Where are you?* "I just need a little time to myself. Time to work out a few things. But I promise I'm fine and that I'll be back home soon. You're sure you looked at the eight track?" Em added.

Leyton added his own frustrated huff to the conversation. "Em, where are you?" he pressed.

"Leyton. Oh, good. You're there with Hadley. I'd hoped you would be. Make sure she doesn't worry too much."

"I am worried too much!" Hadley snapped. "Why'd you leave? What's going on? Where are you?"

"I'll be able to tell you that soon. But for now, please keep an eye on the house until I get back. Oh, and you might want to keep your distance from Sunny's pet duck,

Slackers. She left him there when she went on her trip, and he's been in a sour mood. His food's in the barn."

Hadley huffed loud enough to drain every ounce of breath from her body. She didn't want to talk about a sour-mood duck.

"Where are you? When are you coming back?" Leyton's demands were more like the interrogation of a suspect.

But he was talking to the air, because Em had already hung up.

CHAPTER THREE

LEYTON FIGURED THAT most small-town lawmen dealt with a strange variety of things. Like the accident-causing rooster from the day before. Or a senior citizen taking a mysterious trip and leaving equally mysterious clues in an old eight track. But he was betting what he saw now was a rare occurrence indeed.

The teenage couple was in a truck on what had been dubbed Prego Trail. And it hadn't been named for the spaghetti sauce—it was a make-out place where girls occasionally got knocked up. It was possible that was what had been about to happen today, but there'd clearly been an *interruption*. Leyton had to take care of that interruption and get back to looking for Em.

"Sheriff Jameson," the red-faced boy said when Leyton approached the truck. Or that was what he attempted to say. It came out as a garbled mess. He was Zach Rodriguez, the sixteen-year-old son of the couple who owned and operated the town's gas station.

Zach was shirtless, his neck and some portions of his sweaty chest covered with hickeys. Sixteen-year-old Alyssa Benton, the principal's daughter, was shirtless, too, but thankfully still had on her bra. She was straddling him, her knees levering her up on the seat and her stomach level with Zach's mouth.

"It's stuck," Alyssa said, her voice quivering as much as her bottom lip.

If Leyton had just walked up on this scene without any other info, he would have come to the wrong conclusion about exactly what was "stuck." This wasn't a case of locked male and female parts, however. According to what Alyssa had said when she called Leyton about ten minutes earlier, her navel ring had somehow gotten tangled with Zach's braces.

Leyton looked in the cab of the truck to assess the situation. Alyssa winced and whimpered when Leyton tried to maneuver her back a little so he could see better. She was obviously in pain, but there wasn't any blood on her. But Zach's lip and mouth were swollen and bleeding.

It took a few more maneuverings, but Leyton eventually saw what had gotten tangled. Ironically, it was a notch on a little silver angel wing that was now hooked through one of Zach's front braces.

"The screw's stuck, too," Alyssa said, and while it was spoken clearly enough, it still took Leyton a moment to realize she was talking about the little silver ball that held the navel ring in place.

Leyton gave it a little jiggle to try to dislodge it, but when that didn't work and when Alyssa winced again and groaned, Leyton went back to his truck. "Dun eave us," Zach protested.

"I'm not leaving you," Leyton replied, deciphering what the boy had said.

Leyton rummaged through his toolbox to figure out what he could use. He could try spritzing the screw ball with some WD-40, but he wasn't sure that'd be safe if the oil went in Zach's bleeding mouth. He chose a wire cutter instead, grabbed some tissues from the glove compartment and returned to the teens.

Apparently, the cutter looked scary enough for both of them to make sounds of terror and squeeze their eyes shut. Zach started mumbling a prayer. Or maybe he was cursing.

With one careful snip, Leyton clipped off the angel from the wire that held it, and the teens were freed. But they weren't out of the woods yet. Now Zach had a silver angel dangling from his teeth. Leyton handed the boy a tissue so he could take care of the blood. It didn't look like a bad cut, but Zach might have to endure a little more discomfort when he dislodged the angel. A task that Leyton was going to leave to Zach to handle.

"I'm guessing neither of you wants me to take you to the hospital?" Leyton asked. "Or maybe the dentist?"

"God, no," Alyssa said. "My folks would find out. Everyone would." Zach possibly said something similar, but again it was hard to tell with the tissue pressed to his mouth.

Leyton decided they could handle things from here, so he turned to leave. But he'd barely made it back to his own truck when he saw his brother Austin coming through a tree line toward him. This was Austin's land, the trail cutting through his horse ranch, but Leyton still hadn't expected to see him.

"The twins aren't with you, are they?" Leyton immediately called out. He definitely didn't want his three-year-old nieces to see half-naked teens.

Austin shook his head and walked toward Leyton. It wasn't exactly like looking in a mirror when he looked at his half brother, but it was close. Both of them had gotten a good dousing in Marty Jameson's gene pool. Same dark brown hair, same gray eyes, same lanky build.

Thankfully, what he, Austin and Shaw hadn't inherited was Marty's penchant for creating offspring with his groupies and then being a shitty parent. Leyton didn't have kids, wasn't even sure he wanted them, but Austin was a good dad, and he'd done a damn good job of raising his twin girls, Avery and Gracie, after losing his wife to cancer.

"The girls are at preschool," Austin explained once he and Leyton were standing face-to-face. "I was out checking some fences, and I thought I heard the sound of an engine, so I walked over to see who it was." He tipped his head to Zach's truck. "Trouble?"

"More like a cautionary tale about body piercings." And Leyton left it at that. "I don't guess you or McCall have heard from Em yet?" But he already knew the answer. If Austin had heard anything, he would have let him know ASAP.

Austin gave a weary sigh, shook his head again, and watched as Zach backed out of the trail and headed toward the road. "But McCall should be back here in the next hour or so. She wants to help find Em."

Yeah, a lot of people did, including Sunny, who was also heading back to town today. Leyton wasn't sure what they could do that he and Hadley, Cait, and the rest of the town weren't already doing, but it would probably help Hadley to have her sisters with her.

It had bothered Leyton to leave Hadley alone in the house overnight, even though that was what she'd insisted she wanted. The place was safe enough. Heck, so was the entire town. Still, it'd caused him a restless night.

"You think Em had some kind of mental breakdown?" Austin asked. "Or maybe a very late midlife crisis?"

"I just don't know." But it was one of the many questions

Leyton had asked himself. That and wondering about the possibility of Em being pressured or even forced to leave.

Yeah, she had assured Hadley that she was fine when they'd spoken, but Leyton wouldn't believe it until he saw the woman with his own eyes. And got some answers to explain what the heck was going on.

"We don't have anything else on the black car," Leyton added. "No one remembers the license plate number."

Austin sighed again. "I've been telling McCall not to get too worried, but I know she is. She's worried about Hadley, too. Things haven't been so great for her lately."

Leyton thought about the tit-gate tabloid, and if it was accurate, Hadley had been blackballed. Of course, he wasn't sure the smut rag *Tattle Tale* was the best source for accurate information.

He checked the time and realized it'd been a couple of hours since he'd texted or called Hadley, and while that wasn't a long stretch, it wouldn't hurt for him to go over to Em's and check on her. He was about to tell Austin goodbye and head to his truck, but he stopped.

"Do you have any idea why Hadley would have had a dried flower?" Leyton asked, and judging from Austin's blank look, he knew he needed to give him a bit more info. "It was in a memory box that she and Em buried when Hadley was twelve. I just wondered if you knew if someone had given it to her."

Leyton cursed when he heard himself. Shit. He sounded jealous. Or like an idiot. The flower wasn't important. The only things that would help them figure out what was going on with Em were the items that Em herself had put in that box. Not the damn flower.

And not the picture of him.

Yet it was the flower and the blasted picture that had

been circling and circling in his head. Stirring old memories. Bringing up new questions. Questions and memories he didn't want, but it was hard to push aside those kinds of thoughts about Hadley. Probably because of all the making out that'd gone on between them. It was even harder because Leyton had done some soul baring when they'd been together back then. Even with all of that, though, he'd still thought their relationship hadn't meant that much to her.

But now he had to wonder.

Austin's mouth quirked a little as if he might smile. "Hadley" was all he said, but that was plenty enough. It was like a knowing nudge with an elbow and a brotherly ribbing rolled into one.

Leyton gave Austin a brotherly response in return by saying a single word of really bad profanity before he headed toward his truck. He didn't want anyone, including members of his family, talking to or nudging him about the old heat between him and Hadley.

Maybe if everybody stayed quiet about it, then the old heat would quit pestering him, too.

He drove straight to Em's and was a little relieved when the only vehicle he saw was Em's old truck parked by the house—right where the woman had likely left it. There were a lot of caring but nosy people in town, and he'd thought that maybe Hadley would be overwhelmed by visitors wanting to help. Or those just wanting some potentially juicy gossip. Then again, most still thought of her as Badly Hadley, so maybe folks were lending their help from a distance. He knew for a fact that people were making calls to see if they could find Em.

"I'm up here," he heard Hadley call out. "The door's unlocked."

Leyton looked up and spotted her in the small attic

window, but she almost immediately ducked out of sight. He took her greeting as an invitation and went inside. Because he was a cop, he automatically glanced around, but he didn't see anything out of place as he made his way up the stairs.

He knew that access to the attic was through the closet stairs in Hayes's old room. Once, he and Hayes had been friends. Well, *friendly*, anyway. But Hayes had left town when he was barely eighteen and moved to Hollywood, where he'd become a TV star on a show about a motorcycle gang.

After he made it to the top of the attic stairs, it took a moment for Leyton to pick through the clutter and the dim light and spot Hadley, who was sitting on the floor. She was wearing jeans again but not lace-ups this time, and her baggy top was a dull gray.

The attic window was still open, which explained why she'd heard him drive up. The hot, humid breeze was sliding through the narrow opening, and even though Hadley had turned on the ceiling fan, the attic was sweltering and smelled of dust, old paper and…well, Hadley. She didn't seem to be wearing perfume, but he thought what he was smelling was a combination of her soap and her shampoo. Her hair was still damp, and he didn't believe it was from the sweat but rather a recent shower.

She didn't have on the heavy makeup she usually wore— like a camouflage, to Leyton's way of thinking—and not a jewelry store of bracelets, neck chains and earrings, either, which would clang and jingle, drawing attention to them rather than to her. Today, Hadley was wearing just one pair of earrings. They were silver snakes that looked ready to strike, but still it was minimal and conservative for Hadley.

"This is the box Em used to store her things," she said,

tipping her head to the large cardboard box beside her. It did indeed have Em's name written on it in bold black Magic Marker.

Leyton went closer and glanced into the box, where he saw a mishmash of stuff, including some eight tracks and a stuffed gray cat that had seen much better days.

"Did you find anything?" he asked, shifting his attention to the photo album Hadley was thumbing through. There was another stack of albums next to her on the floor.

"Not really. Well, maybe," she amended.

When Hadley looked up at him, she seemed to do a double take. He heard the slightest hitch of her breath, saw just a split-second tremble of her mouth before she dropped her attention back to the album.

"Maybe?" he questioned.

"Nothing in the pictures so far," Hadley explained. "But these were in there." She lifted a gallon-sized plastic bag filled with cheap-looking bead necklaces. "They're Mardi Gras beads and doubloons," she added. "One of them has a date, and it's from nearly sixty years ago, when Em would have been about eighteen."

Leyton got the connection right off. "And the black car had Louisiana plates. Any pictures of Em in New Orleans?" Though he wasn't sure how that would help. Heck, they weren't even sure if Em's leaving was linked to anything specific in her past.

Hadley shook her head, sending more of her shampoo scent his way. "No, but McCall and I were talking. Em told her that she'd once been involved with a man in the mob. I'm not even sure if it's true, but with the Louisiana plates and Mardi Gras beads…" She stopped, waving that off. "I know, I'm grasping at straws."

Leyton shrugged and sank down beside her. "We'll be

grasping at straws with anything we find unless we get an explanation straight from Em. I've texted and tried to call her several times, but she might call you back if you text her again."

Hadley picked up her phone, which was on top of the photo albums, and showed him the string of texts she'd already sent Em. I'm really worried and need to talk to you was the first one sent shortly after Leyton had left the day before.

No response.

Just call me and tell me you're okay was Hadley's next text.

Em had responded to that one with a thumbs-up emoji.

My neck is sore from the car accident, Hadley had texted next. What meds should I take?

"I know," Hadley muttered. "I was reaching."

Yeah, and Em apparently hadn't fallen for it, because she responded with a thumbs-down emoji.

Leyton moved on to the next text Hadley had sent. I'm thinking about getting married and need to talk to you.

"I was really reaching," she grumbled.

Apparently, Em had figured that out, too, because her emoji response was a pile of poop.

"Well, at least she's kept her sense of humor." He picked up the album on top of the pile and began to thumb through it. The shots were all of the triplets and Hayes when they were little.

"BLC," Hadley provided when she saw what he was looking at. "Before *Little Cowgirls*. The ones below it are photos from during and a few from after. I haven't found any of Em before she married my grandfather and moved to Lone Star Ridge."

Leyton went through a mental inventory of the framed

photos he'd seen over the years around the house. None of those were of a young Em, either.

"A friend at a crime lab is running the letter for me," Leyton said. "He might have something for us by tomorrow."

Hadley's head whipped up, and he could see her practically latching on to the hope that there'd be something in it. Leyton figured there was some kind of explanation, but he wasn't sure it would soothe that worry in Hadley's eyes.

He was looking into those eyes right now, and maybe it was being so close to her and that heady scent, but the question just tumbled out of his mouth.

"Did I hurt you when I broke up with you?" he asked.

She blinked, clearly surprised. "No," she snapped, as if both amazed and disgusted that he would think that. She paused. "No," Hadley repeated. This time it sounded as if she was trying to convince herself.

Leyton kept his eyes connected with hers.

"No," she said for a third time, and this was more a sigh. "It was what I expected you to do."

Which, of course, still didn't answer his question. Em apparently wasn't the only one who could dodge and deflect.

Hadley got to her feet, pushed her hair from her face and looked at everything but him. "Can you help me carry this box downstairs? It'd be easier to go through it if we weren't risking dehydration and heatstroke."

Leyton supposed the smart thing to do would be just to agree and not push to get to the bottom of how Hadley had felt eighteen years ago. What did it matter, anyway?

Because it did—that was why.

"If I hurt you, I'm sorry," he said.

She made a dismissive sound and began to put the albums and beads back into the box. "We were kids. What we had didn't mean anything."

A punch to the gut would have hurt less than that comeback. And Hadley no doubt knew that. He could practically see her putting up those barriers again, and he wasn't having it.

"Bullshit," he spit out. "We were friends. We were close. Hell, I knew you used to sneak off and read those wholesome books that the producers left out as props for Mc-Call."

The barriers dropped, and for a second he got a glimpse of how stunned she was that he had known about that. Hadley probably thought she'd hidden her tracks well, and she had. But he'd followed her a couple of times to the barn and saw what she was doing.

"Little House on the Prairie," he reminded her. *"Pride and Prejudice."*

Her eyes narrowed. "And you and Hayes used to read *Playboy*." *Read* went in air quotes. "Is there a point to this?"

"Yeah." Though Leyton wasn't sure exactly what that point was or why he was poking at Hadley like this. "You put my picture in that tackle box."

"Because I was twelve," she snarled.

"Because we were close," he argued. "And I hurt you because I was embarrassed that the gossips would say I was like my father."

Apparently, that wasn't a revelation to Hadley, because she made a *duh* sound. Then she sighed, paused, sighed again. "Look, Leyton, I don't have any ill feelings about you." She patted his arm. "You're a good guy."

Well, shit. That sounded like a big-ass put-down. Or else she was placating him so he'd shut up.

"Let's just get this box downstairs," she insisted. "And then we can look through it for anything that'll help us with Em."

This time, Leyton kept his mouth shut, but he was figuring on that being a temporary truce. Yeah. This wasn't the end of the conversation. Even if it should be.

Setting his old baggage aside, he helped Hadley put the rest of the items back into the box. When they were done, she set her phone on top of the stuff.

"It doesn't fit in my pocket," she grumbled when he just raised an eyebrow.

It was indeed a big phone, and she obviously thought she was going to need both hands for this particular chore. Leyton didn't intend for that to happen, though. He hoisted the box off the floor.

"Just help me get down the attic steps," he said.

Which wouldn't be an easy feat with a box this bulky. The darn thing was heavy, too. Still, there was no safe way both of them could maneuver down the stairs at the same time. Heaven knew how Em had gotten the box and all the stuff inside it up those rickety steps in the first place, but he was betting Hayes had helped her.

Since he couldn't see where he was stepping, Leyton let Hadley guide him with the motions of her hand. When they made it to the stairs, she went halfway down and did indeed take some of the weight of the box while they inched down. Step by excruciating step. They were still a good four feet from the floor when her phone rang.

Since the screen was right there in front of him, Leyton looked to see if it was Em. It wasn't. Nor was it a normal ringtone. Because he'd heard his nieces sing it, he instantly recognized it was the kids' song "Wheels on the Bus."

"I have to take this," Hadley said, snatching up the

phone. She hit the answer button and sandwiched it between her shoulder and ear while she continued to help him down the steps.

"Hey, Bailey," she said to the caller, and even though Leyton couldn't see her mouth, he could practically hear the smile in her voice. "Is that so?" she said several moments later. "That sounds like fun."

Leyton couldn't hear what the caller said, nor did he try to listen, but he couldn't miss that Hadley was dodging his gaze again. The moment they were at the bottom of the stairs, she moved away from him, going into her brother's bedroom.

"You'll have to save the picture you colored so I can see it," Hadley told the caller, and she was obviously trying to keep her voice low. Another pause, and she glanced at Leyton as he wrangled the box out of the closet and into the hall.

Once again, he didn't mean to listen, and Hadley probably thought he was out of earshot. He wasn't. And that was why he heard her murmur, "Mama loves you, too, baby. Bye-bye. I'll talk to you soon."

Mama?

Baby?

Leyton froze, and even though he tried to tamp down his shock, he must have failed big-time, because Hadley's eyes widened to the size of turkey platters when she came out into the hall and saw him.

She gave a flustered huff, then scowled. "Don't ask anything about that," she warned him.

He no doubt would have done some asking anyway, but Leyton was having a little trouble getting his mouth to work. Hadley had a child?

When the hell had that happened?

Just about the time he got his mouth working, he knew his questions would have to wait. That was because he heard the voices and the footsteps.

"Hadley?" someone called out.

It was Sunny, and he was betting that the second pair of footsteps belonged to McCall.

"Up here in Hayes's room," Hadley answered.

Several moments and many footsteps later, Sunny and McCall rushed in. The pair practically skidded to a stop when they spotted Leyton, and he quickly figured out what was going on in their heads. He and Hadley looked a little disheveled. A little shaken up. And Sunny and McCall might have thought that they'd resumed their penchant for high school lip-locks. That couldn't be further from the truth.

Well, physically, anyway.

But Leyton had indeed given some thought to those kisses *before* the mama bombshell.

"We're looking for any clues to help us figure out what's going on with Em," Hadley explained.

McCall nodded and rushed closer to Leyton and Hadley. "I just got this text from Em," she said, showing them the phone screen.

Hadley and he cursed in unison when they read it.

Make sure to lock all the doors, Em had texted. Don't let anyone you don't know in the house. And just to be sure, have Leyton stay at the ranch with all of you. There could be trouble brewing.

CHAPTER FOUR

THERE COULD BE trouble brewing.

Hadley figured that "trouble brewing" was practically a family motto. She'd certainly gotten into her share of it over the years. Ditto for Hayes and their mother. Occasionally, even McCall and Sunny had contributed to the trouble pool. Em, too. But this was different. This felt like a sucker punch from karma, fate and King Kong all at once.

"What's going on?" McCall asked, the plea in both her voice and expression. She was clearly worried, and while Hadley would have liked to assure her that there was no big whoop of concern here, that text was proof otherwise.

To the best of Hadley's knowledge, Em had never asked that the house be locked down. And she'd certainly never asked that Leyton stay there. Of course, that might have nothing to do with a potential threat. Nope.

This could be Em's backhanded way of matchmaking.

Em had always wanted her and Leyton to be together. Maybe Em thought that being under the same roof with a nameless, faceless bogeyman might send Hadley into Leyton's big, strong, manly arms.

As if.

Well, it might work, Hadley reluctantly admitted. She wasn't a wuss, but after reading that text from Em, having those manly arms around might help her sleep better. But it wouldn't put anything else in the "better" category. Not with that sneaky heat still sparking between them. Heat that could only make Hadley sigh and want to hit herself on the head with a bag of restraint and common sense. She didn't need Leyton. And he didn't need her.

But heaven help her, she sure wanted him.

Hadley looked at Leyton to see if he had the same matchmaking take that she did on the situation, but his eyes were all cop as he reread the text.

"I've tried to call Em multiple times," McCall explained. "So has Sunny. But she's not answering."

"I even lied and told her I was having some trouble and needed to speak to her right away," Sunny said, taking up the explanation. "Trouble with Shaw. Trouble with Kinsley. Trouble with mosquitoes."

Those were all good ploys, since Sunny was in love with Shaw, and they were helping raise Shaw and Leyton's half sister Kinsley, a teenager with an often bad attitude. The mosquitoes went beyond ploy and into the realm of genius. Em loathed the critters and had made it her mission in life to keep them away from the ranch with elaborate traps, a mosquito-repellent garden and even dozens of bats she'd hired someone to bring in. Apparently, those nocturnal winged critters didn't bother her as much as the buzzing, biting mosquitoes.

"Em responded to my texts," Sunny went on. "With poop emoji."

"I used the lie of saying I was pregnant and that I wanted to share the happy news with her," McCall piped in. "She replied with a Pinocchio emoji." She shifted her attention to Leyton. "Is there any way you can trace where she was when she sent this text?"

Leyton gave a heavy sigh. "Em's legally not a missing person, but I could possibly use this text to prove that she could be in some kind of danger." He paused. "Though Em is clearly saying that the threat could be here at the ranch."

"If there was an actual threat to any of us, she'd be here," Hadley pointed out. "That means someone's holding her against her will."

Yes, that last part was a stretch the size of Canada, but maybe it would give Leyton the legal fodder he needed to do a trace. He obviously thought so as well, because he finally nodded.

"Keep looking through the things in that box," he instructed them. "Look for anything that might tell us where she is. I'll go into the office and see what I can do about tracing the text. I need to follow up on the letter, too. Maybe the lab will have something we can use."

"Thank you," McCall said, handing him her phone. "Take it so you'll have the exact time the text was sent. Plus, there might be something in the way she worded things that helps you."

That was another stretch, but right now stretches and speculation were all they had.

"I'll let you know if I find anything," Leyton assured her, heading out the bedroom door. "You do the same for me."

He got mumbled assurances from McCall and Sunny, and her sisters both looked at Hadley as if they expected her to do something. Sunny flapped her hand toward a departing Leyton's back and McCall tipped her head in the same direction. Either the pair had developed sudden urges for gestures or they believed she should accompany Leyton to show him out.

A third possibility was they were matchmaking.

If it was the latter, then it seemed like a wrong-time, wrong-place kind of attempt, what with Em missing. Still,

Hadley went after him, not only so she could be the polite hostess and show him out, but also so she could give him a warning.

Leyton glanced over his shoulder at her, but not with surprise or curiosity. He seemed focused on doing the job. Which was even more reason to warn him about the possible matchmaking. Since he was a good guy with good intentions, he might not see it coming.

"I'll be back later," he said when he reached the front door, "and I'll stay the night."

Hadley huffed. "Not necessary." And she involuntarily glanced at his manly arms. Yes, those very ones that could give her reassurance and the feeling of safety. "Sunny mentioned that Kinsley's been staying with you, and you shouldn't leave her alone to be here."

"She's staying with Austin tonight and helping him watch the twins. Austin wants to help McCall look for Em."

Of course he'd want to do that. In fact, Austin would probably want McCall to stay with him, too, once he heard about the text Em had sent her.

His phone dinged with a text, and maybe thinking it was about Em, he moved fast, yanking it from his pocket. "Shit," he grumbled.

Hadley's heart did a major thud against her chest, and she practically wrenched his phone from him so she could read what had caused him to swear. But it wasn't from Em. It was from Cait.

Zach Rodriguez's mom wants to know why his mouth is bleeding and there's an angel wing caught in his braces, Cait had texted. She's in your office now.

"Don't ask," Leyton said to Hadley in a tone that let her

know this situation was more of a pain in the butt than a reason for heart thudding.

He took back his phone, opened the door and turned toward her. Hadley was about to blurt out for him to beware of matchmakers, but he leaned in and dropped a kiss on her mouth. It was hardly more than a peck, barely qualifying as a kiss, but it generated more than a heart thump or two.

His mouth was apparently more manly and potent than his arms.

"I know your sisters and Em want us together," he said before she could speak. Or protest. Which would have taken some doing, since the air had stalled in her lungs and she couldn't form words. "But if we get back together, I don't want it to be because of them."

Maybe she couldn't speak yet, but Hadley could narrow her eyes. "We're not getting back together."

"Yeah. I keep telling myself that, too."

He made it sound as if his effort wasn't working. That he believed a reunion was entirely possible. Hadley wanted to snarl and say that it wasn't. But her mouth was still tingling from a kiss that was only an almost kiss. Worse, her mind was tingling from the memories. She knew firsthand that Leyton could do a whole lot better than a peck. Better that could lead to sex.

And expectations.

She needed that like she needed another missing grandmother, and that was why Hadley pushed thoughts of the peck, of manly arms and of the man himself aside.

"By the way, I like the look," he drawled in a voice that she was sure had rid many women of their panties.

"The *look*?" she managed.

Leyton only skimmed a finger down her cheek and walked away. Probably because of the steamy fog he'd created in her head… Heck, who was she kidding? The fog was more like a sauna, and it was in her entire body. And because of it, it took her a moment to get what he meant by that.

She wasn't wearing any makeup.

That gave her a jolt of panic. A stupid reaction that she doubted anyone would understand, but before she joined her sisters, Hadley made a quick stop into the upstairs bathroom and slathered on some foundation and mascara. While she was at it, she added another set of earrings and a few bracelets. Now she no longer felt so naked and exposed.

She went back to Hayes's old bedroom and saw that her sisters had already taken some things out of the box from the attic. They were sitting on the floor going through the albums, as Hadley had done. Both of them stopped perusing and looked up when she walked in.

"You put on makeup," McCall said with a sigh. "So, are you going to tell us what's going on between you and Leyton?"

That was the trouble with having a therapist for a sister. Hadley didn't have that whole triplet ESP thing that some multiples had, but McCall had a skill set that made it possible for her to zoom in on vibes, expressions and such. Hadley had a skill set for deflection. She ignored the makeup comment but addressed the Leyton one.

"Nothing's going on between Leyton and me," Hadley insisted. "He's not my type."

"Malarkey," said McCall, as Sunny said simultaneously, "Bullshit. He's a Jameson. He's every woman's type."

Hadley had a quick comeback for that. "You're only saying that because you're both in love with Jamesons."

And for them, it was the right fit. Sunny had been in

love with Shaw since childhood, and McCall had always had the hots for Austin. Those hots had obviously grown into something deeper. Hadley had also had the hots for Leyton, but in her case, the growing wouldn't happen.

Even if she'd felt his kiss all the way to the soles of her flip-flops.

"Instead of weaving fantasies about Leyton and me, let's focus on Em," Hadley reminded them. She couldn't give any more thought to Leyton right now, not with Em doing whatever the heck it was she was doing.

"What have you already gone through in the box?" Mc-Call asked. Obviously, she'd put Leyton out of mind, as well.

"Most of those albums. There's one for each of the DLC years." No need for Hadley to clarify that she meant "during *Little Cowgirls*." "Some BLC and ALC, too." Before and after *Little Cowgirls*.

McCall glanced at Hadley, then Sunny. "Speaking of ALC, are either of you still getting calls from Waterstone Productions about a reunion show they want to put together?"

"Yes," Sunny readily answered. "But they haven't called in the past couple of weeks. Maybe because I've told them I'm not interested."

Good. Because Hadley wasn't, either, and she'd blocked the number when they'd continued to pressure her. Of course, tit-gate might have a nice side effect of Waterstone Productions losing interest. If so, then her *badly* antics had finally led to something good.

Hadley turned back to the photo albums and had another glance at the ones she'd gone through. "None of the pictures are of Em before she moved here."

Sunny's gaze snapped to hers. "You think what's going on now is connected to that?"

Hadley shrugged. She'd already told them about the letter that she found in the tackle box, so they knew the gist. Still, maybe Sunny and McCall didn't want to see the connection that could spell out that Em might be in some kind of danger.

"Em said in that letter that she'd had a life before here," Hadley explained, "that she used to be someone else. I suppose that could be her way of saying that falling in love with our grandfather changed her and made her a new person, but if it's literal, it could mean that she had a past that's now come back to haunt her."

"But how?" Sunny asked.

Hadley had to shrug again. "I don't know, but if we don't find anything in this box, I want to call Marty Jameson. Em put his eight track in that box, so it's possible Marty knows something that'll help us."

"I've got his number. I'll call him," Sunny quickly volunteered. It made sense that Sunny would know how to contact Marty, since she was the illustrator for the books that Marty wrote. Leyton and his siblings likely would have also known how to get in touch with him, but Hadley wouldn't push for that unless Sunny wasn't able to reach him.

Sunny got off the floor so she could take her phone from her pocket, and she pressed Marty's number. Apparently, he didn't answer, but Sunny left a voice mail for him to call her ASAP.

With that ball rolling, Hadley went back to the box, and she tried to pick through anything and everything Em had said in that water-splotched letter, the phone call the night before and the texts. The eight track had come up in the call, so Hadley tackled those next. She hauled the stack out onto the floor with her.

McCall dug in, too, dumping out the rest of the contents of the box, and she began to sort through the plastic bags that Em had deemed important enough to store rather than toss. There was a bag of rubber bands, another of twist ties that had come off bread wrappers.

"Em kept our hair," McCall said, looking at the smaller bags of locks. "And our baby teeth." Each was labeled with a girl's name. There was even a lock of hair and some teeth from Hayes, though Hadley couldn't imagine her badass brother voluntarily giving those up, even to Em.

Hadley continued with her own task. She picked up one of the eight tracks from the stash and peered down into it. Nothing. It was the same for the next one, and the next and the next. But she froze when she saw what appeared to be some paper shoved into the fifth one. A Marty Jameson eight track, *Running Ragged*.

The same album title as the one Em had left in the tackle box.

Maybe this was the eight track that Em had meant to be buried.

It took some doing, but Hadley worked out the paper through the opening, and she saw it had been folded into a tight little square and lodged into the casing. As she unfolded it, she got Sunny's and McCall's attention, and they both dropped down on either side of her.

"It's an old letter," Sunny remarked, tapping the date on top of the page.

Hadley quickly did the math, and if the date was accurate, it would have been written when Em was sixteen or seventeen. But it wasn't Em's name on the page.

"'Dear Patsy,'" Hadley read. "'I miss you so much. All I can do is think about you. Do you miss me, too?'"

"Patsy?" McCall questioned.

Hadley was asking herself the same thing. Had this letter been written to Em? Was Patsy her real name, the name she'd had in that other life she'd mentioned? Or had Em kept this letter for someone else?

"It's signed by someone named Tony," McCall pointed out.

Yes, it was. Hadley spotted that at the bottom. Not an ordinary signature, either. He'd extended the *y* of his name and used it to draw the stem of an upside-down flower.

"'I was thinking about your birthmark today,'" Hadley continued to read. "'The little heart right over your heart.'"

Hadley got another gut punch, and she cursed, her words joining the chorus with her sisters' own variation of profanity. Em did indeed have a birthmark at the top of her right boob.

"Em told me a fairy had kissed her there," Hadley remembered. Maybe the smooch had come from this flower-drawing Tony instead. After all, Em would have to be in her underwear or naked for anyone to see it.

"She told me it magically appeared after she fell in love with Granddad," Sunny supplied.

"Same here," McCall piped in.

Em was definitely good at dishing out BS, but that didn't explain the fact that this Tony had seen it.

"'I think the heart means you're special.'" Hadley kept reading. "'You're certainly special to me, and I should have told you how much I love you, but my words get tangled up when I'm around you. I just wanted you to know I love you and I'm sorry about what happened. So sorry. I didn't know my family was dirty…'"

Hadley paused again, her eyes frozen on the last words before the flowery signed name.

"I didn't know they were in the mob," Tony had written. "I didn't know it'd mess up everything between us. Stay safe, Patsy. Stay in hiding. I'll come for you when I can."

CHAPTER FIVE

LEYTON READ OVER the report he'd just had to write on the incident of Zach Rodriguez and the angel wing caught in the braces.

He'd had no choice about writing it since responding to the teen's call for help and then calming down Zach's mother when she'd come to his office. The report was not only SOP but also a way of covering his butt if it turned out that Zach's injury was more than superficial. It wasn't. But CYA was still SOP.

Even with careful wording, the report sounded like a skit from *Saturday Night Live*, and he'd had to add the part about Zach's mom pressing to find out what had gone on when her son had come home with a bloody mouth. Leyton hadn't had a choice about telling her, either, because Zach was a minor. But he'd managed to keep Alyssa's name out of it. Of course, it wouldn't be hard for Mrs. Rodriguez to figure out who'd been in a lip-lock—or rather a braces-lock—with her son. Still, Leyton hadn't wanted that particular tidbit to come from him.

He hit the save button on the report and looked up when Cait walked into his office. She was carrying a spiral notebook and dropped it onto his desk.

"That was in Hadley's rental car," Cait explained. "It probably fell on the floor and slid under the seat when she wrecked. Barney found it and brought it over."

Barney was Barney Darnell, who owned the towing service that had hauled away the Jeep. Since the wreck had happened over twenty-four hours ago, though, it made Leyton wonder why Barney hadn't seen it sooner.

"Robo-cowboy," Cait said. "It's a sketchbook," she added when Leyton gave his sister a blank stare. "I'm guessing it's Hadley's designs for some kind of robot-cowboy project."

Leyton wasn't sure exactly what a robot cowboy would look like. Or why someone would want such an outfit.

"You looked in the book?" he asked.

She shrugged. "I had to find out if it belonged to Hadley."

"Who the heck else would it belong to?" he grumbled, but he thumbed through it, telling himself he was looking for any damage and any actual proof that it did indeed belong to Hadley.

It was hers, all right. Her name might not have been on it, but the sketches on the first page were definitely those of a costume designer. He didn't need any keen detective skills to piece that together, since Hadley was a designer. This was her book and her work.

Weird work.

The two drawings looked like a long-coat-wearing Wyatt Earp had hooked up with a metal cheese grater. Cowboy on the top and bottom with a hat and boots, but the middle was boxy and with what he thought would be lights and dials. He supposed Cait's description of the robo-cowboy could be accurate if you let the imagination run a little wild.

"There are some kid sketches in the back," Cait pointed out. "I was nosy," she admitted.

Apparently, Leyton was nosy, too, because he flipped to the back and saw what his sister had meant by kid sketches. These appeared to be costumes as well, not for cheese-grater cowboys, but for a winged fairy, an angel and a miniature construction worker, complete with hard hat and toolbox. It made him think of the phone call he'd overheard.

Mama.

And he wondered if Hadley had drawn these for the mystery child who'd been on the other end of the phone line.

"Anyway, I thought you'd want to take the sketchbook to Hadley when you go back out to Em's," Cait said, pulling his thoughts away from the child. "You'll be staying the night there?"

He'd already updated Cait about Em's warning text that she'd sent to McCall, so Leyton knew it wasn't a question that'd come out of left field. If there was any possible threat, Leyton would want to make sure that Hadley and her sisters were safe. Still, Cait seemed to have a gleam in her eye that didn't have anything to do with threats or the search for answers about Em.

"Don't you dare ask me if I'm getting involved with Hadley again," Leyton warned her.

"No need. You're already involved with her. Turd on a tire iron, Leyton," Cait said when he aimed narrow eyes at her. "You're not exactly poker-face guy or man of mystery. I can see it, and I'll bet you've already kissed her."

Since he had indeed kissed Hadley, he didn't acknowledge that, but he could dismiss that he was *already involved* with her. An involvement might happen.

Might.

But not before Hadley fought it every step of the way. Maybe she'd put up obstacles because he'd hurt her way back when. Or it could be because she just wasn't looking for any kind of relationship, even a short-term one that would end when she went back to her life in California. Either way, it would be work to convince her that…

Leyton stopped and tried to figure out how to finish that thought. Convince her to have a fling with him? More than a fling? Have her help him come up with a word that didn't sound as stupid as *fling*?

Or maybe finish the sentence with something that went in a different direction.

For instance, how about they try just having a simple friendship? If that was possible, it might lessen the guilt he felt over how he'd handled their breakup. But he was pretty sure he and Hadley had always been past the simple friendship stage.

"There are one thousand three hundred fifty-three miles between Hadley's place in California and here," Leyton muttered, and the moment he said it, he knew he should have kept the muttering in his head.

Cait gave him a pitying look, whistled out a breath. "Man, you've got it bad."

No, he didn't. Well, maybe. It was sort of bad, but it was only because he'd always been attracted to Hadley. But the mileage was concrete proof that there were obstacles that wouldn't be easy to dismiss.

"Forbidden fruits must look pretty juicy to a straight arrow like yourself," Cait continued, and he detected the smirk that only a younger sister and a prankster poltergeist could manage.

"If you keep bringing up stuff like that, I'll remind you that you once had a thing for Hadley's brother."

Her smirk stayed in place. "Nope. In fact, I was the only woman in town who didn't fall in the sack with Hayes. I don't mind toying with trouble, but I had enough sense to figure out when trouble could toy right back. I steered clear of him."

That was possibly true, possibly, but Leyton seemed to remember catching Cait giving Hayes a long, lingering look or two. And there'd been no smirk in those looks, either. Of course, most women who came within eyeing distance of Hayes gave him at least the once-over.

"Enough about guys who were never on my radar," Cait went on. "You need to know that Mom's worried about Sunny, McCall and Hadley."

It took Leyton a moment to shift gears. That wasn't a surprise about their mother being worried. Lenore was Leyton's adoptive mom, and she was a kind, caring person. But Lenore didn't often express her kindness in ways that others appreciated. Like cooking, for instance.

"Lenore isn't sending over a casserole to Em's, is she?" Leyton asked.

Cait hiked her thumb in the direction of her desk. "She dropped off something that she called pork potato surprise. Yeah, I know," Cait quickly added. "*Surprise* shouldn't be part of anything edible, but she said she wanted you to take it to Hadley, that she wants to make sure she eats right while she's looking for Em."

Well, eating right likely wouldn't happen with pork potato surprise, but he'd deliver it and give Hadley a warning to make sure she had an ample supply of antacids if she decided to risk chowing down on it.

"Anything new on Em?" Cait asked when he stood and tucked the sketchbook under his arm.

"Not really. Hadley called earlier to tell me they found an old love letter that might or might not have been written to Em when she was a teenager. Hadley was going to keep looking to try to find more letters so she can figure out who sent them and if they apply to anything now."

Though it was interesting that Hadley had found that letter in an old eight track of Marty's. Maybe that meant Em had put the wrong eight track in the memory box. She could have intended to put in the one with the hidden letter.

But it didn't appear that particular letter would help them nearly as much as the water-damaged one would have, and Leyton made a mental note to call the lab again and give the tech a push to get the results. Judging from her phone call and texts, Em wasn't in any kind of immediate danger, but that didn't mean time—or the possible threat of danger—wasn't an issue here.

"Well, if you need help, let me know," Cait offered. "I'll be on call tonight if anything pops up in our exciting world of local law enforcement. Who knows, maybe I'll get a call about some other body part getting snagged on braces."

Leyton hoped that Zach and Alyssa had learned their lesson about that, but if not, Cait could handle it. She might have a smart mouth, but she was a good cop. Too bad she hadn't figured out a way to decline Lenore's casserole, because now Leyton found himself picking it up on his way out of the police station. The last time he'd transported a food dish for Lenore, it'd left his truck reeking for days.

Leyton drove to Em's, and hauling out the casserole and the sketchbook, he went onto the porch—where he immediately heard the arguing.

"I'm fine," he heard Hadley say. "I'll be fine."

"What part of Em's warning didn't you understand?" Sunny countered. "You can't stay here alone." Even though her voice was practically identical to McCall's, Leyton picked up on the subtle differences. Sunny had a stronger edge of snark and bite than McCall would have.

Since this was a disagreement that he could perhaps fix, he knocked on the door. After a few moments of grumblings, Hadley threw it open and immediately gestured toward him.

"See? I won't be alone," Hadley said, not to Leyton, but to Sunny.

Sunny shifted, her gaze skimming over the covered casserole dish before it settled on Leyton. "I'm trying to talk Hadley into coming to stay with Shaw and me. Or with McCall and Austin."

"McCall and Austin have a full house with the twins," Hadley reminded her. "And you and Shaw have only one bedroom. I'd rather not sleep on the couch when I have a perfectly good bed right here."

"Is McCall already at Austin's?" Leyton asked. He wanted the whole picture here before he started doling out possible solutions. Of course, the obvious solution was one that Hadley might not like, either.

"She's already at Austin's," Sunny supplied. "She had clients to deal with most of the day."

Leyton nodded. He'd heard that McCall was doing a lot of phone appointments these days. "And you're heading back to your and Shaw's place?" he asked Sunny.

Sunny huffed, folding her arms over her chest. "I want to head back there, but I won't leave Hadley here alone."

"She won't be." Leyton stepped in and set the casserole on the foyer table right between a framed autographed picture of his father and Em and a stuffed toy duck. "I'll be staying the night."

Now it was Hadley who huffed. "I've already told you that isn't necessary—"

"I'm staying," he said, cutting off the rest of an argument that she wasn't going to win.

Leyton figured his tone and expression let her know that, because Hadley gave him another huff. But she also stepped back, turned and headed in the direction of the kitchen.

"Don't let her run you off." Sunny gave his arm a pat and glanced at the casserole again when Leyton picked it back up. "And if that's from Lenore, don't let her eat it."

"I won't," Leyton assured her.

He dropped a kiss on Sunny's forehead when she headed out, and he locked the door behind her. Leyton also fired off a text to let Shaw know that Sunny was on her way back. That way, Shaw could keep an eye out for her. Normally, it wasn't a precaution Shaw would have to take, but nothing about this situation was normal.

After he was certain Sunny was in her vehicle and driving away, Leyton threaded his way through the house and found Hadley in the kitchen. She was looking at the screen of a laptop she had open on the table.

"From my mom," he said, putting the casserole on the counter. "Don't eat it." He laid the sketchbook on the table next to her. "And this was in your rental car."

Hadley looked up at him. "Thanks. I thought I'd lost it." She paused, scowling. "How many laughs did it give you, your deputies and the person who found it?"

He shrugged and sat down beside her. "Interesting designs," Leyton settled for saying.

She snorted out a laugh that wasn't from humor. "I'm at the point where I take any work I can get."

Yes, and also at the point where she would argue with her sister about staying here alone—even when being alone was a bad idea. He got why she wouldn't want to go to Shaw's and sleep on the sofa, but Austin's place was big, and he had a guest room.

He thought of the kid designs in the sketchbook. Thought, too, of that phone call she'd gotten with the "Wheels on the Bus" ringtone. So, maybe Hadley didn't want to be around Austin's twins because they would remind her of the child— *her* child—that she was missing?

But if the missing theory was right, why wasn't Hadley with the child?

"I've been doing computer searches to try to find Em," she said, signaling a change in subject. "There weren't any last names in the letter."

Hadley had the letter right next to her, and she slid it toward him. Leyton had already seen a photocopy of it that Hadley had messaged to him earlier, but he read through it again now. She was right about there not being any surnames. There was a date, however, and he saw that Hadley had used that date and the first names in a computer search.

A very broad one.

Her search had pulled up over a million hits, most of them genealogy records. It would take weeks, if not months, to go through all that, and it was possible that none of the hits had anything to do with Em. Added to that, Tony could be a nickname, so they could be on the wrong track altogether.

"McCall has already called Hayes to tell him what's going on with Em," Hadley continued, "and McCall asked him about what we've learned. He never remembers anyone referring to Em as Patsy. Her middle name is Ann, so that doesn't mesh with Patsy, either."

Leyton had already gone there, too, and he'd taken it a few steps further. He'd asked around among the older folks in town, and none of them ever recalled a Patsy.

"Any chance there's a family Bible or some kind of family history chart lying around?" he asked.

She shook her head. "But I thought maybe you could have the letter dusted for prints. If this Tony sent it to her, then his fingerprints might still be on it. Or maybe there's something in the handwriting that'll give us clues."

Those ideas were well past being long shots, but Leyton nodded. "I can give it to my friend at the lab."

A friend he was going to owe many, many favors, since heaven knew how many prints would be on a letter that old. Plus, Hadley, her sisters and now even Leyton had handled it. And as for the handwriting, the lab would need some kind of comparison for that, which they didn't have, unless this Tony turned out to be somebody famous with equally famous handwriting.

"Any sign of an envelope in the box?" he asked. Then they would at least have a postmark and maybe even a return address.

"No. Only the letter was shoved into the eight track."

Em had obviously hidden her footsteps. Hidden who she was. And it wasn't going to be easy to unravel the past unless Em came forward and spilled everything. He had to believe that would happen soon, though. Em wouldn't continue to put her grandchildren through this.

"Em knows she's worrying all of you," Leyton reminded her. "I suspect she'll be back soon."

He halfway expected Hadley to dismiss that with a huff or an eye roll. But nope. She looked at him, and it was as if she was latching on to the hope of that happening. Maybe latching on to him as the hope giver, too.

"I don't believe Em's actually in danger," she said but then shook her head. On a frustrated groan, she plowed her fingers into her hair. "I don't want to believe she's in danger," Hadley amended. "Do you think she is?"

"No." And he repeated it when he saw the skepticism in her eyes. "I think if Em had been in danger, she would have tried to give us better clues than what was in that buried tackle box. She's a smart woman. A sometimes weird woman," Leyton tacked on to that, "but she would have figured out a way to tell us where she is and what's going on."

Hadley stayed quiet for several moments. "So, it's probably connected to her past." Another pause. "Or maybe our pasts. My mother did a lot of bad stuff, and it could be linked back to something she did."

Leyton nodded. "I've already considered that, but if that's it, I think we would have heard from Sunshine by now. Your mom isn't usually one to suffer in silence."

"No," Hadley softly agreed. Her gaze connected with his. "What if it's because of something I did?" She continued before he could say anything. "Myla Livingston, the singer involved in tit-gate, is half-crazy, and she's really pissed at me. I tried to get in touch with her and ask if she did something to Em, but she wouldn't take my call."

That was an angle Leyton could pursue. "I'll reach out to the LA cops and see if they can find out anything."

He took out his phone to get that started, and since he didn't know anyone in the LAPD, he sent off a text to an old friend in the Texas Rangers and asked him to assist. He showed Hadley the text before he hit the send button.

"Thank you," she said. "Thanks, too, for staying here. Even though I really don't think it's necessary. Or smart," she added in a grumble.

Leyton didn't have any trouble filling in the blanks. "You mean because of that kiss."

With her eyes narrowing, she stared at him a long time.

"Yes, because of that kiss. You did the right thing by breaking up with me way back when. You need to stick to that."

Backing off would certainly be the "smart" thing to do. After all, he'd already spelled out why an entanglement with her wouldn't work. But he just couldn't shake off the taste of her. Couldn't push aside the "what if" thoughts that kept creeping into his head.

"We came close to having sex when you were fifteen," he reminded her. "Maybe if we'd just done the deed, I wouldn't feel that what's between us is unfinished business."

Now she did roll her eyes, but he thought that might be a smile tugging at her mouth. There was sure one tugging at his. "That sounds like a bad pickup line," she commented.

He made a sound of agreement and waited to see if she was going to do anything about it. Especially since that ghost of a smile was still there. So was the heat between them. A heat that seemed to be getting hotter and hotter with her staring straight into his eyes.

She drew in a breath, causing her mouth to tremble just a little. Causing her chest to rise, too. Of course he'd notice that. The moment seemed to be coming together. A moment where they could put the past aside, and he could kiss Hadley the way he'd been wanting to kiss her all day.

But then her phone dinged.

The *moment* vanished, and she practically toppled out of the chair when she scrambled to pull her phone from her jeans pocket. Leyton did some scrambling, too, because he figured this was Em.

It wasn't.

It was a picture of a little girl with dark brown hair. She was grinning and holding a sparkly blue stuffed pony.

Hadley didn't so much draw in her breath this time. She

sucked it in, clearly surprised. Clearly uncomfortable, too, that he'd just seen the picture.

Love it! she texted back, then put her phone away.

He waited to see if Hadley was going to explain anything. She didn't. And Leyton was about to let it drop as well, but then he considered something. It was a long shot, but maybe what was happening to Em was indeed connected to Hadley. Not to the vindictive Myla Livingston.

But to that child in the picture.

"Why don't you tell me about her?" Leyton said, tipping his head to the phone in her pocket. "Because I need to know if what's going on with that little girl is the reason that Em's not here."

CHAPTER SIX

HADLEY HADN'T STEELED herself up nearly enough for Leyton's demand. And there was no doubt about it—it was a demand. One coming from a cop.

Because I need to know if what's going on with that little girl is the reason that Em's not here.

"She isn't connected to Em," Hadley insisted.

But the moment the words left her mouth, Hadley did a mental skidding to a stop. Em didn't know about Bailey.

Did she?

If she did, Em had never mentioned it, and she would have. Wouldn't she?

Maybe.

Hadley frowned because Em certainly hadn't talked about why she had left the way she did and was now being very cryptic about her disappearance. So, perhaps Em had known about Bailey and had simply kept it to herself, waiting for Hadley to spill all. But even if that was the case, Hadley couldn't figure out why knowing something like that would have caused Em to leave.

"She isn't connected to Em," Hadley repeated, and she got another dose of those cop's eyes, which turned into a cop's stare.

Even though Leyton didn't say a word, his silence was just as effective as an interrogation with a rubber hose. Hadley didn't exactly squirm in her seat, but it was close.

"It's not what you think," she finally said, breaking the long silence.

"What is it, then?" he pressed.

He followed his question by doing something that Hadley really didn't want him to do. Leyton slid his hand over hers. Not very cop-like, but it stirred a few old memories of days gone by when he'd touched her so...easily. Since she didn't want *easily* from him, or these blasted trips down memory lane, she eased her hand away and stood.

"It's not what you think," she repeated in a mumble.

Hadley gathered her breath for an explanation she didn't especially want to give him. Still, he might be able to see this from a different angle. An angle that would give them some clues as to Em's whereabouts if there was indeed some kind of connection to Bailey.

"Five years ago, I agreed to be a surrogate for my best friend, Deanna Davidson," Hadley said.

But calling Deanna a friend, even a best one, was like saying the ocean had a little bit of water in it. Hadley had been closer to Deanna than she had her own sisters, and it'd been that way from the first time they'd met at the shoot for a music video. Deanna had been the set designer, and Hadley had created the costumes. That'd been nearly a decade ago, but to Hadley it felt as if Deanna had always been in her life.

And still would be.

"A surrogate?" Leyton blinked with surprise, and Hadley thought there might be some relief in his voice, too.

Relief that riled her. "No, I didn't have a child and then abandon her," she snarled.

He stood, leveling his eyes with hers. "I didn't think you had."

And because this was Leyton—the good guy—she believed him. He hadn't thought the worst about her even if everyone else would if they learned she'd carried a child.

"Deanna and her husband, Carson, desperately wanted a baby," Hadley went on, her voice no longer a snarl. "But Deanna had had eight miscarriages." Heartbreaking miscarriages, and Hadley had seen each one bring Deanna to her knees. "So, I offered to carry their child. *Their child*," she emphasized.

He kept his eyes locked with hers, and she saw something there. Something more than his trying to absorb *their child*.

"It took three tries," Hadley went on, "but the in vitro finally worked, and I carried Deanna and Carson's baby. A girl they named Bailey. She's four years old now." It was impossible not to get that warm, gooey feeling she always got when she thought of Bailey. Love wasn't about DNA, thank God.

"Bailey calls you Mama," Leyton reminded her when she paused.

Hadley nodded and had to take another breath. Then another. That warm, gooey feeling slid away, replaced by the bitter memories. "When Bailey was a year old, Carson and Deanna were killed. They were in a small plane with Carson's boss, and it went down, killing everyone on board."

Leyton cursed and shook his head. "God, I'm sorry."

Lots of people had said that. Lots of people had meant it, too, but coming from Leyton, it felt genuine and more comforting than it probably should have. Even though Deanna had died three years ago, the wound always felt raw and fresh. Hadley figured that wound wouldn't be healing anytime soon.

"Neither Deanna nor Carson had a will," Hadley explained. "Carson hadn't seen his parents in years, so they were out of the picture, and Deanna's father is dead. Both Deanna and Carson are only children and didn't have any other close living relatives. That left her mother, Candice, who petitioned for custody of Bailey. I put in a petition, too, but I lost."

Hadley doubted that her losing was a surprise to Leyton—or to anyone else, for that matter. No judge would consider Badly Hadley mommy material, and every bit of her reputation and every one of her idiot behaviors had come back to haunt her. Her juvie record for joyriding in a stolen car. The time she'd stomped on a paparazzo's camera when he wouldn't get out of her face. And all those tabloid photos and gossip.

So, Hadley had lost her best friend and the child she'd carried for her.

"Candice got full custody," Hadley went on. "She kept referring to me as Mommy's friend Hadley whenever I'd show up to visit Bailey. Bailey latched on to that and started calling me Mama Hadley." She shrugged. "I don't think Candice cares much for her doing that, but she hasn't tried to stop her."

Or rather Candice hadn't been successful in stopping her. Even though there was no genetic connection, Bailey had *inherited* Hadley's stubborn streak.

"I'm sorry," Leyton repeated. He paused. "You did a good thing for your friend by carrying her baby. Now a part of Deanna is living, thanks to you."

Crap. It was the right thing to say. The wrong thing, too, because it caused the tears to threaten. She wouldn't cry. Not in front of anyone, anyway. There'd been plenty of private tears, and there'd no doubt be more. But she wasn't going to boo-hoo now.

"All of this managed to stay out of the tabloids." Hadley squared her shoulders and punched down the grief.

"Deanna's mom is a lawyer in Houston, a rich one, and she saw to that. Candice didn't want her granddaughter's name linked to mine." Hadley gave a dry laugh. "No one wants their name connected to me."

Leyton definitely didn't laugh, and he didn't try to blow it off with a joke or lie to her and say it wasn't true. Instead, he slipped his arm around her and eased her to him. She didn't fight the hug. Couldn't. And this way at least Leyton was looking her in the eyes, where he might see the tears she was fighting.

"I hid the pregnancy," she added when she could speak. "I work from home a lot, so that was easy enough to do. I certainly didn't let anyone in my family know. I didn't think they'd understand how I could carry a child for eight months and sixteen days and then just hand her over. But Bailey wasn't mine. She was always Carson and Deanna's baby."

He made a sound that caused her to believe he understood. Or perhaps he just didn't know what else to say or do. Surrogacy wasn't that big of a deal in a city like LA, but it could be unconventional and perhaps unsettling in Lone Star Ridge.

Leyton continued to hold her, and they stayed that way for several moments. Moments where she felt his breath against her forehead and hair. Moments where she remembered just how good it felt for him to hold her.

"Do you have a picture of Bailey?" he asked, his voice as gentle as his touch. "I got a glimpse of her in the text you received, but I'd like to see what she looks like."

Hadley had to swallow the lump in her throat. Again, it was the right thing to say. It caused her to focus on what she had rather than what she'd lost. And what she had was Bailey. Not custody of her. But Bailey was part of her life, and that had to be enough. When you were Badly Hadley, you didn't get to pick and choose about things like that.

She pulled back enough to take out her phone, but Leyton kept his arm around her. It wasn't hard to find a photo, since Hadley had dozens of them. She tapped the latest one to bring it up fully on the screen. It was the one Bailey had sent her the night before, and she was holding a stuffed pony that Hadley had sent her.

Leyton smiled. "She's beautiful."

"Yes," Hadley agreed, still trying to rid herself of that throat lump.

He took the phone from her, zooming in for a closer look. "Do you get to see her often?"

"Not often enough." Though it was better now that Bailey was old enough to call and even text pictures. "She's in Houston—that's where Deanna was originally from—so I fly in to see her when I can. It's one thousand five hundred sixty-three miles between my place in LA and her grandmother's house in Houston."

Leyton had a weird reaction to that. He laughed, causing her to raise an eyebrow. "It's one thousand three hundred fifty-three miles between Lone Star Ridge and your place in LA."

She nearly asked why he knew such a trivial bit of info like that. Had he thought about making a road trip or something? But then she decided it was probably best not to know. It was obvious that Leyton still had feelings for her.

Correction—he still lusted after her.

Hadley didn't need to know if he had been thinking about attempting a long-distance, blast-from-the-past booty call.

"Houston's a lot closer to Lone Star Ridge," he pointed

out when she didn't say anything. He handed her back her phone. "Maybe you can drive over and see her."

"Maybe," Hadley echoed, fully aware that her response didn't have any oomph to it.

Deanna's mother was nice enough, but Hadley always felt a little like a hooker in a convent around her. Still, it was nice to be this close to Bailey. Nice for Hadley to know she could see her in just a couple of hours.

That closer proximity was one of the reasons she'd considered moving back to Lone Star Ridge. Well, that and she'd basically lost the work she needed to earn a living in ultra-expensive LA. Moving back would have killed a few metaphorical birds. She'd get to see Bailey, could continue to design and would be with Em.

Except now Em wasn't here.

"Bailey isn't part of why Em left," Hadley insisted. "If Em had had any clue about her, she would have said something to me. Em wouldn't have made a secret road trip to see Bailey."

His forehead bunched up as if giving that some thought, and he nodded. "You're right. If that was why she left and she'd wanted to keep up this cryptic stance, I think she would have left you some clues. So far, all the clues have been linked to Em's past, not yours."

It was a relief to hear him say that. She already had too many monkeys on her back without adding any guilt about Em. The relief didn't last very long, of course, because she quickly remembered that they weren't any closer to finding Em.

And that she was still in a halfway hug with Leyton.

Having any parts of their bodies touching wasn't a good idea. Neither was looking up at him when they were still close. But that was what she did. Hadley looked up just as he looked down, and their gazes practically collided. Crap on a cracker—when was she going to be able to get past this thing she had for him?

Maybe never.

She got proof of that when he leaned down and brushed his mouth over hers. It was a peck just like the one he'd given her earlier. Short but still scalding. He might as well have tossed her on the table and had sex with her. That was how her body responded. Thankfully, though, her brain clung to a smidgen of common sense, because Hadley mustered up the strength to step back.

"After we find Em, will you go out with me?" he asked.

Hadley was sure she scowled. "You mean will I have sex with you?"

"That, too," Leyton readily admitted, giving her not only that infamous Jameson charm but the grin to go along with it.

Her brain was having trouble hanging on to that common-sense smidgen, but it was enough for her to recall that she had no more room for back monkeys. Having sex with Leyton would be incredible. She was sure of it. But she seriously doubted he was a wham-bam-thank-you kind of guy. He'd want her to open up. To share. To bare her troubled soul.

Leyton would want pieces of her that she just couldn't give.

"I should get back to that computer search," Hadley muttered, and she sank down into the chair to start scrolling through the screen.

She was pretty sure she heard Leyton sigh.

"If Em left her laptop here, I can search, too," Leyton offered.

"It's in her bedroom on the dresser," Hadley said. "And it's not password protected. I already checked to see if she recently emailed anyone or got any emails that'd help. The last one was sent out two days ago, and it was an email exchange with your mom. They traded recipes."

Leyton gave another sigh, and Hadley had to agree with the sound of disapproval he added to it. No way should anyone be relying on Lenore Jameson for anything edible.

She kept scrolling while Leyton came back into the kitchen, and he set up the laptop right next to her. The close contact was a reminder that she was going to have to deal with this sort of thing until Em surfaced. Heaven help her. Her willpower was already waning, and—

Hadley's attention froze on one of the entries she'd pulled up in her wide internet search for Tony and the year of the letter she'd found in the eight track. It was an archived story from the *Times-Picayune*, a New Orleans newspaper. The date was right, fifty-nine years ago, so Hadley clicked on it and skimmed through it. The name practically jumped right out at her.

Tony "the Iceman" Corbin.

Yes, *the Iceman*. That definitely didn't sound like a friendly nickname.

Her body language must have alerted Leyton, because he leaned over so he could see her laptop screen. "Find something?" he asked.

"Maybe." But it was more than just a maybe. Hadley shifted the laptop so both of them could read the article.

Her nerves were already jumping, and her heart and stomach now seemed to be occupying the same place in her body, but she picked out the gist of the article.

Tony "the Iceman" Corbin and his older brother, Marco, had been arrested for racketeering, and Tony had struck a plea deal. In exchange for testifying against his brother, Tony would get reduced jail time.

"The time, place and first name all fit," Leyton said, his attention still on the article as Hadley scrolled down.

Yes, they did fit, and it also fit with what Em had told McCall about her being involved with a guy in the mob.

There wasn't anything else in the article, so Hadley shifted her search to Tony Corbin, adding the year that the article had been written. And she got more hits from other newspaper articles. She clicked on one, but it was little more than a rehash of the first article.

Except for the picture.

There was a grainy black-and-white photo that appeared to have been taken on the courthouse steps. A tall, dark-haired man. Young, thin and wearing a suit. He had his arm around a woman who had on a flowing dress that hit her midcalf. She was also young and thin, and she had long hair. The couple wasn't looking up at the camera but rather seemed to be hurrying to get away.

Hadley cranked up the magnification on the screen, zooming in on the woman's face. She couldn't see much, but it was enough. Plenty enough.

The woman next to Tony "the Iceman" was none other than Granny Em.

CHAPTER SEVEN

LEYTON FIGURED IT wasn't a good sign that he wanted to shoot a clock. But damn it all to hell, it was taunting him. It sat there with its beady red numbers, numbers that seemed to be stuck at 5:01 a.m.

It was too early to get up. Too late to try to force himself back to sleep. So, he lay there in bed, his eyes narrowed on the blasted clock and his thoughts whirling at the speed of an F5 tornado.

He hadn't expected to have a restful night with the photo of Em in his head and being under the same roof as Hadley. And his expectations had been met. He'd gotten very little sleep, and when sleep had come in short snatches, it'd been a mishmash of dreams about Em as a gangster's moll and Hadley climbing into the bed with him.

Hadley hadn't done that.

In fact, Leyton hadn't heard a peep out of her once they'd ended their computer searches shortly after midnight and had gone off to their respective bedrooms. She to the huge room she'd once shared with her sisters. He to Hayes's bedroom, which was down the hall from hers. Out of sight, out of mind hadn't been true in this situation, though, because he couldn't stop himself from thinking about her.

Or smelling her.

He could swear it was her scent on the sheets in Hayes's

room, and he'd even found himself sniffing the pillow. Which made him a sick, horny SOB. There was no reason for her scent to be here, not when she had her own room, her own bed. No. It was just his stupid body and nose playing tricks on him.

Her confession about Bailey had touched him. He'd known all along that Hadley had a soft side, that she was a whole lot more than Badly Hadley, and the surrogacy proved it. She'd loved her friend enough to carry a child, and she still loved the little girl who called her Mama Hadley.

Leyton had also heard the pain in her voice when she'd said she had lost her petition to get custody of Bailey. Sometimes the past just kept coming at you, nipping at your heels, and he figured that losing Deanna and Bailey had only added more armor to the shield that Hadley had built around herself. Breaking through that armor would be a challenge, but he knew he was going to try to do just that. Even if it was a stupid thing to do.

Finally, the clock showed it was 5:02, and Leyton knew he'd had enough. He threw back the covers, got out of bed, and trying to stay quiet so that he wouldn't wake Hadley, he went into the adjoining bathroom for a quick shower. Thanks to Cait, he had clean clothes and a toothbrush. His sister had dropped those things off the night before. What he didn't have was a razor, so he was going to have to sport some serious stubble until he could make it back to his place.

Whenever that would be.

He didn't want Hadley to be alone, and he figured she'd rather eat one of Lenore's casseroles than stay at his house. She probably wouldn't want to spend the day at the office with him, either. That was where Shaw and Austin would come in handy. Sunny and McCall would likely want to be with Hadley so they could continue their search for Em and give one another the kind of emotional support that only siblings could give. Neither of his brothers would want his significant other to be in a house that no longer felt completely safe, so that would ensure Hadley wouldn't be alone.

"Significant other," he grumbled as he sat to pull on his boots.

Now, that was a term he hadn't expected to say when it came to Austin and Shaw. Just a few months ago, Shaw had been hell-bent on no commitments. Well, except for helping to raise the steady stream of their father's kids. But now Shaw was with Sunny, the woman Leyton suspected that his brother had always loved, and they were planning a family. Austin and McCall were together, too, and their plans were to raise the family they already had—Austin's twin daughters.

Leyton wasn't jealous of what his brothers had found. No way. He wanted them happy. Cait, too. But he couldn't help but feel the whiny tug inside him that said he might never have what they did. He'd certainly never found it with any woman he'd dated over the years, and he'd resigned himself to the strong possibility that he, not Shaw, would be the one with no commitments.

Then Hadley had come back.

She'd stirred up all these old feelings with her scent on the sheets and the quick taste of her that he'd gotten from those equally quick kisses. Now he felt restless, needy and, yeah, whiny.

Pushing all of that aside, Leyton stepped out of the bedroom so he could head downstairs and locate some coffee. That might rid him of Hadley's taste. Would probably get the scent of her out of his nose, too. But he came to a quick stop when he saw her.

Sleeping on the floor outside her bedroom door.

She was on her side, huddled up under a thin blanket, her bare feet sticking out, and she was using what appeared to be a bundled-up shirt and her arm for a pillow.

Even though he'd purposely kept his footsteps light, she obviously heard him, because she jackknifed to a sitting position, her suddenly alert gaze zooming right to him.

"Leyton," she said in what sounded to him like a breath of relief.

Hell. Why hadn't he considered that she'd be on pins and needles? Maybe even scared spitless after the warning Em had given her? So, instead of being in her own bed, Hadley was out here standing guard. Or rather *sleeping* guard. Was that so she would have been better able to hear someone trying to come in through the front door or up the stairs?

He went closer, expecting to see her with some sort of weapon, like a kitchen knife. No weapon, though. But there was a very wary look on her face, making him rethink that whole "breath of relief" thing.

"Did you have a bad dream?" he asked.

Hadley shook her head, pushed her hair from her face and shoved the blanket aside so she could get to her feet. Leyton helped with that, but she immediately looked away from him. He'd been a cop long enough to know when someone was dodging his gaze, and that was exactly what Hadley was doing.

"I had some trouble sleeping," she said, as if that explained everything.

It didn't explain squat, especially why she'd ended up on the floor. There were three beds in her room and—better yet—a door with a lock. If she was this worried about some-one breaking in, she could have used that lock. Or gone to him. Heck, she could have gotten a weapon or a knife that he'd expected she'd have. Most people who were afraid didn't sleep out in the open where an intruder could easily spot them.

So, this wasn't about that kind of fear.

"I always forget how bad the memories are until I'm here," Hadley muttered, and then she cursed under her breath as if she'd said too much and wanted to take it back. But she couldn't take back those words. And Leyton had to wonder what bad memory had put her on the hall floor.

"You're up early," she quickly added. "Couldn't sleep?"

Leyton considered pressing her on the bad memories, but he knew it would only cause her to shut down more. It was a battle he'd need to save for another time.

"The sheets smelled like you, and the clock was piss-ing me off." In hindsight, Leyton figured he should have just settled for a nod.

She quit the gaze dodging and looked at him, maybe debating which of those two things to address. Or ignore. "I've noticed that some clocks do have attitude," she joked.

It was a really bad attempt to lighten things up, but Ley-ton welcomed it. If things got too serious, Hadley would just start building a wall in front of those already sturdy barriers she had in place.

"I guess sometimes sheets have attitude, too," he coun-tered. "Because I swear they smelled like you."

Well, crap. Hadley looked away from him again. "I slept in Hayes's room night before last."

That was almost as much of a surprise as seeing her on the hall floor. "Why?"

She reached down to gather up the blanket and makeshift pillow. "I don't like sleeping in my old room. *Little Cowgirls* wasn't exactly a cheery time in my life, and being in there brings it all back."

"Hell," he mumbled.

He could see that she was telling the truth, and he wanted to throttle himself. Of course this place had bad memories, and the triplets' bedroom had been practically a TV set where producers and her parents had mapped out her life. A life where she lived in a fishbowl, and her every flaw, embarrassment and mistake were put on-screen as entertainment.

"You could have slept in your parents' old room," he suggested. But he stopped, realizing that probably wouldn't have been comfortable, either. No doubt there were memories of her mother and how badly she'd treated her kids.

There was Em's room, too, but obviously Hadley hadn't felt right sleeping there, either. Or the sewing room that had a pullout sofa.

"You should have said something," Leyton told her. "I could have slept in your old room, and you could have taken Hayes's. That's what we can do tonight so you don't have to sleep on the floor."

Her mouth tightened—he'd just reminded her that he wasn't going anywhere until they had all of this sorted out with Em.

"Not all the memories in this house are bad ones," he added.

She didn't jump to agree but finally muttered a "No" as she opened her bedroom door and tossed in the blanket and shirt. They landed on Sunny's old bed. She didn't close the door, however. Hadley stood there and glanced around.

Leyton looked, as well. It'd been years since he'd been in this part of the house. He and Hadley had never made out in here, but he'd gone in with her a few times when she'd needed to get something from her room.

It was indeed like a time capsule, with the large loft-style room divided into three sections. *Distinct* sections that mirrored the image that the producers of *Little Cowgirls* had given them. Sunny's section had her wall posters of boy bands and comedians and the perky colors that meshed with her Funny Sunny nickname.

McCall's area was a showcase of her trophies and awards for the civic causes she'd championed. There were dolls and stuffed animals. Her colors were petal pink to go with her good-girl image.

And then there was Hadley's space.

A *Thelma & Louise* poster hung off-center on a black wall. The poster next to it was a heavy-metal rocker grabbing his bulging crotch. There were no awards, nothing bright and perky. It was as if a dark cloud had settled over that particular spot. It didn't appear that cloud would be moving anytime soon.

"Why'd you leave all of this stuff in here?" he asked.

Hadley made a sweeping glance around the room. "Because it didn't matter. The damage had already been done." And she shut the door.

Leyton wanted to curse again because it was true. The labels the producers had given them had become like self-fulfilling prophecies. That wasn't a bad deal for Funny Sunny or Good Girl McCall, but it had sucked for Badly Hadley. Of course, maybe Hadley would have gotten there without the label. She'd always had more of a rebel streak than her sisters.

A streak that sure as hell hadn't made her happy.

The sadness was practically coming off her in thick waves, and he hated it. Hated that by breaking up with her he'd been part of creating the memories that had led to her sleeping on a hall floor. Yeah, it was a stretch to think it was still bothering her, but emotions like that got all balled up together in one miserable stew.

"Maybe you should look through the box that you and Em buried," he suggested. "Em wanted you to have that so it could cheer you up."

She turned toward him, giving him a flat look. Which was better than the sad expression she'd been sporting. "Don't ask me about that picture of you," she warned him.

"Okay. I'll ask you about the dried flower, then. I never gave you a flower. Did someone else? I figure that flower must be pretty important if you'd put it in a box meant to hold good memories."

Considering that her flat look got even flatter, Leyton figured he should just let it go. Not just for now but forever.

"Why don't you fix us some coffee?" she asked, clearly avoiding any flower discussion. "I'll grab a quick shower."

He watched her as she walked up the hall to the bathroom and realized she'd slept in the same clothes she'd been wearing the day before. The jeans and shirt were wrinkled and were flecked with lint from the blanket. Sort of like a walk-of-shame outfit, except they certainly hadn't done anything remotely shaming. Well, unless dirty thoughts counted.

Leyton cursed his dirty thoughts, cursed himself and headed downstairs to put on the coffee. It took him a few minutes to find everything, since he wasn't familiar with Em's kitchen, so the pot had just finished brewing by the time Hadley came down—bringing the scent of her shower and the soap she used with her.

She'd changed out of her walk-of-shame clothes, too, and was wearing another pair of jeans and a loose dull blue top. Other than her dangling silver spider earrings, there was nothing about the outfit that screamed city, Holly-wood or costume designer. But then, it also didn't scream Lone Star Ridge, and it made him wonder if Hadley fit comfortably in either of those worlds.

"Look, I know you have work," she said, taking the cup of coffee that he poured for her. "Cop work, not just look-ing for a woman who obviously doesn't want to be found. I'll be okay here by myself until McCall and Sunny get here. Or I can call Bernice Biggs and ask her to come over and babysit."

Along with being the most crotchety person in the state, Bernice was Em's part-time housekeeper, and Ley-ton couldn't think of anyone less suitable to be with Had-ley. For one thing, Bernice would give no emotional or search support. Zero. And she was more likely to escalate Hadley's worries by doling out a worst-case scenario or two about Em. Added to that, Hadley despised the woman and vice versa, so having her here wasn't a wise decision.

Of course, he likely fell into the same "unwise deci-sion," too, but at least he didn't despise Hadley. Or vice versa. Hadley's walls might be thick and high, but he knew she was also feeling the old tug of attraction.

"I can be on call from here," he said. "Cait will be in the office today, and if I have to leave, then Shaw or Aus-tin can come over."

He expected her to have a snarly comeback about it not being necessary to have a penis to stay safe and fend off any intruders. Hadley was rolling her eyes and look-ing ready to gear up for that. But she didn't get a chance because her phone rang. She frowned when she pulled it from her pocket, and "Unknown Caller" was on the screen.

Leyton could see the debate she had about answering it.

It was possibly a telemarketer, wrong number or, in Hadley's case, maybe a reporter from one of the trash magazines. But considering everything else going on and the early hour, it could also be connected to Em, which was almost certainly why Hadley hit the answer button. Leyton went one step further and put the call on speaker.

"Hadley," the woman greeted her.

Em.

"Thank God," Hadley murmured. Then she blurted, "Where are you?"

"I'm safe," Em answered.

"That doesn't tell us where you are." Hadley's voice wasn't a murmur now. There was a bite to it. "We're worried sick about you, and we need to know why you're doing this. You need to come home," she added in a snap.

"I will come home," Em answered, "when I can. But I need to work out some things first. You're not staying at the house alone, are you?"

"I'm with her," Leyton answered. He didn't murmur, either, and he used his cop's voice. "Em, a lot of people are looking for you. A lot of people want you to tell us where you are and why you ran off the way you did."

Silence. For a long time. But Leyton moved closer to the phone, trying to tune in to any sounds he could hear. There was chatter in the background, the kind that you'd hear in a restaurant or even a hotel lobby. No music, though, and no announcements like there'd be in an airport. No sounds of her being outdoors, either. Of course, that didn't narrow down the possibilities of where Em had gone.

"I'm safe," Em repeated. "I don't want any of you worrying about me."

"Maybe so, but you know causing worry is exactly what you're doing," Leyton fired back. "You love your grandkids. I know that. And that's why I don't understand why you'd put them through this."

"That's why I'm calling—so they won't worry. Like I said, I just have some things to do first."

"You can do those things from here," Hadley insisted. "Whatever you're going through, I can help. Leyton can help," she tacked on to that.

With the next round of silence, Leyton continued to listen, trying to pick through the background noise. And he finally heard something.

"I have to go," Em blurted. "Just give me another day or two, and I should be home. Love you."

Hadley groaned when Em ended the call, but Leyton took hold of her arm. "Let's go," he told her. "I know where Em is."

CHAPTER EIGHT

"EM'S ON THE San Antonio River Walk," Leyton blurted out as they hurried toward the door. "Somewhere indoors with other people around."

Hadley quickly went back through the conversation she'd just had with her grandmother, and that conclusion just wasn't registering. "How do you know?" she asked, keeping pace with Leyton. She grabbed her purse on the way out of the house, and they practically ran to his truck.

"I heard someone ask about getting tickets for a River Walk cruise. That probably means Em's downtown on or near the River Walk. It was the kind of question someone would ask a desk clerk or waitstaff."

She hadn't heard any mention of that, but Hadley had been focused on what her grandmother was saying. And Em did love that particular part of San Antonio. Still, the River Walk was a big place, and it was jammed with shops, restaurants and hotels.

"Unless we can narrow down where she is, we'll never find…" But Hadley let that thought trail off. This was a lead that would hopefully help them figure out where Em was, and she had to latch on to that.

"What can I do to help?" she asked as he started the drive. It would take them nearly an hour to get to San Antonio, and they might be able to use this lead to zoom in on something.

"Call Cait," Leyton instructed. He handed her his phone,

since Hadley didn't have his sister's number. "She used to date a cop in San Antonio, and they've stayed friends. I want her to contact him and give him Em's picture. Maybe he can pass it on to some beat cops who might have seen her."

That was definitely a good start. Well, for them it was. It was obvious she'd woken up his sister when Cait answered. Hadley relayed what Leyton had told her and got a somewhat grumpy verification that she'd get right on it.

The moment she was done with Cait, Leyton used the hands-free to make a call of his own, and because it was on speaker, Hadley soon heard another sleepy female voice answer.

"Leyton," the woman said. Her voice was almost a purr, and it became even purrier when she repeated his name. "Is everything okay?"

"Sorry to wake you, Elise, but I need a favor."

"Anything," she said, and the woman managed to make that sound like an invitation to sex.

Hadley knew she shouldn't feel even a nudge of jealousy. Leyton was a grown man, and he'd certainly had plenty of women. She just hated that he'd had one who managed to sound like a sexy willing siren even at this ungodly hour.

"I've got a situation of an elderly woman who might be in danger or under duress, and I believe she's in a hotel on or near the River Walk. I know you've got plenty of contacts, and I was wondering if you can check and see if Emma or Patsy Webster is a registered guest at any of the hotels in that area."

Hadley had no idea who this woman was who could manage something like that, but Elise didn't balk. "Is it possible she's using an alias?"

Leyton sighed. "Yes, but if you pull up her driver's license, you'll have her photo, and you could give a description to anyone you might be able to contact. I know it's a lot to ask—"

"It isn't," Elise interrupted. "I'll get right on this. Are you in San Antonio now?"

"On the way there. I just left Lone Star Ridge."

"So, you'll be here in about an hour. I'll see what I can do and get back to you." The woman paused. "It's good to hear from you, Leyton."

He ended the call, but he didn't jump to explain the extremely helpful Elise. "A friend?" Hadley finally had to ask.

"Yeah. She's a PI…and a friend. And, no, I'm not personally involved with her. Not for a long time now," he added in a mumble.

Well, it seemed to Hadley that Elise wanted to do away with that *not for a long time now*, or else the woman had a very helpful nature. Hadley was going to go with door number one.

"Will this favor she's doing cost you?" Hadley pressed.

Leyton shrugged. "We need to find Em, and Elise can help with that."

Which, of course, confirmed that there would indeed be a price to pay. One that Hadley couldn't pony up for him, since the sultry Elise might want to get her payment between the sheets.

"Thank you," Hadley said. "And please thank Elise for me, too."

He looked as if he wanted to say something about that, but before Leyton could get out a single word, her phone rang. Her heart sank a little when she didn't see Em's name or "Unknown Caller" on the screen, but it was something familiar.

Hayes.

Her brother didn't make a habit of calling her—or seeing her, for that matter. In fact, they got together only a couple of times a year, despite living only about twenty miles from each other.

"Any sign of Em?" Hayes asked the moment she answered.

His question wasn't really a surprise, because Hadley knew that, despite rarely coming back to Lone Star Ridge, he loved their grandmother as much as Hadley and her sisters did.

"She called this morning," Hadley explained, "but she wouldn't say where she was. Leyton and I are about to check out a lead now. We think she's in San Antonio."

"Good," Hayes said, and a moment later he repeated it, not with any actual relief in his tone. It was more like a sigh.

She didn't put the call on speaker, but Hadley suspected Leyton could hear at least some snatches of the conversation, since the cab of the truck wasn't that big. They weren't exactly shoulder to shoulder, but it was close.

"It's early for you to call," Hadley commented to her brother.

"I'm just now getting home."

So not early but rather late. That was more the norm for Hayes, too. She knew he didn't have stellar sleeping habits, and he often shot scenes at all hours of the day or night for his TV show, *Outlaw Rebels*.

"I'm not sure what I can do to find her," Hayes went on. "She's not answering when I try to call her."

"She's not answering calls from any of us. I'm worried,"

Hadley added, knowing she could say that to Hayes even if she didn't want to say it aloud to her sisters. Despite his unconventional ways, Hayes was still her big brother.

"Yeah, I'm worried about her, too. And you," Hayes said. "I heard you had to move out of your place and have been staying at your office. Look, Had, if money's tight—"

"It's okay," Hadley interrupted. "I'm fine." That was so not the truth, but Hadley wasn't going to hit up Hayes for a loan even if he was supposedly drowning in the bucks.

"Maybe I can help you get costume design work, then," he went on several moments later—and after he huffed in what was no doubt frustration. "I know people who know people, and I'm sure there's something."

Yes, something that Hayes would likely create just so she'd have a job. "I'm working on a project now, but until we find Em, it's on the back burner."

"I get that. After Em surfaces, I'll ask around." He paused again. "Are you okay being back there?"

She could have sworn she felt Leyton stiffen beside her. There was no way Leyton could know the *depth* of Hayes's question, but he wasn't stupid. Leyton knew something was wrong, that she was out of step just by being back at the ranch with the flood of memories.

"I'll get through it," she told her brother.

That wasn't a lie. It might be hard to have come home, but she wouldn't let the past stop her from finding Em and getting her back where she belonged. After that, well, Hadley had some decisions to make.

Hayes stayed quiet for so long that Hadley thought he might press her on her current state of mind, but he finally said, "Let me know when you find Em."

Hadley assured him she would, ended the call and waited to see if Leyton was doing any "state of mind" pressing.

Even if he hadn't heard every word of her brother's concerns, he would no doubt have picked up on the gist of it. Would have also noticed her uncomfortable body language.

But Leyton didn't say anything. He continued to drive and let the silence settle between them. It wasn't a relaxed settling, either. It was the kind of quiet that made Hadley feel as if she were in a lineup and had to confess all. Or at least confess something.

"Hayes is worried because of my job situation," she said. "You already know what happened with tit-gate."

"I know. Well, I saw the tabloid story about it, anyway. It's really messed things up for you, huh?"

She made a sound of agreement. Oh, yeah. It'd messed things up big-time. "As you well know, I have a long and lengthy track record for doing things that get me in hot water. Badly Hadley," she grumbled. "I've really lived up to that, haven't I?"

He shrugged. "You came home when your grandmother asked you to, and you made her a unicorn hat because she wanted one. Now you're out looking for her because you love her and you're worried about her. And you carried a baby for your friend." Leyton snagged her gaze for a couple of seconds. "You're not nearly as *badly* as you think."

It unnerved her to hear him praise her like that. Even if part of the praise was for that hat. "I have a juvie record," she quickly reminded him.

"So would half the population of Lone Star Ridge, but they didn't get caught committing the various sins and deeds that could have landed them in jail." He gave her another split second of eye contact. "I suspect you wanted to get caught."

He said that last part so casually, but it hit like a thump

of reality. Because it was true. And Leyton was the only person who'd ever called her on it.

"I didn't know for sure that *Little Cowgirls* would get canceled if I got into trouble with the law," she insisted. But that was exactly what had happened. "And I didn't know it would send my parents running once the producers pulled the plug on the show."

Of course, her parents had run with the money when they'd left town, and that had been a big blow to her and her siblings. If Em hadn't stepped up to take them, heaven knew where they would have ended up.

"I wasn't exactly a fan of the show, either, after that cameraman caught us making out," Leyton commented. "I thought it was a raw deal for both of us, but I couldn't stop it from going public."

No, he couldn't. That was because, like most people in Lone Star Ridge, Leyton's mom had signed a contract, and it was one of those catchall deals where Leyton didn't have control over what was filmed or how it was edited. Hadley's mother, Sunshine, had control, more or less, but she certainly didn't back down from airing something that quickly became a fan favorite.

"The only episodes with higher ratings were when McCall wet her pants in kindergarten and Sunny asked if she could grow a weenie like our brother," Hadley reminded him.

He laughed, and while she didn't exactly join in on it with him, Hadley could see the humor in it. That was something at least. Baby steps.

"Some people get over the past just like that." She snapped her fingers, then wished she'd just shut up. Clearly, she'd gotten Leyton's attention, because he kept sliding glances at her.

"Sadly Hadley," he murmured. "That's what I used to call you sometimes."

She shook her head. "I didn't know that." And wasn't sure she liked it. She preferred bad to sad, because the latter meant people might feel sorry for her.

Leyton took the turn off the interstate and then stopped at a red light at an intersection. She had no intention of continuing their conversation about the many words that rhymed with her name, but she made the mistake of looking at him.

Just as he was looking at her.

With a smile on his incredible mouth, he leaned in and kissed her. This wasn't a quick peck. His lips landed solidly on hers, and it was plenty long enough for her to take in his taste, his scent. Long enough for her to remember why she'd once had a very hard time resisting him.

Like now, for instance.

Her body seemed to go into a slide, as if she were on one of those water rides that flung you at a fast speed and then plunged you into a pool of water. In this case, the pool was more of a puddle of feelings that she shouldn't be having. Not at a traffic light, anyway.

She eased right into the kiss, automatically shifting her body and moving closer. Definitely not putting a stop to it. Hadley let him kiss her, and then she took some pleasure of her own by kissing him right back.

They were just getting to the good part, where it was possible the kiss would have gone deep and French, when a car horn blared behind them. Which was reasonable, considering the light was now green. She had no idea how long it'd been that particular color. Maybe minutes. Maybe a week. Apparently, Leyton's kiss could also stop time along with ridding her of any common sense.

Because Hadley wanted him to do it again.

Heck, who was she kidding? She suddenly wanted a whole lot more from her former crush.

"There," he said, driving through the intersection. "I just had to get that out of the way. Now that it's out of my system, it won't happen again."

She frowned. "You kissed me two other times."

"I'm still getting it out of my system. In fact, it might take me a while to rid myself of these…urges I get."

For some stupid reason, that made her smile when there was nothing to smile about. Well, maybe that kiss was something. But it was also a reminder that she was going to have one heck of a time resisting any *urges* he might aim in her direction.

The traffic was still fairly light, and Leyton was weaving his way through it when his phone rang. The screen on his dash showed the caller's name.

Elise.

That melted away any traces of heat left over from that scorcher of a kiss, and it was a poke to remind Hadley that her mind shouldn't be on a lip-lock with Leyton but on the reason they were in his truck.

"I might have something," Elise said when he hit the answer button. Like before, the call was on the truck's speakers. "Try looking at the Pacifico. It's a little boutique hotel on the River Walk, and there's someone registered under the name of Patsy Franklin."

That sounded promising, even though Hadley had never heard Em mention that particular surname. Still, she felt a little tingle of hope.

"Don't ask me how I got the info," Elise went on, "but I found out the room is being charged to a prepaid credit card."

Leyton didn't ask, but Hadley could guess that Elise had either done some hacking or else she'd bribed someone to give her the name. That was against the law, of course, but Hadley didn't care. She was just thankful to have a lead, any lead.

"I figure if this woman you're looking for wanted to keep her real identity hidden," Elise went on, "then that would be the way to do it."

"Yeah, it would," Leyton agreed, and when they stopped at another traffic light, he programmed his GPS to take them to the hotel. They weren't far away from it at all.

"Thanks for this, Elise," he told her. "I really appreciate it."

"Let me know if you find her. Then maybe we can meet and catch up."

Here was the bill that Elise had just handed Leyton. The payment the woman wanted for services rendered.

"I'm seeing someone right now," Leyton said, and he made a point of tossing a glance at Hadley.

Despite everything, that gave her another ripple of warmth. Warmth that made her silently curse. He was seeing her, literally, but they weren't seeing each other in the way he'd just implied to Elise.

But they would.

Hadley figured that if she stayed around Leyton much longer, they'd do more kissing, and the kissing would land them in bed for some wild nights. Soon, very soon, she was going to have to figure out if she would fight that. Or just give in to it. Maybe Leyton had a point about getting this out of their systems.

That was BS, of course.

She didn't mind lying when it was necessary, but Hadley made a point of not lying to herself. If she had a longer, hotter sample of Leyton and his incredible mouth and body, it wouldn't cool her appetite. Well, not until the fling— or whatever it would be—ran its course and fizzled out. Which it would do. And then she'd be raw, possibly broken and in a whole world of hurt.

Even knowing that wouldn't stop it from happening.

"Oh," Elise said after a long pause. "Well, good for you on seeing someone. If that changes, you know where to find me."

"Thanks, Elise," he repeated and ended the call.

Hadley didn't want to talk about any part of that conversation. Especially the parts about a yet-to-happen relationship between her and Leyton. Thankfully, Leyton didn't seem to be in a "pouring out his heart" mode, either. Following the directions of the GPS, he drove to the River Walk and found a parking space about a block from the Pacifico Hotel.

Even though it was barely seven in the morning, it was hot, the temps in the eighties, and the cafés they passed were already bustling with the people who were having breakfast before heading into work. The scents of strong coffee, sugary baked goods and fried eggs all clashed together, but Leyton and she didn't even pause as they made their way down the cobblestone walkway that coiled around the river.

Hadley had been to the River Walk plenty of times when she was growing up, but she didn't remember the small hotel sandwiched between two larger ones. They stepped inside, the air from the AC immediately spilling over them, and she glanced around the small lobby. It was clean and decorated in soft muted colors that meshed with the English translation of the hotel's name: *peaceful*.

There was no sign of Em, but there was a couple at the

desk. Two women were seated on the small leather sofa and were studying a city map. Once the clerk finished with the couple, she and Leyton went closer, and Leyton unclipped his badge from his belt so he could show it to the clerk. He also flipped through his phone and came up with the photo from Em's driver's license.

"Have you seen this woman?" Leyton asked. "She's possibly using the name Patsy Franklin."

According to the clerk's name tag, he was David Mendoza. He was young, only in his twenties, and the alarm instantly went through his eyes. "I, uh… Do I have to say? I mean, do you need a warrant or something before I tell you that?"

Bingo. It meant Em was there. Or at least she had been. It took a lot of willpower for Hadley not to latch on to the clerk and demand to know where Em was.

"It's possible the woman's in danger," Leyton went on. His voice stayed calm, but it was all cop. "She disappeared from her home, and no one has seen her for nearly forty-eight hours."

The clerk's eyes widened. "Could something bad happen here? I mean, could someone come in shooting or something?"

"No. We just need to bring the woman home," Leyton replied.

"She's a senior citizen, and it's possible she's experienced some memory problems." That wasn't true, but Hadley thought this situation called for a lie or two. Anything that would help them find Em.

"You mean like dementia," the clerk muttered. "My granddad has that, and he sometimes has a hard time remembering." He nodded and turned to his computer screen. "The woman is here, and you're right—she said her name was Patsy Franklin. She's in room 212. I'll call security and have him go with you."

"Not necessary," Leyton assured him. "She's not violent." He tipped his head to Hadley. "This is her granddaughter, and the woman will want to see her."

That was another lie, of course. If Em had actually wanted to see Hadley, then she would have just come home.

The clerk shifted his attention to Hadley, and his forehead bunched up before he grinned. "Hey, didn't you used to be on that TV show about cowgirls? My mom watches the reruns. You look like the one who used to get in trouble all the time."

Hadley wasn't sure if playing the celebrity card would help them or not with getting any further cooperation from the clerk, so she just settled for a noncommittal nod and muttered a thanks.

She and Leyton took the stairs to the second floor, and when they reached the door to 212, he motioned for her to step to the side. He did the same, taking up position on the other side of the door. It took Hadley a moment to realize he'd done that so they wouldn't be seen from the peephole. He then knocked on the door.

"Housekeeping," Leyton said, clearly trying to disguise his voice.

Hadley pressed her ear to the wall, listening for any sound of footsteps and, yes, praying. Judging from what Leyton had overheard during Em's phone call, she'd likely been in the lobby at the time, so it was possible she'd gone out since then. Heck, she might have been at one of those breakfast places that she and Leyton had walked by along the way. But just when Hadley's anxiety couldn't soar any higher, the door opened.

They immediately moved out from cover. And Hadley

froze. Em was wearing a long dark-haired wig and a short body-hugging yellow dress that seemed much more suited for someone younger. Like a teenager.

"Hadley," Em said, sighing. "Leyton."

Em's mouth went in a flat line of disapproval that only emphasized her smeared red lipstick. Either Em hadn't used a mirror when she'd put it on or else she'd been making out. Hadley figured there was no chance it was the second one.

Until she saw the man who stepped up behind Em.

An elderly man with a squat build who had some smears of lipstick on his mouth.

"Come in," Em said, sighing again and stepping back. "I'm guessing we need to talk."

CHAPTER NINE

THERE WAS NO guessing about it, as far as Leyton was concerned. He, Em and Hadley were definitely going to talk. And part of that talk was going to include Em explaining who the man was hovering by her side.

But Hadley didn't even wait until they were actually inside the hotel room before she started spouting out the questions. "Why did you leave? Why did you worry us like this?"

They were both excellent questions, but Em's response was another sigh, another motion for them to come in. Leyton did, but he kept an eye on the man.

The guy was at least as old as Em, maybe older, and his thick sugar-white hair stuck up in what appeared to be multiple cowlicks. Either that, or this was his attempt at a disguise. If so, it was the only part of him that seemed to be camouflaged. The rest of him looked normal, ordinary even, in his khaki pants and plain blue shirt that was the same weathered color as his eyes.

Leyton glanced around the room and didn't see anything out of place, anything that shouldn't be there. Well, except for Em herself and the man. Still, Leyton kept his hand near his service weapon. It was probably overkill, since Em didn't actually seem to be in danger, but he didn't know this guy from Adam, and Leyton wasn't taking any chances. After all, it was still possible the guy had coerced or even forced Em into coming here with him.

But nothing looked forced.

There were no signs of struggle in the room. No restraints of any kind. There were two queen-size beds, both unmade, which indicated to him that Em and the man hadn't slept together. Still, there was a coziness, maybe even an intimacy, between them when he took hold of Em's hand. Added to that, with Em's smeared lipstick and the traces of that lipstick on the man, it didn't take a cop to figure out that kissing had been going on.

"Why?" Hadley repeated as Em shut the door. Her expression and tone of concern had more than a tinge of anger in it now. Leyton couldn't fault Hadley for that, because Em had indeed put her and her siblings through an emotional wringer.

A wringer that might not be over.

"Tony, this is my granddaughter Hadley," Em said, making introductions. "And this is Sheriff Leyton Jameson, Hadley's boyfriend."

Leyton figured Hadley wanted to object to his boyfriend label, but both of them latched on to what Em had called the man. "Tony?" Leyton questioned. "As in Tony 'the Iceman' Corbin?"

Tony gave what Leyton thought of as an "aw, shucks" grin. "That's me, but nobody calls me that anymore."

The easy grin didn't put Leyton at ease. Apparently, not Hadley, either. "You're here with a man from the mob?" Hadley demanded.

Em scratched her head, causing her wig to shift a little. "Tony isn't in the mob. That was his past, and he really couldn't help it. He was born into it." She looked at Hadley. "By the way, did you bring the unicorn hat I asked you to make?"

In the grand scheme of things, that didn't seem to be at all important, and Hadley's flat stare let Em know that.

Em shrugged. "I just thought I could use it while I was here."

Since Hadley looked ready to implode, Leyton copied Tony's gesture and took her by the hand. He sat with her on the foot of one bed, and Tony and Em sat on the other so they were all facing.

"Start from the beginning," Leyton instructed, aiming his attention at Em. "Tell us why you left Lone Star Ridge."

Em dragged in a long breath that Leyton figured she'd need. Before this was over, there'd be a lot of answers, and Em would be providing most of them.

"Some of this was in the letter in the happy memory box," Em said.

"The letter has water damage, and we couldn't make out a lot of it," Hadley snapped. "Besides, you put that letter in the box years ago, so what does it have to do with what's happening now?"

"It pretty much has everything to do with it," Em replied on a sigh. "I guess you can say that I've been on a first-name basis with fudging the truth for a while."

Leyton had to take a moment to interpret that. "You've been lying for a long time. Why?"

"Because of me," Tony answered. He gave Em's hand a gentle stroke. "Poor Patsy. That's her real name, by the way. She just got caught up in my family mess."

Leyton thought of the picture in the newspaper of a very young Em and this man. At least it was this man if Tony was telling the truth about who he was. Leyton couldn't figure out a reason why he would BS them about that, but there appeared to be layers to this mess. Something that'd happened decades ago was now coming back to haunt them.

"Again, start from the beginning," Leyton insisted, and he made a quick glance at Hadley to see if she was okay. She wasn't. She looked as if someone had punched her.

Em scratched her head again, and the wig must have been itchy, because she yanked it off. Her natural gray hair caused the heavy makeup to flash like a beacon. Leyton wanted to know why Em was wearing that getup in the hotel room, but he didn't intend to get the woman off topic. As it was, he suspected Em would be taking a meandering route to tell this tale.

"Maybe this would be better coming from me," Tony piped in.

His voice was meek, and he certainly didn't sound or look like someone who'd earned the moniker of the Iceman. He was about as far as you could get from the stereotype of a mobster.

Em seemed to consider what the man had just said, and she gave Tony a nod.

"Patsy—uh, I mean, Em—and I met when we were teenagers. She worked at the Dairy Dip over in Beaumont, and I had a fondness for curly-top cones." He smiled at Em. "She was as pretty as a picture. Still is," he added, causing Em to blush. "We fell in love." He paused, frowning. "But things didn't end well."

"Your brother, Marco, was convicted of racketeering and some other crimes," Hadley supplied when Tony paused. "We found a newspaper article about it."

Tony nodded. "My brother always did have a nose for trouble, and he got mixed up with some very bad men. He mixed me up in it, too. I'm not saying I was squeaky clean.

I wasn't. But I guess the prosecutor figured I was the little fish they could use to get bigger fish, including Marco."

Leyton wanted to get the trial records and have a better look at them, but plea deals like that were common. Still, he wanted to know specifically what crimes Tony had committed, and he didn't want to rely on Tony to give him those details.

"I learned what Marco and Tony were doing," Em said, picking up the story. "And I asked Tony to stop. He said he already had, that he didn't want anything more to do with his brother and his business dealings, but before he could go to the cops, he and Marco got arrested."

"Em got pulled into it because of me. She did nothing wrong," Tony quickly added. "Nothing other than fall in love with me, that is."

Em smiled again, and there was plenty of lovey-dovey on her face when she looked at Tony. Hadley cleared her throat, no doubt her way of getting their attention and telling them to get back to topic.

"Em and I testified against Marco," Tony continued, "and my brother was convicted and went to jail. Em and I went into witness protection."

Hadley sucked in her breath, hard, and the sound she made was a cross between a gasp and groan.

"It was necessary," Em said. "Because Marco could have had us hurt, or worse." She said it almost flippantly, as if describing how she'd made one of the curly-top cones that Tony had liked.

Hadley made another of those sounds, and this time Leyton was on the same page with her. "The cops actually believed that Marco could and would hurt you?"

Em and Tony nodded at the same time. No hesitation whatsoever.

"My brother isn't a good man," Tony supplied. "So, the Marshals gave Em and me new identities and told us that we couldn't be together, that it would be too easy for Marco to track us that way. Even though he was in jail, Marco still had connections."

Hell.

When Em had gone missing, Leyton had come up with plenty of scenarios, but he hadn't truly believed that the woman was in actual danger. Or at least she had been in danger. Leyton wasn't sure if that was still the case, but Em must have had a reason for leaving and wearing a disguise.

"I couldn't see Em because I didn't want her hurt," Tony emphasized. "So, I moved on with my life and tried to forget her. I didn't manage to do that," he mumbled.

"I moved on, too," Em said. "Well, as much as I could. I didn't have any family. I was living in the state home for girls when Tony and I met."

"It's true that you were an orphan?" Hadley asked. "Because I'm not sure what to believe anymore."

"I know, and I'm sorry." Em definitely wasn't flippant now. "I didn't lie about that. I never knew who my father was, and my mom died of pneumonia when I was twelve. There wasn't any family to take me, and foster care didn't work out, so I went to live in a state home."

Leyton didn't know what kind of experience that had been for her, but it couldn't have been an ideal one, and it might explain why she'd gotten involved with a man with such a shady family.

"The year after I went into witness protection," Em continued, "I met your grandfather, married him and moved to Lone Star Ridge. I loved my husband, but I never forgot Tony."

Tony and Em smiled at each other again, but he and Hadley sure as heck weren't doing any smiling.

"I'm guessing something happened with Marco?" Leyton prompted. "Something that would cause Em to leave her home with you and come here?"

Em nodded. "Marco served his time and got out of jail."

Yeah, that was exactly where Leyton had thought this was going. So he'd need to do research on Marco, too, even though by now the man had to be in his late seventies or even his eighties. In this case, though, age didn't mean Marco wasn't still dangerous.

"Do you know where your brother is?" Leyton asked Tony.

Tony shook his head. "Marco was supposed to report in with his parole officer, but he didn't. I figure he went under so he could look for Em and me and do a little payback."

Well, that would be one reason for Marco to disappear, but Leyton was going to try to see this through rose-colored glasses. Maybe the man wanted to get out of the country and spend his last years in peace.

"When I learned Marco had gotten out of jail, I hired some PIs to find Em," Tony explained. "I wanted to warn her and to try to keep her safe. I found out where she was, and I went to see her."

"How'd the PIs find her?" Leyton asked.

"Em had left a letter with an old friend of hers. A letter she wrote shortly after she got married. The friend gave it to the PIs."

"I wanted Tony to have the letter," Em insisted, "but I couldn't give it to him myself because I didn't know where he was. I figured if he ever came looking for me that he'd know I'd gotten married and that I was happy."

"Reading that letter meant a lot to me," Tony continued. "And he helped me figure out where she lived." He paused, giving Em's hand another squeeze. "I went to see her, and we decided we had to do something. I mean, if I could find her, then so could Marco."

"Why didn't you just tell us all of this when you called?" Hadley demanded, aiming a glare at Em. "Why didn't you tell me where you were?"

"Because I didn't want you to come looking for me. I thought it was best to put some distance between me and anyone in the family."

As explanations went, it sucked, but he doubted Em was thinking straight right now. Plus, Tony probably helped convince her that coming here was the right thing to do.

It wasn't.

"Marco could have come to Lone Star Ridge," Leyton said, hoping to put the fear of God into Em. "He could have done that while Hadley was there."

"And that's why I insisted you stay with her." Em certainly wasn't smiling now. In fact, she was blinking hard. Either she was trying not to cry or the gunky makeup was causing her some trouble.

"You should have come to me with all of this," Leyton insisted, keeping his voice as calm as possible. That was because Tony looked to be on the verge of tears, too.

"Maybe," Em muttered, though she certainly didn't seem convinced that going to him would have been the right thing to do. "But Tony and I thought we could lure Marco here. That's why I used my real name, Patsy Franklin, when I checked in. I figured if Marco was looking for me, he wouldn't know to look for Emma because that's the name I got after going into witness protection."

Em motioned toward the wig and then fanned her hand over the dress. "I tried to make myself look like I did when

Marco knew me, and Tony and I went out, making ourselves as visible as possible so we might be spotted."

Hadley huffed. "You tried to make yourself bait for a
dangerous man who might want to hurt you?"

Tony and Em nodded in unison again, and Tony provided the explanation. "If Marco tries to make a move on
us, we could have him arrested again, and then you and
your sisters wouldn't be in danger."

That wasn't the dumbest plan Leyton had ever heard,
but it was close. "If Marco finds you, he could hurt both
of you before you manage to call the cops. Or if he doesn't
follow your bread crumbs here to the hotel, he could go
to the ranch and try to use Hadley, McCall or Sunny to
get to you."

The color drained from Tony's face, and Leyton thought
maybe it had done the same to Em. With the makeup, it
was hard to tell.

Em stood up from the bed. "Tony and I need to talk
about this," Em said. "Maybe we can go down to the coffee shop."

"No," Leyton and Hadley said in unison, and Leyton
figured they both had the same concern. They didn't want
Em trying to sneak off.

"But I need to talk to Tony," Em insisted.

"And you can, but you're staying here," Leyton insisted right back. He went to the window and looked out
to make sure there wasn't a fire escape. There wasn't, and
it'd be a long jump down to street level. In other words,
Em wouldn't be able to escape.

"Hadley and I will wait in the hall," Leyton decided,
"and don't you dare try to lock us out. If you do, I'll break
down the damn door."

Hadley went to the window and had a look for herself

before she followed Leyton out of the room. They didn't go far, only a few steps into the hall.

"Don't do anything else stupid," Hadley warned her grandmother as Em shut the door. Hadley huffed and took out her phone. "I need to text McCall so she can let the others know Em is safe."

Good idea. Leyton did the same to Cait. Between his sister and McCall, the word would spread soon enough that they'd located Em. That would relieve a lot of worry, and then he could try to figure out a fix for this mess.

"I told McCall we found her and that I would explain everything else when I could," she relayed, then looked up at him. "Thank you for doing this."

The thank-you actually riled him some because he didn't want or need it. This wasn't the job, damn it. Em was important to him. So was Hadley. Even if he hadn't been a cop, he would have done whatever it took to find the woman.

"Do you think Tony's on the up-and-up? Do you really think he's here to make sure Em doesn't get hurt?" Hadley asked before he could vent his anger. And the question cooled his riled mood. That was because he could still see the worry all over Hadley's face.

"Hard to tell." But he crafted a follow-up text to Cait to have her get started on the court records for Marco's trial and a background check on Tony Corbin. Of course, Leyton didn't know the name the man was using now, but once he had it, he'd send that to Cait, too.

"We'll talk Em into coming back with us," Leyton went on after he'd put his phone away, and he made sure Hadley had eye contact with him before he added the rest. "And I'll be staying at the ranch with you and Em until I'm sure you're both safe."

He thought maybe she'd argue about that, but Hadley seemed to take a breath of relief, and much to his surprise, she stepped toward him, sliding her arms around him. She pressed her face to his shoulder.

"Thank you," she murmured.

This time, those words didn't rile him at all, and Leyton pulled her closer to him. It felt as if a huge weight had just dropped off him. He and Hadley were going to work on this together, and while he doubted this moment would cure whatever was eating away at her, it was a start. Ironic that it'd been Em and her situation to put that into motion.

Leyton brushed a kiss on the top of her head and might have considered taking that kiss to her mouth, but Em opened the door. The woman gave them the once-over and smiled.

"I seem to remember the two of you getting caught cuddling up like that when you were teenagers," Em remarked.

No, that hadn't been cuddling. That'd been full-on making out.

Hadley stepped away from him, and Leyton could see that she was gearing up to grill Em on the conversation she'd just had. First, though, Leyton wanted to get in one question.

"What name has Tony been using all these years?" Leyton asked.

"Bobby Caldwell," Em readily supplied, "but he doesn't want to use that anymore. He wants us all to call him Tony. And I'll be Em, just like I've been for the past sixty years."

"You're coming back to Lone Star Ridge with Leyton and me," Hadley blurted out, obviously ignoring what Em had just said.

"Yes, I am," her grandmother answered.

Leyton hadn't expected the quick agreement or Em's

smile to continue as she reached behind her, taking Tony's hand and pulling him into the doorway with her.

"Tony will be coming with us, too," Em added, both of them smiling. Tony dropped a quick kiss on Em's mouth. Leyton could have sworn he saw little hearts in their eyes.

"He's coming to the ranch?" Hadley asked, and there were definitely no heart eyes for her.

"Yes," Em repeated, beaming now. "Tony and I have decided to get married."

CHAPTER TEN

HADLEY DECIDED TO do something she rarely did—look on the bright side. Em was home and safe. Later, after the shock had worn off some, Hadley figured the bright side would take a nosedive and reality would set in, but for now she just stood back and watched as Sunny and McCall engulfed Em in a flurry of hugs.

There were tears, mainly from Sunny, and they were definitely of the happy, relieved variety. There were even some cautious welcomes and congrats to Tony when Em introduced him as her fiancé. McCall and Sunny both seemed puzzled about that announcement.

Welcome to the club.

But neither of her sisters bellowed out objections. Those would likely come later.

Thankfully, Tony looked nothing like a former mobster or even someone who'd had even a mild brush with the law. In fact, going with the bright side again, he looked like a senior citizen who was in love. Also, if his feelings for Em were all just an act, then the man was putting on an Oscar-worthy performance.

Hadley would keep an eye on him. On Em, too. And she had no doubts that her sisters and Leyton would do the same. Even now he was eyeing the newly engaged couple as Hadley was.

"The engagement happened fast," Tony told McCall

and Sunny. "But I'll be getting Patsy, I mean Em, a ring real soon."

It was a huge understatement about the engagement happening fast. Then again, teenage romances had a way of sticking with you. That was what it seemed to be doing with her and Leyton, anyway. Maybe it was hard to cool down that kind of heat.

Hadley frowned.

And she so wished she hadn't thought of her grandmother and Tony as having any kind of heat.

"You don't worry about me moving off," Em piped in. "Tony and I will be making our home right here."

Well, that was something at least. Of course, Hadley had no intention of letting Em go anywhere. She was already considering if she could put alarms on the door and Tony's car in case the couple decided to skip out again. But Hadley didn't think they would. Not with the threat of Marco Corbin looming over them.

A threat that Em had somewhat minimized when she'd told Sunny and McCall why she'd left Lone Star Ridge.

Instead of saying Marco might want to hurt them, as she'd told her and Leyton in the hotel, Em had toned it down with the chance that Marco *might* still be angry with them. Em had further insisted that she'd wanted to coax Marco into finding her so they could hash out the past and have a good air clearing. A *showdown* would have been a better term for it.

McCall and Sunny didn't seem to buy that toned-down version, which was good, and Hadley would make sure her sisters understood that they should all take precautions. Exactly what precautions, she didn't know yet, but Hadley knew that was where Leyton would help.

"Come on to the kitchen," Em said, motioning for them

to follow her. "We can have some iced tea and cookies while we talk about wedding plans."

Hadley didn't want either, but like the others, she went with her grandmother. Em stopped, however, when she saw what was sitting on the kitchen table—the unicorn hat, which she promptly picked up and put on.

Em grinned and modeled it by bobbing her head side to side. "If I'd had this in San Antonio, I could have worn it and really drawn attention to myself. Marco would have had no trouble spotting me…and then we could have had that air clearing."

So, that was why she'd wanted the hat. It made sense, but only in an Em sort of way. "I'm surprised you didn't go to the Dairy Dip in Beaumont," Hadley remarked. "Marco probably looked there for you."

Em dismissed that with a flippant pooh-pooh sound and the flap of her hand. "The Dairy Dip burned down years ago, and I always told everybody how much I loved San Antonio. Marco knew that's where I lived when I was a little girl, before I ended up in the state home. Guess he's not interested in finding me after all, or he would have headed straight to San Antonio."

That was still to be determined. Marco could indeed be in San Antonio trying to find Em. It was a big city with lots of places for someone to hide. Or try to put a spotlight on themselves to use as a lure. If Tony's PIs could manage to track her down, then Marco could, too.

She thought of the sultry-sounding Elise and how quickly she'd managed to get a lead on Em staying at the hotel. Under what had been her real name, no less. A name that Marco could search for, and it could lead him to the same hotel. After that, the clerk or someone else who'd seen them might tell Marco that Em had left with a cowboy cop. That wouldn't be a direct lead to Leyton and Lone Star Ridge, but it could be a straight line to her, since the clerk had recognized her. Marco wouldn't have any trouble finding out where *Little Cowgirls* had been filmed.

Leyton's phone rang, and when he glanced at the screen, he excused himself and walked out to take the call. He didn't exactly invite Hadley to go with him, but she figured this might have something to do with Em's situation.

"Keep an eye on Em," Hadley whispered to Sunny, and she went after Leyton.

Hadley found him on the front porch, and he was pacing while he talked. Or rather while the caller talked. Hadley couldn't hear what was being said on the other end of the line, but she could definitely hear Leyton. His occasional responses were short and not very sweet. They included a *shit*, a *sonofabitch* and a snapped out *what the hell?* By the time he finished his call, it was obvious to Hadley that whatever he'd heard from the caller wasn't good.

"That was Cait, and she confirmed that Marco's indeed out of prison," Leyton told Hadley before she could ask. "And no one has a clue where he is. The man apparently has magic skills, because he just vanished."

That tightened her stomach and chest and caused her breath to go thin. Now she understood why Leyton had cursed. "The cops must be looking for him."

Leyton nodded, scrubbing his hand over his face. "His disappearance is a parole violation so, yeah, they're looking. In the meantime, he could be any damn where, including out looking for Em and his brother."

More tightening in her chest. Hadley couldn't see any of this falling on the "bright side" of things.

"The Houston cops say that Marco was a model prisoner," Leyton went on. "No violence, no serious infractions, but that doesn't mean he won't be a risk now that he's out."

No, not if he wanted to pay back his brother and Em for testifying against him. They were the reason he'd spent decades behind bars.

"I'm guessing Marco has enough money so he can hire PIs and such?" Hadley pressed.

"Yeah, there's money. Not long after he went to prison, he inherited about a hundred grand from an uncle who passed away. Since that money couldn't be tied to any of the criminal activities, it's been sitting in an account for about fifty years and collecting a boatload of interest. Marco got that money a couple of days after he was released."

Each bit of info she was hearing only made her worries skyrocket.

"What about Tony?" she asked. "Or I guess that'd be Bobby Caldwell, since that's the name he's been using for most of his life. Did you find out anything about him that caused you to use all those curse words?"

Hadley knew that Leyton had asked Cait to run a background check on the man, because he'd done that on the drive back from San Antonio.

"No criminal record since he testified against his brother," Leyton explained. "Well, no record unless the Marshals hid something, and I can't see why they'd do that. He's a widower, no kids, and he's been living in Dallas since he went into witness protection. He's retired, but he used to own a flower shop."

"A flower shop," she repeated. That definitely didn't mesh with the image of a mobster. So, maybe he wasn't. Perhaps Tony had truly just been a teenager who'd made bad decisions.

Something that she knew plenty about.

"What do we do now?" she asked, but it was a question more for herself than Leyton. So were the questions that followed. "Do I just stand back and let Em marry him, or should I put my foot down and say all of this is a stupid idea and that she should take a breath before she says 'I do'?"

Leyton didn't jump to answer, and he did his own "taking a breath." He walked down the porch steps and into the front yard, and he glanced around. Of course, he knew the grounds, but he seemed to be looking at it with a fresh eye. Or rather a cop's eye.

"There's no proof that Marco actually ever killed or seriously hurt anyone," Leyton said. "The reason his sentence was so long was because he had connections to men who did hurt and kill. They're all dead," he added. "They were a lot older than Marco and Tony, and they died in prison."

Well, that was something at least. Marco wouldn't have a pool of his old cronies to help him do whatever it was he was planning.

"And while Marco has money," Leyton went on, "he's also eighty-three. It's possible he just wants to live out the rest of his life in peace and not have to report to a parole officer. He could already be out of the country."

Hadley went down the steps to join him. "But you don't believe that."

"No," he readily admitted, and he turned to lock eyes with her. "That's why we'll all take security precautions."

"No argument from me on that. Though Em might give us some grief."

Not because her grandmother believed that all was well. No, Em might have some odd ways, but she wasn't stupid; however, she might want to continue to make them believe that there was no possible threat, only a potential air-clearing encounter with a convicted felon.

"I'll talk to both her and Tony." Leyton started walking again, this time toward the barn, and he motioned toward the pasture. "Remember, there are old trails on the backside of the ranch. Marco won't know about those trails, but if he wanted to sneak up on Em, that'd be the way to do it."

Hadley was sure her heart skipped a couple of beats. She wasn't a scaredy-cat, but, like Em, she also wasn't stupid. There was a possible threat, and they had to be aware of how that threat could get to them.

"Until Marco's found, it's best if Em, you and your sisters all stay indoors as much as possible," Leyton went on. "If Em balks about that, lay a guilt trip on her. Tell her how worried you are and ask her to stay inside as a favor to you."

That was a great suggestion and the perfect way to play Em, so Hadley made a sound of agreement as they walked to the corral. There were no horses in there, but two were grazing in the pasture off the side of the barn.

"Is Joshua Spicer still taking care of the livestock for Em?" Leyton asked.

She nodded. "He was here yesterday when you went into the office."

"Good. So, there's no reason for any of you to come out here." He said it like gospel, which was fine with her. It'd be fine with her sisters, too.

"While the guilt trip might work on Em, it might not work on Tony," she pointed out.

"I'll talk to him," Leyton said, going into the barn, where he did the same look around as he'd done on the grounds. "If he's really as much in love with Em as he seems, then I can convince him to keep her inside where she'll be safe. Does Joshua also muck out the barn?" he added without so much as a pause. He was definitely in cop mode now.

"I'm not sure, but if not, I'll hire him to do that until…" She wanted to say *until things get back to normal*, but that might never happen. Even if Marco was found and put back in jail, it was possible that Em would indeed marry Tony. "Until," Hadley settled for saying.

There must have been some nerves in her voice, because Leyton turned to her. His steely gray eyes went a little soft. "I'm sorry. I don't want to scare you, but I want you and your family to be safe."

There were some nerves in his voice, too, and she didn't like that pitying look of sympathy she saw on his face.

"I've taken self-defense classes," she said, and without warning, she kicked at him, stopping right before her foot would have connected with his balls. Hadley followed it up with an open palm bash in the direction of his nose. She got close enough that he probably felt the air coming off the movement.

Leyton didn't duck, didn't even flinch. Instead, he smiled. It was slow, confident and incredibly sexy. Of course, breathing was often incredibly sexy when it came to Leyton.

Uncertain of why she'd amused him or caused that smile, Hadley drew back her hand. Or rather that was what she was in the process of doing when Leyton took hold of her wrist and pulled her to him. His mouth swooped down on hers before she could even get out a gasp of surprise.

And the swooping down was just the start.

The man could create magic with that mouth, and his lips moved over hers as if he had some secret knowledge to unlock every erogenous zone in her body. He didn't wait to deepen the kiss, either. Leyton went right in, not in the brutish, overpowering way of some kissers. No. This was all finesse, and he tasted as good as he looked.

With all the energy—and, yes, some fear—zinging around them, the kiss wasn't as hungry and urgent as it could have been. He took his time, sampling, even giving her bottom lip a nip, and it was darn effective. By the time he eased back to look into her eyes, Hadley could feel the slow slide of heat all the way from her mouth to her kneecaps.

"Is that your way of disarming a bad guy?" she asked with what little breath she managed to muster.

The corner of his mouth lifted. "No, only you."

It had worked, but she was surprised he hadn't gone for the obvious by saying it was his way of disarming Badly Hadley. Either way, she was definitely in the disarmed mode.

"You do still remember that kissing me isn't a good idea?" Hadley threw out there. Oh, man. She sounded like the breathy, sultry Elise.

"Isn't it?" he countered.

She frowned, not sure if he was agreeing or disagreeing with her, and Hadley didn't have time to sort it out because he kissed her again. There was no lapse in between this one starting and going full French, but this time the slide of heat was more like a slam.

The kiss alone would have been plenty effective enough at making her crazy, but Leyton upped the stakes by upping the contact. While their mouths and tongues were fooling around, he turned her, putting her back against a stall post, and he followed that up by pressing his body to hers.

Oh, this she remembered. He was magic at this, too, and

he hadn't lost an ounce of flair in that department. Even though he was a good seven inches taller, he seemed to be able to use his body to touch and tease the parts of her that were already begging for that sort of attention.

She should stop this. That was what the sane region of her brain was telling her. But it'd been so long since she'd been touched like this. So long since she'd felt needed. That should have been a big red flag to get her to back off, but she stayed put, steeling herself up as if to weather this scorching storm.

With the kissing and touching still going on, Leyton shifted his right leg between hers, which added a special kind of pressure. She remembered it as his signature move of sorts, something he'd done to her way back when, but it seemed even more effective now. Effective enough to make her realize this had just gone beyond the mere making-out stage.

He slid his hands over her jaw and into her hair, tilting her head to re-angle the kiss. Not that it needed such measures, but it seemed to fire up the heat another notch. So many notches that Hadley gave in to it and threw her arms around him.

Now there was some hunger and urgency.

Leyton made a husky sound of approval and pressed even harder against her, and, mercy, she could feel every inch of him. Every inch. That included not only his manly part but his badge. Since it was clipped to his belt, it dug into her belly. And it was just what she needed to jolt her back to reality.

They shouldn't be doing this. It was many steps past playing with fire, and that was why Hadley untangled herself from him. It was impossible to stop all the touching because he didn't move back. But he did quit kissing her.

Leyton definitely wasn't smiling now as he looked down at her, and his breath was a little uneven. Their hearts were thudding like war drums.

"Are you going to tell me why you're fighting this?" he asked.

Good question, and she just happened to have a good answer. "Because it can't work out between us. My reputation would take the shine right off of this." She ran her fingers over his badge.

Because she was looking right at him, she saw him grimace a little. That probably had something to do with the badge being so close to his erection. Her fingers had grazed that area.

"I say we risk it," he told her.

Before Hadley could object, he kissed her again. This one was somehow more scalding than the other one, and it involved just as much touching. Hadley went from having 60 percent control to having none.

That was when Leyton stepped away from her.

"I say we risk it," he repeated. He took hold of her hand, leading her back toward the house.

CHAPTER ELEVEN

I SAY WE risk it.

Leyton knew that it'd been a pretty bold statement for him to make. One brought on by the fierce ache and need he had for Hadley after he'd kissed her lights out in the barn.

But even at the time Leyton had said it with so much cocky confidence, he'd known that the particular *risk*—sex and more sex—would have to wait. After all, Em's house was filled with people. Concerned people. And it had taken him hours to assure McCall and Sunny that they should go home and be with their respective fiancés, where they could have their own sex and more sex.

Of course, he hadn't actually spelled out that *sex and more sex* to Sunny and McCall. Best not to let them think that his hormones had gotten the better of him. But they sure as hell had. His dick could come up with some very convincing arguments, but at least he hadn't made a dick out of himself by rushing Hadley's sisters along. Or by rushing the security measures. He wanted everyone safe and tucked away in bed.

And in Hadley's case, he wanted the tucking in to be with him.

Now he'd made it through the afternoon, and Sunny and McCall were finally gone, leaving Leyton with just one more obstacle.

Dinner.

Considering that this was a homecoming meal of sorts for Em and Tony's first night at the ranch, Leyton had expected, well, better.

For reasons that would fall under "a mystery for the ages," Em had allowed Leyton's mother to supply the food, and Lenore had sent over what appeared to be a mixture of peas, canned mushroom soup and unappetizing cubes of beige tofu. There was also a Jell-O mold, but this one was green with large black olives suspended in it like eyeballs.

Em ate as if it were fine fare, but Leyton, Tony and Hadley weren't nearly as enthusiastic about digging in. They were basically moving the food around their plates, which wasn't easy to do with the Jell-O. Instead, they were chowing down on the crackers and beer that Hadley had suggested might go well with the meal. Wise choice on her part, but the crackers and beer hadn't helped with the conversation.

"Tony and I don't want to wait to get married," Em said, and it wasn't a newsflash. She'd given variations of that throughout the day. In fact, she'd given many variations of many wedding plans, including which spot on the ranch they'd use for their I dos.

Leyton suspected it was Em's way of not talking about the threat looming over them. Marco. But by not acknowledging it, it hung like a stench over the kitchen table. Well, a stench that couldn't be attributed to the casserole.

"I'm glad you're happy," Leyton settled for saying.

That wasn't just lip service. Em did indeed appear to be a happy bride-to-be excited about her upcoming wedding. But he'd also tossed that out there to gauge Tony's reaction. The man smiled, but there were nerves behind it and the gleam in his eyes that he aimed at Em. And those nerves were the reason Leyton volunteered him and Tony to clean up the dishes after the dinner was finally over.

Hadley picked up on the glance Leyton gave her, and she took hold of Em's arm. "Why don't we go in your sewing room so we can talk about your wedding dress? I could maybe do some sketches for you."

Leyton was certain there'd be other things in that discussion and that Hadley would manage to get to the bottom of how Em was truly feeling. And maybe get to the bottom of any other secrets that Tony and Em might have. Leyton thought the pair was being level with him, but it didn't hurt to press.

Which was what Leyton did the moment Hadley and Em were out of the room.

"Will Marco come after you and Em?" Leyton asked him point-blank.

Tony took a deep breath and sighed as if he'd been expecting Leyton to bring this up. "I don't know. That's the truth," Tony emphasized while he took some of the dishes to the sink. "I haven't seen him in years. I don't know what's in his heart."

"Then guess," Leyton insisted. He took the rest of the dishes to the sink, mainly so he could make direct eye contact with Tony. "Because I want to be able to prepare Em and Hadley for the worst."

"So do I," Tony said in a barely audible voice, and then he repeated it with another of those sighs. "My brother used to be a bully," he went on. "But a lot of years have passed since then."

"You think prison reformed him and he's no longer a bully?" And, yeah, some sarcasm went along with that.

Tony shook his head and started loading the dishes in the dishwasher. "No, I think that if he finds Em and me, he'll come here to try to start some trouble. I want to be ready for that, and it's one of the reasons I'm not leaving Em's side."

Leyton thought about that a moment. "*One* of the reasons?"

"The other is because I'm in love with her. Always have been."

"You were married," Leyton reminded him.

"I was. I had a good wife, and I loved her. That doesn't mean my feelings for Em went away." He paused. "I think you might know something about that. Em filled me in on how you and Hadley used to be together."

Leyton nearly snapped out that their *together* had been years ago, but he doubted he could put much conviction behind something that wouldn't even dismiss the truth. That he did indeed still have feelings for Hadley. Not love. He'd never actually been in love with her—or in love with anyone else, for that matter—but there were feelings.

"I know Em and Hadley are important to you," Tony went on. "Hadley's important to me now, too, because Em loves her so much and vice versa. I want to help you keep them both safe."

"How?" Leyton asked. "By arranging another lure so you can have an air clearing with your brother?"

Tony didn't fully wince, but it was close. "The lure seemed the right thing to do while Em wasn't here, while her granddaughters weren't in Marco's possible path."

"No, the right thing would have been to come to me," Leyton argued. "I could have arranged for protection for you and Em along with finding your brother."

Which was what Leyton had done. Or rather what he was trying to do. He hadn't had any luck finding Marco, not yet, but the protection would happen.

"I'll be staying here as much as possible," Leyton explained. "And when I'm not here, I want the house locked up tight. I don't want Em, Hadley or her sisters going outside alone. My brothers can take care of McCall and Sunny. I'll do the same for Em and Hadley. You just have to make sure Em does the smart thing and takes precautions."

"Agreed," Tony readily said. "That's why I'll be staying in Em's room tonight." He stopped, and the man actually blushed. "I don't mean it like that. I won't be in bed with her, but I don't want to leave her alone. I plan on using a sleeping bag on the floor next to her."

While that wouldn't be comfortable, especially for a man Tony's age, it would make Leyton rest a little easier to know that Em had a second pair of eyes and ears to stay on alert for a possible break-in.

"You'll be staying in Hadley's room?" Tony asked.

Leyton thought about Hadley sleeping in the hall and what she'd said about the memories haunting her in her old room. So, maybe the solution was for him to coax her into his bed. If that failed, then Leyton might be looking for a sleeping bag of his own so he could join her on the floor.

"I'll take care of Hadley," Leyton assured him. Now, the trick would be for her to let him do that.

They finished loading the dishwasher and made their way to Em's sewing room, which he remembered was by her bedroom suite. Before he and Tony could make it there, though, Em came out.

"Hadley got a phone call," Em whispered. She not only closed the door behind her but also took hold of Leyton's hand. "Tony, could you excuse Leyton and me for a sec?" She didn't wait for Tony to agree, and there was some urgency in her steps when she led Leyton back into the kitchen.

"Did Hadley have a baby?" Em demanded.

Well, he certainly hadn't expected that question. Hell. Leyton guessed that Em had heard Bailey's "Wheels on the Bus" ringtone.

There was no good way to answer this. Even if he told Em she should ask Hadley about that, he'd practically be confirming not only that there was a child but also that he knew about said child. Silence would be its own confirmation, too, which Em must have realized, because she groaned.

"Is it your baby?" she added.

Now Leyton groaned and went through the possible responses he could give to that. Best not to tell Em that he and Hadley had never done the sex deed. Like everyone else in town, she probably wouldn't believe him. Since there were no good options that would keep Hadley's surrogacy secret, he just shrugged and said, "Hadley has a right to her privacy."

"Well, that's malarkey."

Leyton gave her a flat look. "This coming from the woman who kept her real identity hidden for decades."

Em dismissed that with a grunt. "That was necessary. I couldn't risk anything getting back to Marco. That's why I always refused to be filmed on the TV show. The Marshals agreed that it was okay for the filming to go on at the ranch as long as I didn't appear on-screen or give any interviews."

"Maybe Hadley considers her privacy a necessity, too," he argued just as he heard the movement behind him.

Hadley.

She didn't say anything, but Leyton figured she'd heard at least part of the conversation. Volleying glances between him and Em, she hiked her thumb in the direction of Em's bedroom.

"Tony's looking for the sleeping bag," Hadley told Em.

Em did some glance volleying on her own, and for a moment Leyton thought the woman would dig in her heels and demand some answers, but she finally grumbled something about secrets and went toward her bedroom.

"I didn't mention or confirm anything about Bailey," Leyton quickly whispered to Hadley. "But Em asked if you'd had a baby and if the baby was mine."

Her reaction was a weary sigh, and she pushed her hair from her face. "I'm sorry about that. She won't say anything about it to anyone in town. Even if I tell her about Bailey, which I will, Granny Em will make sure everyone around here knows that Bailey's not yours."

Once again, Leyton wasn't sure how to respond to that. Part of him didn't give a rat's ass if folks believed he'd fathered a child with Hadley. But then he thought of Marty, his own father, who was an irresponsible turd when it came to knocking up women. For Leyton, it'd always been a hard line to walk to uphold the Jameson name. Not Marty's name. But the one that Shaw, Austin and Cait had chiseled out for themselves.

Hadley had said she didn't want to take the shine off his badge, but if he followed in Marty's irresponsible footsteps, that'd certainly dull it more than a bit. Of course, fathering one child wouldn't put him in Marty's league, especially since Leyton would take care of and love any child who was his.

Still, to some, the smudge would be there.

To Leyton's way of thinking, it would be a darker smudge for him than it would be for Shaw, Austin and Cait. But his half siblings hadn't had to live with being born to a woman Marty had cheated with.

"I'll tell Granny Em about Bailey," Hadley repeated, drawing his attention back to her.

She was staring at him, maybe trying to figure out what was going on in his head. No way would he bring up that whole smudge thing. Hadley had enough of that kind of crap to deal with without him adding his own baggage.

"Is Bailey all right?" he asked. "Did she call because something is wrong?"

Hadley's mouth relaxed into a near smile. "She's fine. She wanted to tell me about a book her grandmother bought for her." She paused, shook her head and drew in a long, tired breath. "But I do need to change that ringtone. Best not to advertise that sort of thing if I happen to be in town when she calls again. If Em can make the leap to you being her father, then so can others."

She gave his arm a pat when he didn't say anything. "I think I'll go up to my room. I can work on some sketches for Granny Em's wedding dress."

He raised an eyebrow. "You'll actually go in your room? You won't sit out in the hall?"

"In my room," she assured him. She came up on her toes, brushed a quick kiss on his mouth, then hurried away as if to avoid him making that kiss a whole lot hotter and deeper.

Which he would have done.

There was a lot of worry on his plate, but there was also a lot of lust. Even with the threat of life smudges and serious complications, Leyton wanted her way too much. That want, however, couldn't get in the way of what he had to do. And, no, what he had to do didn't include getting Hadley in his bed.

Leyton checked the doors and windows again, to make sure they were all still locked. They were, and there wasn't any old guy lurking around outside. Of course, with the money that Marco had, he could hire younger, tougher guys to lurk around and try to get to Em.

He grabbed his laptop, which he'd left in the dining room, and did a quick glance at Em's room—the door was shut, and he could hear her and Tony talking. So, all was well for now.

Leyton made his way up the stairs, where he halfway expected to see Hadley sitting in the hall. But nope. Her bedroom door was shut, as well. That was something at least. After he went through his emails and read reports from his deputies, he'd check on Hadley to make sure those old memories weren't haunting her—

He practically tripped over his own feet when he saw her in his room. Or rather her brother's old room. She was sitting on the side of the bed.

She was wearing those loose black jeans that she favored and a sleeveless black top. No shoes. She'd kicked those off by the door, and she was swinging her bare feet, the movement causing her red toenail polish to stand out like little beacons. Of course, Hadley was plenty beacon enough, and she had his complete attention.

"Don't," she said. Her mouth stayed pursed as if she was considering how to finish that. *Don't read anything into this. Don't tell me that I'm an idiot for being scared of a room. Don't look at me that way. Don't judge.*

Leyton figured this was one of those times when he should just stay quiet. And quit gawking at her. He put the laptop on the dresser, shut the door and went to sit beside her.

The silence stayed between them, but it wasn't the awkward tell-a-joke-to-cover-it kind. It felt more like, well, cuddling. Like two people who were just fine with nothing to say. Then again, if they'd been actually cuddling, Leyton figured there'd be plenty to say.

"I considered just stripping off my clothes and getting in bed with you," she muttered.

Instant heat, and, yeah, it went right to that brainless part of him behind his zipper. "You're dressed," he pointed out. "So you changed your mind? Or maybe you're still mulling it over?"

Brainless voted for the mulling over. Leyton tried to temper that with common sense, even if lust had nothing to do with common sense.

"Still mulling," she confirmed.

Instant erection. Just like that, he was sixteen again and very much needed to get her out of those clothes.

"I want you," she went on. "You know that already. You can tell by the way I look at you."

He risked touching her by gently putting his fingers under her chin and turning her head so they were facing each other. Yeah, he could tell by the way she looked at him that she wanted him. Could also tell that it was causing a war inside her. Leyton wanted sex, but he didn't want this to spin her into a bad place. That made him a good guy. A very hard, very frustrated good guy.

The silence came again, but she didn't look away. Hadley kept her eyes locked with his, and he waited—not easily, though—for her to make the first move. Or rather the second one. She'd made the first move by coming to this room.

"I can handle something casual," she added a moment later. "Something that won't mean more than just sex."

His erection thought that was a damn good idea, and had this been any other woman but Hadley, he would have already had his mouth on her. But Hadley was different.

Fragile. And it would piss her off to know he thought of her that way.

"It can be casual," he said. "The first time, anyway."

She pulled back her shoulders, frowned. "You're getting ahead of yourself. This could be a onetime shot, ace."

He nodded, skimming his finger over the bunched-up lines on her forehead. "But if it's not, if it's more than once, then you might have to accept there's more than just lust between us."

"It is just lust," she insisted.

As if to prove it, Hadley took hold of the back of his hair and dragged his mouth down to hers. That sure didn't soften his erection. The kiss was hard and rough, and more than a little desperate. The kiss of people who were starved for each other.

Leyton felt the starvation. The need. Felt, too, that whatever she had in mind could take care of that need. For now. And *for now* was what he would settle for.

He sank right into the kiss and soaked up even the desperation. Desperation could make for a good round of sweaty sex. So could the touches she added with the kiss. Her hand went to his chest, and Hadley started unbuttoning his shirt.

"The door," he managed to say. It wasn't locked, and he didn't want Em walking in on them.

Without breaking the kiss, Leyton hauled her to her feet, and in a clumsy groping kind of way, they made it across the room. He locked the door, putting her back against it while he did some desperation kisses of his own. He lowered his mouth to her neck and was pleased when Hadley moaned in pleasure. It'd been a while, but he still remembered her hot spots.

Obviously, Hadley remembered his hot spots, too, because she tongued his ear and slid her hand over the front of his jeans. Brainless went crazy, demanding that Leyton take her now, but the rest of his body wanted to savor this for at least a few more minutes. He finally had Hadley hot and willing, and he didn't want to rush that. He wanted to taste, touch and—

"Hell." Leyton added some more curse words under his breath when it got through his thick skull what would happen after all that tasting and touching. "I don't have a condom."

Her breath was gusting, her eyes unfocused, but she stopped and stared at him. He saw, and heard, the moment that reality sank in, because she cursed, too. Then her gaze fired around the room, specifically to the nightstand.

Leyton knew what she was thinking. Her brother could have left some condoms behind, but if so, using one that old would be as risky as having unprotected sex.

"I'm guessing that's not something Tony would have," she grumbled.

Leyton had no intention of asking him, and he wasn't going to run to the store, either. No way could he leave Em and Tony here alone while he and Hadley hurried off to buy Trojans.

"Let's try this," he said, kissing her again.

She made a sound of protest. Until he slid his hand into her jeans. For once, he was very thankful for the baggy fit, because he had no trouble getting past the waist and making his way into her panties.

And he found exactly what he was looking for.

Leyton had made it this far with her before. When they'd been teenagers, they'd gotten well past first, second and even third bases. Lots of touching, first through their clothes, and then skin on skin, which had resulted in an orgasm or two.

Those other times, though, they'd been in the dark, either in his old truck or else the barn. Plus, he'd been so caught up in the lava-heat pleasure that he hadn't taken the time to watch her face.

He took that time now.

Leyton slipped his fingers inside her. Into all that wet, warm, tight heat. Her breath hitched, more than a mere sound of pleasure. She dropped back her head until it thudded against the door, and her eyes glazed over.

"I could do this myself," she muttered. "But you're better at it."

He would have smiled had his own body not been aching from need. But Leyton pushed his own ache aside and continued to slide his fingers in and out. While he kissed her. While he ran his other hand up to cup her right breast.

Her nipple was hard, pressing against her shirt, making it easy to find. He gave it a gentle pinch and got a nice reaction. Her moan of pleasure was a lot louder, and Hadley thrust her hips against his fingers.

Hoping to get another moan, he shoved up her top, pushed down the cup of her bra and replaced his hand with his mouth.

Yeah, the moan was louder.

Hadley dug her fingers into his back, anchoring him, holding him in place. But Leyton had no intention of going anywhere until he carried through on this no-condom version of getting her off.

It didn't take long. Just a few more strokes, the flick of his tongue over her nipple, and he felt her climax clamp onto his fingers. He finished her off with a deep kiss.

Hadley cursed, but it didn't seem to be aimed at him.

He'd been with women who talked dirty, and that was fine with him, but he didn't remember that being the case with Hadley. Of course, it'd been years since he'd given her an orgasm.

"Yes, you're better at it," she said and practically melted against him. She dropped her head onto his shoulder. "I can be better with you, too."

Even if Leyton hadn't known what she meant by that, he would have gotten it when she slid her hand over the front of his jeans. A hand job was tempting—very tempting—but the timing felt off. It seemed as if Hadley needed...

Something.

He just wished to hell he knew what it was.

"We'll wait on that," he said, easing her hand away. "I can get some condoms tomorrow, and we can do this together."

Leyton thought she might argue, might even try to convince him turnabout was fair play when it came to hand jobs. But she didn't.

"I don't want to sleep in my room," she said with her head still on his shoulder. "I'm so tired, but I don't want to sleep in there."

He got a buzz. A buzz to warn him that whatever the *something* was that she needed was connected to that room. He wanted to press her, to make her tell him what had happened, but it wasn't what she needed from him now.

Maybe not ever.

So that was why Leyton scooped her up, and cuddling her against him, he carried her to bed.

CHAPTER TWELVE

SHE'D SCREWED UP. Hadley didn't need anyone to tell her that, and it wasn't even a hindsight thing. She'd known from the moment she'd gone into Leyton's room that things would happen between them.

Sex things.

They had no willpower and were seriously stupid when it came to each other. Always had been. Yet she'd gone in there, had fooled around with him in a one-sided carnal sort of way and then had slept with him. It didn't matter that the *sleeping with* had been in a non-carnal way. It didn't matter because there'd been a blasted connection.

An intimacy.

And that would lead them down a very bad road, one paved behind her with secrets.

Well, one secret, anyway. She'd shared the whole surrogacy thing with Leyton, but there were things she just couldn't share. Not without baring her soul and explaining… everything. Some things were best left unspoken and unanalyzed.

At least Leyton had made the morning after as easy for her as possible. He'd gotten up before dawn and slipped out to shower in the hall bathroom. That'd been thoughtful of him not to use the en suite and wake her, but Hadley had already been awake. In fact, she'd gotten even less sleep next to him than she had on the hall floor.

She didn't want to analyze that, either.

But there were some things that she could explore, and Hadley saw one of those *things* when she finally got dressed and went downstairs.

Tony was in the kitchen. And he was alone.

"Your grandmother's in the sewing room," Tony said, giving her a quick glance over his shoulder. He was at the sink and appeared to be cleaning up after breakfast. A meal she'd intentionally missed. "Leyton's in the dining room handling calls and reports from work."

So, that was where he'd gotten off to. Hadley was fine with that because she figured this was her chance to have a private chat with the man who was aiming to become her step-grandfather.

Tony turned toward her as she went closer to him, and he disarmed some of her steely resolve to get answers, since he was smiling and wearing a Kiss Me, I'm Irish apron. He also didn't look like a threat to anything or anybody, but Hadley knew that looks could be deceiving.

"I was just trying to clean up this old memory box," he said.

That was when she saw the old tackle box that she and Em had buried. Minus the letter, it still had the contents inside, but Tony was scrubbing a dry steel-wool pad over the rust flakes. So, not breakfast dishes after all.

"Can we talk?" she asked.

"Of course." Nothing alarming about his voice, either. It was as welcoming as the gesture he made for them to sit at the table. He even poured them cups of coffee before he joined her. "I'm guessing you have concerns about your grandmother. I can tell how much you love her, and you're worried about her. Worried about me, too, because you don't know if I have the best intentions."

Well, the man had certainly laid it all out there for her. The only thing he hadn't addressed were the hasty marriage plans.

"You'd probably feel better if Em and me delayed our vows," he went on, making her wonder if he had ESP or if he was just very good at reading her expression. "She's got her heart set on getting married next month, but I think I can talk her into holding off on that if it'd make you feel better about all of this."

Hadley had a list of things that would need to happen before she could feel better, including delaying the wedding. But that wasn't at the top of her worry list. "What are the odds that your brother will come here and cause trouble?"

He bobbed his head as if he'd been expecting that question. And he probably had. In fact, Leyton had almost certainly pressed him on it. "I don't know, but if he does come here, I won't let him hurt Em."

Okay, that was a good answer. It still didn't fix squat, though.

She put on her scariest Badly Hadley face and then leaned in to violate Tony's personal space. "If you're scamming Em in some way or if you hurt her, I'll kick you in the nuts. Understand?"

The man just smiled at her and patted her arm as if she were a child who needed soothing. "I love Em, and I'd kick myself in the nuts rather than scam or hurt her."

Hadley continued to study him to try to see if there was any tinge of untruth to that. There didn't seem to be, but she still wasn't ready to hand him a blanket "Okay, I trust you."

With that ghost of a smile still on his mouth, he turned

back to scrubbing off the rust. He used the steel-wool pad to point to the picture and then to the bagged dried flower.

"Leyton gave that to you?" Tony asked, the pad lingering in the direction of the flower.

Hadley mentally groaned. "No."

And she wished people would stop asking her about it. There wasn't a cool backstory behind it. Only an embarrassing one that would make her seem needy. Of course, she had been pretty pathetic back when she was twelve and she and Em had buried the box. In those days she was still trying to break out of the Badly Hadley mold. Or rather some days she tried. Others, she just gave in to it, since that seemed to be the path of least resistance.

Her way of distinguishing herself from her sisters, too.

She loved McCall and Sunny, but some saw them as interchangeable parts. People were always mixing them up or talking to them as if they were a single unit. It didn't matter that inside they were as different as the seasons of the year; most people saw only the identical faces.

After she'd become a teenage Badly Hadley, though, no one mistook her for her sisters.

"I wanted Leyton to give me a flower," she said. "So, I pretended it was from him."

There it was. The sad-sack truth. And why she'd blurted it out to this man she didn't trust further than she could spit, she didn't know.

"That's sweet," Tony concluded. He smiled that grandfatherly smile. "Does Leyton know how much you care for him?"

This was an easy answer. No, he didn't know. And she had zero intention of blurting that out to Tony and especially to Leyton. She'd already bared enough of her soul today.

Hadley plucked the flower and Leyton's photo from the tackle box and shoved the small bags into the front pocket of her jeans. It would cause the dried petals to crush into dust and probably bend the picture, but at least she wouldn't have to answer any other questions about them. Out of sight would hopefully go a long way to being out of mind.

Figuring she'd clued Tony in enough that he'd better be on the up-and-up when it came to Em, Hadley left him in the kitchen, and taking her coffee with her, she went in search of Leyton. Maybe, just maybe, he'd managed to locate Marco along with solving any other problems that had to do with Granny Em and Tony. That way, Leyton could go home, and she could...

She was still a little fuzzy about her future, but one thing was for certain: she would keep her eye on Tony. He might have an easy way and a truth-serum smile to make her confess dumb childhood things, but she wouldn't just hand over a blessing for him and Em.

Leyton was exactly where Tony had said he would be, the dining room. He'd set up a makeshift office with his laptop, some notepads and papers, a pen, and a huge coffee mug on the table. And he was finishing up a call when she walked in. He smiled at her. The kind of smile that let her know he was glad to see her. The kind of smile that hinted at the *intimacy* they'd had the night before.

Hadley didn't get a chance to ask him for any updates, because the moment he put his phone away, Leyton stood, went to her and kissed her.

She frowned. "You keep doing that."

"I kiss women who sleep with me. It's just a little quirk of mine."

"We didn't sleep," she pointed out. "We slept. Some," Hadley added in a grumble.

He winked at her, but the smile faded. "I figure eventually exhaustion will take over and we'll both sleep. There's only so much that multiple cups of coffee can do."

True, the half cup she'd just drank hadn't put a dent in the fatigue or the fuzzy brain. Strange, though, that Leyton's quick kiss had managed to clear a few cobwebs along with giving her body a sexual nudge. A nudge no doubt meant to remind her that he was more than capable of giving her another orgasm or two.

Sipping his own coffee, he plucked her sketchbook from the office stash on the table and handed it to her. "Em brought it to me earlier. She didn't want to wake you up and said I should give it to you, that you'd left it in her sewing room."

"She probably wanted you to bring it to me in bed," Hadley mumbled. Her grandmother was definitely trying some matchmaking, and Em would have probably been as pleased as punch to know that Hadley had indeed ended up in bed with Leyton.

She set her coffee aside so she could thumb through the pages. The most recent one was a sketch for Em's wedding dress. A sketch for which Em had given her plenty of input. The result was a flowy maxi dress in a flowery print that looked like something straight out of the sixties. It was the polar opposite of Hadley's taste and the sketches that followed.

Cyborg Cowboy.

She flipped through the rough drawings that she'd done on the flight to San Antonio. *Rough* being the operative word. She had a long way to go.

"I have to turn in some sketches by the end of the week,"

she said, talking more to herself, but then she shook her head when she realized Leyton was looking at the drawings, too. "Yes, I know it's a lame job."

He shrugged. "I had to unhook part of a navel ring from a guy's braces. Some would consider that lame."

Hadley couldn't help herself. That made her smile. "You're the town hero, the cowboy cop. No one thinks you're lame."

And there it was again. The great divide in how they were perceived. Leyton could untangle a thousand navel rings and still keep his shiny reputation intact. He deserved that. He'd paid his Jameson dues, and other than his high school relationship with her, he'd kept above the gossip fray. She could stub her toe, and folks would call her falling-down drunk. Of course, she deserved the judgment, even when it came in harsh behind-the-hand whispers.

The sound of an approaching car caught Hadley's attention. Leyton's, too, and she got a quick kick of adrenaline when he slid his hand over his holstered weapon and hurried ahead of her to the door.

"It's Cait," he said, peering out the side window. "She'll stay here while I go into the office."

Hadley cursed the disappointment that slicked over the adrenaline jolt. Disappointment that Leyton was leaving. Stupid. Stupid. Stupid. His leaving was a good thing, she mentally insisted. And it wasn't as if Em would be unprotected, since Cait was a cop, too. Still, Leyton wouldn't be there.

Leyton unlocked the door to let his sister inside, and Cait immediately handed Hadley a white bag. "Golightly Donuts," Cait said. "I picked them up from Tiffany's on the way here."

Tiffany's was short for Breakfast at Tiffany's, the town's diner, and the owner, Hildie Stoddermeyer, was obsessed with the author Truman Capote. Hildie had painted the diner the signature Tiffany color of robin's-egg blue, and she had items on the menu that paid tribute—in Hildie's own kind of way—to characters in the famous novel. Go-lightly Donuts were obviously part of that tribute and were also one of Hadley's favorites. Either Cait had remembered that or she, too, had a fondness for the overly sugared treats.

"Let me get my things, and I'll go," Leyton said, leaving her and Cait alone in the foyer.

Hadley watched him walk away, and when she turned back to his sister, she realized that Cait had noticed her watching.

"You're sleeping with him?" Cait asked her.

Cait rarely pulled punches when it came to, well, anything. It was one of the reasons Hadley had always liked her.

"Technically, yes," Hadley answered.

Cait bobbed her head in what seemed to be a mix of approval and *I figured as much*, and she helped herself to one of the doughnuts from the bag. The reach inside left sugar crystals on her hand.

"Are you going to lecture me about it?" Hadley asked. She set down her coffee so she could claim her own doughnut—which she immediately bit into. Hildie might have a strange Truman Capote obsession, but the woman knew how to create fat-and-sugar nirvana. "Or tell me not to hurt him?"

"Nope." Cait took a big bite of the doughnut. "Everybody's screwing something or somebody. Both technically and for real. I try to stay out of that. Besides," she said, licking the sugar goo off her fingers, "if anyone was to get hurt in this, it'd probably be you."

Hadley dismissed that with a snorting laugh that might

have been fueled with the serious sugar rush she got from the doughnut. But she thought that might be true. *Might.*

"Not with my thick hide," Hadley argued.

Cait looked her straight in the eyes. "I try to stay out of assessing hide thickness, too. Hey," she said without pausing, and she waved at Tony, who stepped into the foyer. "Cait Jameson," she added.

"Tony Corbin." He came forward and shook her hand despite the sticky sugar spots. "You're Leyton's sister, the deputy."

"That's me. No, I don't carry a gun," Cait said when he looked down at the waist of her jeans, where she had her badge clipped. "But I have three older brothers, so I know how to kick ass." She lifted her keychain and showed him the tiny can she had clipped there. It was a travel-size container of Mighty Hold hair spray. "Plus, one squirt of this will glue your eyelashes together so you can't see."

Hadley sincerely hoped it didn't come down to a situation where a butt kicking or Mighty Hold was required, but she had no doubts about Cait's abilities. And it didn't have a lot to do with her older brothers. Hadley remembered Cait and her smart mouth being able to defuse some incidents in elementary and middle school that could have turned physical. She'd done that without the use of Mighty Hold, too.

Leyton came out of the dining room, his computer and notebooks tucked under his arm. It was a reminder that Hadley hadn't asked if there'd been anything new on the investigation. A reminder, too, that he was leaving. He hadn't said how long he'd be gone, but it was possible that Cait would be staying the night. After all, Leyton was the sheriff, and he had a job to do—

"I'll be back in a few hours," Leyton said, nipping her

thought in the bud. He didn't nip other things, though, because as if it was the most natural thing in the world, he dropped a kiss on her mouth.

Cait made another of those *I figured as much* sounds, but the sound Hadley made was more of frustration. And she blamed it on the frustration when she kissed him right back.

Leyton smiled, licked his bottom lip, then had a bite of the doughnut she was still holding. "Progress," he concluded. He added to his sister, "I'll drop by my house on the way to the office and should be back before lunch. Lock the door behind me."

Cait did just that, but she didn't take her eyes off Hadley. "Technically sleeping with him?" Cait muttered with her eyebrow raised.

Even though Cait kept her voice low, Hadley suspected that Tony heard her just fine, because he said something about wanting to find Em, and he hurried away.

Hadley finished the rest of her doughnut and washed it down with her coffee before she responded. "I thought you said you tried to stay out of things like this."

Cait shrugged. "I *try*," she emphasized, "but now that Austin and Shaw are both hooked up with your sisters, Leyton and Kinsley get the bulk of my attention. Kinsley's got a bad attitude about me poking into the personal details of her life, but Leyton tolerates it enough." She paused. "The betting pool is up to forty-seven bucks and change that you and Leyton will be lovers by the end of the week."

So, there was a betting pool and the gossip that went along with it. That didn't surprise Hadley, but it seemed to her that folks had plenty more to gossip about with Em than with her and Leyton. Especially since she and Leyton were old news. Still…

"What are people saying about Em?" Hadley asked.

And just like that, Cait's expression changed from chatty old pal to concerned cop and friend. "Folks are worried," Cait admitted. "Not just about Em but about themselves. The hardware store sold out of locks and had to order more. Willa Lee Sanberry is offering to teach self-defense classes at the library."

Willa Lee was built like a Mack truck and had fists the size of hams. Her mere presence was her self-defense, but that didn't apply to most people in town. Hadley could see them taking precautions like extra locks and classes.

Worse, those precautions might be necessary.

"Is there anything at all about Marco's whereabouts?" Hadley pressed.

Cait shook her head. "Sorry, but lots of people are looking for him. Trust me, if he shows up in town, someone will see him, and I can arrest his sorry butt for worrying everybody like this." She stopped, drawing in a breath. "Between you, me and these doughnuts, I'm worried, too. If Marco's still a sack of shit, I don't want him anywhere near my nieces."

Neither did Hadley. She'd met the nieces, Avery and Gracie, about a month ago. They were Austin's twin daughters, and they were too young to be aware of a threat if Marco went to Austin's place instead of coming directly to Em.

Hadley's phone rang, and because she was in such deep thought—or rather deep *worry*—the sound startled her. Obviously, she was more on edge than she wanted to admit, and the edge got a little sharper when she saw the name on her phone screen.

Candice Monroe, Bailey's grandmother.

Since it'd been months since Candice had called her,

Hadley's first thought was that something had happened to Bailey. Bailey had her own phone. A simple kiddie one that she could use only for calls and texts to Hadley, and the girl was very good at keeping Hadley informed about all the little things going on in her life. Candice, however, rarely got in touch with Hadley.

Hadley practically threw the bag of doughnuts onto the entry table, and while mumbling "I have to take this call" to Cait, Hadley hurried into the parlor.

"Mrs. Monroe," Hadley greeted her, using her surname, since Candice had never once invited her to use her given name. She didn't blurt "What's wrong?" but instead forced herself to wait for Candice to speak.

"Hadley." But that was all she said for several way-too-long moments. Moments during which Hadley's thoughts started to run wild. "Bailey said you were in Texas."

Still tamping down her worries, Hadley made a sound of agreement. "I'm at my grandmother's ranch in Lone Star Ridge."

"Good," Candice answered after another hesitation. "Does this mean you'll be coming to visit Bailey?"

Hadley very much wanted to do that, but the timing was awful. "Soon." God, she hoped it'd be soon, because that would mean things would be resolved with Em. But then something occurred to her.

Candice had never invited Hadley to Houston for a visit.

"How soon?" Candice pressed, and that was when Hadley got confirmation that something was indeed wrong.

"I'm not sure. My grandmother's having some personal issues," Hadley settled for saying. "What happened? Is Bailey sick or something?"

"No, Bailey's fine." Her answer was quick and certain, causing Hadley to release the breath she'd been holding.

"Then what is it?" Hadley demanded. "Why do you need me to come?"

Candice didn't jump on the fast-answer train this time. The silence dragged on and on before she finally said, "Bailey and I will come to you. Text me the address of your grandmother's ranch."

Well, that didn't help ease any of the tension that had settled in every nerve and muscle in her body. "Tell me what's wrong."

"I will. But not over the phone." Candice paused again. "Bailey and I will be there tomorrow. I need to see you, Hadley. It's…important."

"What's wrong?" Hadley repeated, but she was talking to the air because Candice had already ended the call.

CHAPTER THIRTEEN

CONDOMS. THAT WAS on the top of Leyton's list as he threw some things into an overnight bag that he'd take from his place back to Em's. Condoms and a change of clothes—both necessary items, as far as he was concerned. He didn't want to be unprepared like he had been the night before.

Of course, there were no guarantees that he and Hadley would have a repeat of near sex or sex, but then, guarantees were rare when it came to Hadley. When he thought of words that applied to her, *predictable* wasn't one of them.

But *trouble* was.

Yeah, she was trouble, all right, and he didn't need any cop skills to know that it wasn't just Em's situation bugging her. She had secrets, ones that haunted her, which was no doubt why she'd ended up sleeping in the hall. And then in bed with him.

What had happened to give her those kinds of demons?

Unfortunately, his cop's mind took a bad direction to come up with answers. She'd never had a good-girl rep like McCall, but Hadley had upped her acting out when she was fifteen. There'd been a series of events that had maybe brought that on. His breaking up with her, her joy-riding in that stolen car, her arrest, the cancellation of *Little Cowgirls* and then her parents leaving.

That was a heck of a lot to happen in such a short period of time. Mere weeks. Any one of them alone would have been a lot for a teenager, but she must have felt as if twelve hundred rugs had been pulled out from beneath her feet.

He sure as hell hadn't helped with that.

No.

He'd done the breaking up, probably crushing her heart in the process, which was something he would have to live with. But he thought whatever she was going through went beyond crushed teenage hearts. Beyond all those other things that he knew had happened.

But what?

His cop's mind took over again. Acting out and trouble sleeping. Plus, Hadley had mentioned those bad memories, leaving him to wonder what the hell had happened in her bedroom. The first thought that came to him wasn't a good one. Unfortunately, it was a common one. Had Hadley been sexually abused or molested?

Hell. He hated that the possibility was even on his radar, but it added up. And just the thought of it sickened him.

There was a knock on the door, and before Leyton could answer it, he heard the door open, and someone called out, "You have to say yes."

It was Kinsley, his fifteen-year-old sister.

Leyton had to groan. He and Kinsley got along just fine, but he'd wanted this trip to his house to be a quick in and out so he could then finish his work at the office and head back to Em's.

"You have to say no," someone else added. His brother Shaw.

Carrying his overnight bag, Leyton went into the living room to see what was going on. Shaw was still in the doorway, looking as beleaguered as Leyton felt. Kinsley was helping herself to a Coke from his fridge. Her hair was pink today, which was somewhat conservative for her. Usually she went for multiple colors.

"I want to stay here at your place," Kinsley told him. "Say yes."

Leyton didn't say anything. He just shifted his attention to Shaw so he could get an explanation. In the Jameson family, Shaw was not only the oldest, but he was also level-headed and reasonable. If Shaw wanted Leyton to say no, then Leyton would be saying no. He just wanted to know what he was agreeing to and nixing.

"Sunny, Kinsley and I have been staying at Mom's," Shaw told him. "I thought that was best until this thing with Em is sorted out."

"It is best," Leyton assured him. He didn't want any of them, including his mom, alone.

"But I want to stay here," Kinsley insisted, burping from the large gulp of Coke she'd swigged. "You've let me stay plenty of times before. It's quieter here, and it doesn't matter if you'll be at Miss Em's. I'll be fine here by myself."

Leyton gave her a flat look. "No."

Kinsley huffed as if that were the most unreasonable answer she'd ever heard instead of the one she should have expected. "I'm almost sixteen," she fired back.

He had no idea what that had to do with this argument. Em was a senior citizen, and he didn't want her alone, either. "No," Leyton repeated. There was little chance that Marco would come here, but a *little chance* wasn't worth taking.

"I didn't bring her over here so you could state the obvious," Shaw added a moment later. "I figured you were swamped with work and Em, so Kinsley and I are going to check on your horses."

"Thanks." There were plenty of good things about having family, and this was one of them. They all pitched in and helped.

And speaking of family, it'd been only a few months since Kinsley had found out she was a Jameson, but Leyton knew she already felt some of those bonds. Bonds he could use.

"If you don't want to stay at Lenore's, Cait might be looking for some company," Leyton suggested to Kinsley. "But you can't stay there unless she's with you. Say yes, that you understand that you can't be there alone." He gave her a warning stare to go along with that order.

Kinsley rolled her eyes and grumbled something he didn't want to catch, but Leyton knew he'd made himself clear. Now he'd have to make it clear to Cait, too. In the Jameson family, Cait was not the most levelheaded one, but at least she would know how to defend herself and Kinsley.

"Is there anything you can tell me about Em that'll help relieve Sunny's mind?" Shaw asked.

It was obvious that Shaw was worried about his bride-to-be, but Leyton had to shake his head. "Lots of people are looking for Marco Corbin. Including me. I'm heading to my office now."

That seemed to be enough of a cue to get Shaw heading toward the barn, but Kinsley took out her phone. To call Cait, he realized when he heard Kinsley start the conversation with "Say yes."

Leyton had barely made it to his truck when his own phone rang, and he wondered if Cait had put Kinsley on hold so she could call him. But it was Hadley. And just like that, the bad scenarios came. He hit the answer button and got behind the wheel.

"Are you okay?" he immediately asked.

"It's not Em or Marco," she said right off. But that wasn't an *I'm okay* tone in her voice. "I got a call from Bailey's grandmother Candice."

Of all the subjects he'd thought Hadley might bring up, this hadn't been on his radar. "The one who fought you for custody."

"Yes," she verified in that same tone. "Candice said she was bringing Bailey here for a visit."

Again, not on his radar, and apparently it hadn't been on Hadley's, either. "Is that usual?" he added. "Does she bring Bailey to see you—"

"She's never done that, and Candice hung up before I could press her to explain why it was so important that she come here with Bailey. She didn't answer her phone when I tried to call her right back, so I called Bailey instead. She was very excited and said she'd get to see me soon. I asked her why they were coming, and she said she didn't know but that her grandma was talking to someone on the phone and that she'd been crying."

Hell. Leyton started driving back to Em's ranch. "This probably isn't connected to Marco," he reminded her.

But there was a connection. A loose one. Candice was living in Houston, and that was where Marco had been released from jail. Still, it was a huge leap to believe the man had learned about Hadley being a surrogate and was now using that in some way. If he wanted to have some leverage to use to get back at Em, there were more direct routes— such as Hadley, McCall, Sunny or even Em herself.

"I'll be at Em's in a few minutes," Leyton said. "In the meantime, take Cait aside and tell her about Bailey. She can get started on calling the Houston cops, and they can go out and make what we call a welfare check on Candice and Bailey. They'll make sure they're okay."

Leyton would follow that up with some calls of his own, including one to Candice. It was stupid of the woman to worry Hadley this way, but then again, Candice might not be aware of the possible threat from Marco.

He skipped swinging by his office and went straight to Em's. Leyton didn't even have to knock on the door because Cait was right there to let him in, and she was already on the phone. "Houston PD," she mouthed.

Good, and since there didn't seem to be any alarm in Cait's expression, Leyton went in search of Hadley. He found her pacing in the living room.

"Candice, call me back right now," Hadley demanded, and she hit the button on her phone. "I left her another voice mail."

Unlike Cait's, Hadley's expression held plenty of alarm, and Leyton went to her. He set his overnight bag aside so he could pull her into his arms.

"I can drive you to Houston so you can check on Bailey," he said.

When she looked up at him, he saw the tears shimmering in her eyes. Hell. Hadley wasn't a crier, so this was obviously shaking her already shaky ground.

"You'd do that for me." Not a question, but there seemed to be a sigh along with it. Maybe because she thought this was a huge favor, one that she would have to pay back.

"There are no strings on what I said I would do, but I think you should tell Em about Bailey," he advised. "Just in case Candice shows up here with Bailey before we get back."

That dried up her tears, and her eyes widened. "You're right. I didn't give Candice the address, but I'm sure she could have found it online because of the show being filmed here."

Hadley stepped back and probably would have headed straight to Em's room if her phone hadn't rung. "Candice," she blurted and nearly dropped the phone when she fumbled to answer it.

Leyton certainly didn't breathe any easier, not yet, but he hoped it was a good sign that the woman had finally gotten back in touch with Hadley.

Much to his surprise, Hadley put the call on speaker and stood close to Leyton so he could hear. That let Leyton know that Hadley believed this conversation might be something a cop would want to listen in on.

"Has anyone threatened you?" Hadley demanded. Because her body was right against his, he could feel her muscles trembling.

"No," Candice answered, and judging from her shocked tone, she hadn't expected the question. "Why would you think that? Did Bailey say that'd happened?"

"No." Hadley blew out a long breath. "No," she repeated, "but she did say you'd been crying."

Candice didn't deny it, and he thought he heard the woman take a long breath of her own. "I was crying because I got some bad news. Personal news," she clarified.

That clarification didn't cause Hadley to relax, though. Probably because Candice's cry-generating personal news affected Bailey. Or maybe it was even about Bailey, since Candice wanted to bring the child here for a visit.

"What happened?" Hadley asked.

"A close friend of mine needs surgery to have a tumor removed. It could be cancer."

"I'm sorry about that." Now Hadley's muscles did ease up a little. So did Leyton's. Cancer was a bitch of a diagnosis, but this meant Bailey and Candice weren't in danger.

"If it comes down to my friend needing treatments, I

want to be with her," Candice explained. "Not just for a couple of hours a day but 24/7 until…well, until."

"I understand," Hadley said. "What do you need me to do?"

"I planned to ask you this in person, but I wanted to see if you could come here and watch Bailey for a couple of weeks. She has a nanny, of course, but Bailey asked if you could be with her, too. Actually, Bailey insisted."

Hadley opened her mouth. Closed it. And Leyton could see the debate she was having. She no doubt wanted to do this for Bailey—it was obvious how much she loved the child—but there was the issue of Marco.

Leyton wanted to assure Hadley that he'd make sure Em stayed safe, but if he spoke up, Candice might not appreciate that he'd been listening in on their conversation. Thankfully, Candice continued before either he or Hadley could say anything.

"I know you told me your grandmother was having some problems. That's why I offered to bring Bailey to Lone Star Ridge tomorrow. Bailey really wants to see you, and we could maybe work out a schedule of when you can be here." Candice paused. "Like I said, I wouldn't need you to watch Bailey until next week. And maybe you could even have her stay with you at your grandmother's ranch. *Maybe*."

Candice definitely didn't sound enthusiastic about that last option, and Hadley hesitated, too. But Leyton figured her hesitation was simply because no one in her family knew about Bailey. With the little girl calling her Mama Hadley, there'd be questions. And probably gossip, something that Hadley hated.

"I wouldn't want you to take Bailey all the way to California," Candice went on, "but Lone Star Ridge is only a couple of hours from Houston. I think I'd be okay with that."

"Come tomorrow, and we'll talk," Hadley finally said. "I'm sure we can work something out."

"Thank you." Candice sounded as if she'd blown out a breath of relief. "I'll call you when we're on the road."

Hadley hit the end-call button and looked up at him, and Leyton thought he could give her that assurance that he hadn't been able to give while Candice was on the phone. But he didn't get a chance to do that because Cait stepped into the room.

"We've got a sighting," his sister said, excitement in her voice. "The San Antonio cops spotted Marco."

CHAPTER FOURTEEN

HADLEY'S MIND WAS already whirling with what Candice had told her, but for news about Marco, she didn't mind adding more whirls to the mix. Finding him was at the top of her wish list, and once he was arrested, it would put an end to a good chunk of this worry she had for Em.

She stood back and listened to the flurry of phone calls that Leyton and Cait made. Em and Tony were doing the same since Hadley had alerted them the moment Cait told them about the sighting, but with each passing minute, each bit of conversation she heard, Hadley's hopes started to dim.

"I'm sure everything's going to be hunky-dory," Em declared, slipping her arm around Hadley.

Hadley wasn't sure anything would be hunky, much less dory, but she tried to keep that mental opinion off her expression. Tony, however, was looking as if he had some dimming hopes, as well.

"Once they find Marco, you'll have a clear mind to help me with wedding plans," Em went on.

True. But even if Marco wasn't found, Hadley still needed to get some focus for Bailey and Candice's visit. That meant telling her sisters and Em all about the little girl. Hadley wanted to spend time with Bailey, and she thought the girl would enjoy the ranch, but the timing beyond sucked.

Leyton finished his latest call, and when he turned to

face them, Hadley knew it wasn't going to be good news. "Marco went to the hotel in San Antonio where you were staying," he said to Em. "The same clerk, David Mendoza, was on duty when Hadley and I went there looking for you. He got suspicious that Marco was asking about you, or rather about Patsy, and he called the cops. Marco left, though, before the cops could get there."

Hadley groaned and wanted to know why the clerk hadn't just wrestled Marco to the ground and restrained him, but she thought of David's scrawny build. He probably hadn't wanted to get into a skirmish even with a guy Marco's age.

"How did Marco know that Em was staying at that hotel?" Hadley asked, but she immediately waved off the question. If Leyton's PI friend could find Em, then Marco could hire someone to do the same.

"The cops will continue to look for Marco," Leyton continued a moment later. "But we know now that Marco is looking for you. Probably for you, too," he added to Tony.

"The clerk didn't know what name Em is using now," Tony pointed out.

Leyton shook his head. "I mentioned Em's name to him, and I showed him my badge, so he knows I'm from Lone Star Ridge."

"He knows, too, that I'm Em's granddaughter, because he recognized me from *Little Cowgirls*."

Another head shake from Leyton. "The clerk didn't say anything about that to Marco." He paused. "But if Marco has any kind of age-progression photo of Em and he shows it around, the clerk or someone else could tell Marco that Em left the hotel with us."

True, and that would lead him not only to the name she was using now but also to the ranch. Well, crap. She wanted a showdown with Marco, but Hadley sure as heck didn't want it happening tomorrow while Bailey and Candice were here.

"I had a baby," Hadley blurted out and immediately realized she should have put some thought into how to better break the news about Bailey.

Everything went quiet, and all eyes landed on her. Even Cait, who was still on the phone, hushed and turned to Hadley.

"Leyton's baby?" Em asked.

Of course, her grandmother would leap to that wrong conclusion, and she'd jumped to it with what seemed to be some hope in her tone and her eyes.

"No," Hadley answered. "And she's not my baby, either. I was a surrogate for a friend and her husband, and I carried their daughter for them because my friend couldn't."

Hadley paused to give them a chance to absorb that, and when there weren't any questions, she continued. "When the baby, Bailey, was a year old, my friend and her husband were killed, and Bailey's grandmother Candice now has custody of her. I know it's not a good time for this, but Candice wants to bring Bailey here tomorrow for a visit."

"That's wonderful," Em declared, pulling Hadley into a hug.

Hadley should have realized this would have been Em's reaction. No judgment, no real shock. Still, that wouldn't be everyone's reaction. Some would see what she'd done as weird, something that didn't happen in a place like Lone Star Ridge. That was okay as long as none of that talk met Bailey's ears. Hadley didn't want the child feeling the least bit uncomfortable because of the way other people felt.

"I'm sorry about your friends, though," Em added, "but

how nice that I'll get to meet the baby you carried for them."

So, her grandmother didn't have any reservations. But Tony and Cait obviously did. Hadley could practically hear their objections about the timing of the visit. It made her rethink her decision to stay put and not go to Houston. She didn't want to be away from Em, but she also didn't want Bailey having an encounter, even one from a distance, with Marco.

Tony stepped forward. "While Bailey's here, I can go into town and make myself…visible. That way, if my brother comes to Lone Star Ridge, he can deal with me there and not be near the rest of you."

"No one's making themselves *visible*," Leyton insisted after a huff. "No bait, no taking risks. I need to work in my office for a while today, but Cait will stay here. Then both of us will be here tomorrow when Bailey and her grandmother visit. Understand? No one makes themselves a lure."

Leyton stared at Tony and Em until they nodded, and then he motioned for Hadley to follow him to the door. She figured he'd give her another lecture about precautions, but he kissed her.

"Are you okay?" he asked.

Her nerves were jangling like a sleigh full of Christmas bells, but she doubted that would ease up. At least not until after Bailey was safely back in Houston.

"I'm fine," Hadley partially lied. "I have to throw myself into the sketches for the rest of the day. Along with being hard work, outfitting a gunslinging cyborg will be a good distraction."

He smiled and kissed her again. This one was a little

longer, a little hotter. "I want you in bed with me tonight," he whispered.

The third kiss he gave her was significantly longer and hotter, and while she'd had no intention of turning him down, that gave her a hard nudge to mutter a yes. It certainly seemed the right thing to say, what with this new round of searing heat he'd sent through her body.

But right wasn't necessarily right.

Yes, it would no doubt be amazing sex with Leyton, but the little voice in the back of her head kept telling her that a deeper involvement with him was the wrong way to go. Whether it was a good thing or not, plenty of other parts of her could drown out that little voice.

Hadley locked the front door, watched as he drove away, then went straight to the sewing room, where she could start the sketches. She could throw herself into the work and push all thoughts of Leyton aside.

She thought of him.

Damn him and his pretty face that he rode in on. There needed to be some kind of vaccination to build up a resistance to the Jameson men. She couldn't even ask for help on that, either, since her sisters had both dived headfirst into that particular gene pool. Heck, maybe it was some weird primal DNA thing that had created a pull so strong that Hadley was certain of one thing.

That she would indeed be in Leyton's bed tonight.

Cursing herself, cursing him and cursing everything primal in the universe, Hadley shoved aside thoughts of Leyton and got to work.

It took her a few minutes and some strokes of her pencils, but she finally got into it. This wasn't her favorite part of the job. The actual sewing was, but she wouldn't be able to start that until the sketches had been tweaked, retweaked and then tweaked again by committee. After that, the sewing would go through multiple retweaks, as well. Even with all that, it was still the only job she'd ever wanted.

And that was why it stung so much that she'd been blackballed.

It was her own fault, of course. She hadn't intentionally sabotaged Myla's costume, even after Myla had pissed her off by screaming at her and calling her a "fourth-rate has-been reality-show slut who shouldn't be allowed to own scissors." Not even after Myla had torn off a costume in the final fitting and threatened to shove the garment up Hadley's "untalented twat."

Hadley hadn't exactly held her tongue and had fired back that her twat had more talent than Myla did with her pus-coated vocal cords. Or something along those lines.

Myla's personal circle-of-hell employees—her agent, handler, spiritual adviser, therapist and personal spray tanner—had interceded and gotten Myla calmed down. Then the handler had talked Myla into putting the costume back on, saying there wasn't time to come up with anything "suitable," since Myla was to go onstage in fifteen minutes.

During that handful of minutes, Hadley had repaired the costume, but she hadn't been too particular when it came to the stitching in the tit area. Clearly, she should have done more to make sure something like that wouldn't happen, but her extreme dislike of Myla had colored her work.

Which was basically the story of her life.

Too many times she'd let her emotions, especially her anger, cause her to keep digging a hole that she was already in. Sometimes, being the queen of sarcasm and the princess of badassery didn't play in one's favor.

Using the descriptions that the scriptwriter had given her, Hadley worked her way through the scenes, doing a rough sketch for each one. Yes, they were stupid, but then, this was a stupid project.

Perhaps her last one.

She had no other jobs lined up, and even though her brother had offered to ask around, Hadley wasn't sure Hayes had much pull in that area. Yes, he was a TV star, but he owned the king of sarcasm and the prince of badassery titles. Women wanted to fall into his bed, men wanted his rebel edge, but those same men and women wouldn't necessarily want his sister to design stuff for them.

Sometimes—like now, for instance—her heart felt as if someone was squeezing the life out of it. Being a costume designer was the only thing she'd ever been good at. The only thing she'd truly ever wanted to do. It was a pipe dream that had oozed out of the pipe to become real.

Losing it put her right back in that pipe.

A pipe that Leyton apparently wanted to share with her. And here she was again. Right back to thinking about the hot guy.

"Someone's driving up," Cait called out.

Thoughts of the hot cowboy vanished, and in their place came the fear. "Someone" meant that it wasn't a person Cait recognized, and since she knew everyone in town, then this was a visitor. Perhaps a bad kind of visitor with ties to the mob.

Hadley practically threw her sketchbook aside and grabbed her scissors, and she broke one of Em's childhood warnings by running to the foyer with them. She hurried to the side windows to peer out with Cait.

A large black luxury SUV came to a stop in the driveway, and Hadley didn't think it was her wild imagination that it was a vehicle a mobster might use. Apparently, Cait thought the same thing, because she reached for the baseball bat in the umbrella basket by the door.

"Who is it?" Em asked, coming into the foyer.

Hadley glanced behind her to see that her grandmother was carrying a cookie sheet in one hand and a can of nonstick spray in the other. By her side, Tony was brandishing a cast-iron skillet and a huge metal spatula. Either they'd been about to cook something, or they'd grabbed kitchen weapons of opportunity.

Hadley turned to the window in time to see the SUV driver step out. He was a tall, beefy man in a white shirt and jeans with a belt the size of her right butt cheek. Iron-gray hair peeked out from beneath a blinding white Stetson.

Em and Tony went to the window, too, and both looked out. "Well, son of a biscuit eater," Em grumbled after she huffed.

Hadley didn't detect any fear in her grandmother's voice, but there seemed to be plenty of annoyance.

"Should I call Leyton?" Cait asked.

"No." More annoyance pulled Em's face into a scowl. "It's Herb the turd, that director from Waterstone Productions."

It didn't take long for Hadley to fill in the blanks. This was the guy whose number she'd blocked because he'd kept calling her about doing a reunion show for *Little Cowgirls*.

Now Hadley had some annoyance in her own expression.

She remembered him, of course. Hard to forget the oily man who would have sold his left nut if it helped increase the ratings for the show.

"Did you know he was coming here?" Hadley kept her

gaze nailed to the man as he hoisted up that big-ass belt buckle over his bulky belly, which shifted like a water balloon when he moved.

"No, and I certainly didn't invite him," Em snarled.

Good, because that meant they could send him on his way. Once he got a look at all the weapons that were trained on him, he might even make the departure a very speedy one.

"What were you going to do with that?" Hadley asked when Em set the can of cooking spray on the foyer table.

"If it was Marco or one of his goons, I was going to blind him," she readily admitted. "Oil on the eyeballs acts just as good as pepper spray. Then I was going to whack him with the pan."

Tony made a sound of agreement to verify those were also his intentions, but he evidently wanted to add some white-knight stuff, too, since he'd moved protectively in front of Em.

Em stepped around her protective honey and was about to unlock the door, but Cait put her hand over Em's to stop her. "Wait. He has somebody with him," Cait said in a whisper.

That had Hadley, Tony and Em all snapping back to the window, and Hadley did indeed see the passenger door open. Another man stepped out, and, like the driver, he was also wearing jeans. No cowboy hat, though, and that allowed Hadley to better see his hair and face.

Hadley's breath stalled in her lungs. Her knees went weak. And her heart stuttered through some slow, thick beats.

"Are you all right?" Cait asked, and what would have likely been a mere glimpse at Hadley turned into a gaping stare. "You look like someone just doused you with gasoline and is about to set you on fire."

Close, but no fossil fuels of any kind involved in this. It was memories that had caused this particular reaction. Pure, bad memories.

Cait's grip tightened on the bat. "Are these guys trouble?" she demanded.

They were. Well, one of them was, anyway, but not the kind of trouble that would require a deputy to do any bat bashing.

"That's the guy who used to be a cameraman," Em said, giving visitor number two the once-over. "Wayne something-or-other."

"Dempsey," Hadley provided, though she wasn't sure how his surname made it through the muscles in her throat. Muscles that seemed to be trying their level best to choke her.

"I'll get rid of them," Em insisted. This time when she tried to open the door, Cait didn't stop her. Neither did Hadley. But that was because it would have required the muscles in her hands to work, and right now Hadley couldn't force her grip to ease up on the scissors.

Oh, God.

And those two words continued to repeat in Hadley's head as Em opened the door.

"Herb McGrath," Em said, and it wasn't a greeting. It had the tone an executioner would use to someone whose head she was about to lop off.

"Granny Em," the man greeted her, outstretching his arms in an "old friends" kind of way.

Wayne Dempsey didn't offer any such gesture, but he did walk in Herb's wake toward the porch.

"No need for either of you to come any closer," Em said,

stepping onto the porch. Cait went right along with her. Then Tony. Hadley moved to the doorway, but she stayed back, making her feel like a coward. "I've already told you I don't want to do business with you."

"Em, Em, Em." Herb stopped and lifted his hands palms up. "You haven't even heard my latest offer. *Our* latest offer," he amended and tipped his head to Wayne, who moved to his side. "Wayne's come up in the world. He's no longer just a cameraman, and I'm no longer just a director. We're partners at Waterstone. It's our production company."

It surprised Hadley that she could add yet another feeling to the avalanche of emotions slamming down on her. But she did. And what she felt was…well, shame.

"In fact, Wayne thought he'd be able to change your mind about us doing that reunion show," Herb went on, sparing Hadley a glance. "Sunshine's on board with it."

Em rolled her eyes and huffed. "If you think that's a good bargaining chip, you got it all wrong. Having my idiot daughter on board is enough of a reason for me to steer clear of it."

"I know you two didn't have the best of relationships at times—" Herb said.

"Sunshine's about as welcome here as a porcupine in a nudist colony, and you're hollering down an empty well if you think I'd budge on having her around her girls and me."

Hadley wasn't sure what part of that caused Wayne to smile, but that was exactly what he did. Not a big, shiny grin. It was small and sly, and he aimed it at her.

"Maybe I can have a word with Hadley," Wayne said. "Just a word," he emphasized when she didn't move or say anything.

"Anything you got to say to Hadley, you can say to me," Em spit out.

Wayne just smiled again, and that was when Hadley knew that whatever he was about to say, she definitely didn't want Em to hear. Or anyone else, for that matter.

"I'll talk to him," Hadley agreed, and she hated that she had to clear her throat and repeat it. Her first attempt was breathy and broken.

She'd never particularly thought of herself as brave, but it took every ounce of courage she could muster to move out of the doorway. She had already reached the steps when she realized she was still holding the scissors. Wayne noticed, too, and when his attention drifted down to them, that slick smile finally faded.

"You can get back in your SUV," Hadley told Herb. That didn't take courage at all. He wasn't a demon from the past but rather a bug she could flick away with a cold, hard Badly Hadley glare.

"I'm not giving up on this," Herb declared, but he did go back to the SUV and stand by the door.

Hadley forced herself to keep walking until she was only about two feet away from Wayne. Too close, but this way anything they said might have a chance of remaining just between them.

"Hadley," he greeted her, and it had that same slick, sly tone as his earlier smile. He wasn't smiling now, though. "Long time, no see."

"What do you want?" she snapped. No need to repeat that, and she considered it a victory that she sounded strong. At the moment, sounding strong was about as good as she was going to get, but she sure as heck felt no such strength inside her.

He leaned in, putting his mouth closer to her ear. "I

want you to convince your grandmother and your sisters to reconsider doing the reunion show."

"None of us wants anything to do with *Little Cowgirls*," she snapped.

Wayne pulled back, their gazes connecting, and damn it all to hell, those brown eyes flooded her with memories.

Bad, bad memories.

"Either you go along with this reunion," Wayne said, lowering his voice to a secretive whisper, "or everyone, including your grandmother, will know exactly what happened."

CHAPTER FIFTEEN

LEYTON DECIDED THIS was one of those days that he didn't want to repeat. It was as if all the weird people and crap in the universe had joined together in a "let's mess with the sheriff" day.

He'd gotten two calls before he'd even made it to the office. One from Bernice Biggs, Em's part-time housekeeper, who'd complained that someone had TP'd her house and yard. That wasn't unusual. The crotchety woman often pissed off people, but Leyton concluded that this must have been a major pissing off.

Since Leyton was nearby Bernice's when the call came in, he'd responded and had soon discovered that there wasn't a single spot on her house, yard, shrubs or flowers not covered with toilet paper. Not dry stuff, either, but rather wet globs that appeared to have been hurled by those with good aims.

Leyton figured at least a hundred rolls had been used, so that meant the culprits had likely pooled their money, since TP wasn't cheap. His chief suspects were the entire baseball team that practiced on the diamond just behind Bernice's house. Bernice had admitted the team had it in for her since she'd refused to give them back any baseball that landed in her yard. She had also admitted that she slept like the dead and hadn't heard what would have likely been a dozen or more teenagers smacking wet toilet paper against her house.

While Leyton had been taking Bernice's report and trying to calm the woman down, he'd gotten another call. This one was from Zach and Alyssa, who apparently hadn't learned their lesson, because this time her navel ring had gotten caught on his zipper. Since it wasn't even lunchtime, it was obvious that the two didn't wait until night to do their fooling around on Prego Trail.

The oddball calls had continued even after he'd finally freed Zach and gotten to his office. There was a loose rooster on Main Street squawking at people and trying to peck them. That was followed by complaints of—surprise, surprise!—rooster shit on the sidewalks. Followed by more complaints of there not being a single roll of toilet paper for sale anywhere in town.

Some days they didn't pay him enough for this job.

Leyton figured, though, that all of that wouldn't have dragged him down so much if he'd managed to get some good news about Marco. But nothing. Marco had gone into the Pacifico Hotel, which didn't have security cameras in the lobby, asked about Em and, when he'd gotten the answer that she wasn't there, vanished again. As long as Marco was in the wind, Em, Tony, Hadley and her sisters wouldn't be resting easy. Which meant he wouldn't be resting, either.

He would be with Hadley, however.

That was definitely a ray of sunshine in his day. That morning he'd left her with a reminder, a suggestion that he wanted her in his bed tonight. One way or another she would be, since he had no intention of letting her sleep on the hall floor, but having her in his bed didn't mean sex. Still, the possibility of it made that sunshiny ray a little brighter.

He pulled to a stop in front of Em's, and after hauling

his work out with him, he went to the door. Just as he'd known she would be, Cait was right there to open it.

"Everything okay?" he asked her.

She nodded, already collecting her things so she could head home. "Hadley's in the sewing room, and Em and Tony are watching a movie in the living room. I think they're making out."

"Thanks for the heads-up." No way did he want to walk in on that, especially not after what he'd already witnessed with Zach and Alyssa.

"No phone calls from anyone who shouldn't be calling," Cait continued. "Those two TV guys didn't come back, and Em didn't have any other visitors."

Good on all of that. Cait had called him after the two men from Waterstone Productions left, and she'd filled Leyton in on the short visit. Apparently, Em was sticking to her guns on there not being a reunion of *Little Cowgirls*. That fell into the "good" category, too, because Leyton knew that Hadley wanted nothing to do with it.

Cait hoisted her computer bag onto her shoulder and then glanced around as if making sure they had the foyer to themselves. They did. "Look, this might be nothing, but I thought you should know. When the Waterstone guys were here, one of them asked to speak to Hadley. *In private*."

That got his attention. "What'd he want?"

"I'm not sure, but, Leyton, Hadley looked very shaky after he left."

"Shaky?" he questioned.

"She wouldn't talk about it, but I could tell that whatever he said upset her." Cait stopped, shaking her head. "Actually, Hadley got upset the second she laid eyes on him."

Again, that snagged his attention. "Who is this man?"

"His name's Wayne Dempsey. Apparently, he used to

be one of the cameramen for *Little Cowgirls*. Now he's a partner in the production company."

Leyton first thought like a cop and wondered if the guy had maybe threatened Hadley in some way. Then he thought like a man and wanted to bust the moron's ass for doing whatever the hell he'd done to get to Hadley that way.

"You didn't hear anything this Wayne Dempsey said to Hadley?" Leyton pressed.

Cait shook her head. "They had a very short whispered conversation in the yard, and then the two men left." She paused again, rolling her eyes. "Apparently, Sunshine wants to do this reunion."

Great. So maybe that was what had upset Hadley. There was definitely no love lost between Hadley and her mother, and the idiot Wayne Dempsey might have hit some raw nerves. Or hell, Sunshine could have sent some sort of veiled threat through the guy. Either way, Leyton hoped that Hadley would tell him what'd happened.

"The other guy's name is Herb McGrath," Cait added a moment later, "and he and Dempsey didn't leave town. They checked into the inn, so they must be expecting to put some kind of sweet talk or pressure on Em to get her to change her mind. On the triplets, too."

Yeah, the men would likely try that. *Try*. But McCall and Sunny wouldn't cave, either.

When Cait headed out, Leyton locked the door behind her and went in search of Hadley. While avoiding the living room. He found her exactly where Cait had said she would be. In the sewing room. And she was surrounded by…weird shit.

Hadley had obviously been sketching, but she'd taken those sketches to great heights. Literally. She'd stapled together pages, each with a piece of the drawing that made up a whole costume, and then she'd taped the costumes to the walls. Another two were on the floor. There were eight in total, all at least seven feet tall, which explained why there was an open stepladder in the center of the room. One of the sketches was taped to it.

Hadley looked up at him, but her eyes didn't actually meet his. Her gaze sort of skimmed over him, and he hoped that was because she was deep into the work and not because she didn't want him to see that she was troubled about that visit from the Waterstone guys.

"I thought sending photos of these would do better than just emailing the sketches," she said, still not looking at him. "It's hard to get the impact of how stupid these are from just drawings."

She had a point. A single page couldn't give you the effect of having seven-foot-tall figures looming over you. Figures that would have looked at home in an old science-fiction movie. Well, if those figures had also found some tacky Western wear, that was. There were massive boots, chaps, holsters and guns. Heck, one of them was even wearing a badge, and Leyton had a closer look to make sure it wasn't supposed to be some kind of replica of him.

"It's not you," Hadley said, obviously noticing that he was staring at it. "There's a lawman in the video. A lawman with a bulging crotch," she added in a mumble.

Yeah, he'd noticed that, too. "What kind of video is this, anyway?"

"A bad one." She sighed, standing back to eye the figures for a few more moments, and then Hadley started taking pictures with her phone. "I'm hoping when the director sees how ridiculous these look, he'll rethink his vision for the project and want them toned down."

Leyton wasn't sure toning down was possible, but it

was obvious Hadley had put a ton of work into this. She looked tired. No, it was more than that. She looked weary, and he hated that.

He waited until she was done with the photos before he went to her. He eased her around to face him, and she immediately went into his arms, pressing her face to his shoulder. Normally, that would have suited him just fine, but he couldn't help but think she'd done that to avoid something more intimate. Like a conversation, complete with questions about what was eating away at her.

"How's the cop business going?" she asked.

He obliged her by giving her a wrap-up, hoping it would help her settle. "Well, Alyssa's navel ring got hung up on Zach's zipper. I wish she'd put some safety gear on her body piercings. Oh, and there's a serious shortage of toilet paper in town."

Leyton looked down at her and saw the ghost of a smile on her mouth. "You have an interesting job," she commented.

Interesting was one word for it. "I do. I didn't even get into the part about Hildie stepping in rooster crap and wanting to sue."

When he got a second ghost smile from her, Leyton tipped her head so that she was facing him. "How was your day?" he asked.

She opened her mouth as if she might give him the stock "okay" answer—which would have almost certainly been a lie—but she didn't say anything stock, anything that flicked away the concern he saw written all over her.

"It was a rough one," Hadley admitted. She paused one beat, two beats. After three he stopped counting and just waited her out. "I told McCall and Sunny about Bailey."

He couldn't imagine her sisters' reactions being so bad that it'd put Hadley in this mood, but something certainly had.

"They were fine with it," she continued. "Just a little frustrated that I hadn't told them sooner."

Leyton could see that. It wasn't as if the surrogacy was a bad thing. Just the opposite.

He waited for her to continue, but when she didn't add more, he gave her a prompt. "Cait told me about the visit you got today from some TV production company. Two men. She said they want to do a *Little Cowgirls* reunion episode."

Hadley nodded and stepped away from him. She went back to examining the sketches. Sighing, wishing that they'd gotten past this habit of hers not to share her feelings with him, Leyton turned her back to face him.

"There's nothing you can tell me that'll make me think less of you," he assured her. "There's nothing that'll make me believe you're a real Badly Hadley."

She stayed quiet a moment. "Then you'd be wrong."

Well, hell. Her comment was like opening a big-ass door that sounded as if it might have a ton of old baggage dumped just on the other side. He was more than willing to walk through that door and, if possible, help her sort out whatever had put that look of dread on her face.

But the dread look instantly changed. At least he thought it did. It was hard to tell, because she came up on her toes and kissed him. This wasn't a "shut up" kind of kiss. All right, maybe it was, but if so, then Hadley still managed to put a lot of heat into it. A lot of tongue, too. It was deep and plenty long enough to let him know that he'd been kissed by a woman who knew how to fire him up.

Even when he could be cooling down and finishing this conversation.

As quickly as the kiss had come, it ended, and she ducked away from him to go to the door. Not to leave, he quickly realized. But to lock it. She whirled back around, in the same motion catching onto a handful of his shirt and yanking him to her. Of course, she didn't have to yank especially hard, since he had no trouble going in that direction.

A direction that led straight back to her mouth.

This kiss had a needy edge to it. Much more than mere foreplay. This was a "get naked now" kiss, complete with frantic touches.

Her grip stayed tight on his shirt as if she thought he might try to get away. He wouldn't. Even if it was possibly the right thing to do, he wouldn't. Hadley had flipped his switch, and now he wanted her more than any *possibly*. More than reason. That was why he made a grunt of protest when she stopped the common-sense-evaporating kiss and looked up at him.

"Please, tell me you have a condom," she murmured in a voice that could have qualified as an eighth deadly sin.

Leyton nodded. He'd put two in his wallet and had more in his overnight bag.

"Then let this be casual," she added with her breath gusting and her face flushed with arousal. "Let it only be sex."

At the moment, with his erection pressing hard against her, he probably would have agreed to a lobotomy. Or eating one of his mother's casseroles. But he didn't have to agree to or say anything. Because Hadley's mouth came back to his, and her hand slid to the front of his jeans.

Common sense was definitely going to have to wait its turn.

HADLEY TRIED NOT to think about what she was doing. It wasn't hard to rid her mind of thoughts, because Leyton's mouth had a way of unzipping reality and sending her to a steamy world where there was a strong likelihood of great sex. Sex that would stop him from asking her any other questions.

For now, anyway.

She figured this was merely prolonging a chat that he would want to have with her, but that chat might go down easier if she could cool this fire he'd started inside her.

He took control of the kiss, devouring her with the hungry need she could feel coming off him in waves. She had that same need, maybe even more than he did. Yes, he'd given her an orgasm the night before, but that had simply awakened an ache that she'd thought was long since gone. Apparently, Leyton had awakening skills to go along with the superior kissing.

And touching.

Yes, he touched her, too. He slid his hand down the front of her shirt, cupping her breast and then swiping his thumb over her nipple. Just that simple gesture robbed her of what breath the kiss hadn't already taken.

"Hadley," he said like a groan against her ear.

It was possible he was fighting this, maybe trying to do the right thing. The right thing in his mind, anyway, of getting to the bottom of what was troubling her before they went at each other like horny teenagers.

Hadley made sure he lost that battle with his willpower by grinding her body against his. It was playing dirty, but as so many dirty plays did, it felt amazing, and it sent that heat spearing right to her center—which in no way needed more heat.

He cursed her. That was a turn-on, too, but she had to concede that, at this point, pretty much everything would be.

Leyton shoved up her top, went lower and did some

tongue kisses on her breasts. The man certainly knew how to do foreplay, but if she'd been able to speak, she could have told him that it wasn't necessary. That he had already primed her and she was ready to go.

Maybe literally.

When he took her nipple into his mouth, Hadley thought she might have a crashing orgasm right then. That would relieve the need clawing away at her, but this time around she wanted Leyton in on the big finale.

Knowing she couldn't take any more of those kinds of kisses, Hadley took hold of him and pulled him to the floor. They landed on one of the sketches, a seven-foot-tall bad guy in all black except for his chrome-colored cod-piece and breastplate. Not the most comfortable place to have sex, but she and Leyton had already moved past the point where comfort, bad sketches and codpieces mattered.

Thankfully, Leyton jumped on the hurry train with her. He stripped off her top and went after her jeans. He was good at it, too. His nimble fingers had her unzipped in no time flat while she continued to fumble with his shirt buttons.

He didn't help with her fumbling when he moved back so he could shimmy off her jeans and panties. Of course, he managed that just fine, too. Then he froze.

For a couple of horrifying moments she thought he might have gotten grossed out by the stretch marks from her pregnancy. But no. He was staring at the baggie that'd fallen out of her jeans pocket. The one with the crushed and crumbled-up dead flower.

"It's not what you think," she said. "It's not drugs. Or tea." Though she seriously doubted his mind had gone to the latter option.

"It's the flower that you had in the memory box," he provided.

Bingo. And while she knew he had questions about that, her body just wasn't interested in having a lengthy discussion unless it had to do with sex or Leyton talking dirty to her. She thought she might like that kind of action from the guy with the shiny reputation.

"It's a flower that I wished you'd given me," she rattled off, her words practically running together. "It doesn't make sense, I know, but I was twelve."

To put an end to the subject, she followed that up with a rough French kiss and a palm press to his erection.

It worked.

On several levels.

The flower discussion ended, he talked dirty, and he took that dirty-talking mouth right between her legs. Talk about spearing heat and rippling waves of pleasure. Leyton managed both, and it was so good that Hadley nearly lost her fight to have them end this together.

It was like backing away from Christmas presents, birthday cake and chocolate all at once, but Hadley latched on to Leyton and pulled him back up so they were mouth to mouth. She didn't kiss him, though. She wasn't much of a multitasker when it came to stuff like this, so she focused on getting him out of his shirt.

Her hands were trembling now. Her body was one giant aching fire, and she wasn't sure she would have gotten off his shirt if he hadn't helped. A couple of shoves, a shift and some maneuvering, and he was bare chested.

Oh, my.

A bare-chested Leyton was indeed a thing of beauty. All those toned muscles. Plus, the bonus of chest hair. He hadn't had much of that when he was sixteen, but he certainly had it now. Despite all the aching and need, she took a moment to run her fingers through it, letting her fingertips graze his nipples.

Apparently that upped his urgency, because he went after his own jeans. She stopped fondling his chest long enough to help with that. Down went the jeans. The boxers.

And her mouth went dry.

She mentally strung together some *oh, my*s and would have done some fondling there, but he took hold of her wrists and put her on her back. What he didn't do was follow on top of her, something that made her talk dirty, too, but hers was tainted with frustration.

"Condom," he growled.

Oh, yes. That. And it suddenly occurred to her why there were so many unplanned pregnancies. The body in urgent need of an orgasm could shut down the mind.

Leyton fumbled in his pocket, yanked out a condom from his wallet and had that sucker on in seconds. Seriously, it had to break some kind of speed record. A thought that barely had time to register, because he moved onto her.

Then into her.

And the speed record came to a stop. He stopped. Maybe giving her body time to adjust to this sweet invasion by one very hard hard-on. Maybe giving himself time to adjust, too.

He looked at her and smiled. Not a ha-ha kind of smile but one that was part grimace from holding back, part *I've died and gone to heaven*. She totally got that. What she was feeling was amazing along with being the best she'd ever had. Hadley wanted it to last, but she needed it to finish. She couldn't ride this razor-blade edge much longer.

Leyton began to move, his stroke inside her way too slow for what her body was begging for. But he stayed with it, taking her right to the edge, again and again. One wave of pleasure after another. Until she was at a place where it wasn't possible to feel anything else.

He thrust into her, releasing her.

The climax racked her body. Her muscles clamped around him as her arms and legs did the same. Hadley returned the favor and released him, too.

CHAPTER SIXTEEN

LEYTON FULLY EXPECTED Hadley to be dressed by the time he made it back to the sewing room after a pit stop in the bathroom. But she wasn't. Much to his delight, she was still lying naked on the floor.

She was stretched out on top of one of the sketches. In fact, her left butt cheek was resting on the bulging crotch of what appeared to be...hell, he didn't know, but it certainly made an interesting contrast. The naked artist with the incredible body on one of her creations.

Her arms were tucked beneath her head, and her eyes were closed. One leg was stretched out and the other bent at the knee. She looked so relaxed that for a moment Leyton thought she was asleep, but then her lids lifted and her gaze zoomed to his. She smiled. A very short-lived one, though, because she seemed to remember that she was naked, and she sat up.

Oh, man. He hadn't thought he could get dick stirrings this soon, but he'd been wrong about that.

"Oh," she said. "I didn't hear you come back in."

He'd intentionally stayed quiet, even resorting to tiptoeing to the bathroom because he hadn't wanted Em or Tony to hear him. If they did, Leyton figured they would immediately clue in to the fact that he'd just had sex with Hadley. He didn't mind them knowing. He and Hadley were adults, after all. But he didn't think Hadley would want that news spread around even to members of her immediate family.

Even though the floor was a long way from being comfortable, he went to her and sat down beside her. He got a gut punch when he looked at her naked body, but he got one just as strong when he looked at her face.

Always did.

Hadley was beautiful, even more than her sisters, though some would say that wasn't possible, since they were identical. But Leyton had always been able to tell the triplets apart, and despite those identical looks, Hadley had been the only one of the Dalton women that Leyton was attracted to. Good thing, since Shaw had claimed Sunny and Austin had claimed McCall.

He pushed a strand of her hair from her cheek and gave her a soft kiss. "Are you going to tell me what's wrong?"

Without breaking their gaze lock, Hadley dragged in a deep, weary breath. "No."

That was it. Nothing else. And he could tell from her expression that she meant it. She wasn't going to talk about what was eating away at her. Well, that didn't mean he couldn't keep trying.

"Is it about Bailey?" he asked. "Are you worried about her visit tomorrow?"

"No." It was another quick answer, but this one didn't have nearly as much resolve as the other. "Maybe. A little worried, anyway."

Okay, they were getting somewhere, though Leyton wasn't sure this was the right *somewhere*. He didn't push now. He just waited for her to continue.

"Candice might need me to watch Bailey soon. Like maybe as early as next week. And with Marco still out there, I don't want Bailey cooped up in here all day. I don't want her afraid of this old fart who might be out to settle a grudge."

It definitely wouldn't be ideal for Bailey to not be able to go outside. "Maybe I could talk to Austin, and you and Bailey can stay there."

Of course, Leyton would be staying, too. Or Cait. His brother's house was big, but all those people would make it a tight fit. Still, Austin's twin girls would be playmates for Bailey.

"Let me think about that," Hadley said, moving away from him so she could get to her feet.

She held her arms over her breasts and turned away so she wasn't flashing him, but he took enough of her in to make him feel like a horny teenager. Since getting horny would soon make him hard again, he got up as well, reaching for his boxers. He stopped, though, when he heard the crunch beneath his foot.

It was the flower in the plastic bag. Or rather the *flower that I wished you'd given me*. That was how Hadley had described it, anyway. He figured she didn't want to have another round of talk about it, so he picked it up and slipped it back into her jeans pocket. He also made a mental note to get her some flowers, something his sixteen-year-old self hadn't thought of doing.

He pulled on his jeans and watched her do the same, and because he couldn't stop himself, he kissed her. She didn't pull away. Not physically, anyway. But she was definitely trying to slap up some barriers. It wasn't going to be easy, since they'd soon end up together in the same bed.

"It wasn't casual sex, Hadley," Leyton told her. "We have too much history for casual."

And there went another brick in her barrier. Her mouth

tightened, and she yanked on her shirt with a little more effort than necessary.

"I need to grab a shower," she said, but she did brush a quick kiss on his mouth before she hurried out.

He didn't go after her, since it was obvious she wanted some alone time. Maybe even time to make sure all of her many barriers were in place, and he'd give her that. For now. Soon, though, he would need to know why she had that haunted look in her eyes.

Leyton finished dressing and was about to head upstairs for his own shower when his phone rang. Cait's name popped up on the screen, so he answered it right away.

"It's not about Marco," his sister immediately said. "I don't have anything new on him, but I got a call from Carter Bodell, and he said those two guys from the production company are at the bar. Apparently, the pair is trying to drum up local support for the reunion show they want to do."

On the surface that didn't sound worthy of a call from Carter, which in turn had prompted Cait to get in touch with him. His sister wasn't one who overreacted to things, however. Well, unless he counted that time when she was six and he'd put a lizard down her back. Sometimes, he could still hear echoes of her shrieks.

"Hadley and her sisters don't want to do the show," Leyton said.

"Yeah, I got that. But these two, Wayne Dempsey and Herb McGrath, are talking about how much money will be funneled into the town with the production crew around."

There had indeed been extra income when *Little Cowgirls* was being filmed. The businesses had definitely profited and so had plenty of locals who got paid anytime they ended up on-screen. After the show was abruptly canceled, the town went through sort of an economic depression, and Hadley had caught most of the blame for that. Which got Leyton thinking.

"Please tell me these two clowns aren't trying to stir up trouble for Hadley," Leyton snarled.

"Bingo. According to Carter, Wayne Dempsey's a dick, and since Carter can be a dick himself, I think he recognizes one of his own kind. Wayne apparently challenged the folks in the bar to talk Hadley into changing her mind about doing the show. And he did that after he bought everyone a couple of rounds."

Yeah, definitely stirring up trouble, and the only reason those tipsy folks hadn't called Hadley yet was because they didn't have her number. But he was betting Sunny, McCall and his brothers would have those tipsy, greedy townsfolk reaching out to them.

"Are Herb and Wayne still at the bar?" he asked.

"No. Carter said they left about fifteen minutes ago and were heading back to the inn. According to Thelma Medford, they've booked rooms there for two nights."

Thelma would know, since she was the inn's owner and was somewhat less gossipy than some. Too bad about that, though, because Leyton would have liked to know anything and everything about these two visitors.

"Anyway, I thought you should give Hadley a heads-up about this," Cait added.

Oh, he would do just that, but Leyton thought he should take this one step further. Tomorrow, he needed to have a little chat with the shit stirrers from Waterstone Productions.

HADLEY WOKE AROUSED.

And that was an understatement. She woke up to Leyton's hands on her. His scent surrounding her. His mouth on her stomach. He was planting some amazing tongue kisses there, and she suddenly felt like melting gold.

"Good morning," she managed, noting the sunlight sliding through the edges of the blinds.

"Good morning," he muttered back, creating an even better sensation when his breath hit against the damp spots his mouth had left on her stomach. She'd never gotten what was essentially a belly BJ, but it was seriously effective. She'd gone from a deep sleep—which in itself was a surprise—to wanting morning sex with Leyton.

She reminded herself that she should be distancing herself from him. Of course, that was hard to do, since they were sleeping in the same bed. Even harder because of his magic mouth.

And his hands.

Oh, yes. They were magic, too, and she got a reminder of that when he slid his fingers down the outside of her thigh. Then the inside. Then into her panties.

Then into her.

There wasn't enough time to brace herself for the jolt of pleasure. Heck, ten years might not have been enough time for that. He made sure his fingers landed on the most sensitive part of her body at the exact moment she was wet, hot and so very ready. The climax was on her before she could do anything about it.

She got lost in those ripples of pleasure. No choice about that. The moment was primal and mindless—two things she'd come to expect of her reactions to Leyton.

Hadley opened her eyes and met his. He was looming over her, watching her. Smiling. The smug toad. He knew exactly how to make her an orgasm junkie, with a more than adequate supplier whose initials were *LJ*.

Then again, she could turn the junkie table on him, so she slid her hands between their bodies and found him hammer hard. His eyes crossed, and he called her a few bad names in between some manly grunts.

"You'll have to hold that thought," he rumbled out. "It's after seven, and Cait will be here soon to relieve me."

Hadley's frown was for several reasons. It'd been years since she'd slept this late. Or slept this well. And she didn't like starting her day with a first-class orgasm when Leyton would get no such release. It felt a little icky, as if she now owed him.

He rolled off her, sitting on the side of the bed as he tugged on his boxers. How he got the underpants on over that massive erection, she didn't know. Hadley got up, too, and looked down at her exposed belly. More specifically, at the stretch marks and the C-section scar.

"From my pregnancy," she said, only because Leyton was looking in that direction, too.

"Yeah. I figured as much. You had complications when you were pregnant?" he asked, standing to pull on his jeans.

She nodded and located her own jeans on the back of a chair. "Bailey was breech. I probably should have warned you that I no longer have that fifteen-year-old body you used to fool around with."

He leaned down and kissed one of the stretch marks. It was sort of like an unspoken *no warning necessary*, and it touched her far more than it should have. Damn him. He was such a nice guy.

"You're the first man who's seen them, so I wasn't sure what the reaction would be," she grumbled.

Then she froze.

Crap, crap, crappity-crap. Why in the name of all things

holy had she said that? Because her orgasm junkie condition had obviously left her stupid, that was why.

She hoped that Leyton had gotten temporary hearing loss or that she'd blabbed that softly enough that he hadn't realized what she'd said.

But he did.

His slightly raised eyebrow morphed to less slightly and more raised. If there was a picture of a curious/puzzled hot guy in the dictionary, Leyton would be the visual example. A visual example, too, of someone doing mental math. Bailey was four, and taking in the nine months of pregnancy, Leyton had no doubt figured out that it'd been nearly five years since she'd gotten naked with a man.

It'd actually been six. Maybe closer to seven.

"I've been in a dry spell," she muttered and hoped that lame explanation would suffice.

She continued to dress. Continued, too, to cast glances at him. He was still curious/puzzled hot guy, but it had lessened some. He leaned in and dropped a kiss on her mouth.

"One day you can tell me about the dry spell," he said, not in a "holy shit" kind of tone. Not a "poor pitiful you" tone, either.

It was worse.

It was the tone of a man who seemed to believe that she would indeed spill all about why she'd been abstinent longer than some Victorian prudes. And the kick? She would do it. Hadley just knew it. Heck, he probably wouldn't even have to push her on it. With a simple "Why?" she would gush like a geyser and tell him that sex just wasn't that important to her.

At least it hadn't been.

Then she'd have to tell him that he was the reason the importance of it had skyrocketed.

Crap, crap, crappity-crap.

No more morning orgasms for her, since they left her brain so mushy that she couldn't keep a lid on the Pandora of all boxes.

He tucked in his shirt, zipped up. "I can come back when Bailey gets here," he said, drawing her attention away from what was behind the zipper.

Yeah, her mushy mind had gone to gutter mode.

"Or Cait can be here if you'd rather I not be around," he added.

She pushed aside the mush and gutter to grasp what he'd just said. Or what he might be saying. "Are you worried how I'll introduce you? Because if so, I wasn't going to go with *closet boyfriend.*"

He smiled. "I just thought Candice might pick up on some vibes between us. I wasn't sure if she'd object to Bailey staying over here if she noticed that you and I were lovers."

Hadley hadn't considered that maybe she was wearing an invisible sign that read Orgasms Three Days in a Row, but Candice was perceptive and might pick up on the sexual stuff zinging between Hadley and Leyton. Still, that was enough reason for him to stay away.

"If possible, I'd like for you to be here. I get a little shaky and defensive sometimes when I'm around Candice," Hadley confessed.

Shaky and *defensive* were Badly Hadley synonyms for *bitchy.*

"Candice looks down her nose at me, so I take verbal jabs at her. Not in front of Bailey," she quickly added. "But I need to go cold turkey on Candice jabs because I don't

want Bailey to overhear or pick up on the messy under-
currents."

"Then I'll be here," he said, making it all sound so simple. Maybe it was for him. Hadley wanted him there for
this visit, and he would be.

But she knew that wasn't a blanket offer she could make
to him.

"Call me when Bailey gets here," he said, giving her another kiss. "I'll be in the office or at my place until then."

Hadley stood there a moment, trying to pick her way
through what she was feeling. And what she was going to
do about Leyton.

About Wayne's threat.

She wasn't one to pull the ostrich-head-in-the-sand ploy,
but for now it was all she had. When she finally started to
unravel the threads of her life, she'd need time, and there
wouldn't be much of that today with Bailey's visit.

Forcing herself to get going, she went by her old room,
where she'd left her suitcase. Her head wasn't so sand
deep that she didn't see the irony of leaving her bags in
a baggage-filled room. But she just hadn't been up to the
questions she would have gotten from Em had she left her
stuff in the hall.

She grabbed a quick shower and put on a fresh change
of clothes. Even slathered on some makeup and swapped
out her serpent earrings for a pair of gold sewing needles.
They'd been a gift from Deanna, and Hadley thought she
might need that little piece of her friend with her today
while she entertained her friend's daughter and mother.

Hadley dropped by the kitchen to grab a cup of coffee and say a quick good-morning to Em, but she wasn't
there. There were some fresh blueberry muffins, however,
so Hadley grabbed one along with her coffee and headed

to the sewing room so she could clear up any "evidence" that she and Leyton had left behind. Like suitcases in the hall, that was yet something else she didn't want to have to explain.

The sound of Tony's voice stopped her.

The door to the sewing room was slightly open, but it was enough for her to see Tony. His back was to her, and he was looking up at one of the costume sketches she'd taped to the wall.

"I don't see another way around this," Tony said, and she realized he was talking on the phone. "I can't keep this up."

Since she was still suspicious of the man, Hadley frowned and leaned in to listen. *I can't keep this up* wasn't exactly the confession of a potential ax murderer, but it didn't sound like the musings of a man in love, either.

"No, I don't want to wait," Tony went on a moment later, obviously responding to something said on the other end of the conversation. "It's best if I just leave right now."

Her temper snapped like a flick of a bullwhip. The little creep was running out on Em, and he wasn't even going to tell her goodbye.

"I'll be at the first gas station at the John's Road exit in Boerne off I-10 in thirty minutes," Tony said. "Meet me there."

Tony put his phone away, turned around and came to a dead stop when he saw Hadley. She figured he had no trouble noting the more than a glimmer of fire in her eyes.

"I can't keep this up," she repeated, her voice rising with each word. *"It's best if I just leave right now."*

Tony groaned softly, shaking his head. "I can explain."

But he didn't do that. He just stood there, looking down at the costume sketch as if he hoped it would gobble him up.

"Explain it, then," Hadley snapped, and she didn't even have to muster up a Badly Hadley glower. This one came straight from her heart. "Was that a lackey of yours on the phone, someone who'll whisk you out of harm's way while Em stays here and faces danger?"

Tony shook his head again. "No. Not a lackey. It was Marco."

CHAPTER SEVENTEEN

LEYTON FIGURED IF he'd had more time, he could have won this argument with Hadley. But time had been in short supply because of the thirty minutes Tony had given his brother. Boerne wasn't exactly a stone's throw from Lone Star Ridge, and it would take nearly all of those minutes just to get there.

That was why Leyton was now driving Tony's car to the rendezvous with a gangster. Not alone, either. Em, Hadley and Cait were in the back seat, and Tony was riding shotgun. Cait was not only his backup, but while Leyton drove, she was also on the phone with the Boerne cops, requesting a quiet-approach assistance from them. In other words, no blaring sirens and flashing lights. They didn't want Marco running before they had a chance to corner him.

Of course, Leyton also didn't want Marco shooting at them, so hopefully that wasn't what the man had in mind when he'd agreed to a meeting in a public place. Maybe Marco simply wanted to speak his mind, vent or—best-case scenario—bury the hatchet. If it was something that didn't involve violence, then maybe Tony would come in handy.

Hadley and Em wouldn't.

There was no *handy* consideration for them, and Leyton would have preferred them out of potential harm's way. But as Hadley had so adamantly argued, this could be a ploy for Marco to come to the ranch. And since there hadn't been time for Leyton to arrange a deputy to stay with her and Em, they came along.

It hadn't even helped when Leyton reminded Hadley that Bailey and Candice would be visiting today, but it had prompted Hadley to call Candice, who assured her that it'd be early afternoon before they arrived. In other words, Hadley had a green light to go with Leyton.

"What you were going to do is so sweet," Em said, and after a glimpse in the rearview mirror, Leyton saw her blow Tony a kiss. "You were going to sacrifice yourself for me."

"It's not sweet," Leyton snarled, and he paraphrased something he'd already said. "It's stupid, and I don't want either of you to pull anything like that again."

Hadley made a sound of agreement, and Leyton didn't think it was his imagination that she gave Tony the stink eye when she looked at him. Leyton was on the same stink-eye page with her. Except he preferred to think of his particular expression as more of a badass glare. Maybe the looks would drill it home with Tony that he wasn't going behind their backs again.

"Did Marco say how he got your phone number?" Leyton glanced at Tony to let him know that question was directed at him. There just hadn't been time to ask Tony that before they'd hurried out of the house.

"He didn't say, but I suspect it's something a PI can get."

True, though Elise hadn't been able to find a phone for Marco. That was probably because the man was using a burner cell, one that couldn't be traced. Cait had started a trace on the number, but Leyton wasn't holding out much hope on that. Tony, on the other hand, hadn't used a burner.

He was using the same number he'd had for years, so it wouldn't have been that hard for Marco to get it.

"Go over everything Marco told you," Leyton insisted, though it was something he'd already had Tony do. Still, he wanted to see if the story changed or if Tony remembered any new details.

"Like I said, his name didn't show up on my screen, but I answered it. The moment he spoke, I knew it was him. He said we should make arrangements to meet, that we had some old business to settle."

From the rearview mirror, Leyton saw Hadley pull back her shoulders and eye her grandmother with concern. Again, he and Hadley were on the same page. Old business to settle could mean violence.

"I told him that I'd rather us go ahead and meet," Tony went on. "I didn't want to wait." He paused. "I didn't want to keep putting Em through this."

Leyton considered giving him another blasting reminder that meeting his gangster brother was a dumb-as-dirt thing to do, but six times was probably enough. *Probably.*

"And Marco didn't say anything about knowing you were in Lone Star Ridge?" Hadley pressed, doing some rephrasing of her own.

"No." As with his other responses to that question, Tony didn't hesitate. "He didn't even ask where I was and didn't mention Em. He just said he wanted us to get together and talk. He suggested tomorrow, but I told him I'd rather see him now. I told him where and when I wanted us to meet."

Marco might have preferred to set things up, to have whatever he wanted in place before the meeting. That likely would have included choosing the place, too. But even though Marco hadn't had a say in either the time or the place, it didn't mean he wouldn't come prepared.

"The Boerne police have an unmarked car with two officers on the way to the gas station," Cait informed them when she finished her call. "They should arrive about ten minutes ahead of the meeting."

Leyton checked the time. They would be only a couple of minutes behind the Boerne officers, but Marco could already be there. After all, they didn't know where Marco had been when he'd made that call.

"I also had Willy go over to Em's to keep watch," Cait added. "You know, just in case Marco shows up there."

Willy was Deputy Willy Jenkinson, and while he wasn't the best lawman in town, he'd do for duty like this. If someone even resembling Marco drove up, Willy would call for backup.

"Okay, what are the rules?" Leyton asked when he was getting ready to take the exit off the interstate. This should be easy, since he'd done plenty of repeating with them, too.

"Stay in the car no matter what," Tony provided.

"Don't try to give Marco a piece of my mind," Em contributed. "Like telling him just because a chicken has wings, it don't mean it can fly worth a darn. Marco and his meanness won't fly with me."

Leyton wanted to groan. This was basically a police op, and he had a senior citizen loose cannon in the back seat. Thankfully, Em was in the middle between Hadley and Cait, and Leyton was reasonably sure they could keep Em inside.

"Granny Em, Cait and I are to slink down on the seat so we won't be visible," Hadley piped in.

She shot him a look as if she wanted to include him in on that slinking, so Leyton tapped his badge. This was his job. Not just that, of course. Hadley and her family were more than the job, but he wouldn't be getting down on the seat if things went wrong. Tony, however, would. Leyton had made that clear to the man.

Leyton spotted the first gas station and glanced around. No sign of anyone matching Marco's description, but there were four cars. Two at the pumps and the other two on each side of the building. He motioned for Hadley, Cait and Em to ease down lower, and they did. Marco might not show if he had the place under surveillance and saw a car full of people.

"The cops are in the dark blue sedan," Cait supplied.

That was the car at one of the pumps, which would give the officers inside a good vantage point for seeing not only the gas station itself but also the road that fronted it. One of the cops was in plain clothes and was pumping gas. Leyton drove past him, making eye contact to let him know they'd arrived, and he parked Tony's car on the far side by the machine that dispensed air.

And the waiting began.

Leyton had been on stakeouts before, and he knew they could get boring fast, but he had a personal investment in this, so it kept his body revved. Just as Hadley had been doing for the past couple of days.

Revved and wired.

Sleeping with a complicated, attractive woman could do that. Sleeping with a complicated, attractive woman that he'd wanted since he was old enough to want such things added another level to this. Once he had this meeting sorted out with Marco, Tony and Em, he really needed to focus on Hadley and see if she was going to let this sleeping together go past the mere *sleeping* stage. It would take plenty of convincing for that to happen. Plenty of getting to the bottom of what'd happened in her past, too.

Leyton didn't have an ounce of proof, but he felt in his gut that *what'd happened* had something to do with those two clowns from the production company. Somehow, he needed to fit in that chat with them before they checked out of the inn. Oh, and meeting Bailey and giving Hadley some moral support for what would likely be a tense visit with Candice.

A full plate indeed. But maybe it wouldn't include rooster crap or Alyssa's navel ring.

He continued to glance around the gas station, and beside him Tony did the same. He had to hand it to the man—Tony didn't look especially nervous. More like determined. Of course, the stakes were pretty darn high for him.

Leyton automatically put his hand over his weapon when the front door of the gas station flew open. Cait reacted, too, and from the corner of his eye, he saw her lift her head and zoom in on the young man who was firing glances around the area. He was way too young to be Marco and possibly worked there.

"Marco?" Em asked, and she would have lifted her head, too, if Hadley hadn't pulled her back down.

Leyton was about to mumble "good" to Hadley for doing that, but then Hadley did some head lifting, as well. "It's not Marco," she said, ending her comment with a huff.

The young man continued to look around, and his attention finally landed on the car. Specifically, on Tony. He hurried toward them, causing Leyton to make a split-second decision about what to do. The guy wasn't visibly armed. In fact, the only thing in his hand was a yellow sticky note. So, Leyton didn't draw his gun. Nor did he take his attention off their surroundings, because this note-carrying man could be some kind of decoy that Marco was using to distract them.

"Tony Corbin?" the man asked when he was closer to the car.

Leyton saw then that he wasn't a man at all but a kid. Probably eighteen or nineteen. And he had no criminal vibe whatsoever.

"Tony Corbin?" he repeated, waving the sticky note. "I have a message for you if you're Tony Corbin."

"Stay put," Leyton said, and he meant that not just for Tony but for everyone else in the car. He opened the door, stood and looked at the teenager from over the top of the car. The two plainclothes officers were closing in, too.

"What message?" Leyton snapped.

The kid froze, probably because Leyton was sure he sounded like a cop. Also, the kid noticed the other two badges approaching. "Uh, it's from some guy who just called." His voice cracked on practically every word. "He said I needed to give a message to Tony Corbin, who'd be sitting in a parked car out here. He said it was real important."

Leyton motioned for the other officers to keep watch, and he went around the car to take the note. The kid's hand was shaking. Heck, so was most of his body, and he nearly dropped the note before handing it to him. Leyton glanced down at it and cursed when he read it.

"You brought friends. I wanted this to be a private meeting between you and me. We'll have to get together some other time. Marco."

CHAPTER EIGHTEEN

THE RIDE BACK to Lone Star Ridge felt as if it lasted six years. Hadley knew that it'd been only a fraction of that, but with all the broody silence in the car, it had given her plenty of time to think.

And contribute to the broodiness.

For instance, why had Marco sent the note with the gas station clerk instead of just calling Tony? Marco had his brother's phone number and could have easily called him to deliver the message himself.

And where had Marco been while Leyton and the rest of them sat in the car waiting for him? Nearby? Close enough to see them? Or had he sent a lackey to take a peek for him? Even though she didn't know the man, she thought maybe he was the lackey-having type.

There was also the unspoken elephant in the car. The concern that Marco might have spotted Em and now knew that she and Tony were together. Of course, he might have been aware of that before today, too.

Em and Tony hadn't exactly remained shut up in their hotel room on the River Walk. In fact, they'd tried to draw attention to themselves and likely had succeeded. If Marco's lackeys showed Tony's picture around, someone could have mentioned that Tony was with a woman. It wouldn't have been much of a stretch for Marco to believe that the woman was Em.

All of those questions and worries kept circling through Hadley's mind, but she quickly pushed them aside when they arrived at Em's, and she saw the three vehicles in the driveway. One was Cait's SUV. Then there was a truck that must have belonged to Deputy Willy Jenkinson, who was standing on the front porch, and the other one was a sleek silver luxury car that had Candice written on it.

Literally.

The woman had vanity license plates with her name.

At that exact moment, Cait's phone rang, and she relayed that it was Willy calling to let them know Em had company. Considering that Candice and Bailey hadn't even gotten out of the car, it meant they'd likely just arrived. And much earlier than Candice had said when Hadley spoke to her earlier. Hadley had hoped she'd at least have some time to freshen up. Any concerns about her appearance vanished, however, when Candice stepped out and helped Bailey out of her car seat.

Hadley could feel her heart fill with love.

It was the same reaction she had every time she saw Bailey, and yet every time it was still a surprise. It was so hard to believe that she could care this much for a pint-size cutie.

"Mama Hadley!" Bailey called out the moment she spotted Hadley getting out of Tony's car.

Bailey ran toward her, and Hadley scooped her up in her arms. Noisy exaggerated kisses were a must, so Hadley made sure she got in her share of them. Bailey did the same, and Hadley got so caught up in the giggling moment that she hadn't realized everyone had stopped to watch them. Not watching with soft smiles and "oh, how cute" grins, either, but more like surprise. Then again, it wasn't every day that they saw Badly Hadley have some fun.

"We rided a long time," Bailey told her, ignoring the stares they were getting. "And I painted you a picture."

"I can't wait to see it." Hadley sneaked in another kiss.

Bailey took that as a "see it now" request and ran back toward Candice's car. Candice came closer to Hadley. As usual, Candice was dressed to perfection in her sky blue dress and silver sandals. Not a strand of her blond hair was out of place, and the makeup was flawless. No needle earrings for her. Just classic pearl studs. But she did have on a silver necklace with her name spelled out. Apparently, Candice liked to have reminders of who she was.

"I'm sorry we're early," Candice said. "Bailey was anxious for us to leave." She slid her gaze over Hadley's black pants and top, and Hadley suddenly felt as if she were on an episode of fashion disasters. Candice then turned scrutinizing glances at the others. "Is, uh, everything okay?"

"Of course it is," Em piped up. "I'm Hadley's grandmother. Just call me Em."

"Candice Monroe," she reciprocated.

"This is Tony, my beau," Em continued, "and that's Cait, a deputy around here." She pointed to Leyton. "And that's Leyton Jameson, Hadley's beau."

Well, so much for holding back the tidbit about her and Leyton being lovers. But other than a nod of greeting, Candice didn't seem to have much of a reaction. The same couldn't be said for Bailey. She hurried back to them, and she handed the drawing to Hadley while she went up to Cait.

Bailey pointed to the badge Cait had clipped to the waist of her jeans. "You the police?"

Cait grinned and hitched her thumb in Leyton's direction. "I am, and so is my brother. He's got a badge, too."

Bailey ran to Leyton. The girl just didn't know how to

move slowly. An all-velocity, no-vector kind of kid. She had to practically skid to a halt to stop herself from running straight into him.

Leyton unclipped his badge and handed it to her. Judging from the way Bailey's eyes widened and the loud *ooh* she made, she was impressed. Bailey darted back to show it to Hadley, presumably so she could be impressed, too.

"Why don't we all go inside?" Leyton asked, and he said it in such a way to remind Hadley that they all shouldn't be out in the open like this. If Marco had managed to spy on them at the gas station, then he could do it here, too.

A creepy thought.

"I'll head back to the station," Cait called out to them. "If I hear anything about, well, anything, I'll let you know."

Maybe *anything about anything* would include Marco's whereabouts, though Hadley doubted they'd get lucky and spot him on security or traffic cameras.

Leyton continued to fire glances around the yard while he ushered them toward the porch. No easy feat. Bailey loved to move fast, but at the moment she also wanted to continue to show Hadley the badge.

"Tell me about the picture," Hadley said, putting her hand on Bailey's shoulder to maneuver the girl into the house.

"It's a cossume. Like yours," Bailey added.

It took Hadley a moment to figure out that she meant costume, and, yep, that was what it was, all right. A big red dress that billowed out like a sail on a ship. The "model" who was wearing it had either a tiara or some kind of serpent coiled on the top of her head. It was more realistic than Hadley's Cyborg Cowboy sketches.

"I love it," Hadley told her, leaning down to drop a kiss

on the top of Bailey's head. "Who knows, maybe you'll be a costume designer, too."

Candice had been examining the foyer and its odd mix of contents, but she practically snapped toward Hadley. And Hadley knew why. Candice wanted something loftier for Bailey, and Hadley had no beef with that. She had nothing against lofty, but she also wanted Bailey to be happy. Sometimes, Hadley didn't think that was Candice's top priority when it came to the child.

"I'll be in the parlor," Tony said, excusing himself as he walked away. "I want to make some phone calls." No doubt to see if he could get in touch with his brother. "It was good to meet you, Mrs. Monroe."

Candice spared him a polite glance and a nod, then went back to her disapproving perusal of the foyer.

"I can draw you a badge," Bailey offered, handing Leyton back his real one. "What's a beau?"

Hadley hadn't even thought the girl heard Em's comment, but obviously she'd been wrong about that.

"It's sort of a friend," Hadley answered when no one else said anything. That wasn't a lie, but she hoped Bailey didn't apply the word to kids in preschool who were just plain old friends.

Apparently, that answer seemed to suit Bailey, because she shifted her attention to the foyer. She was looking at stuff, too, but there was no scrutiny in her gaze. Her eyes lit up when she saw a stuffed duck.

"It's Slackers," Bailey said, making quacking noises.

"It is," Hadley verified, and she was about to say that her sister Sunny did the illustrations for the popular *Slacker Quackers* graphic novel series for kids, but Candice's mouth had gone tight.

"The preschool had some of the books," Candice said.

Definite disapproval. "But I'm not sure they're suitable for a child Bailey's…" Her words drifted off when she caught sight of the photo of Em with Leyton's father.

"Is that Marty Jameson?" Candice asked, her hand flattening on her chest.

"It is," Leyton verified with no enthusiasm whatsoever. "Em's a fan."

"And he's Leyton's father," Em gladly provided, lifting the picture to better show it off.

Hadley expected plenty of disapproval from Candice about that, too, since Marty didn't have an angel reputation. Well, unless you counted fallen angels. But that wasn't disapproval on her suddenly flushed face.

Crap.

It was a groupie look. Hadley had certainly seen enough of them when female members of the *Little Cowgirls* filming crew would see Marty during the handful of times he visited the ranch. Who knew that the high-horse-riding Candice would have the hots for a country-rock star with the morals of an alley cat?

"You're Marty Jameson's son," Candice said. She got a goofy smile, clearly not picking up on the hesitant confirmation of that from Leyton. "I used to go to his concerts. I love his music."

"I'll see about getting you his autograph," Leyton grumbled. No enthusiasm in that, either.

Em saved the day by switching the subject and taking hold of Bailey's hand. "You want to see your Mama Hadley's room, and then we can find some toys?"

No way would Bailey turn that down, and she headed up the stairs while she chattered away to Em and Slackers. Candice might not think the stories were appropriate for Bailey, but the kid obviously loved them.

"You told your family you were a surrogate," Candice commented as they started up the stairs to follow Em and Bailey.

"I did. They're okay with it."

Leyton cleared his throat. "I need to make some calls, too," Leyton said, staying back. Obviously, he thought she and Candice needed some privacy to continue this conversation.

Hadley glanced at him, and even though he didn't say it aloud, she figured he was silently reminding her to let him know if she needed him.

Maybe she would need him, but Candice wasn't doing her supreme uppity act today. She'd doled out some flashes of it, as if she just hadn't been able to keep them all contained. But she was subdued by Candice standards. Probably because of her friend being sick. Things had to be pretty bad in that area for Candice to make this trip to Lone Star Ridge.

"This is where Bailey would stay if I left her here with you?" Candice asked.

"Probably. I'm not sure if I'll be going back to California anytime soon."

Hadley wouldn't get into her somewhat dismal financial situation. A situation that would ease considerably if she could sublet the office space that she was still paying for. Ditto for getting paid for the latest work she'd done.

"My grandmother needs me right now," Hadley added. "That's why it'd be easier if Bailey came here instead of me going to Houston to be with her."

Though if Candice dug in her heels about that, Hadley would see what she could work out with Leyton and her sisters. She'd only go to Houston if there was no other choice and if she could be absolutely sure that Em would be safe.

Candice slowed her steps on the stairs, and Hadley followed suit. It was obvious the woman wanted to chat, and Bailey was fine with Em. Hadley could already hear Bailey squealing with delight, which meant she was likely in Hadley's old room. Hadley could never see the appeal, but she remembered Austin's twin daughters loving the junk they found in there.

"And what about Marty's son? Leyton," Candice added as if stretching her memory to recall his name. "Does he stay here with you, too?"

Well, this was a giant can of worms. Hadley had a five-second debate with herself and decided not to mention Marco. If Bailey ended up coming here for a visit and Marco was still at large, Hadley would come up with a safe solution and tell Candice about it then. What she didn't want was the woman backing out and maybe coming up with someone else to watch Bailey while Candice's friend was in the hospital.

"Leyton could end up spending some nights here," Hadley settled for saying. "But I'm not going to let Bailey see anything she shouldn't see."

Candice made a sound that Hadley couldn't quite interpret. It didn't sound like agreement, though.

"Look, Leyton's a good guy," Hadley said, feeling the need to defend him. "You can ask anybody around here, and they'll tell you that."

For some reason, hearing those words aloud caused them to sink in. *Really* sink in. He was a good guy, and that made her wonder even more what the heck he was doing with her.

They made it to the top of the stairs and then to the

bedroom, following the sound of Bailey's laughter. She and Em were playing with some dolls that were in Mc-Call's section.

"Could I sleep in all the beds?" Bailey asked the moment Hadley stepped in.

She looked at Bailey's big smile in this room drenched with bad memories, and it, well, helped. The memories were still there, but Bailey had brightened them a little.

"You want to take a nap?" Hadley teased, knowing that Bailey wouldn't care for that.

"No, I wanta sleep and play. All night." Bailey shifted her attention to Candice. "Can we stay the night, Grandma?"

"Not this night but maybe soon."

Candice's answer earned her a groan from Bailey, who obviously wanted the sleepover to start now, but at least Candice didn't seem put off by the idea. Of course, Candice likely thought that Hadley would be staying in here with the child.

And she would.

If it came down to it, she'd push back those memories and do what was best for Bailey. That pretty much described her entire outlook when it came to the child she'd carried.

Candice gave the large room the same kind of once-over she had the foyer, and she frowned when she looked at the section with the black walls. "Yours," Candice said, her voice a sigh.

Since it wasn't an actual question, Hadley sighed, too. Black had been the obvious choice for the walls, since it was the color of most of her clothes. Hadley liked fading into the decor when she was forced to be in the room when they were shooting scenes in there.

"Em, would it be okay if Bailey played up here with you while Hadley and I talk?" Candice asked.

"Of course," Em readily agreed. "Bailey and I are going looking for treasure in here. The girls have boxes of stuff beneath their beds."

There were indeed some boxes. Sort of like mini time capsules in the bigger time capsule of the room itself. From time to time, the producers and scriptwriters would order other props to be brought in, and the old stuff would be boxed up. Hadley couldn't remember anything embarrassing or inappropriate that would be in any of the areas, but hopefully if there was something, Em would hide it before Bailey could see it.

Hadley led Candice back downstairs, passing through the foyer, where Leyton was talking on the phone with someone. She could also hear Tony doing the same in the living room.

Hadley's gaze connected with Leyton's, and since she could see the worry in his eyes, she gave him what she hoped would be a reassuring smile. An actual one, since this visit with Candice was going better than expected. Yes, the woman was making those judgmental expressions, but she hadn't nixed the idea of Bailey coming here. Maybe Leyton's calls would go better than expected, too, and they'd find Marco today.

She took Candice to the kitchen and put on a fresh pot of coffee to brew before she sat at the table with her. "How's your friend doing?" Hadley asked. "When will she have the surgery and find out if it's cancer?"

Candice did something that Hadley had never seen the woman do. She dodged Hadley's gaze. In fact, Candice got very interested in the surface of the table and began to trace her fingers around the wood grain.

That put a knot in Hadley's stomach.

Maybe it was the already heightened concern about Em,

but Hadley's mind jumped straight from gaze dodging to worst-case scenario. "Is something wrong with Bailey? Is she sick? Does she—"

"It's not Bailey," Candice said, and Hadley was thankful for both the interruption and the assurance. Crap. Being an almost mom wasn't a job for sissies. It was pure agony to think of anything being wrong with the precious child.

"Okay." Hadley repeated that a couple of times to steady herself. Mercy, she was the walking, talking definition of being on edge. "Tell me about your friend."

Candice didn't do any interrupting this time. Nor did she jump to answer. She did more tracing of the wood grain before her eyes finally came back to Hadley. "It's me. I'm the one who needs surgery."

Hadley froze for a moment, staring at the woman. "You might have cancer." She shook her head. "But you don't look sick." Which, of course, was a stupid thing to say, but Hadley's mind was starting to whirl again with scenarios. Some of them worst-case.

"Not yet, but I've been told many patients don't have symptoms in the early stages. But if it is cancer, the treatments will have some side effects."

Chemo. Maybe even radiation.

"The tumor is in my uterus," Candice went on, "and my surgery is scheduled for next week. My doctor wanted it sooner, but I had to work out Bailey's care with you first. Bailey's nanny, Janet, could bring Bailey here a week from today."

Hadley figured it wasn't a wise medical decision to delay something like that, but she would have done the same. "I'll watch Bailey for as long as you need."

"Thank you," Candice muttered. She paused, took a

deep breath and finally lifted her eyes to meet Hadley's. *"As long as you need* might be…forever. If I don't make it, Hadley, I'll need you to take custody of Bailey."

CHAPTER NINETEEN

LEYTON LOOKED UP from his laptop when he heard the sound of a car engine. But before he could make it out of the dining room, where he'd been working, Hadley stepped in.

"It's okay," she said. "It's Candice leaving."

Leyton would have bolted for the front door, since he didn't want them going outside alone, but Hadley stopped him. "Cait's with them. She pulled up as Candice was getting ready to go. Just as I was about to come and get you," she added.

He hadn't heard his sister's SUV, but then, Cait had likely parked on the side of the driveway because Candice's and Tony's cars were out front.

Leyton knew that Cait could handle something like this, but he still went to the door and looked out. Candice and Bailey were already driving away, and his sister was making her way to the porch. Maybe just to check on him, maybe for an update.

He very much wanted to hear what his sister had to say, but for now Hadley was his concern. For the past couple of hours, he'd stayed out of her way so she could spend the day with Bailey, but after a careful look at her face, he knew that'd been a mistake.

Every bit of her expression showed worry and fatigue.

"Did something happen to Bailey? Is she all right?" he asked, taking hold of Hadley's shoulders.

"Bailey's fine," she assured him.

He would have felt a whole lot more relief had her expression not stayed the same, and Leyton would have definitely pressed her for more info, but Cait came in. It took his sister a split second to pick up on the tension, and she volleyed glances at them.

"Something I should know?" Cait asked.

Leyton was wondering the same thing, but Hadley quickly shook her head. That told him that whatever was going on with her needed to be talked about in private. With him. Or at least it'd better be with him. No way did he want her holding whatever this was inside her.

"Any updates on Marco?" Leyton asked his sister. Best to get business out of the way first.

"Nada. No one in or near the gas station spotted anyone matching his description. Nothing on the traffic cameras, and the gas station security cameras aren't working."

That last part would have frustrated Leyton a whole lot more if he'd thought there was any chance whatsoever that Marco would have actually gone inside the building. But it would have been a stupid thing to do, since he would have essentially been trapped. Marco had to have assumed that his brother might bring a cop or at least some muscle with him.

"Is it possible for you to stay here for a while?" Hadley asked Cait.

"Sure." Cait tossed a few more suspicious glances at them, her attention settling on Leyton as if she was trying to read his mind. *Good luck with that.* There was nothing in his mind right now that would explain things, because he didn't have a clue what was going on. But it was possible that Candice had said something mean-girl style that had hurt Hadley.

Hadley turned to Leyton. "You think we could go to your place? I just need to get out of here and get some fresh air."

He was about 100 percent sure that she didn't have fresh air on her mind, but it was obvious she needed to talk, and whatever was bugging her, she didn't want to get into it here.

Leyton nodded, looking at his sister to make sure she was okay with holding down the fort for what might be hours. Or all night. Not only was Cait okay with it, but she must have sensed there was some kind of urgency for Hadley.

"You want me to tell Em that you and Leyton are heading out?" Cait asked Hadley.

Hadley nodded. "Yes. Thank you." Now the worry and fatigue had made it into her voice and seemed to be growing with every passing second.

Hadley didn't even grab her purse but instead started out the door with Leyton right behind her. He didn't ask her what was wrong, figuring if Em's house wasn't the right place for this discussion, then the driveway sure as hell wasn't, either. Leyton just waited until they were inside his truck and then waited some more while he drove away from the house.

"Candice might have cancer," Hadley finally said.

Leyton had come up with a mental list of possible things bothering Hadley, but that hadn't been one of them. Cancer. Hell. That could be anything from treatable to a death sentence. Hadley no doubt knew that as well, and it explained that stark look of dread she was still sporting.

"It's bad?" he asked.

"To be determined. Candice's surgery is next week.

They'll know then if the tumor is cancerous, and if it is, what kind of treatments she'll need."

Leyton tried to process all of that while he drove to his house. He'd known people who'd survived, and died from, cancer. Including Austin's wife. That'd been an ordeal from hell where his wife had just withered away. He hoped Candice didn't have that in store for her.

"Candice wants Bailey's nanny to bring her here on Monday," Hadley went on. "And Bailey will stay here with me in Lone Star Ridge until…well, until."

In other words, maybe Bailey wouldn't be going back to Candice ever. That was what Hadley was obviously trying to come to terms with. Which confused him a little. She clearly loved the little girl and had wanted custody of her. So, that couldn't be causing this dark mood. Maybe she was feeling guilty because she and Candice hadn't gotten along and now the woman might have a disease that could kill her.

Hadley didn't say anything else until he pulled to a stop in front of his ranch. She sat there, looking out at the one-story limestone-and-cedar house, and he realized this was probably the first time she'd seen it. The place hadn't been here when she lived in Lone Star Ridge, but Leyton had bought it and the land nearly a decade ago. He'd added the barn and corral and made it his home.

"It's really nice out here," she murmured.

Until she said that, Leyton hadn't realized just how much he wanted her approval. Which made him feel a little bit stupid. He couldn't be weaving fantasies about Hadley spending long chunks of time here. Hell, it was best not to weave any fantasies, period, when it came to Hadley. Still, her comment felt good.

"Candice is doing some paperwork," she went on when

they got out of the truck. "She wants to give me custody of Bailey if the worst happens."

Well, at least Candice was thinking ahead. That was a decision best made now, and it'd been the right one to make.

Leyton unlocked the door, and Hadley stepped in, looking around. It definitely wasn't a fancy place, but it wasn't a man cave, either. In part, that was because of the toy chests he had sitting around for when his nieces visited. Also in part because his mother had gotten in on the decorating, and it had resulted in the denim-colored sofa instead of a dark leather one that he would have chosen.

Hadley smiled a little when her gaze landed on that and then on the "artwork" that he had taped to the stone mantel. Again, thanks to his nieces. Apparently, a couple of the drawings were of him, but looking at them now, Leyton thought they would have fit into Hadley's Cyborg Cowboy project.

"Bailey should be with you if something happens," Leyton assured her, hoping that would ease some of the worry that seemed to be building inside her.

It didn't.

In fact, her worry seemed to spike to a panic level. "I'm not a good enough person to raise a child." Groaning, then cursing, she went to the fireplace and caught onto the mantel as if she needed it to hold her up.

Leyton hurried to her, but she turned away from him when he tried to pull her into his arms.

"Don't," she said in a hoarse whisper. "Don't touch me right now."

He didn't. But it took every ounce of his willpower not to try to comfort her. Maybe because he had enough sense to realize that a hug wasn't going to fix this.

Whatever this was.

"I'm like an onion with lots of bad layers," Hadley went on several moments later, and she let go of the mantel long enough to swipe away a tear that streaked down her cheek. She cursed the tear, too, as if disgusted with herself. Which she probably was. Hadley likely saw crying as a weakness.

"You're not bad," he assured her, knowing it wouldn't help, either, but it was something he wanted her to hear. "You're here in Lone Star Ridge because Em needs you. And don't say it was because it fit in with your plans or some other bullshit."

The glance she gave him confirmed that had been indeed what she was about to say.

"Em asked you to come, and you did," he went on. "Now Candice has asked you to take care of Bailey, and you will. Just because you acted out when you were a teenager, it doesn't mean you don't deserve to be happy."

She stayed quiet for a long time, her gaze glued to the mantel again. "I don't deserve to be happy. You don't know the half of what I did."

Until she added that last part, Leyton had been ready with another round of arguing to give her examples of all that goodness that he knew was beneath her barrier. And those tears that were still coming.

"There's nothing you can tell me that'll make me think you're a real Badly Hadley," he settled for saying.

She made a hollow laugh. "Want to bet?"

"Yeah, I do," he snapped.

"Then it's a bet you'll lose."

Well, shit. What the heck was this about? He'd gone a long time without seeing her, and other than the tidbits he heard from Em, Leyton had to admit he knew very little about her life in California. Obviously, something bad had happened.

But maybe not in California.

Maybe the bad had happened right here in Lone Star Ridge.

Groaning, Hadley stepped back from the fireplace, went to the sofa and sank down. Leyton stayed put, watching her, hoping he could deal with whatever the hell it was she was about to say.

"Did someone molest you when you were a teenager?" Leyton came out and asked.

He halfway expected her to clam up again or tell him to mind his own business, but she made another of those hollow laughs, and the sound of it, the pain in it, cut him bone deep.

"Who did it?" he demanded, wishing that he sounded less like a cop or a boyfriend who wanted to beat the shit out of whoever had hurt her.

She looked him straight in the eyes. "I wasn't molested."

Leyton was already so worked up that it took him a moment to understand what she'd said. It took more than a moment to realize she was telling the truth. That took some time for him to process, too. How the heck had he been so wrong about that? And if it wasn't sexual abuse, what was all this bad-onion bullshit about?

Hadley leaned back on the sofa, but she was no longer looking at him. Her gaze was now on the ceiling. "Remember the night you broke up with me?"

It was a question, but there was no reason for Leyton to confirm that he did indeed remember it. In every shitty detail. It was his own version of a bad-onion layer. He'd gotten embarrassed over the making-out episode that'd aired, and he'd handled it the way an immature idiot would. By breaking up with Hadley and therefore making her feel as if it had been all her fault.

"What does that have to do with why you think you're not fit to raise Bailey?" he asked, hoping to get right to the heart of the matter.

"Everything," she readily answered, but then she shook her head. "It was the start of everything," she amended. "And, no, I'm not putting one ounce of blame on you. You had no part in what happened after our breakup. That was all on me."

Once again, his brain started whipping out a mental list. The breakup had happened about a week or so before her stolen-car joyriding arrest. But maybe it had taken her a week to get into that kind of trouble. If so, then he had more than an ounce of responsibility in this.

"I was hurt and very pissed off," Hadley went on, and she aimed her index finger at him when she saw his face— which no doubt included a tight jaw and a riled expression. "That's not on you, either. Most teenage girls handle something like that with a crying jag, pigging out on ice cream and bitching to their girlfriends or sisters. I didn't do any of those things."

She stopped, and he had to wait to find out how exactly she'd tried to mend her broken heart. A heart he'd broken.

"I seduced one of the guys on the crew," Hadley said, her voice hoarse, her breath thin. "Or rather I tried to do that. I didn't have a lot of experience in that area."

Because she'd been a virgin.

Leyton knew for a fact that he wasn't going to like how this attempted seduction had turned out.

"This guy was setting up some lighting and sound in my bedroom," she continued. "McCall and Sunny were off shooting a scene somewhere with Sunshine, so I had the place to myself. I stripped off my clothes. Most of them, anyway. And I went in, offering myself to him."

He'd been right about not liking how this had turned out. Leyton felt a mixture of anger, hurt and dread that the worst was yet to come.

"When he didn't jump to take me up on my offer, I kissed him." Her voice dropped a notch, and her gaze drifted from his. "He kissed me back at first. I mean, he was a guy, after all, and he had a naked woman throwing herself at him."

"Girl," Leyton corrected. "You were fifteen. You weren't a woman."

"Semantics," she argued. "I had a mostly filled-out body, and I'm pretty sure he wanted it. He might have had it, too, if a production assistant hadn't walked in." She paused. "The assistant was his wife."

"Shit," Leyton grumbled.

"Yes, that about summed it up. She pitched a fit, of course. I mean, here was her husband in the room with a naked teenager, and she didn't believe him when he said that I'd come on to him." Hadley paused, moistening her lips. "Bottom line is that his wife filed for a divorce, and he had to pay her a settlement to keep her from putting anything about me in the divorce papers."

"Settlement?" Leyton asked. "You mean money?"

"Money," Hadley confirmed. "The guy went to Sunshine and told her what'd happened. She was furious, of course, but it didn't tamp down her bottomless pit of greed. Sunshine knew that if this became public, there'd be a scandal and *Little Cowgirls* would be canceled. She siphoned off ten grand from our accounts and paid the guy so he could pay off his wife."

Leyton couldn't imagine any of that encounter with

Sunshine would have been pleasant for Hadley. On her best days, Sunshine was just a partial bitch instead of a full-fledged one.

He went to the sofa and sat down next to her. "You didn't go to Em?"

"God, no. I was already humiliated, mortified and plenty of other adjectives that I preferred my grandmother not know about. It was bad enough that Sunshine knew. Bad enough that I broke up a marriage because I was acting out."

He paused a moment to figure out the best way to say this. "I'm guessing the marriage wasn't very strong if the woman didn't believe her husband when he told her what'd happened."

Hadley shrugged, and he could tell what he'd said didn't lessen her guilt one little bit.

"I swear I didn't intentionally set out to get the show canceled when I got in that stolen car," she went on. "I just wanted to do something…bad. Something that would make the outside of me match what was going on inside. I wanted to prove I truly was Badly Hadley."

Well, she'd succeeded. Or so most people thought. But Leyton had always believed there'd been something else under the surface. And he'd been right.

"I didn't think," she added a moment later. "I definitely didn't think things through. I was just so relieved when I got arrested and the show was canceled. Relieved until I realized what it all meant. Without the show, there was no money coming in. That sent my spineless, lazy father running. Well, running with what money he could drain from the accounts. Sunshine wasn't far behind him."

This was something he could help with, and Leyton slid his arm around her. "Your folks were idiots, and trust me, I have plenty of personal experience when it comes to idiot parents."

"They were idiots," she agreed. "But they would have stayed and wouldn't have taken the money if the show hadn't been canceled."

Hell, there was no way he was going to let her put all of this on her shoulders. Leyton turned her to face him. "You made a mistake," he said. "Okay, a couple of them, but you were a kid who was in pain. This is just as much or more on Sunshine and your dad as it is on you."

The sound she made told him she wasn't buying that. So, he kissed her. A kiss wasn't going to solve squat right now, but at least she wouldn't be able to keep bad-mouthing herself. Plus, the kiss settled him, and he sure as hell needed that right now.

Hadley didn't exactly slide into the kiss. Not at first, anyway. Then she sighed and kissed him back until he felt as if at least some things were right with the world. Hadley was certainly the right woman, as far as he was concerned. He doubted, though, that she would see things his way.

When Leyton finally broke the kiss, he looked down at her. The tension was still there, but it had eased some. Unfortunately, he would hike it right back up with the question he had to ask her. Still, he had to know.

"Who was the guy you came on to?" Leyton asked.

She blinked and moved away from him, but Leyton had already seen the answer in her eyes and body language.

"It's that clown from the production company," he grumbled.

And he mentally went through the info of the two that he'd gathered. Herb McGrath and Wayne Dempsey. Herb was in his sixties, so he was probably out, but the other one was in his late thirties, which meant he would have still been in his twenties when all of this mess went down.

He thought about Hadley's mood after the pair had visited the ranch. Cait had also said that Dempsey asked to speak to Hadley in private, and afterward Hadley had been upset. Had the jerk brought up what'd happened? Maybe threatened her with it in some way?

It was possible.

Hadley had said the guy had kissed her, and Leyton was betting he would have gone through with sex if his wife hadn't come in and interrupted them. Then he'd put all the blame on Hadley. Clearly, she was in the wrong, but so was this Dempsey, since he'd kissed her back.

"I don't want you to do anything about this," Hadley insisted. Obviously, she'd picked up clues from his body language, too.

Because he didn't want to outright lie to her, he kissed her again. Yeah, it was playing dirty, but he was too pissed off right now to have a reasonable conversation about this.

As soon as he could, Leyton was going to pay that asshole Dempsey a visit.

CHAPTER TWENTY

HADLEY KNEW SHE should just go back to Em's so that her grandmother wouldn't worry about her, but she wasn't sure she could face seeing her just yet. Em would know something was wrong, and she'd want Hadley to spill. She couldn't.

Not now while her nerves were right at the surface.

If she talked about all of this again, there was no way she could hide her feelings. Hide the guilt. And it didn't matter that Leyton was saying she shouldn't feel guilty. She did, and there was nothing he could do to fix that. Nothing she could do, either, except shove it back down just as she'd done for the past eighteen years.

She supposed that if it'd just been the failed seduction and payoff, she would have maybe gotten over this. But the incident had snowballed into a bitch of an avalanche that had smothered her siblings and her. It was the avalanche that had caused her parents to leave and rob them blind, and later it'd almost certainly been the reason her siblings had left, too.

"Can I just stay here for a while?" she asked Leyton.

He gave her a "you don't have to ask" flat look. "Of course. I have to go out and take care of something, but I can have Shaw and Sunny come over and stay with you until I get back."

"No." She couldn't say that fast enough. Hadley didn't

want to face her sisters just yet, either. "Whenever it's time for you to leave, you can take me back to Em's." Where she could hopefully hide out. That probably wouldn't be hard, since Em and Tony were always sneaking away to do some making out.

"I don't have to go for a while," he assured her. "I can fix you something to eat if you're hungry."

She wasn't. In fact, her stomach felt as if a thousand butterflies had invaded it. Hadley doubted she'd be able to keep any food down. "Thanks, but no thanks."

Her nerves were still jangling, and she had those stomach flutters, but that didn't stop her from taking a long look at him. Of course, he was right there, right next to her, so she didn't have to look far, and despite everything, she smiled.

And lusted for him.

Leyton had a way of taking her mind off her troubles and putting it on another trouble. One that he created with this fire and ache he put inside her. She considered just giving in to that fire—the ache, too—and kissing him again. It wouldn't take much for it to lead to sex, but she was afraid it could also lead to her having thoughts—and guilt—about that other failed seduction.

Apparently, Leyton wasn't having any debates, because he leaned in and kissed her. It was classic Leyton. Clever, hot and designed to make her incapable of thinking. But just as Hadley was about to cross over the line where thinking wouldn't have happened, something occurred to her.

Something bad.

She pulled back to look at him. "You're not going to try to kick Wayne Dempsey's butt, are you?" Hadley asked.

He stared at her a long time. "No."

The breath of relief she released came out like a gust.

Leyton was levelheaded, and a cop, so she'd thought he would handle this by, well, not handling it, by letting the past stay in the past. But she'd wanted to make sure.

Now Leyton obviously wanted to make sure that he robbed her of any air she had left in her lungs, because he kissed her again.

Even though they'd been lovers for only a short time, her body already knew where this was leading, and she could feel herself rev up. Along with going hot in all the places that Leyton would appreciate. She certainly appreciated it, and not just because of the way he made her feel, but because, along with the feelings, the guilt inside her got pushed away.

The guilt would be back, of course.

Along with her worries about Candice and Bailey. Worries about Em, too. For now, Leyton would make her forget all about it. And she was going to let him do just that.

She slid her hand around the back of his neck and brought him closer to her. He didn't resist, didn't break the kiss, either, when he made some adjustments of his own. He dragged her into his lap and went after her neck like a man on a mission. A good mission. Where he was tongue kissing some very sensitive spots.

Hadley went after his sensitive spots, too. Just below his ear, kissing him there while her fingers trailed down his chest. He certainly had more finesse now than when they'd been teenagers, but those spots still did it for him. She heard his breath hitch, felt the muscles tighten beneath her touch.

She could have kept up that torturing pace if Leyton hadn't started touching her, too. Apparently, her spots hadn't changed, either, because her mind and body went crazy when he shoved up her top and kissed her breasts. A couple of seconds of that, and she wanted to speed things up. She needed to have him naked and inside her.

But Leyton didn't go along with speeding up.

In fact, he took his time. One torturous nipple kiss after another. Slow and easy. No desperate urgency to get to the finish line.

It didn't help when she pressed the center of her body to his erection. He just kept kissing. She had to fight through the fiery haze, along with fighting with his belt buckle. The darn thing was as effective as a chastity belt, and Hadley ended up cursing it before she got it undone. Of course, her curses were very breathy and coated with desperation.

She wanted to cheer when she finally got her hand in his pants, and she smiled because it finally put an end to those slow, insane kisses. He grimaced and made a husky sound that she wanted to hear again and again. So she stroked him. Again and again.

He finally seemed to snap, and cursing her, he took hold of her, cuffing both of her wrists in one of his hands. He used his other hand to go after her jeans.

"I can help you with that," she managed when he went after her zipper.

His answer was nonverbal—a turnabout fair play with his hand in her pants. Or even better, his fingers in her. It was even more amazing than the breast kisses, but Hadley knew if he kept it up, she'd have an orgasm while they were fully dressed. It wasn't a bad way to go over the edge, but unlike in high school, they had a private place where they could do a heck of a lot more than hand jobs.

Apparently, Leyton agreed with her on how to finish this, and he moved fast. One second she was on his lap, and the other her back was on the couch. He pulled off her top and shimmied off her jeans and panties. He didn't totally nix the kisses, though. He got in a few of those while he stood to get rid of his own clothes.

And get a condom.

He took one out of his wallet—always be prepared—and he handed it to her, no doubt intending for her to put it on him.

"I've practiced doing this," she said. Great day—being fully aroused had made her stupid. "I mean, Sunny and I used to practice putting them on bananas." Since that put a nice gleam in his eyes, she added, "With our mouths."

"Later, I'd like a demonstration of that," he drawled. "For now, I think it'd be too much for my dick to have your mouth on it."

She considered testing that theory, but her body had no interest in playing around. That primal beat inside her was getting louder, like an ancient drum, pounding and pounding. Demanding that she take what she needed.

So, she took.

The moment she put the condom on Leyton—with her hands—Hadley pulled him down onto her. Lining them up in just the right way so he could thrust into her. The primal drum approved, but it didn't stop. Nope, it was just getting started.

And apparently so was Leyton.

He drew out those strokes, making the most of them. Making this last, which disproved his theory about not lasting. He would have lasted, all right. Just as he was doing now.

The drums pounded harder. Pushing and throbbing to the pulse of her body. Pushing just as Leyton was doing. Until the edge came and she went over it.

Leyton hadn't lied to Hadley. That was what Leyton kept telling himself, anyway, as he drove away from Em's after dropping her off.

When Hadley had asked, "You're not going to try to kick Wayne Dempsey's butt, are you?" he'd said no, and that was the truth. If it got to the point of Dempsey needing an ass kicking, there'd be no *trying* on Leyton's part. He'd kick, period. First, though, there needed to be a discussion about what this dickhead had said to Hadley to put her on another guilt spin cycle.

Leyton understood the guilt. He was a card-carrying member of hauling around too much of it. Guilt because he'd broken Hadley's heart and embarrassed his family and himself with that making-out episode with Hadley. But guilt could crush the good stuff if one wasn't careful.

Leyton was certain that he and Hadley could get some good stuff—stuff more than sex—if she could just let go of the past. He thought a starting point for that might be spending more time with Bailey. More time with him, too. Leyton believed, however, that one Wayne Dempsey might have a contribution to the guilt-removing process, too, and that was why he drove straight to the inn.

There was a postage-stamp-sized parking lot next to the inn, but there was no car there that he didn't recognize, so he kept driving. This time to the town's old bar with the unoriginal name of the Watering Hole. The parking lot here was much bigger, but Leyton pulled in and soon spotted what he was looking for.

Bingo.

The car that the Waterstone Production team had been in when they'd gone to Em's to harass her and Hadley into doing that reunion show. He parked, got out, and went inside to the blare of George Strait and the smell of draft beer. Of course, it always smelled of beer, and George Strait was often playing, since the bar owner, George Garcia, believed in paying tribute to the singer with the same name.

Like all the other businesses in Lone Star Ridge, this was a friendly place, and Leyton immediately got some hellos and nodded greetings. He doled out some hellos and nods of his own while he looked around. He spotted the older man, Herb, standing by a table at the back, and he appeared to be shooting the bull with the two couples who were seated there. Wayne Dempsey was at the bar chatting with Carter, the mortician, and Ella Fortenberry, the kindergarten teacher.

"There could be walk-on parts for both of you," Leyton heard Wayne boast. "Heck, for anybody who wants them. Herb and I want to do plenty of the scenes right here in town. Maybe in this very bar, since the triplets are plenty old enough to knock back a few and rub some local elbows. Legally knock back a few," he emphasized, then chuckled as if that was a fine joke.

Leyton hated the guy on sight, and, yeah, it had plenty to do with what had happened with Hadley. He walked closer, well aware that every eye and ear in the bar was suddenly tuned to him. That was probably because Leyton figured he was sporting an ass-kicking expression, and it was aimed at Dempsey.

"Sheriff," Carter greeted him as Leyton approached.

With his beer in hand and a shit-eating grin on his face, Dempsey turned to Leyton to give him the once-over. His grin widened when he saw the badge.

"Oh, the law's here," the idiot announced, then had another sip of his brew. "Actually, I've been meaning to come talk to you, but you're a hard man to catch. Haven't been in your office much today."

"What'd you want to talk to me about?" Leyton asked, and he didn't add even a smidge of friendliness to that question.

"The reunion show, of course." Judging from his continued grin, the idiot didn't pick up on Leyton's lack of hospitality and charm. "I've heard things about you and Hadley and thought you might be able to put in a good word for me."

"A million hells could freeze over a million times, and I still wouldn't do that," Leyton snarled. Yep, snarled. He could hear his own voice, and others heard it, too. "Hadley, her sisters and her grandmother don't want to do that show, and I want you to stop pestering them about it."

Well, at least that got the dickhead to stop grinning. His eyes locked with Leyton's, and the tension in the air went up. Maybe not to the million-hells level, but it soared more than a mere bit.

"Did Hadley say I was pestering her?" Dempsey asked. With his gaze still on Leyton, he set his beer down on the bar.

Leyton skipped answering that and gave the man his bottom line. "I know that's what you're doing, and I want you to leave her and her family alone."

Apparently those were fighting words, because Dempsey pulled back his shoulders in a ploy that roosters and other less-than-bright animals used to make themselves look bigger and therefore more capable of winning a fight.

It didn't work.

He just looked like a bully dickhead who'd confirmed that he had indeed been pestering Hadley. And more. Trying to intimidate her by using the past as a bargaining chip. Or worse—a threat.

"Is there a problem here?" Dempsey's partner said, approaching them at the bar.

Leyton spared him a glance, only to size him up and see if idiot two was going to try to sucker punch him or something. But McGrath was still sporting what he probably thought of as his good-ol'-boy smile. One frayed a little at the edges because he'd no doubt picked up on the busting-some-ass vibe.

"The sheriff here thinks he needs to involve himself in our business proposal with the Dalton family." Dempsey didn't glare at Leyton. It was more of a sneer.

McGrath went for a friendly chuckle. "Well, that's understandable. He's the sheriff, after all, and probably just wants to make sure we've got the town's best interest at heart. Which we do." He propped his hands on his fleshy hips. "Say, you think you could get your dad to make a cameo appearance in the reunion show? It'd give his career a little boost along with helping out with the ratings."

Leyton took his eyes off Dempsey long enough to give McGrath a look that would have iced the sun, and then he shifted his attention back to Dempsey. "There'll be no reunion show."

Dempsey's sneer continued. "You're sure about that? Well, I think you should have another chat with Hadley. I believe she could be on the verge of changing her mind, and if she gets on board with it, she could convince her sisters and grandmother to go along, too." He leaned in and dropped his voice to a whisper. "Hadley will change her mind when she realizes what's at stake."

Leyton's glare continued. "How do you figure that?"

"I think Hadley would like to keep her private life private."

Leyton had to fight a very powerful urge to plow his fist into this asshole's face. Many, many times.

"Like I said," Dempsey went on. "You need to talk to Hadley." His eyes lit up, but he was looking over Leyton's shoulder. "Maybe now would be a good time for that, since she just walked in."

Shit. Leyton knew it was too much to hope that it was McCall or Sunny dropping in for a drink and that Dempsey had mistaken her for Hadley. Nope. One glance back confirmed not only that it was Hadley but that she was making a beeline toward them.

And she was pissed.

Thankfully, though, she wasn't alone. A frazzled-looking Willy was trailing along behind her, so obviously Hadley had pressured the deputy into coming with her while Cait stayed back with Em and Tony.

"We need to talk," Hadley insisted, aiming that at Leyton.

"Told you it was a good time for a chat," Dempsey said, a smirk in his voice.

Leyton upped his cop's glare when he turned back to face the man. Dempsey didn't drop back a step, but he did lose the glare-down when he looked away. Maybe the idiot finally realized that it just wasn't a smart idea to rile a small-town cop when he was surrounded by friends and acquaintances of that cop. Even George, who was tending bar, had taken on some defensive posture.

"We need to talk," Hadley repeated. "Now."

Yeah, they did, but Leyton didn't like the *now* part. Not when he wasn't finished with Dempsey.

Hadley huffed when Leyton didn't budge, but she did

move between him and Dempsey. "I didn't figure it out until I got back to Em's," she said. Her voice wouldn't have been loud enough to be audible had every patron in the bar not gone silent. "That's when I realized that you'd want to confront him. But it isn't necessary."

"To hell it's not. He's trying to bully you."

She opened her mouth, maybe to deny it, maybe to try to put a spin on it that would defuse this, but Leyton wasn't in a defusing sort of mood. Nowhere near it.

"I can handle this," she finally said.

"Yeah, you can," Dempsey piped in. He moved to Hadley's side, aiming glances at them both. "And you have only one option, Hadley. You know exactly what that option is."

Leyton was glad to see the anger that blazed through her eyes. This situation definitely called for some Badly Hadley, the woman who wouldn't take shit from anyone for any reason. But she also glanced around the room and realized this was as far from being a private conversation as it could get.

"We're taking this outside," Hadley said with eyes narrowed to slits. "Just us," she snapped when McGrath started to follow them.

She didn't snap for Leyton to do the same, but it wouldn't have worked anyway. McGrath stayed put, and Leyton went with Hadley and Dempsey out the back door and into the parking lot.

"If you lay a hand on me, I'll sue," Dempsey warned Leyton.

"And that's supposed to stop me?" Leyton warned him right back, and he nearly told the idiot that if there was to be any laying on of hands, it would most likely come from Hadley.

Something that Leyton couldn't let her do.

Dempsey deserved a punch or two from both of them, but Leyton didn't want to give him any kind of fodder he could use to manipulate Hadley into agreeing to this re-union show. That was why Leyton positioned himself right next to Hadley so he could hold her back if necessary. He also took her hand and gave it a gentle squeeze to remind her that she wasn't in this alone.

Leyton expected her to sling off his grip, to let her temper sling it off with more force than necessary. But she looked at him, and despite the crappy situation, he had to admire the picture standing there in the milky moonlight, her black clothes and spitting-mad expression. She looked like a fierce warrior who was capable of kicking whatever ass needed it.

Hadley's gaze held with his for a long moment. Just held. And while he didn't know exactly what she was seeing now when she looked at him, he thought it might be favorable.

"Thank you," she said, surprising Leyton and causing Dempsey to huff.

"Don't know why you're thanking him," Dempsey griped. "He didn't get your butt out of the sling it's in."

Together, Hadley and Leyton shifted their attention back to Dempsey, and Leyton would have demanded to know what the hell that meant if he hadn't heard a familiar voice. A voice he damn sure didn't want to hear.

"There you are," Em said.

Groaning, Leyton glanced back and saw Cait, Em and Tony making their way toward them.

"Trust me," Cait said. "Short of arresting them both, I couldn't have stopped them from coming."

"Then you should have arrested them," Leyton grumbled.

But he knew this wasn't his sister's fault. Em could be a

formidable force when she set her mind to something, and apparently she'd set her mind to coming here.

"I knew something was wrong with Hadley." Em went to her granddaughter and slid her arm around her waist. She also eyed Dempsey as if he were a pile of smelly fresh cow shit. "Then I got a call from Gayle Silverman, who said y'all were in the bar and that this man was acting like he was about to cause trouble." She tipped her head to Dempsey. "Are you about to cause trouble?" Em asked in a tone more suited for a Wild West gunslinger than a grandmother.

"No, ma'am," Dempsey assured her. "I was just about to remind Hadley why she should do the reunion show."

"Sounds like causing trouble to me," Em concluded. "We aren't doing that show, and that's that."

Em turned as if she might try to lead Hadley out of there, but Dempsey maneuvered himself in front of the woman.

"I don't know how much of this Hadley told you," he said, "but right before *Little Cowgirls* was canceled, your granddaughter took off her clothes and tried to seduce me. I resisted her, but my wife walked in on it, and it ended up costing me my marriage. It nearly ruined my life."

Shit. Em shouldn't have had to hear that, especially not like this. But Em didn't react. Neither did Hadley, but Cait came forward so fast that Leyton thought she might go at the idiot who'd just spilled such a nasty little secret.

"Sounds as if you didn't have much of a marriage or a life if something like that could ruin them," Em remarked, staring at Dempsey. "You're the kind of strutting rooster who thinks the sun comes up just to hear you crow."

Em turned again and got Hadley to turn, too. Hadley

no longer had that pissed-off warrior look in her eyes. No tears, but Leyton figured those would fall in private.

"You should know that I was setting up lighting and sound that day when Hadley came sauntering in and stripped off her clothes," Dempsey called out to them. "I've got the audio, a recording."

That stopped them, but only Cait and Leyton looked back at the man.

"If the Daltons don't do the reunion show," Dempsey said, the smugness back in his tone, "I'll release the recording. And everybody will know exactly how bad Badly Hadley can really be."

CHAPTER TWENTY-ONE

HADLEY'S BURST OF temper and the adrenaline that had come along with it vanished in the blink of an eye. Or rather it'd vanished with the threat that Dempsey had just made.

And she didn't believe the threat was a hollow one.

I'll release the recording. And everybody will know exactly how bad Badly Hadley can really be.

Dempsey had up-close and personal knowledge of her bad side. Apparently, he was willing to spread that knowledge around, and he didn't care a rat about how it would affect her family or anyone else.

Hadley managed a weary breath, but the fatigue that hit her hard and fast seemed to seep through every cell in her body. Still, she knew she needed to muster up some energy and strength to deal with Leyton and Em. Both might do something to wipe that "What do you have to say to that, huh?" look off Dempsey's face. Hadley didn't want either of them to get in legal hot water for defending her.

"Please, let's go," Hadley said to them. Tony was obviously all for that because he took hold of Em's hand, but Hadley had to grip onto Leyton's arm to get him moving. It wasn't easy. It was like budging a boulder, but when she repeated her *please*, he finally walked away with her.

"I hope your balls turn to dripping pus and your dick rots off," Cait snarled to Dempsey.

Hadley couldn't help it. The image of that had her making a face, and it turned her stomach a little. Cait certainly had a way with words, and Hadley had to use her other hand to pull Leyton's sister away from a possible fight. Or a smackdown of trash talk.

"Anything we say or do right now will be something Dempsey can use against my family and me," Hadley reminded them.

That seemed to be enough voice of reason to get Cait to go along with them. Or so Hadley thought. But the moment they reached the truck where Willy was waiting, Leyton turned to go back to where they'd left Dempsey. The rest of them followed, creating a sort of stampede with their shoes and boots smacking and thudding against the pavement. Somehow, Em and Tony managed to keep up.

"I can't let him get away with threatening you like that," Leyton snapped when Hadley latched on to him again.

"Yes, you can." She got right in his face so he could see that she wasn't going to budge on this. "You can do this for me because it's what I want you to do. What I *need* you to do," she amended.

Leyton didn't bolt forward. He stopped and let out a string of curse words that had Em smacking him on the arm.

"Language," Em scolded. "Call him a flamin' bunghole instead."

"I'm sorry," Leyton grumbled, proving that he was indeed a good guy if he could apologize to her grandmother while the anger was still coming off him in hot, mean waves.

"Let's just go back to the ranch," Hadley insisted, "and we can discuss this." She was glad she didn't sound the way she felt. Frustrated and furious with herself for laying the foundation for something like this to happen. She had screwed up her life eighteen years ago, and she hadn't even learned her lesson, because the screwups had continued. Now many butts could get bitten because of it.

No one budged, not even Dempsey, but he was glancing around as if he might make a run for it. Especially when Cait growled at him. Yes, growled. Hadley suddenly knew why the woman didn't feel the need to carry a gun. She could manage intimidation just fine without one.

"If any of you hit me, I'll sue you for every penny you've got," Dempsey yelled.

Cait growled again and took a step toward him, and Dempsey did indeed take off running. He headed out of the parking lot and to the other side of the bar, and he just kept on running.

Hadley didn't think for a second that it was the last she'd see of him. No way. Dempsey had what he considered the ultimate bargaining tool, and now Hadley would have to figure out what to do about that.

Thankfully, no one went after Dempsey, but Hadley knew that Leyton wanted to do just that. She couldn't allow it, though. No way did she want Leyton risking his reputation and his badge by punching Dempsey's lights out, and that was exactly what would happen if the two men had another run-in.

"Willy, why don't you go home?" Hadley suggested. "Cait can drive Em and Tony back. I'll ride with Leyton."

That'd give her a chance to try to soothe his temper before they had what would no doubt be a big discussion about this. Hadley didn't want to talk about it. She wanted to find a quiet place so she could think, but Leyton and Em deserved better. That was the problem with caring about people—you had to give a piece of yourself whether you wanted to or not.

"You should have told me what happened," Em muttered as they walked back to their vehicles.

Hadley made a sound of agreement, but she knew there was no way she could have told Em. Especially not then. Her shame at fifteen had been a huge dark cloud, and it had colored everything. Hadley had wanted to hide that from Em, not share it with her.

"I'm sorry," Tony said to Hadley, his voice a barely audible whisper. He gave her a somewhat awkward pat on the back, which he probably thought would help. It didn't. It only reminded Hadley that there was yet someone else who could get dragged into all of this.

"You're sure you don't want me to go back to Em's with y'all?" Willy asked, his question aimed at Leyton.

Leyton shook his head, though Hadley wasn't sure how he managed such movement with his muscles still stiff and hard. "Go on home. I'll call you if I need you."

Willy gave a suit-yourself shrug and thankfully didn't ask any questions about what was going on. He got into his truck and drove off. Several moments later, Cait, Em and Tony did the same. She and Leyton got into his truck, but he didn't drive. He just sat there with a white-knuckle grip on the steering wheel.

"You know I can't let that asshole get away with this," Leyton said.

Hadley sighed, knowing it wouldn't do any good to beg Leyton to let her handle this. He wanted to protect her, and that was her fault, too. She'd let him get too close to her.

And that made Leyton another potential casualty in this messy life she had created.

Hadley wished she could do something to keep him

from being hurt, but at the moment she didn't see a way around it.

Leyton finally started the drive to Em's, which wasn't far. Of course, nothing was far from anything else in Lone Star Ridge. When they made it there and went inside, Em and Tony were waiting in the foyer. No sign of Cait, but she'd probably—wisely so—gone somewhere else in the house so they'd have some privacy. Leyton, however, didn't budge.

"If it were just me, I'd agree to do the reunion show," Hadley let them know right off. She kept her gaze on Em. "But I don't want to pull you, Sunny and McCall into it. Plus, it'd give Sunshine an excuse to come back here for what could be weeks or even months."

Em's mouth tightened. "Your mother's about as welcome here as a strong breeze coming off an outhouse."

That was true, and Hadley had no intention of forcing her family into dealing with the likes of the woman who was a master at creating havoc.

"I'll look into what criminal charges we can file against Dempsey," Leyton spit out. "This is extortion, and if there really is a recording, it's possible to have it suppressed."

Filing charges took time. Time that Dempsey could use to release the recording. Of course, once he released it, he'd lose his leverage, and he wouldn't get an ounce of cooperation from her, Em or her sisters for the reunion show. But his lost leverage would be her own public humiliation.

She thought of Bailey. God, Bailey. Having that recording released would unleash a town filled with gossip. Bailey was only four years old, but some of it might get back to her. Not exactly a sterling example to set for a child.

"Maybe I should have a talk with Dempsey's partner?"

Tony suggested. "I'm the outsider here, and his partner might listen to reason."

Might. But again, it wasn't the partner who was holding the cards here. It was Dempsey. Plus, McGrath might be willing to do whatever it took to make sure this project happened.

"I'll consider that," Hadley told Tony even though she knew she wouldn't. She didn't want to involve the man in this when he had his own family concerns.

Hadley turned to her grandmother next, knowing that Em wasn't going to like what she had to say. "Could I talk to Leyton alone?"

Yep, Em didn't like it at all. She wanted to fix this or maybe just go after Dempsey and give him a piece of her mind. Something that definitely wouldn't end well. But Em finally nodded, and she gave Hadley a kiss on the cheek.

"I don't care what's on that recording," Em said, the fury still in her eyes. "I don't care what you did or didn't do. I love you, and I'm not going to let that pissant spread his piss over my family."

Hadley mustered up a smile and returned the cheek kiss. "Thank you," she whispered, and Hadley waited until Tony and Em were out of the foyer before she tackled her next concern.

Leyton.

Anything she said to him would likely cause an argument, but she didn't see a way around it. "I need some time to think," she told Leyton. "It'd probably be a good idea if Cait stayed here for the night."

"You mean instead of me." And, yes, the argument was in his tone and steely expression.

She touched his arm, rubbing gently. "You and I both know if you're here, we'll be in the same bed. We'll have sex, and while that would be a very effective way to take my mind off things, it wouldn't give me time to think."

"You can think after sex," he quickly replied.

Hadley managed a thin smile and gave him one of those cheek kisses that she and Em had exchanged. Because this was Leyton, she extended the kiss to his mouth and made it something much more than assurance and comfort. Of course, it made her feel the heat.

And the guilt.

It felt a little like leading him on, but heaven help her, he seemed to need that kiss as much as she did. She'd take that from him now and give him what she could. But Hadley thought that, at the end of her thinking time, she was going to have to do something that would be the ultimate Badly Hadley move.

Walk away from Leyton and shut him out of her life.

She didn't say a word about that now. That would have to come later, when she'd figured out the best way to say it.

"I just need time to think," she repeated.

Leyton stared at her, studying her with those cop's eyes as if he was trying to suss out what was going on in her head. He wouldn't be able to do that unless he could pick through the tornado of thoughts she was having.

"Let me talk to Cait," he finally agreed. "If she can stay, then I'll leave. But I'll be back first thing in the morning, and we'll talk then."

Hadley was too relieved and exhausted to give him any lip about that. Besides, she knew what a huge concession this was on his part.

He kissed her, and it certainly wasn't one of the cheek variety. It was much hotter and deeper, and bolder, considering they were in the foyer. It was better suited for the last moment of foreplay before having sex. He left Hadley more than a little breathless when he strolled away to find Cait.

She cursed the moment he was out of earshot.

This was the proverbial rock and a hard place. If the recording leaked, there'd be another scandal, one of her making. Whether Leyton would admit it or not, some of that scandal would splash onto him. Onto her family, too. Heck, onto the whole town. Dempsey could mess up a lot of people by hitting the play button on whatever it was she'd said to him that day. Hadley couldn't remember her exact words, but she was certain they'd be cringeworthy.

Once McCall and Sunny heard about what was going on, they'd offer to agree to the reunion show if there was no other way to stop what was happening. Em would fall in line, too, if all else failed. They could stave off a scandal, but the cost would be sky-high. Then there was the possibility that Dempsey could just continue to hold the recording over her head.

Dempsey might want more than one reunion show, and this could be the start of sucking her family back into a life that none of them wanted. Well, none except Sunshine, and her wants and wishes didn't matter.

She turned when she heard Leyton's footsteps, and he joined her in the foyer. "Cait can stay. She'll sleep in your old room."

That meant Leyton had explained at least something to his sister about her preferring to stay in Hayes's old room. Cait would be curious, but she wouldn't push. In fact, Cait would give her that thinking time without hovering.

Leyton did some hovering, though. He kissed her again, this one not quite as scalding as the other.

"Promise me that you'll go home," she said, "and not try to confront Dempsey."

He stared at her. A long time. "Promise me that you'll stay put and talk to me in the morning."

She nodded. That seemed to be enough for Leyton, because he gave her a nod in return. And another knee-weakening kiss.

"Lock the door behind me," Leyton reminded her, and just like that, he was gone.

Despite Hadley wanting him to go, she immediately felt the loss. Not just in her body but in her heart. Damn it. She should have guarded her heart better. She should have stopped these feelings from happening. Because it wasn't just her who'd be getting hurt from this. Leyton would be, too.

Hadley was still standing there and cursing herself when Cait came in. She was drinking a beer and eating a brownie. Not an ordinary food pairing, but Cait seemed pleased with it. She still seemed a little pissed off, as well.

"Em and Tony are in the living room," Cait told her. "Tony's probably just trying to settle her down, but there's a lot of displays of affection going on. If that's something you'd rather avoid seeing, I'd advise you to steer clear for at least the next couple of minutes."

Hadley frowned. She wanted her grandmother to be happy, but no granddaughter should witness her grandmother in a lip-lock.

"You want to get drunk and watch some mindless TV shows?" Cait asked. "We can bad-mouth the rat bastard Dempsey and try out some voodoo curses on him. I suspect there's one designed to make his dick rot off."

"Tempting." Hadley mustered up another smile. "But I think I'll take a rain check on that. Besides, I'm not sure he has a dick."

Cait hooted with laughter and gave her an appreciative

poke with her elbow. "Then I'll grab my laptop, take it up to your old room and get some work done. You don't mind if I get brownie crumbs in there, do you?"

Hadley shook her head. "Crumb all you want. I'm going to get something to drink and then I'm heading to bed, too." Where she wouldn't sleep, that was for sure. But at least if she was in the bedroom, she wouldn't have to face anyone else tonight.

She left Cait, and avoiding the living room, Hadley made her way to the kitchen. She didn't want anything with alcohol but instead got a glass of water. Sipping it, she stood at the kitchen window and stared out into the darkness. Suddenly, the sprawling house felt too small, as if it were smothering her. Her heart and breathing started to race, and even though she'd never had a panic attack, Hadley thought she might be on the verge of one.

She practically stumbled to the back door and had to unlock it so she could go out onto the porch. The night breeze was far from cool, but it seemed to help. She stood there, taking long, deep breaths, and forced her nerves to settle. She was close to getting there when she heard a creaking sound, and she practically snapped in the direction of it.

It'd come from one of the rocking chairs.

One that wasn't empty.

The man who'd been sitting in the one on the far end of the porch stood, turned and faced her. Even in the dim light seeping from the kitchen window, she saw him smile.

And knew exactly who he was.

"You must be Patsy's granddaughter," he said, his voice with more gravel than a country back road.

Marco Corbin walked toward her.

CHAPTER TWENTY-TWO

LEYTON WASN'T THE sort of man to break his promises. But in this case, he would have to make an exception. He couldn't just go home and put aside what Dempsey was trying to do to Hadley, and that was why he called the Watering Hole to find out if the man had gone back there. He hadn't.

So, Leyton headed to the inn.

He didn't waste any time trying to talk himself out of this. He went inside, got Dempsey's room number from Thelma Medford and went straight to the second floor. Leyton knocked. Then he knocked again when Dempsey didn't answer.

"If you don't open the door," Leyton warned him in a voice loud enough for anyone else in the building to hear, "I'm going to assume you're trying to avoid arrest, and I'll come in after you."

That got the sound of footsteps storming toward the door, just as Leyton figured it would. A moment later, Dempsey opened up, but there was an "I'm ready to rumble" glare in his eyes.

"Arrest me?" Dempsey snarled. "You've got no cause, and if you think you can come in here and assault me, think again. I've got a witness." He hiked his thumb in the direction of his business partner, who was in the sitting area on the other side of the room. McGrath got up and went to

Dempsey, maybe thinking that this twofer show of support would get Leyton to turn tail and leave.

It wouldn't.

He had no intention of punching this moron, but he wasn't going to stand by and do nothing, either. In fact, Leyton didn't do any standing at all. He pushed past Dempsey, and once he was inside, Leyton shut the door. He didn't want Hadley's personal business served up to the other guests or anyone who might be listening.

"Get out," Dempsey demanded, and he took out his phone as if he might call someone. Probably the cops. Then he must have remembered he was dealing with a cop. "I'm recording this," he snarled on a huff.

"You're good at recording stuff," Leyton reminded him and made a show of moving closer to the phone so he could speak right into it. "That's why I'm here to remind you of something you maybe didn't consider."

"What the hell are you talking about? I know what I'm doing," the man insisted.

That was debatable. "You recorded a minor without her permission, and, yes, you could maybe claim her contract gave you permission, but you weren't filming footage for *Little Cowgirls*. You were in a teenage girl's bedroom, where you happened to record what she believed to be a private conversation. You didn't inform her that you were recording her and that you'd keep what was property of *Little Cowgirls* to use against her if she didn't kowtow to your wishes."

Dempsey went a little stiff, and Leyton could practically see the wheels turning in his head to create some spin on this. "Hadley came on to me. She threw herself at me," he finally snapped.

Leyton gave him a flat look. "That's the best you can

do?" He didn't wait for the idiot to attempt an answer. "Some who hear that recording might consider you were exploiting a teenager. I certainly do. And it doesn't help that you kissed and fondled that teenager."

Dempsey huffed, looked back at his partner for support, then huffed again when McGrath only shrugged. "I was just surprised, that's all, when she came into the room half-naked," Dempsey claimed, whirling back to face Leyton. "I reacted like any other red-blooded male would."

It made Leyton boil to hear Dempsey try to put all of this on Hadley, but he reined in his temper. "Wrong. Not every red-blooded adult male kisses and fondles a teenager even if that teenager comes on to him. In fact, we lawmen call that a jailbait situation, and the adult in that situation should face the consequences if he wants to act like a dick."

The fury returned on Dempsey's face, and his eyes narrowed. "You can't put me in jail for that. You can't put me in jail for anything."

Again, Leyton kept his voice calm, a big contrast to Dempsey. "The statute of limitations has passed for me to file charges against you for making that recording and for sexually assaulting a minor. Using that recording now to bully her is a problem, though. A problem for you," he emphasized. "It's called blackmail and extortion."

"I didn't blackmail her." But it was obvious it was starting to sink in that his sorry ass could be in very hot water. "I simply told Hadley about the recording and then informed her I wanted her agreement to do the reunion show."

Oh, that tested his temper nearly all the way to its limits, and Leyton had to take a moment and count to ten. Better that than a couple of face punches to teach Dempsey a lesson.

"I heard what you said to her, and I'll make a very credible witness with a spotless reputation if this goes to trial," Leyton managed. "Now, listen carefully to this. If you make the recording public, along with me having you arrested for extortion and harassment, you'll be crucified in the press. Everyone will know what you did with a fifteen-year-old girl." He shifted his attention to McGrath. "How much business do you think you'll get after that, huh? And what do you think I'll do after I've decided that my mission is to make your fuckin' lives a living hell?"

McGrath had the sense to look very concerned about that possibility. He cleared his throat. "Wayne and I need to talk," he finally said.

"Yeah, you do." Leyton would have added more, like shoving a pitchfork up Dempsey's ass, but his phone rang. Annoyed, he snatched it from his pocket and hoped like hell that it wouldn't be another call about Alyssa and her navel ring.

But it was Cait.

Since his sister was with Hadley, he immediately hit the answer button and stepped away from Dempsey and McGrath.

"You need to get to Em's right away," Cait blurted out. "We've got a problem."

Leyton heard something in the background. Moaning maybe. And it caused his stomach to drop like a stone. "Is someone hurt?"

"Sort of. Just get here," Cait repeated, and she ended the call, but not before he heard Cait shout, "Em, put down that shotgun now!"

Hell. Hell. Hell.

Leyton didn't even bother saying anything to the two men. He just hurried out and ran to his truck. He considered trying to call Hadley so she could tell him what was going on, but if there was a gun involved, he didn't have a second to waste with a phone call. He hit the police dash lights on his truck, something he rarely did, and he drove as fast as he could.

The distance between the inn and Em's might be short, but there was plenty enough time for Leyton's concern to build. *A shotgun.* Shit. Cait wasn't armed, but apparently Em thought whatever was going on was enough of a threat to bring out a weapon.

Leyton doubted Cait would have called him if this had been just a coyote straying too close to the property. No. He could also tick off a possible threat from Dempsey, since Leyton had been with the man when Cait had sent up the alarm. So that left him with one possibility.

Marco.

Tony's thug brother could have broken into the house and was maybe holding them hostage. Or worse. Maybe Hadley, Em, Cait or Tony had already been hurt. That thought sure as hell didn't do anything to punch down his fear that he wouldn't get there in time to save them.

The moment he braked to a stop, Leyton got out and drew his gun while running to the porch. Thank God the door opened just as he reached it or he might have busted it down. He saw Hadley and realized she was the one who'd opened it. The next thing he realized was that she wasn't hurt. But she did look…pissed off. That was a far better reaction than anything his panicked brain had come up with, and he hauled her into his arms for a quick hug of relief.

"You're okay," he blurted out, breathing deep so he could calm the shit down. "What happened?"

"Marco," she said, taking him by the arm and leading him through the house and into the kitchen.

Leyton had tried to prepare himself for just about anything, but he hadn't prepared himself for this. Thankfully, Em wasn't armed, but her shirt was unbuttoned, and he could have sworn there were multiple hickeys on her neck. Tony's clothes were askew, too, and he was hickeyed up, but neither Em nor he was harmed. Ditto for Cait. No askew clothes or hickeys for her, just a riled expression that was a close match to Hadley's.

Then there was Marco.

Leyton had no trouble recognizing him from the records he'd gotten from the prison. The man was in one of the kitchen chairs that had been dragged into the center of the room. He looked every one of his eighty-plus years, and he was holding one Ziploc bag of ice cubes to his jaw.

And another bag to his crotch.

He didn't look pissed but rather in pain. He was grimacing and moaning.

"What happened?" Leyton repeated, and this time he sounded much calmer. Because he was. No one had been hurt. Well, except for Marco, but he didn't count when it came to doling out any concern.

"When I went on the back porch for some fresh air, Marco was there," Hadley explained. "He came toward me, and I kicked him in the nuts. I followed it with a punch to his face."

Good. That was Leyton's first reaction, anyway. Hadley had seen a threat and had defended herself, but it twisted at him to know that she'd even had to do something like that.

Because he needed to touch her, Leyton ran his fingers over the back of Hadley's hand. Later, he'd check to make sure she hadn't bruised her fist or broken anything. For now, though, he holstered his gun and went closer to Marco.

"He's not armed," Cait said. "I frisked him while he was writhing on the back porch. Then the three of us hauled him in here because the mosquitoes were about to eat us alive."

So, maybe not hickeys on Em and Tony but rather mosquito bites. Leyton decided he'd stick with that option because he didn't want the images of them making out in his head.

"You checked his boots to make sure he doesn't have a knife?" Leyton pressed his sister.

She nodded. "The only things in his boots were his bunioned feet. He's not even carrying an ink pen or anything that could be used as a weapon."

Leyton nearly asked if Marco had had a chance to toss any weapons, but he wouldn't have had time to do that in between writhes and moans.

"I wanted to hold him at gunpoint," Em piped up. "Figured it'd deter him from trying to run off."

"And I was going to beat him up if he attempted to escape," Tony added.

"It appears that Hadley's kick and punch made sure he wouldn't run," Leyton muttered, and taking a deep breath, he went to stand in front of Marco. "How the hell did you get here?" Leyton demanded, giving his badge a tap in case Marco hadn't figured out that he was in a boatload of trouble.

It took a few more moans and some grunts before Marco finally started speaking. "I had my driver drop me off at the end of the road, and I walked." He stopped and uttered more moans and sounds of discomfort. "No one answered the door when I knocked, so I had a walk around the place and decided to rest in the rocking chair. I must have drifted off."

Leyton mentally ran through that to see if it made sense. It didn't. But considering the source—this moaning old man—it could have happened that way. Marco didn't look like any more of a threat than Em's pet duck. Still, Leyton had to get a bigger and clearer picture of what had gone on.

"How'd you know Em lived here?" Leyton snapped.

"Private investigator," Marco answered. At least that was what Leyton thought he said.

"Get him some water," he instructed Cait. Maybe that would get enough of the breath and rust out of his voice so he'd be easier to understand.

Cait went to the sink and got the water, and since both of Marco's hands were filled with ice bags, she held it to his mouth for him to drink. "Thank you," Marco murmured to her after he'd had some sips. "Thank you," he repeated, lowering the bag from his face. He worked his jaw as if testing it.

"I hired a PI to find Patsy—I mean Em—and my brother," Marco continued a moment later.

"Why?" Leyton demanded.

Marco looked at him as if the answer was obvious. "Because I wanted to find them."

Leyton huffed. *"Why?"* he pressed.

"Oh." Marco visibly relaxed a little. "Because it'd been a long time since I'd seen them, and I wanted to talk, to find out what they'd been up to all these years."

Marco made it sound like a social visit, but it obviously wasn't. "You broke the law by not reporting to your parole officer."

"I know. Probably not a smart thing to do, but I got caught up in looking for Em and Tony. I really wanted to see them."

"Then why didn't you meet us at the gas station, huh?" Tony asked, sounding very skeptical.

"Because I wanted to see you alone, and you brought people with you. I figured you were going to have me arrested, and I wouldn't have been able to give you and Em what you deserve."

Coming from a former mobster, that had a sinister ring to it. *"What they deserve?"* Leyton questioned. "And what exactly is that?"

Marco sighed and glanced down at the front right pocket of his pants. "I'd like to take something out, but I'd rather not get kicked in the nuts again." He cast an uneasy glance at Hadley.

"Hey, I wouldn't have kicked you had you not scared me," Hadley quickly pointed out.

"I know," Marco admitted on a sigh. "I was kind of groggy when I woke up, and I wasn't thinking straight. That's why I walked toward you like that." He paused, frowning. "You really thought I was after my brother and your grandmother because I wanted to hurt them?"

"Yes," Hadley, Em, Tony and Cait all said in unison.

That truly seemed to surprise Marco, and he shook his head. "You thought that because they testified against me all those years ago?"

There was another chorus of yeses along with a muttered *damn straight* and a *duh* sound.

"You can't make me believe you weren't mad about them testifying," Leyton insisted.

"Oh, I was mad," Marco admitted. "That probably lasted for the first twenty years or so that I was in jail, but after a while, you just have to let go of the past and get on with your life."

That sounded reasonable, but Leyton still had his doubts.

"So, just like that you decided to let bygones be bygones?" he snarled.

"Yes, pretty much. Of course, every now and then I'd have twinges of being riled. I mean, Tony's my brother, and it hurt that he didn't come to see me the whole time I was in jail."

"I put you in jail," Tony quickly pointed out. "Em's and my testimony helped convict you."

Marco shrugged, and apparently his balls were feeling better because he laid the ice pack aside. "You did what was right for you and Em." His eyes watered a little, and Leyton didn't think it was a leftover effect of the kicking he'd gotten. "I just thought you would have come to see me."

"Witness protection," Tony reminded him, but Leyton thought he heard some regret in the man's voice. "Besides, I didn't think you'd ever want to see me again."

"We're brothers," Marco said, his gaze locking and holding with Tony's. "And when I got out, I wanted to find you so I could give you what's in my pocket."

Leyton looked at Cait to see if she knew what this was about, but she shook her head. "I patted him down, but I didn't feel anything in that particular pocket. I took those out of his other pockets." She tipped her head to the items on the counter.

A wallet, a black comb, a handkerchief and some Tic Tacs.

"No car keys," Cait pointed out.

Yeah, and Leyton would want to know more about this driver that Marco had said had dropped him off at the end of the road.

"I don't have a weapon." Marco huffed, then shifted his attention back to his brother. "It's a ring. Our mother's engagement ring. I had it in a safe-deposit box, but she wanted you to have it. Remember?"

Tony nodded and muttered a yes. He turned to Leyton. "Our mother intended for me to give her ring to the woman I married. She left her wedding band to Marco and the engagement ring to me."

Sliding his hand over his gun, Leyton motioned for Marco to reach into his pocket. He did, and he came out with a ruby-and-diamond ring that he then handed to Tony. As if to show that was all he had, Marco turned out his pockets.

"Mom's ring," Tony said, his voice taking on a dreamy quality. His eyes took on a dreamy look, too, when he turned to Em and offered it to her. "I know you've already said yes, but I want to hear it again. Will you marry me?"

The dreaminess was obviously catching, because Em sighed and looked at Tony with stars in her eyes while he slipped the ring onto her finger. "Of course I'll marry you," Em said, and that launched them into a new round of kissing.

Leyton ignored them and turned back to Marco. He wasn't done with the man just yet. "If you just wanted to give them the ring, why'd you violate parole to do it? Why didn't you wait until you could find them and ask them to come to you?"

"It would have been a lot less threatening than you sneaking around to try to find them," Hadley contributed. "Or trespassing on private property and getting your balls busted." She was obviously trying to avoid looking at her grandmother and Tony, too.

Marco made a quick sound of agreement. "I sneaked around because I didn't want the cops to find me until I'd gotten a chance to talk to Tony."

Leyton gave him a flat look and felt he had to state the obvious here. "If you'd stayed in Houston and followed the rules, the cops wouldn't have been looking for you."

Marco nodded. "But I wanted them to look for me. I just didn't want them to find me until I gave Tony the ring."

Leyton glanced at Hadley to see if she was following this any better than he was, but she just shook her head. "You wanted to be found?" Hadley asked.

Another nod from Marco. "I don't like being out." His mouth tightened as if he'd tasted something bad. "Too many decisions to make. Plus, there's a nice lady who comes to see me, and she won't see me now that I'm out of jail. She said it's one thing to visit me behind bars, but it's not nearly as exciting now that I'm a free man."

Leyton had indeed heard about women who were attracted to prisoners, but this was the first he knew of a man who wanted to be in jail because of a woman. Maybe Marco was BSing about that, but Leyton couldn't figure out why he'd do something that stupid.

"You do know I'm taking you into custody?" Leyton asked Marco.

"Yes, I know. I think I can stand now." And that was exactly what Marco tried to do. He wobbled a bit, grimaced and took the cautious steps of a man dealing with the lingering pain of making a bad decision. He offered his wrists to Leyton.

Leyton sighed. "Go ahead and say goodbye to Em and your brother." He stepped away to give them a few moments. Moments that he needed with Hadley.

He could still see the tension in her face. That was expected. She'd had a hell of a night, what with Marco showing up and Dempsey threatening her. Leyton considered telling her about his visit with the a-hole, but it could wait.

For now, the best thing he could do for her and Em was get a convicted felon out of the house.

"Do me a favor," Leyton whispered to her.

His mind just stopped while he considered how to finish that. He could say, *Don't worry too much.* Or *Give me a chance to finish working out things with Dempsey.* Or *Don't think about leaving.*

That last one was especially important.

But Leyton went with something totally different.

He leaned in, kissed her and stunned them both by saying, "I love you."

CHAPTER TWENTY-THREE

I LOVE YOU.

Hadley hadn't thought hearing those words could feel like a kick to the gut, but it did. It had been like Leyton throwing down a gauntlet. An unspoken *I love you* and *I want you to feel the same way about me.*

She did care for him. Deeply cared for him, she mentally amended. But it couldn't be *I love you.* Leyton might believe that was what he wanted to hear, but it would come back to bite him. She wasn't the good woman that he should have in his life.

And that was why she was leaving.

Thankfully, Leyton hadn't come back to Em's after he'd left the night before. Apparently, there was a lot of paperwork and phone calls involved in the transfer of a prisoner, so Leyton had spent the night at the police station. According to Cait, who'd called Hadley with some updates, he would likely spend a good chunk of the morning there, too, which gave Hadley the perfect opportunity to leave.

Well, maybe not perfect.

There wasn't anything about this situation that fell into the totally perfect category. Still, it would be easier for her to sort through her feelings for Leyton if she put some distance between them. She could spend that thinking time in Houston with Bailey and Candice. She could be there for both of them and do herself a serious favor in the process.

Since Hadley wanted to avoid Bernice, the housekeeper who was cleaning today, she tiptoed down the stairs and made her way to the kitchen. Em was there as expected. No Tony, though. Hadley had heard him say earlier that he was going to the police station to check on the status of his brother's transfer. Hadley hoped that the two would be able to have a long chat before Marco was taken away.

Em turned when Hadley walked into the kitchen. Her grandmother was already frowning, and it deepened when her gaze slid to the suitcase. "This is a mistake," Em said. "You oughta stay and fight for what you should have."

Em had already told Hadley that same thing multiple times and had done her best to try to talk Hadley into staying, but in the end, Em had agreed to let Hadley use her truck until she could arrange for a rental car. It'd been a huge concession for her grandmother. So was Em not telling Leyton or Cait about Hadley's planned departure.

Cait wouldn't rush over to actually stop her from leaving, but she'd want to try to talk Hadley out of it. Hadley couldn't go through another conversation about what she should or shouldn't have, what she should or shouldn't fight for. She just needed some peace, and Hadley doubted she'd find that here in Lone Star Ridge.

Em came to her, handing her the keys, and in the same motion she brushed a kiss on Hadley's cheek. There was such sadness in her grandmother's eyes, and it tugged at her. Still, it wouldn't make her change her mind.

"You should talk to your sisters again," Em advised.

No, she shouldn't, but Sunny and McCall were clearly on the "let's keep Hadley here" page. Hadley had hashed this out with them the night before and again in another morning call she'd gotten from Sunny. She loved her sisters, but right now they were at a stalemate.

"At least see Leyton before you go," Em pressed. "I can see the way you light up around him. That has to count for something."

Hadley frowned at the idea of lighting up, and she was almost positive Leyton didn't make her visibly glow. He did make her happy, however, and that might have some kind of effect. But it was because he made her happy, because she cared for him, that she couldn't saddle him with yet another mess.

"I'll call him once I'm on the road," Hadley promised. And she would. She'd call him and listen to him rant about why she hadn't had the conversation in person with him. He'd be hurt. Hadley wished she could take his hurt onto her own shoulders, but she couldn't.

Hadley kissed her grandmother's cheek. "It'll be easier if I do things this way."

There was plenty of skepticism in the small sound that Em made. Disapproval, too. Hadley had to push both aside and leave.

"Oh, I nearly forgot," Em said when Hadley started for the door. Her grandmother stepped in front of her. "I got you a job."

Hadley stopped, certain that this was some kind of stalling ploy. "A job?"

Em nodded and beamed out a proud smile. "I sent a picture of that unicorn hat you made to a friend in San Antonio. She wants to hire you to do costumes for a little theater group for kids. She's loaded and can afford to pay you your asking rate for such things." She took a business card from the counter and handed it to Hadley. "Just give her a call and work out the details."

Considering her job outlook, Hadley would have probably called the woman, but it wasn't something she could do right now. Maybe after Candice's surgery. Maybe, well, after she sorted through her feelings and figured out what she wanted. She couldn't imagine giving up costume design, but an offer like this felt like an anchor designed to keep her here.

"Thank you." Hadley put the business card into her purse. "I'll go out back." That way she would avoid Bernice. But Hadley didn't even make it a step before Bernice appeared in the kitchen doorway.

Bernice speared Hadley with her narrow-eyed gaze. "There's some fella here to see you." Everything the woman said sounded like a gripe. "He's from that production company."

Crap. Hadley didn't want to see either Dempsey or McGrath, though she figured she hadn't seen the last of Dempsey. No. The man wasn't just going to give up on the notion of the reunion show when he had her over a barrel.

"Just so you know, if y'all start up filming here again, I'll quit," Bernice complained, "and I'll expect some severance pay. I don't want to be dealing with those TV people again."

Hadley thought that maybe this was the one and only time she'd agreed with the crotchety woman. She didn't want to be dealing with them, either, and that was why she started to just slip out the back. That was also when she saw Dempsey pacing across the backyard. Her groan must have snagged his attention because his head whipped up, and he snared her gaze.

"I thought you might try to avoid me," he said at the same moment that Hadley demanded, "You need to leave."

Dempsey nodded but didn't budge. It wasn't much consolation, but it didn't look as if he'd slept since she'd seen him the night before at the bar. Considering that he was trying to blackmail her, Hadley wasn't going to have a lick of sympathy for him.

His attention lowered to her suitcase, and he sighed. "I'm guessing you weren't coming to the inn to talk to me."

"No," Hadley snapped.

She walked down the porch steps and headed toward Em's truck. She considered just driving away, but she'd already fulfilled her cowardly quota for the day by not seeing Leyton, so she had to at least deal with one of the things in her growing heap of problems.

"I can't do the reunion show," she said. "I can't put my family through that again."

There. She'd spelled it all out for him, and now he'd no doubt remind her of the recording he'd made of her failed seduction. He didn't get the chance, though, because of the SUV that came to a screeching halt. Not Leyton. But rather McCall and Sunny, and her sisters practically barreled out the vehicle, hurrying to each side of her to create a united front against Dempsey.

"Em called you," Hadley grumbled in a whisper. She set her suitcase down on the ground.

"Don't blame her," Sunny whispered back. "Blame yourself, because you should've let us know what you're doing." Her sister shifted back to face Dempsey. "We're not doing the show."

"And you're not blackmailing Hadley," McCall added.

Dempsey nodded as if that'd been exactly what he'd expected them to say. There was also none of his usual smugness in his expression.

"I'm not going to release the recording," he said. "It wasn't right for me to say that I would to get all of you to cooperate."

Hadley stood there in stunned silence, and she figured her sisters were having a similar reaction. This was a complete turnaround from the night before, and her shock quickly turned to suspicion. Was this some kind of ploy to try to gain their trust?

"I would like the three of you to consider doing the show, though," Dempsey went on. "I think it'd be a money-maker for everyone concerned. But the recording won't play into this." He started to walk away. "Call me if you change your minds about doing the show," he added from over his shoulder.

"Wait!" Hadley called out when he started walking again. "What about the recording? What are you going to do with it?"

"Nothing." Dempsey shook his head, cursing softly under his breath. "I'll destroy it," he explained, and he headed toward the front of the house, where she was guessing he'd left his vehicle.

She wanted to demand that he destroy it in front of her so that she'd be sure he'd never try to use it against her again. But something was off here. Maybe McGrath had interceded and told Dempsey to back off.

Or maybe Leyton had.

Hadley silently cursed. Leyton wouldn't have had a lot of time to confront Dempsey, what with the whole Marco fiasco, but maybe Leyton had managed to say or do something. That made her want to hurry to the police station to ask him about it, but then she'd have to tell him she was leaving. Face-to-face with Leyton wouldn't go well. Not with her current state of mind.

"You think he's lying?" McCall asked as they watched Dempsey drive away.

"Even if he is, it doesn't matter," Sunny said. "If he releases the recording, we'll deal with it. Together," she emphasized. "Right?" she asked Hadley.

"Together," Hadley verified after a long pause. Then she sighed. "But I still need to leave."

She expected her sisters to argue, which was the reason she hadn't wanted to see them before she left for Houston. But it had felt good having them stand with her against Dempsey. Maybe that was the start she needed. Ditto for the job that Em had gotten for her. It was just a start, however, and she needed to get her head on straight. Not just sort out her feelings for Leyton but also figure out how to handle things if Dempsey had a change of heart and released the recording.

Hadley turned first to Sunny and hugged her, and then she did the same to McCall. "I love you," she murmured and was surprised when she didn't feel the need to brace for a lightning bolt or hell freezing over.

Apparently, it hadn't disturbed the cosmos after all to peel aside a badly layer and admit that she loved someone. Especially these two someones.

When she pulled back from McCall, Hadley saw the tears shimmering in her eyes. She didn't ask Hadley to stay, though. Neither did Sunny. Hadley doubted they could totally wrap their minds around why she felt the need to do this, but they didn't stand in her way. With their arms looped around each other, her sisters stood there and watched Hadley as she went to Em's truck.

And she drove away.

LEYTON WANTED TO kick some ass. Too bad there wasn't a deserving one around so he could vent and get that kicking urge out of his system. The paperwork for Marco's transfer was moving slower than a snail's pace, which meant Leyton was tied up badgering people to hurry the hell up. He wanted Marco out of Lone Star Ridge so he could move on to other tasks.

Like making sure Dempsey wasn't doing something else to require his ass being kicked.

Leyton thought he'd put the fear of God into the man, but one never knew with idiots like that. Dempsey could be trying to figure out a way to save his own butt while still screwing Hadley over.

Then there was Hadley herself.

She was at the top of those "other tasks" that Leyton wanted to take care of. She was probably getting ready to run. Her fight-or-flight response was faulty when it came to causing possible smears on what was left of her family's reputation. Hadley wouldn't run from Dempsey. No, she'd likely go with the fight response there. But she might try a hasty departure to put some distance between herself and Lone Star Ridge until she could come up with a way to fix things.

Leyton looked up from the latest round of paperwork when someone stepped into the doorway of his office. It was Cheryl Milton, the dispatcher.

"He's asked for a broom," Cheryl said.

Because his mind was elsewhere, it took Leyton a moment to figure out the *he* in this comment was Marco.

"He wants to sweep the floor in his cell," Cheryl added.

Leyton wasn't totally surprised by the request, since Marco had already asked for a change of sheets. Cheryl had accommodated the man and had also given him a dust rag when Marco said he wanted to clean the baseboards. Apparently, the ex-mobster liked things tidy even when incarcerated in a temporary jail.

"No broom," Leyton said. He didn't think Marco was a

risk for an attempted escape, but it was best not to become a laughingstock in the cop world by allowing a prisoner to break out with a cleaning tool that they'd provided him.

"All right," Cheryl said, shaking her head, "but he's gonna be a mite disappointed."

Leyton didn't care about mites, disappointment or dust. He wanted the man gone, and he needed to make yet another call to find out what was holding up the transfer. But his phone rang the moment he took it out, and he saw Em's name on the screen.

"You didn't hear this from me," the woman said when he answered. "But Hadley left, and we couldn't talk her out of it. She's headed to Houston in my truck."

Shit. He'd expected this, but he thought he would have more time. "How much of a head start does she have?" he asked, already getting to his feet.

"Only a few minutes. She just had a talk with that TV fella, the younger one who's acting like a bunghole."

Dempsey. He wanted to hit himself, because he'd expected that, too. Leyton thought he'd made progress with Dempsey by reminding him that his ass could be on the line if he released the recording, but maybe Dempsey had decided to take the risk. If so, Leyton was going to have to hurt him.

"Find Hadley and convince her to stay," Em insisted.

He'd do his best, but Leyton figured it wasn't going to be easy. Still, he had to try and try fast before she made it to the interstate. Leyton grabbed the keys to the cruiser, rattled off "I'll be back soon" to Cheryl and ran out the door. The moment he was in the cruiser, he turned on the siren and lights and took off hot after Hadley.

Leyton knew he had to focus on the drive, but it was

impossible to turn off his thoughts. The bottom line to all of this was that it hurt.

Bad.

Hadley should have trusted him, and herself, on this Dempsey matter. Her first instinct shouldn't have been to run. Not after what they'd had together. They were lovers, for crap's sake, and if that hadn't been enough to get her to stay, the fact that they were also friends should have done it for her. But no, not only was she leaving him behind, but she was also putting her family in her rearview mirror.

Leyton took the road out of town, hit the accelerator and thanked all his lucky stars that Em's truck was basically a piece of junk. That was because he spotted Hadley only about a mile from Lone Star Ridge. The truck was chugging along, and he saw Hadley's head whip up when she heard the sirens. Leyton suspected she was cursing him, but at least she wasn't mad enough to try to outrun him. Hadley pulled the truck onto a ranch trail, and Leyton came to a stop right behind her.

They stormed out of their vehicles at the same time. "Why are you leaving?" he demanded at the same moment she demanded, "Why are you doing this?"

Leyton waited, and waited, for her to respond first. "Because I need to go."

As responses went, it sucked, so he provided her with an equally sucky answer. "Your taillight's burned out, and that's a violation."

Her expression flipped between a frown and a scowl when she tossed a glance at the taillight. "There's no way you could have known it was out until I braked. Your cop lights were on before that."

Since Leyton couldn't dispute that, he shrugged, went to her and hauled her into his arms. It was a caveman move, one that he generally hated, but, damn it, he was pissed, too. Pissed enough to give her one very angry kiss.

Her response was anger riddled, as well. It was a little mean for a lip-lock. A little too hard. But man, did it pack a wallop. Apparently, mean kisses could fire up his body when Hadley was the kisser.

He felt the exact moment when things changed. She'd probably see it as going south, but she tore her mouth from his and sagged against him. All the pent-up emotion seemed to leak out of her body. She cursed him, but there was no bite to it. More like desperate sighs and moans.

Leyton's grip gentled, but he kept holding her. Kept her pressed to him. For one thing, she didn't seem too steady on her feet, and for another, he needed to feel her in his arms.

"I'm leaving," she insisted, her whispered voice a tangle of emotion and nerves, "because all I do is cause trouble when I stay."

Leyton could actually follow the logic. Well, *her* logic, but what she was seeing was only part of the big picture.

"So, if you go with that theory, then you'll cause trouble when you get to wherever it is you're going," he pointed out. "You're sure it's a good idea to take that sort of thing to Candice and Bailey?"

She opened her mouth, then closed it, and her eyes narrowed some. "I don't want to cause you trouble."

"Yeah, I got that." And it was time they had an air clearing about it. First, though, he had to wave at Elmer Henderson, a nearby rancher, who honked when he drove by them. "You've got this idea that Dempsey trying to screw you over will cause people to think less of me. It won't. It'll only cause people to realize the man's a dick."

Hadley huffed, then sighed. "It's not just Dempsey. It's

tit-gate. It's my reputation. I have a police record, for Pete's sake, and you're a cop."

Leyton couldn't help himself. He grinned. "You do know that's sort of a fantasy for some people. That whole opposites-attract sort of thing." He dropped the grin before he continued. "But guess what, Hadley. We're not opposites. We both had shitty parents, and both of us got banged around when we were growing up."

She stared at him as if he'd sprouted a third eye. "And that's supposed to justify what's going on now? Every time people see me with you, they'll think—there's Badly Hadley with the sheriff. Doesn't he know he can do a hell of a lot better? Doesn't he know she'll soon drag him down into the gutter with her?"

Well, hell. She really believed that, and sadly, some part of it was true. "I wouldn't mind dipping a toe in the gutter with you."

She poked him on the arm with her index finger. "I'm serious."

He poked her back. "So am I. Do you think I'd choose a better spin of gossip over you? No way in hell," he added before she could say anything. "People are going to talk. That's a given. But when they figure out just how I feel about you and that you make me happy, then the gossip will move on to other things. This town is a regular hotbed of gossip topics, and not all of them involve us."

That only seemed to frustrate her even more, and Hadley located the nearest rock and kicked it. "You told me you loved me," she grumbled.

And there it was. The real reason she'd tried to run. The Dempsey crap was a low blow. So was Candice's surgery. Maybe even the tit-gate mess was dribbled into this emotion stew. But none of those other things scared her spit-less like him loving her.

Leyton went to her, and this time he used a much gen-tler touch when he pulled her into his arms. There was no anger in the kiss that he brushed on the top of her head. If he could have cradled and protected her for a lifetime, that was what he would do, but cradling, offers of protec-tion and declarations of love triggered all sorts of dark fears for Hadley.

"You don't have to do anything different just because I love you," he said.

"Yes, I do. If you love me, then I have to stay," she quickly pointed out.

He cursed the interruption when Rowley Blake, Shaw's ranch hand, drove by, honked and waved.

"No. I *want* you to stay," Leyton corrected. "I want you to be part of my life. I *want* you to be my lover. But we can do that on your terms."

When she looked up at him, there was suspicion in her eyes. "What do you mean?"

"I mean if you feel the need to go to Houston, then go. I can come and see you on my days off. I just don't want you shutting me out of your life or driving away in a really old truck because you believe you'll make a mess of things." He slipped his arm around her waist to lead her to the cruiser. "Besides, you still haven't shown me how skilled you are at putting on a condom with your mouth."

She poked him again, but her lips quivered a little as if fighting a smile. The smidge of humor didn't last, though, and her next sigh told him he still hadn't convinced her that he was the best thing since sliced bread. Well, the best thing for her, anyway.

He opened the cruiser and took out the box he'd spotted on the floor of the passenger seat. Something that Cait had likely left behind.

"You're giving me lunch?" Hadley asked when he handed her the Burger Barn take-out container.

"No." As expected, when she opened it, it was empty except for a napkin, the discarded paper that'd once been wrapped around a cheeseburger and two packets of ketchup, the condiment his sister hated. "This will be our memory box."

Judging from the way her forehead bunched up, he'd lost her.

"We'll make the real one soon, but for now, this is a stand-in," he explained. "We're going to put in things that make us happy. Personally, I'm putting in a picture of your face after I've kissed you. Hell, I'll put in one before I've kissed you, too, because the idea of your face, of you, makes me happy. Now it's your turn to put something in the box."

Hadley certainly didn't jump to play this game, and for a couple of heartbeat-skipping moments, he thought she might slip right back into a deep, dark place where even he couldn't reach her.

"I'm afraid I can't make you happy," she said, her gaze connecting with his. She tossed the Burger Barn box onto the hood of the cruiser.

Leyton smiled. "You already do." He meant every one of those three words, but Hadley searched his eyes as if looking for some smear or inkling that he was BSing her.

She shook her head. "But how? Why?"

These were probably the easiest two questions he'd ever had to answer. "Because I love you." He leaned down and kissed her. Okay, it was playing a little dirty, but he added some heat to it, to help ease her into what he had to say next. "And I believe you love me, too."

Leyton waited. Waited some more. And he finally had to release the breath he was holding, but his chest was starting to hurt bad. The lungs didn't like it when you deprived them of oxygen.

"You don't have to say the words back to me," Leyton assured her. "You don't have to—"

"I do love you," she interrupted. But this wasn't in a jump-for-joy kind of tone. It was a tone he totally got, however, just as he got Hadley. "Shit. I love you," she repeated, groaning.

He wanted to smile, wanted to even do a little jumping for joy, but he held back on that. "Love doesn't fix squat," he pointed out. "It won't make our lives easier. But it'll give us a shot at something we've never had. Being truly happy," he provided in case she hadn't clued in to that.

Again, she stared at him. "You really think we can be happy?"

Again, he could have scolded her for posing such easy questions. "Oh, yeah. I'm pretty sure we can."

"Pretty sure," she repeated, as if considering just how much of a guarantee that truly was.

"Pretty sure," he confirmed.

She stood there a long while, the conflict raging through her. Him or not him. Here or not here. A risk or same ol', same ol', which could turn out to be a risk, too.

"Shit," she repeated, and he thought she'd finally come to the conclusion that they had an honest-to-goodness shot at that truly happy life.

Then Hadley called him a bad name before she caught onto a handful of his hair and yanked him down to her for a kiss.

"We've lost our minds," she mumbled.

Or that was possibly what she mumbled. Leyton couldn't be sure, because French-kissing and conversation weren't a good mix. But there was one very good mix standing there on the side of the road—him and Hadley.

Maybe soon he'd convince her of just that.

EPILOGUE

Two Months Later

THERE WAS A lot to be said for quickies. Actually, Hadley could say a lot about non-quickies, too, with Leyton, but she'd learned that he could sure make the most of a handful of minutes.

For this handful she'd ended up against his glass shower wall, her legs wrapped around his waist, the steamy hot water spewing all over them and with Leyton pounding into her as if a quickie was the cure for every ill in the universe. Hadley thought that wasn't just hype, either. There were certainly some ills cured when his deep, urgent thrusts brought her to peak and released her into that flying orgasmic whirl of pleasure.

Leyton was extremely good at flying orgasmic pleasure whirls.

He whirled in right behind her, finding his own peaking pleasure while giving her the last couple of thrusts so that he could enjoy some pretty amazing aftershocks. There was a lot to be said for aftershocks, as well.

They stayed there, locked together in as many ways as two bodies could be locked, their breaths gusting, their muscles lax. The latter was a nice perk from a quickie, but it had one big pitfall in that it was a challenge to stay upright.

"Steady," Leyton whispered, his voice also lax.

Since they often seemed to end up having shower sex, Hadley knew what he meant. To prevent them from busting their butts and risking possible concussions, they took it slow. She slid down her legs while he kept her anchored to the wall, giving her some nice postsex chest-to-chest action.

He was extremely good at that, too.

Heck, there was no reason for her to spell out Leyton's sexual virtues, because he was a bright, shiny winner at everything.

By the time Hadley's feet touched the floor, they'd disengaged in that intimate way that made her immediately miss him, and she wondered if there was time for a second quickie. Leyton was usually game for that sort of thing after only a few minutes, and they wouldn't need a condom.

After they'd done the whole "I love you" thing, and had tests to make sure they were both clear, Hadley had gone on the pill so that quickies wouldn't require the frantic search for condoms. It had felt like a huge step for her to take, but it'd been a step that hadn't made her feel panicky and hemmed in. Of course, that might have something to do with the superior orgasms Leyton was giving her.

Or maybe it was just Leyton himself.

He kept his arms around her as the last of the aftershocks wore off, and he looked down at her. Not an ordinary look, but she'd realized that Leyton just wasn't capable of anything ordinary. It didn't matter that they'd had sex often in the past two months; he gave her that look, that smile, each time, as if she were the greatest thing since, well, orgasms.

"I love you," he said to go along with that look he was giving her.

The words seemed to slide right off that silver tongue of his. Which she'd learned could also produce incredible orgasms. Her tongue wasn't so silver, though, and the words didn't slide so easily for her, because they still seemed a little foreign. As if she'd suddenly been called on to give a heartfelt toast at a party for someone she cared deeply about.

Someone she loved.

Still, she had to make her throat work, but that didn't make her response any less heartfelt. "I love you, too."

Leyton smiled, not gloating or reveling in victory, but in that "you're the greatest thing since orgasms" sort of way. It always had the strangest effect on her because it made Hadley want to say it again. Often again and again. Until she sounded like a very sincere broken record.

"You're still a little surprised about that," he drawled when she said *I love you* for the fifth time.

"Yes," she admitted with a touch of panic. More than a touch of wonder and a whole boatload of *What did I do to deserve this?* "And you're surprised that I'm surprised, so it goes both ways."

His smile turned to a grin. "We're not talking sex now."

And there it was. That easy way he had of defusing the panic. He'd been chipping away at that for the past two months since the day she'd tried to leave Lone Star Ridge, and the panic was little more than a tiny squeak she could tamp right down. She wanted this incredible hot cowboy. Needed him. Loved him. And in what could only be called a miracle, he felt the same way about her.

Hadley held on to the moment awhile longer, getting

in another kiss, just looking at him until she felt the hot, steamy water lose some of the steam.

Leyton muttered some profanity. "I really need to get a bigger hot-water tank."

She made a sound of agreement and sneaked another kiss, but more hot water wouldn't have helped today. They needed to get out of the shower and get dressed because it wouldn't be long before Candice and Bailey arrived. Hadley didn't want the rosy afterglow of an orgasm still lingering around her during their visit.

It'd been less than a week since she'd seen Bailey, but Hadley could see her every day and it wouldn't be enough. Bailey was sort of like Leyton in that Hadley loved and needed her, and now that things were better between her and Candice, it was easier to get visits with Bailey.

Too bad it'd taken cancer to help with that.

Candice had indeed had a malignant tumor but had already finished up her first round of treatments. Apparently the woman felt well enough to travel, since she'd insisted on bringing Bailey to Lone Star Ridge, with the nanny doing the actual driving. Hadley had offered to go to Houston, but Candice had nixed that, saying she needed to get out. She only hoped Candice wasn't coming to deliver some bad news about her health.

Hadley was more than willing to step in and take care of Bailey either permanently or short-term as she'd done right after Candice's surgery. But she didn't want to get those custodial rights at the expense of Candice's health. Bailey loved her grandmother, and Hadley wanted the child to have Candice around for a long, long time.

With her thoughts turning to Bailey, Hadley got dressed, getting distracted only three or four times by the hot cowboy who was dressing next to her. Maybe in another decade she'd be able to look at his amazing body and not feel the need to drool. Or haul him back to the shower for another quickie.

Leyton must have seen the gleam in her eye because he hooked his arm around her neck, angled her to him and kissed her. He was still kissing her when they maneuvered out of his bathroom, through his bedroom and into the living room. Where they immediately heard someone clear their throat.

Crap.

Hadley jolted, probably looking very much like someone who'd just had shower sex.

Sipping a Coke and munching on some Cheez Doodles, Cait had her feet propped on the coffee table in a pose that made it seem as if she'd been lounging there for a while.

"Let me guess," Cait said, crunching down on another Cheez Doodle. "You were trying to save on your water bills, so you showered together?"

"No, we were having sex," Leyton readily admitted, though there was some annoyance in his tone. Maybe because Hadley unhooked herself from his grip. She didn't mind Leyton's sister knowing they were lovers, but she still had trouble with this whole PDA thing.

"That was my second guess," Cait commented, and she apparently wasn't the least bit concerned with her brother's mild annoyance. Or the PDA. She did frown, however, when she reached for what was apparently the last of her cheesy snack.

"Bailey and Candice will be here soon," Leyton told her, no doubt as a way of nudging his sister out the door.

But Cait stayed put, and using her pinkie—which was the only digit on her right hand not coated in Cheez Doodle—

she caught onto a small padded manila envelope and slid it across the coffee table toward Leyton and Hadley.

"This arrived at the police station about a half hour ago," Cait explained. "I thought you'd want me to bring it right over."

Both he and Hadley went closer for a better look, and she instantly spotted the return address. And she groaned. Because it was from Dempsey.

Hadley certainly hadn't forgotten about the former cameraman turned producer who'd tried to blackmail her into doing a *Little Cowgirls* reunion show. But it had been two months since he'd left Lone Star Ridge, and he hadn't contacted her once during his absence. She'd started to believe that Dempsey wouldn't try to use the recording against her after all, but obviously he hadn't forgotten about her. Or Leyton, since the package was addressed to him.

Leyton took the envelope and gave it a cop's once-over. Maybe looking to see if it was booby-trapped or something. He must not have seen anything to cause that kind of alarm, because he opened it and spilled out the contents onto the coffee table. A handwritten note and a crushed USB drive. It looked as if someone had bashed it with a hammer.

Hadley didn't know what Dempsey had used to record their "conversation" the day she'd thrown herself at him, but maybe the pieces of this USB had something to do with that?

"Why would Dempsey send this to Leyton and not me?" Hadley asked.

Cait shrugged, stood, then went into the kitchen to toss the Cheez Doodle bag and empty soda can. Hadley thought that maybe she'd done that to give her and Leyton a moment alone to discuss the recording and what'd happened with Dempsey. But if so, it wasn't necessary, since Hadley had already told her sisters, Em and Cait not only about what she'd done but also about Dempsey's blackmail attempt.

Leyton didn't answer her question, either, but he picked up the note and read it aloud. "'Here's the recording of Hadley and me. I transferred it to this USB years ago, and there aren't any other copies. I thought if you saw that I'd destroyed it, there wouldn't be any need for you or Hadley to worry. Wayne Dempsey.'"

Hadley took the note from Leyton and read it for herself. He hadn't left out a single word, but this still didn't make sense.

"Why would he send this to you?" Hadley repeated, but the moment the question left her mouth, she got an inkling why. "You threatened him?"

Leyton shrugged. "I merely stated the truth."

"You threatened him," Hadley confirmed on a sigh. For just a split second, the old Hadley defense kicked in, and she nearly blurted out that she could fight her own battles.

And she could.

She could take names and kick ass at the same time. But it was nice to have someone like Leyton to help her with that ass kicking.

"I hope you scared Dempsey enough to make him piss his pants," Hadley murmured.

"Pretty much." Leyton smiled and kissed her. "I don't think you'll have to worry about him again, but I'll keep my eye on him just in case."

Since Em, Tony, her sisters, Shaw, Cait and Austin had all said something similar, she obviously had lots of people in that proverbial court. It didn't erase her shitty childhood, but it made for a somewhat stellar present and future.

"All's well in paradise?" Cait asked, slowly making her way back into the living room.

Hadley nodded and kept her gaze on Leyton a moment longer before she shifted her attention to Cait. Leyton's sister was no longer munching on snacks but was instead holding a gold padded lightning bolt.

"Please tell me this isn't some kind of otherworldly penis?" Cait asked. "Because if so, then ouch, just ouch."

"No penis." Hadley took it from her and put it back in the sewing basket that she'd left on Leyton's counter. "It's part of the lightning-bolt wings that'll be on a goddess superheroine costume. It'll have a cape of gold and red flames to go along with it."

Hadley was making it and other outfits for the little theater group. An actual paying gig as it'd turned out—thanks to Em. But other jobs had come in from Hollywood, too. Only a trickle of work, for now, but it all played into that somewhat stellar present and future.

"Sweet," Cait declared. "Can you make me one for Halloween?"

Since Hadley had already agreed to outfitting Austin's twins for trick-or-treating, she'd add one more costume to her to-do list.

The sound of an approaching vehicle had Hadley going to the front window to check it out. It was Candice's car, and Janet, the nanny, was behind the wheel. Hadley hurried back to the coffee table to gather up the USB pieces and the note, but Leyton had already beaten her to it. He shoved it all back into the envelope and put it in his pocket.

"Gotta go," Cait said, grabbing a banana and an apple before she headed to the front door to open it.

"Cops and bobbers!" Bailey squealed with delight the

moment she spotted Cait. She ran to Cait, giving her a leg hug.

Hadley didn't need a clarification as to what Bailey had said, because she knew that the little girl had played cops and robbers with Cait and Austin's twins, Avery and Gracie.

Cait assured Bailey that they'd play the game again soon, and she greeted Candice and Janet before she said her goodbyes and went to her SUV.

Hadley and Leyton did the greetings as well, and both got leg hugs from Bailey before Hadley scooped her up for a kiss. Bailey returned the kiss, but she was obviously anxious to get inside and have a go at the stash of books and toys that Leyton kept for his nieces. He'd even added a few things in there just for Bailey. Something that Hadley figured would have melted her heart had he not already melted it.

Candice stepped closer, surprising Hadley and Leyton with yet another round of hugs. The woman had definitely looked better, but then, she'd also looked worse. The treatments had obviously taken their toll, but she seemed much stronger than she had just a week ago when Hadley had gone to Houston to stay a couple of days. Leyton had gone with her for one of those days. They had plans to do the same trip in another two weeks.

Since the temps were well past the sweltering stage, Hadley motioned for the women to come in, and she got yet another hug from Janet.

"Bailey insisted I bring this." Candice handed Hadley a metal cookie tin. "It's not cookies," she quickly added.

"It's a memory box," Bailey and Leyton said together, and Hadley was the only one who seemed surprised that he'd be in on this.

"I told Bailey about the memory box Em did for you, that Em wanted you to have something to make you happy whenever you thought of it. And she said she wanted one, too."

"We gonna buried it," Bailey proudly announced. "You gonna buried yours, too."

Leyton grinned. "I told her about the one I gave you."

The box from Burger Barn, which was now sitting on top of his fridge. Hadley had brought it back here with her after Leyton had chased her down and *convinced* her to stay. He'd done part of that convincing on the side of the road and added a second and third round of persuasion in bed. And on the sofa. The floor. The shower. Heck, there weren't many spots they'd missed in his house.

"I show you," Bailey continued, and clearly she was excited when she took the cookie tin, sat right on the floor in the foyer and muscled it open. It was filled to the brim with pictures, tiny stuffed animals and even a cookie with a bite out of it.

Hadley sank down beside Bailey, but Leyton pulled over a chair for Candice. Janet sat on the chair arm, and Leyton took the floor spot on the other side of Bailey.

"Me," Bailey explained, showing them a picture of her as a newborn. "Mommy and Daddy."

It was a familiar photo, since Hadley also had a copy of the wedding photo of Carson and Deanna.

"Grandma," Bailey went on, taking out another picture. Then another. "Mama Hadley."

Again, it was a familiar shot of Hadley holding Bailey when she was a newborn. Bailey took out a more recent photo of them next. Then one of Leyton.

"She asked for a picture of me," Leyton explained. "One of me wearing my badge."

It was a great picture of him in uniform, and Hadley made a mental note to ask for her own copy. Apparently, she had a thing for hot cops as long as that cop was Leyton.

"Mr. Wiggles," Bailey continued, moving on to the tiny plastic worm. There was a theme here as the girl brought out a small fuzzy cat named Miss Purr and a dog on a keychain named Mr. Barkie.

Since all the animals and the photos made Bailey smile, Hadley figured they were perfect to go into a memory box.

"Grandma's got a box, too," Bailey prompted, nudging Candice to take an Altoids mints tin from her purse. It had miniature photos of Bailey, Deanna and Carson, and much to Hadley's surprise, there was even one of her.

"I kept mine small so I wouldn't have to do as much digging," Candice remarked.

"So did I," Janet provided, and she produced her own Altoids tin.

"Can we bury them now?" Bailey asked, looking up at Leyton.

"Sure. I already put a shovel on the back porch. But let me get Hadley's first, and maybe your grandmother can watch us from the window."

Candice gave a nod of approval, one layered with relief, and Leyton went to the fridge to retrieve the Burger Barn box. Hadley was hoping that she didn't have to explain everything inside just as Bailey said "Open it."

Rejoining them on the floor, Leyton did just that, and Hadley had no trouble seeing the disappointment on Bailey's face. No photos or Mr. Wiggles but rather the napkin, ketchup packets and the paper wrapping that'd once been around a burger.

"That napkin was there the first time Hadley told me she loved me," Leyton pointed out to Bailey.

The little girl brightened some, but clearly it was no match for the importance of Mr. Wiggles.

"And I added this," Leyton said, fishing out a photo from beneath the Burger Barn debris.

It was a photo of her. Not of the cute toddler she had been. Not of her as an adult. It was Badly Hadley with a mega dose of surly thrown in. She remembered one of the production assistants had taken it, and it had captured every ounce of her teenage angst.

"I got it from Em," Leyton explained. "I thought it might be fun for you to know what you left behind."

She smiled, because that definitely wasn't her any longer. Yeah, she might still have some angst, even some smidges of surliness, but she wasn't that bitter, heartbroken girl with an f-you attitude. It was definitely something she wanted buried.

"You gonna buried this, too?" Bailey asked, pulling out a small matchbox.

Hadley couldn't be sure, but she hadn't noticed that in the Burger Barn box two months ago. Then again, things had gotten so heated between her and Leyton that she hadn't looked at it that hard.

Just as she'd done with the cookie tin, Bailey worked hard to open the matchbox, and she made an *ooh* sound. That was when Hadley saw the ring nestled inside. She did a double take. It was a ring, all right.

And she smiled again.

This time, she felt the smile all the way to her toes.

It wasn't a traditional engagement ring. This one had a row of what appeared to be black diamonds set in white gold.

"I thought it'd match your clothes," Leyton said, nudging her with his elbow. "Well, it will if you wear it."

"You not gonna bury it?" Bailey asked with some disappointment.

"Uh, why don't we give Hadley and Leyton a few minutes?" Candice asked. She was smiling as well, and she got to her feet, taking Bailey's hand. "Let's go to the window. Look out, and you can pick a spot to bury your memory box."

That got Bailey moving fast. Talking fast, too, about burying it thirty hundred feet deep. Apparently, Leyton had his work cut out for him, but for now, he had work of a different kind.

"Is this a marriage proposal?" Hadley asked the moment they were alone.

He kissed her first. "It is."

If he hadn't already robbed her of her breath, that would have done it. Hadley totally hadn't seen this coming. Of course, she knew they were in love, knew they were spending every possible moment together. Heck, Leyton had even moved her things into his house. But marriage?

"Don't ask me if I'm sure," he blurted before she could say anything. "Because I'm sure. You are, too, but you're worried that you're not good enough for me. Well, maybe I'm worried I'm not good enough for you." He paused. "All you have to say is yes."

He kissed her again, and she recognized this ploy. He was making her mindless. And it was working. Of course, she wanted it to work.

"The only thing that matters here is that I love you and that you can say those words right back to me. Multiple times." He stopped, his forehead bunching up in mock contemplation. "Or maybe that only works if you're naked. Prove me wrong, Hadley. Say it while you've got on your clothes and this." He slipped the ring onto her finger.

Since the mindless kisses had indeed worked, it took her a few seconds to come up with the right answers in the right order. "Yes, I'll marry you. And, yes, I love you."

She got just a flash of Leyton's grin before his mouth swooped down on hers.

"Don't worry," he mumbled. "We're not going to screw this up."

At least that was what she thought he said, but it was hard to tell since she was kissing him as if there was no tomorrow.

* * * * *

Turn the page for Hot Summer in Texas, *a special bonus story from* USA TODAY *bestselling author Delores Fossen!*

HOT SUMMER IN TEXAS

CHAPTER ONE

LANA WATLEY SMELLED a rat the moment she stepped in front of the jail cell. A *rat* with two legs, a sly grin and blue eyes that were a genetic copy of her own.

She definitely wasn't smiling. Lana was frazzled and out of breath. She'd hurried into the Lone Star Ridge police station with a mountain of worry and concern—and confusion—but apparently the grinning man didn't see a reason for any of the emotional reactions she was having.

"Granddad, what are you doing in here in this cell?" Lana asked. She gave him a long once-over, making sure he wasn't injured, and she thankfully didn't see a scratch on him.

"You came," he said, totally ignoring her question.

He slowly rose to his feet. There was no other way to describe it. Benji Watley—aka her grandfather—moved as if he had all the time in the world to amble the two yards from his cot to the front of his cell. Even though he was now eighty-one, he wasn't feeble, far from it. He wrapped his fingers around the bars, peering out through them with his wrinkled narrow face, and he flashed her another smile.

"I wasn't sure you'd come," he added a moment later. "You've been so busy."

Now, along with the other things she was feeling, Lana got a hefty dose of guilt. She had indeed been busy with her law practice and hadn't made it to Lone Star Ridge in nearly three months. Way too long. But when Benji had called her today, it hadn't been because he'd wanted a visit from his granddaughter. It was the lawyer he'd requested.

"You said I should get here ASAP," Lana reminded him, "that you'd been arrested."

"I was," he readily admitted, and he hung his head as if remembering he should also be feeling some shame over whatever it was that had gotten him locked up here in jail.

Which was no easy feat for a man like her grandfather.

To the best of her knowledge, Grandpa Benji had never had so much as a traffic ticket. Plus, the town sheriff, Leyton Jameson, was as fair a cop as they came and wouldn't just arrest someone on a whim. Lana was certain of that.

Even though she hadn't lived in Lone Star Ridge in years, she still had plenty of friends here who kept an eye on her grandfather and kept her updated on the town talk. Lana included Leyton in the pool of "plenty of friends." Also, his sister Cait, who was one of the deputies. It was Cait who'd ushered Lana back into the jail area, but despite their friendship, the deputy had stayed mum on the charges, saying that it was something her grandfather had wanted to explain to her. However, Cait had spilled that Benji had refused bail even though many people, including Cait herself, had offered to pay it.

Yes, Lana smelled a rat, all right.

Her grandfather was up to something. Something that would no doubt involve getting her to move back to Lone Star Ridge. Lana was still mulling over the possibility of doing just that, but she sure as heck hadn't wanted to be lured here and given a hard sell by the man who'd raised her. By the man she loved.

And she remembered that now.

She loved him and owed him. He'd been the only one in

her family to step up and raise her after both her parents had been killed in a car wreck when Lana was ten. It'd been a hefty task for a widower who'd already hit the sixty mark, but he'd done it, and she would be forever grateful to him. That was why she softened her voice when she asked the next question.

"What happened?" Lana stroked her hand over his.

Her grandfather opened his mouth, but he didn't get a chance to answer before Lana heard the sound of footsteps behind her. She glanced over her shoulder, expecting to see Cait or the sheriff, but instead she got another shock. Not as much of one as seeing her grandfather behind bars, but it still gave her heart a jolt.

Along with a little flutter.

Marco Becker could cause reactions like that. Not just for her but for most women. He had rock star looks and a cowboy's swagger, all wrapped up in a nice package with his dark brown hair and amazing blue eyes. Yes, amazing, though Lana had heard many women call them bedroom eyes, followed by little sighs to go along with the heart flutters. Simply put, Marco was one hot cowboy.

And he was trouble.

Trouble for her, anyway, as ex-lovers often were. After all, there was a reason he was an ex, and that reason was slathered thick with old memories. Old wounds. And the heat, of course. That, too, was still obviously simmering between them.

Lana would have liked to deny that the attraction was even still there, but no way could she do that. Not when her body went haywire whenever she was around Marco. Like now.

In hindsight, it wasn't a surprise that he was there. Marco owned the ranch nearest to Benji's. They even shared a property line that included the creek. Also, according to Cait, Marco often helped Benji with running his own ranch, so they'd managed to stay friendly despite the breakup between Marco and her. Then again, the breakup had happened over a decade ago, so maybe she was the only one remembering it.

"I'm not filing charges against Benji, but he insisted that Cait arrest him," Marco grumbled.

Now Lana had more than a split second of speculation. She volleyed glances at Marco and her grandfather. "Why would there need to be charges or an arrest?"

Judging from the silence, neither man wanted to answer that, but it was finally her grandfather who responded. "I punched Marco."

Lana immediately whirled back around to look at Marco, specifically at his face, and she spotted the bruise.

"You hit Marco?" she asked Benji.

Her grandfather nodded, and he did the head-dip maneuver again as if trying to prove he was sorry about that. He didn't prove it very well at all. There was still some slyness in his expression, and since Lana didn't want to play Twenty Questions with him, she turned back to Marco.

"What happened?" Lana demanded.

Marco dragged in a long, weary breath and scrubbed his hand over his face. He winced, though, when his fingers brushed against the bruise. "Benji came over to my place this morning, and he was mad about one of my bulls breaking fence and messing up his garden. I tried to tell him I'd fix it, but he punched me. Then he called Cait and told her to come out and arrest him."

There were so many things wrong with that explanation. For starters, bulls broke fence, period. That happened on ranches, and she knew of at least two incidents where

Benji's livestock had done the same to Marco's property. Well, not to his garden, because to the best of her knowledge, Marco didn't have one. Ditto for her grandfather.

"Since when do you have a garden?" she pressed Benji. "And since when do you get mad and punch someone?"

Her grandfather shrugged. "I've taken up tending roses, and when I saw his Angus bull had trampled my Mr. Lincolns and Buff Beauties, I just lost it. I went right over to Marco's and slugged him." He was quick to answer, which made her wonder if he'd rehearsed it.

Mulling over that info, she shifted back to Marco, and she could tell from his frustrated huff that he hadn't made any more sense of this than she had. It also told her that whatever was going on, Marco wasn't part of it. Nope. He wasn't a happy camper right now.

"Benji's up to something," Marco concluded.

Yep. She was back to smelling that rat, and both Marco and she aimed a long stare at Benji.

"Start talking," Lana insisted. "Tell me what's going on."

Her grandfather had the nerve to act surprised that they wouldn't believe his righteous ire over trampled roses. "Nothing's going on. Like I said, I just lost it."

They continued staring at the old man until Cait stepped back in. The deputy went straight to the cell and opened the door. That was when Lana realized it hadn't even been locked. Apparently, Cait knew that Benji wasn't a threat to the safety of others. However, he had slung out some prime BS with this story he'd concocted. That said, the punch had been real.

"Marco's not filing charges," Cait repeated, motioning for Benji to come out of the cell. "Which means you owe him an apology."

Her grandfather didn't budge. "I already told him I was real sorry, and now I'm ready for my punishment. I figure I should get at least a day or two behind bars."

That brought on frustrated sighs from everyone outside the cell.

"Consider yourself punished," Marco assured him. "Now come out of there so we can all get to work."

Benji looked at Lana then. "You'll be leaving right away, I guess?"

Lana checked her watch. She had an appointment with a client in a little less than two hours, and it'd take her an hour to get back to San Antonio. That gave her some time but not much.

"Come out of the cell, and we can have some coffee and talk," Lana offered.

Benji nodded but still didn't budge. This time when he lowered his head, he shook it. "I'm afraid I'm losing it. You know, like old people do."

Lana felt the spike of concern from head to toe. Was her grandfather talking about dementia?

"What do you mean?" she asked just as Marco said, "Say what?"

Marco's obvious surprise meant he hadn't picked up on anything off with Benji. Well, nothing other than being assaulted by him. And until this second, Lana had thought that maybe it'd been a ruse to get her here. But maybe it was something more. Like a cry for help.

"I can't take care of my place any longer," Benji went on. "It's just getting too hard."

Lana swallowed the lump in her throat and hated that she'd ever believed this was a ploy. "I can hire someone to help you," she offered.

Though she wasn't sure how she could afford it. She

wasn't pulling in a huge income since most of her legal services were for low-income families. Still, she'd manage it somehow.

"I can help more," Marco added. "You just tell me what needs to be done, and I'll do it."

Lana muttered a heartfelt thanks, but she had to do that over the buzzing of her phone. She intended to hit the decline button, but when she looked at the screen, she realized she couldn't do that.

Matthew Devane's name popped up on the screen.

Lana got another slam of concern because it was the middle of the day. A school day, at that. Which was exactly where Matthew should be—in his fifth-grade classes at the elementary school in San Antonio. The boy definitely shouldn't be calling Lana and likely wouldn't unless this was some kind of emergency.

"I need to take this," Lana said, stepping away. "Matthew, what's wrong?" she immediately asked.

"I left my science project at the house and wondered if you could bring it to me," Matthew answered. His words were so rushed they ran together.

Lana frowned, mentally reminded herself of the day of the week. "It's Monday. Your dad should be working from home today. Why can't he bring it to you?"

"Because he'll get mad at me for forgetting it."

Yes, he would. Nolan Devane, Matthew's father, could be testy when something threw off his schedule. Setting aside whatever architecture project he was working on to help his son would definitely result in fussing.

"Mom's out of town on a business trip, so I can't ask her. Plus, it's not her week. It's Dad's. Please, Lana," Matthew went on. "You wouldn't have to do it right now. I just need to turn it in before the end of the day."

The end of the school day was probably four o'clock. It was doable, but Lana had to deal with her grandfather first and then meet with her client. There was also the issue of whether this "favor" would even do any good.

"If I go by your house, your dad will know about the science project," Lana pointed out.

There were several seconds of silence. "Maybe you could use your key to get in? The project's in a box on the foyer table."

Lana sighed. "I don't have a key. I haven't had one since your father and I stopped seeing each other a year ago."

"There's one in the flowerpot at the end of the porch," Matthew immediately assured her.

"I'm not sneaking into your house." Lana sighed again. "But I will get the project and bring it to you."

"Thanks, Lana. You're the best. Love you," the boy rattled off.

"Love you, too," Lana said, even though Matthew had already ended the call.

Lana turned and realized that everyone had been listening to her. Of course, the area was postage-stamp-sized, so that shouldn't have been a surprise.

"Trouble?" her grandfather asked.

Lana shook her head. "That was…"

And her explanation ground to a halt. *My ex-boyfriend's son* was the simple answer. What wasn't so simple was what Lana felt for the child. No. Nothing simple about that. Besides, it didn't apply here. She needed to finish up with her grandfather, take him home, and then she could hurry back to San Antonio for her appointment and to help out Matthew.

"That was Nolan's little boy?" her grandfather asked.

She nodded and left it at that. Benji knew that she'd dated

Nolan for nearly two years, and Lana had told him about Nolan's eleven-year-old son. But Marco and Cait probably didn't know those details, and judging from Marco's slightly raised eyebrow, he was curious about that conversation. Not for long, though. When Lana didn't add anything else to her nod, Marco turned back to Benji.

"I'll help out on your ranch," Marco repeated. "I'll replace any of the roses the bull trampled and repair the fence. Just let me know if there's anything else that needs to be done."

Lana felt the tightness in her chest ease up some. It was a generous offer on Marco's part. She'd make the same offer, and on the drive back to the ranch, she could have Benji write a list of anything else that might need to be done.

"Let's go," Lana said, opening the cell door even wider.

Once again, Benji stayed put. Their eyes met, their gazes holding for a few seconds, before he finally muttered some profanity under his breath.

"I did hit Marco to get you here," Benji admitted.

Lana groaned. She'd just about decided there was no rat to smell after all, and now this confession.

"Sorry I used you like that," her grandfather quickly added to Marco, "but I thought this was the fastest way to get Lana here."

Since Marco didn't say anything, Lana decided he must have been too shocked or riled to speak. Lana had no such problem.

"The fastest way," she repeated in a snarl. "Why was it so important that you get me here?"

Her grandfather didn't hesitate. "Because I needed to

get started on a project. An important one." He paused, sliding glances at both Marco and her. "I need the two of you to get married."

CHAPTER TWO

MARCO WASN'T SURE who repeated the word *married* in the loudest voice. Lana, Cait or him, but Marco knew he had to be the most shocked.

Or maybe not, he amended when he looked at Lana.

Her mouth was open, literally, and her wide, stunned blue eyes were fixed on Benji as if he'd lost his mind. Which Marco believed Benji had, if the man truly believed Lana and he should get married. And here Marco had thought that the punch Benji had thrown and his self-arrest were the craziest parts of his day. Apparently, though, the crazy was just getting started.

"Is this a joke?" Lana finally managed to say to her grandfather.

Benji shook his head. "I've been trying to get you to come home for weeks now so we could talk about this, and I figured it shouldn't wait any longer. You've got to marry Marco."

Lana kept up her intense stare and muttered something about hell having to freeze over before she said *I do* to Marco. He tried not to let that sting. After all, Lana and he hadn't exactly had an easy breakup, but he didn't like being lumped in any hell-freezing scenario.

"Uh, I think I've got something else to do," Cait insisted, already heading out as she added the rest from over her shoulder. "When you're finally ready to leave the cell, just stop by my desk so we can do some paperwork. No hurry. It appears you've got some talking to do."

Yeah, he did, and Marco figured Cait was wise to bow out of…well, whatever the hell this was.

"You're going to need to explain just what the hell you're talking about," Marco advised Benji.

Benji nodded and gathered his breath in a way that made Marco think he was steeling himself up for the flak he was about to get. "My ranch has been in the Watley family for eight generations, and as it's passed down, each heir has had to promise two things. That the ranch wouldn't be sold to outsiders and that only a male heir could inherit it."

Marco took a moment to process that and then tried to pick through his memory to see if Benji had ever mentioned this. He hadn't. Apparently, he hadn't said anything about it to Lana, either, because the sound she made was a gasp of surprise. She followed it with an almost frantic shake of her head.

"A male heir," she repeated in a hoarse whisper. "This is a provision in a will?"

"There's no will," Benji assured her. "Just the promises. In my case, I made them to my daddy when he was on his deathbed two years before you were even born. Of course, I'd known all along that I'd be taking the ranch, since by then I was already running it. And at the time, I thought your father would be in line to inherit it after me."

That had gone to hell in a handbasket when Lana's father, Benji's only child, had been killed when Lana was just a kid. Added to that, Lana didn't have any siblings.

"A male heir," Lana said again, but this time it wasn't a whisper, and it had a smidge of anger to it. "What kind of crock is that?"

"An outdated crock," Benji readily admitted, "but the

conditions were set over a hundred and fifty years ago. Guess my ancestors weren't big on gender equality way back then."

Obviously not, and it was ironic since there were many women ranchers in the area. Heck, Cait was one of them. She operated a small horse ranch along with helping her brothers run the much larger family one.

"So, a deathbed promise," Lana said, and Marco knew she was trying to wrap her head around this shocking turn of events. "But no actual paperwork."

"A promise is more binding than paperwork," Benji muttered.

That caused Lana to make a frustrated sigh before she paused. "Why didn't you tell me any of this sooner?"

"Because I kept thinking you'd get married and I'd have that male heir."

Everything inside Marco went still, and he glanced at Lana to see how she was handling that comment. She didn't appear to be handling it well. She'd gone a little pale and clammy looking, which confirmed that the subject of heirs and babies was still an open wound.

It was for Marco, too.

Marco cursed under his breath. "What made you think Lana and I'd be getting married? We broke up years ago."

"And you still have feelings for each other," Benji pointed out just as quickly.

Lana rolled her eyes, but Marco didn't hear any denial coming out of her mouth. Then again, it wasn't coming out of his, either. That was because there were indeed feelings.

Lust.

Even though neither Lana nor he had gotten out of their relationship unscathed, the lust just kept lingering. Like now, for instance. Certain parts of his body seemed to get all kinds of stupid notions whenever he was around Lana. So did his mind. It made sure to give him very clear images of the memories he'd made with Lana. Specifically, the memories of her being stark naked and in his bed.

In his truck, too.

Oh, and in his barn.

That was the trouble with a fierce physical attraction. There hadn't been many places off-limits when the urge hit them. And that urge had hit pretty damn often before things had gone to hell in a handbasket and Lana had walked out on him. Marco made sure he remembered the walking-out part, too, because she'd done a number on his heart. Like the lust, the hurt was also still there.

Lana glanced around before her attention settled on Marco. Maybe she was looking at him to see if he had a solution. He didn't. However, he did have some more questions.

"Does all of this have anything to do with the doctor's appointment you had this morning?" Marco asked.

Benji suddenly looked about as comfortable as a bare ass on an especially thorny cactus.

"What doctor's appointment?" Lana snapped when her grandfather didn't say anything. And by not saying anything, Benji said it all. Yeah, this sudden need for them to get married was indeed connected to the doctor's visit.

Hell.

Was Benji sick? Or maybe it was something worse. Why else would he be trying to get his affairs in order?

"Why don't I get that paperwork done for Cait and we can go back to the ranch and discuss this?" Benji offered.

Lana checked the time, no doubt calculating if she could have this chat with Benji and get back to San Antonio to take care of that errand for her ex-boyfriend's kid. Or maybe the guy wasn't her ex. According to Benji, they'd broken up, but it was obvious Lana had stayed connected to the boy. After all, she'd told the kid she loved him.

Which didn't surprise Marco.

Lana had always loved children. Had always wanted them. So did he. And that had been the reason she'd walked out on him over a decade ago. Well, maybe it was the reason. He'd never gotten a clear picture of what had gone on between them nearly eleven years ago.

Marco pushed all of that aside. Old water, old bridge, and he didn't need to be making mental treks like that. Right now, he needed to focus on Benji, on getting him home so he could figure out what the heck was happening.

As Cait had instructed, Benji closed the cell door before they made their way into the squad room where Cait was waiting for them. "If one of you could give me a lift home, I'd appreciate it," Benji told Marco and Lana, and he sat in the chair next to Cait's desk. "I'll just get these papers signed and meet you outside."

Marco didn't especially want to go outside and wait, but he needed to talk to Lana, and it was best if that didn't happen in the police station. Cait wasn't a blabbermouth, but Marco couldn't say the same for today's dispatcher/receptionist, Myrtle Crenshaw. Anything said around the woman's ears would become information for any and all. Lana must have realized that as well because she stepped outside with him without putting up so much as a groan of protest.

Marco did some groaning, though. It was June in Texas, which meant it was hot. Too damn hot to be lollygagging around and waiting for news about Benji's health. News that could possibly take a big painful bite out of him.

Benji was as close to family as he had, since his own

folks hadn't shown much interest in him or his life. The month after Marco had turned eighteen, they'd given him the ranch and taken off in an RV. Their leaving hadn't been a surprise, though. His mom and dad hadn't kept it a secret that they'd never planned on having kids and that they didn't especially enjoy parenthood.

Or the ranch, for that matter.

The ranch had been an inheritance, too, from his maternal grandfather to his mother, but his mom had shown even less interest in raising Angus cattle than she had in raising Marco.

It'd been three years since he'd last seen his folks and he had no desire to now. Or ever, for that matter. But Benji was different. Benji had been there for him. Had taken much more than a mere interest and had made Marco feel…well, wanted. That was powerful stuff. It'd be a powerful loss when it was gone, too. While Marco knew Benji wouldn't live forever, he hadn't considered that losing him might be coming so soon.

"You didn't know anything about this?" Lana immediately asked him. They walked to a shade tree just a few yards from the door.

"No. And you don't know what happened in his doctor's appointment?" Marco countered.

Lana shook her head. "No. But it must be bad for him to pull a stunt like punching you."

"It wasn't much of a punch," Marco admitted. Not much of a stunt, either. If Benji had just told Lana that he had health problems, she would have put her work aside and come home.

"FYI, I'm not marrying you to save the ranch," Lana continued while she glanced around.

Marco didn't hesitate answering her on that. "Same here."

He did some glancing around, as well. Not because there was anything new to see. Things stayed pretty much the same in Lone Star Ridge, and you could take in the entire town in one long sweep.

Main Street was flanked with the mom-and-pop shops and stores and had just one traffic light. Hardly a beehive of activity, but Marco did notice that Lana and he had caught some prying eyes. A handful of folks stopped to mill around, perhaps hoping to catch a tidbit about what was going on.

"Same here," Lana repeated, muttering it under her breath, and her tone had Marco looking at her again. He didn't think he was mistaken that there was some bitterness in those two words.

Yep, bitterness, he confirmed when he studied her expression. And that riled him. In fact, it riled him so much that he didn't keep his mouth shut when he darn well should have.

"I wasn't the one who left," he pointed out.

"And you know why I left," she pointed out equally fast. Lana muttered some profanity and lifted her long blond hair off her neck—which was probably sweaty.

Since Marco was sweating, too, he hitched his thumb to his truck. "Let's sit in the AC while we wait for Benji. Best not to end up in the ER with heatstroke."

Lana didn't argue with him. She started in that direction ahead of him, giving Marco a nice but unwanted view of her great butt and equally great legs. The plain blue dress skimmed along some curves that he also knew fell into the "equally great" category.

"Are you looking at my butt?" she grumbled.

Marco was sure he looked as if he'd just got caught stealing some cookies. "Well, it's right there. Hard not to look."

He expected her to scowl at him or snap that he should keep his eyes on something else. She didn't. Lana smiled. It wasn't exactly a beaming grin. More like a weary resignation. Then she stopped, waiting for him to go ahead of her.

"I'm just returning the favor," she admitted, and he glanced back to see that she was indeed ogling his backside.

Now it was Marco who smiled. Yeah, there was still something between them, whether they wanted it there or not. It was a nice moment. One that ended as soon as they were in his truck.

"I never told my grandfather about the baby," she blurted out.

For just a handful of words, they sure packed a wallop along with giving Marco another of those blasts from the past. Not lust this time. But what their lust, and love, had created. A baby.

Their baby.

One they'd lost when Lana miscarried at six weeks. For those few weeks, he and Lana had gone back and forth on what to do. They'd been young. Damn young. Barely twenty-one, and Marco had been struggling to run his ranch on his own. Lana had been in college, studying pre-law. She'd had hopes and dreams of being a lawyer and helping people, and even though they'd wanted the baby, the timing had sucked.

During that time, she had poured out her fears and her worries to him, but she'd finally started to see how it could work out. How they could have a baby and start their lives together. Then she'd miscarried and broken things off when Marco had still been reeling from the loss of their child.

Yeah, that was an old wound, all right, and he totally got why she hadn't told her grandfather about it. Too painful. And she might have worried that Benji would have thought less of her.

As he'd pushed aside the lust, Marco gave all of that a mental shove as well, and he turned on the truck's AC full blast.

"I won't say anything to Benji about the baby," Marco assured her.

"Good," she murmured and leaned in to get closer to the vent. "That was all a long time ago anyway. No need to bring it into the mix." She paused, groaned. "Sweet heaven, do you believe something's seriously wrong with him?"

The answer was yes, he did believe that. But he kept it to himself because that wouldn't help ease the worry he saw on Lana's face. For reasons he didn't want to explore, he wanted to do something to ease that worry. Which was probably why he did something stupid.

Marco reached out and pulled her into his arms.

The moment her body landed against his, he realized the mistake. Realized, too, that it gave him a lot more comfort than it should have. But the real shocker was that Lana didn't back away. Just the opposite. She sort of melted, dropping her head on his shoulder.

"I should have come sooner," she muttered. "He kept asking me to come, and I put it off. I shouldn't have put it off."

Marco let her go through that self-bashing for a couple of seconds before he eased her back so he could look her straight in the eyes. "Benji could have asked me to take him to see you. He didn't. I think he had to come to terms first with whatever's happening with his health."

He hoped that would comfort her. Hoped, too, that it was true. But Marco had no idea why Benji had decided to play things out this way.

"I'm not ready to lose him," Lana whispered.

On this they could agree. "No, and things might not be as bad as they seem. Just hold off on the worrying until Benji tells us what's wrong."

Marco knew that was advice he wouldn't be keeping. He was worried, and it was going to stay that way until he had answers. Answers that he must have thought he'd find in Lana's eyes because his gaze stayed locked with hers. While they were hip to hip and with plenty of her touching plenty of him.

That touching was something his body definitely noticed.

Lana was right there. Her face only inches from his. Her scent brushing over him as her breath landed against his mouth.

He felt the stirring in his blood. Heck, he felt it below the belt, too. And another wave of stupidity washed over him. Before Marco could talk himself out of it, he leaned in and kissed her.

The moment his mouth met hers, the jolt came. Of course it did. Lust only kicked up when there was kissing involved. That alone should have been a good enough reason for him to pull back.

He didn't.

Marco stayed the course, his mouth moving over Lana's as if he had a right to do just that. Even worse, her mouth was moving, as well. Until a stupid mistake became a full-fledged kiss. A kiss that probably would have gotten a whole lot hotter if the passenger's-side door of his truck hadn't opened.

Lana made a strangled sound. Part gasp, part groan. And she practically shoved away from him, turning to meet her grandfather's puzzled gaze. Well, maybe it was puzzlement, but Marco thought Benji might be having to work hard not to smile. If he did, it was only going to make this whole situation a lot worse. Neither Lana nor he needed Benji rubbing in this mistake.

Or making them believe it wasn't a mistake at all.

"Uh, sorry," Benji muttered, and he got in the truck, forcing Lana right up against Marco again. Thankfully, not breasts to chest this time, though. Instead, it was arm to arm, and Marco could feel Lana's tight muscles. Mentally, she was no doubt kicking herself because he was doing the same damn thing.

"Since Lana's got to get back to work," Benji continued, "I'll make this quick. The appointment I had this morning didn't go so well. The doctor thinks it's time I retire. And this is why." He tapped his heart. "The ticker's gone bad. I need bypass surgery for starters, but there's damage. Can't undo that."

The sound Lana made this time wasn't of surprise. But rather sadness and shock. Marco was right on that same page with her.

Benji opened the door and stepped out. He motioned for Lana to get out, too. "Why don't you go ahead back to San Antonio? I'll have Marco take me home so I can get some rest."

Both his voice and his expression were weary, and Marco saw something he'd never before seen on Benji's face. Genuine worry. It seemed to go bone deep.

Benji took a deep breath before he looked at Lana and

continued. "Tonight, after your work and errands are done, could you come back here?"

She nodded. "Of course." Lana brushed a kiss on his cheek, gave his arm a gentle squeeze. "I'll be back. And then we can figure out how to fix this."

CHAPTER THREE

LANA PULLED UP in front of her grandfather's house, but she didn't get out of her SUV. She needed a moment to gather her thoughts. Doing that might help her come up with a better solution to this problem with the ranch.

Might.

But she wasn't holding out much hope she could actually manage it, considering she hadn't been able to gather her thoughts all afternoon or on the drive to and from San Antonio.

She glanced at Marco's truck that was parked at the side of the two-story white house. There was no sign of him, which was good. She needed to do some thinking about Marco, too. Of course, after that kiss, it was impossible to get him off her mind. She just hadn't been able to steady herself long enough to put that kiss and this situation in perspective.

Damn him and that incredible mouth. He'd stirred up not only the old heat but the old memories as well, and she already had enough to handle without adding to the mix.

Her grandfather was probably counting on that heat, though. That was why he'd suggested marriage as a fix to his deathbed promise to his own father. But while the attraction between Marco and her might still be there in spades, the love wasn't.

Well, it probably wasn't.

Marco couldn't still be in love with her. Not after what she'd done by leaving him. And she couldn't love him again until she'd learned to forgive herself. Too bad that might never happen.

With that dismal thought running through her head, she started to get out of her SUV, but some movement in the corral caught her eye. She spotted Marco with one of the Appaloosas that her grandfather loved. He certainly made a picture in his black Stetson, jeans and a work shirt that strained with the flexing of his muscles. Pure cowboy. All man.

That stirred memories as well of the times she'd had her hands and her mouth on that manliness.

She was just seventeen when she lost her virginity to him. Even though Marco hadn't given her a lot of details about it, his sexual initiation had happened a year or two before. Lana wouldn't admit it to anyone, but she'd waited for him to make his way through the bevy of girls who'd eyed him as if he were a tempting, tasty dessert. She'd waited because she'd thought he was "the one."

Now she knew that sex with "the one" was a heck of a lot easier than dealing with the aftermath of their relationship. She'd been a miserable failure at that, and she had ended up hurting Marco in the process. That hurt was still there. Probably always would be, which was why he would nix any marriage notions, as well.

Her phone buzzed, and she absently answered it without taking her attention off Marco. If she had looked at her phone screen, she probably wouldn't have answered because the caller wasn't someone she wanted to talk to right now.

Nolan.

"Lana," he said. "Just calling to make sure you're okay."

She didn't want to talk to her ex again, especially not while she ogled her first ex in the corral. Not that the chat they'd had at Nolan's house when she'd stopped by to pick up Matthew's science project had been unpleasant. He hadn't gotten angry. Instead, Nolan had taken one look at her face and immediately asked her what was wrong.

The man could be impatient and self-absorbed when he was in work mode, but she'd never once doubted that he cared about her. Maybe still did. But since Lana had been the one to end their relationship, too, that wasn't a discussion she wanted to have with him. Nor was this one about her grandfather.

"I just got to Lone Star Ridge," she answered, making sure she sounded as if she was pressed for time. "I'm going in to talk to Benji now."

"Well, give him my best, and if there's anything I can do, let me know."

She was feeling lousy enough that she nearly pointed out that he could help by not being so snippy with his son when he forgot things like a science project. But that was a battle she could no longer fight. She couldn't entangle herself in Nolan's life because she loved the boy who'd nearly become her stepson.

"Thanks," she murmured and got distracted when Marco peeled off his shirt to hose himself down.

Mercy.

The man could still make her mouth water.

"You said your granddad's having trouble and wants you there at his ranch," Nolan added a moment later.

"Yes," she answered, though it was hard to focus on the conversation when she couldn't take her eyes off Marco. She had indeed told Nolan that when she'd lowered her defenses after he'd expressed some concern for her. "Granddad needs to retire, but he has to turn over the ranch to a male heir. Since I'm obviously not a male, he'd planned on giving it to my spouse."

Nolan laughed as if that were a joke, but then he cleared his throat. "You're serious?"

She refrained from using the clichéd answer of "as a heart attack." Lana didn't want to think of anything to do with the heart right now.

"I'm serious," she settled for saying. "Granddad wants me to get married so he can leave the ranch to me and my spouse." She stuttered a little when a shirtless Marco started toward her grandfather's house. "I have to go, Nolan. Thanks for checking on me."

She ended the call while he was mid-goodbye and stepped out of her SUV. Marco immediately spotted her, and he muttered something under his breath. Probably profanity and aimed at her because seeing her was a reminder that he was regretting that amazing kiss he'd laid on her back at the police station. He must have also regretted being bare chested because he ended her peep show by putting his shirt back on. What he didn't do was button it, which meant she got a limited peep show.

Which was still amazing.

There were tiny beads of water clinging to the fine mat of chest hair. Chest hair that she used to run her fingers through—

And she couldn't go there.

"You're ogling my chest," he commented.

His tone was as dry as dust, but there was a glimmer in his eyes. Eyes that lowered to her breasts. They were playing tit for tat again, and Lana felt her nipples tingle in response. Heck, a lot of her body was tingling.

She shook her head to clear it. "Uh, my grandfather's inside?"

That glimmer stayed in place a few seconds longer before he nodded and started for the house. Lana fell in step alongside him. "He took a nap, and I had the diner deliver something for dinner so he wouldn't have to cook." He glanced at her. "Did you finish your business and deal with the science project?"

She didn't miss the shift in tone when he mentioned the science project. Probably because he knew it was for her ex's son. Maybe the tone was Marco's way of asking her what was going on there. But Lana didn't want to talk about that any more than she wanted to discuss the fact that she still had the hots for him.

"I did deal with my business," she answered, "and I cleared my schedule for the next couple of days." Which hadn't been as hard as she'd thought it would be. Lana had rescheduled some of her appointments to conference calls and had shifted a few projects that would allow her to work remotely from the ranch.

"Good. Because I think Benji's going to need you here," Marco muttered.

Lana stopped on the porch and looked at him. "Did he say anything else about his heart—"

"No. And I didn't push. I figured he'd want to talk about this tonight." He paused. "But if you think I shouldn't be here when you two discuss it, just let me know."

Lana wasn't sure if his hesitancy was simply a courtesy to not impose during a "family" chat or if he wanted to cut and run because of that kiss. And because of the ogling. But if that was it, he was just going to have to deal with a little discomfort because anything they might work out would almost certainly involve Marco.

Not marriage.

But maybe keeping an eye on the daily operations of the ranch until Lana could learn how to do that herself.

"You should be here," she told him, and trying to steel herself up, she opened the door and went in.

Home. That was her first thought as she stepped inside the foyer with its rich wood floors and paintings of the prizewinning horses her grandfather had bred and raised over the years. She loved the place, and even though her life was in San Antonio, this would always be home.

Her second thought was the guilt over not having been here in so long.

They made their way through the foyer and into the sprawling living area that hadn't been redecorated in more than a decade. Then again, the caramel-colored leather sofa where her grandfather was seated never seemed to go out of style.

However, she did see some changes. There was a stack of mail and magazines on one of the end tables and the furniture had a fine coating of dust. Normally, her grandfather stayed on top of keeping the place clean, so it was an "in the face" reminder that he was indeed not feeling well. Maybe not feeling well for months—something she would have known had she visited him.

Her grandfather smiled at them, causing some of her worry to ease. He didn't look sick, and that was good, but that didn't mean something bad wasn't going on inside him.

She went over and hugged him before sitting down. "How do you feel?" she asked.

"I'm not ready to keel over or anything, so you can take that gloom-and-doom look off your face." He patted her hand, aimed another smile at Marco. "Thanks for seeing to the mare."

Marco nodded. "Anytime." He didn't sit, and when her grandfather motioned for him to do that, Marco fanned his hand over his shirt. "I hosed off, but I'm still plenty sweaty."

Yes, he was, and despite the situation, Lana remembered just how hot of a look that could be on him.

"Sit down anyway," Benji insisted. "I'll grab us some beers, and we can talk."

Lana caught onto her grandfather's hand when he started to stand. "Did the doctor say it was okay for you to drink alcohol?"

His mouth flattened, which told her the answer to that was no.

"I'll get us some ice water in a minute," she offered. "First, though, I want to know what the doctor told you about your heart."

"I already gave you the condensed version. Not much else to say." He paused as if gathering his breath. "I'll be scheduled for bypass. It's not as much of a big deal as it used to be," he quickly added. "There's not much risk. But I will have to take it easy and not do as much as I'm used to doing."

Marco finally did sit, taking the chair across from them. "I've already made some calls, and I can have some part-time help here by tomorrow morning. I can fill in, too."

"And so can I," Lana volunteered, causing both men to look at her as if she'd just sprouted another nose. "I can," she insisted.

"Well, thank you," Benji said without a whole lot of conviction.

"I can," she repeated in a grumble. "Ranching might

not be a strong skill set for me, but I can learn, and I can do some parts of my job from here."

She got the sprouted-nose look from them again. Maybe because in the past she hadn't made an effort to help out. But in her own defense, that was because her help hadn't been needed. It was now, though. Not just helping with the ranch, either, but with the legalities of ownership, as well.

"I'm looking into maybe the ranch being placed in a trust," she explained. "That way, it can be held for future male heirs."

"I'd rather leave it to you," Benji quickly stated.

She'd expected this argument. "Well, unless I'm going to start spontaneously growing male parts, that's not going to happen. Or unless you're planning on breaking the promise you made to your father. Which I know you aren't."

Lana wouldn't ask him to do it, either. Her grandfather was an honest man. Well, except for luring her back to town under the pretense that he'd been arrested. But she figured that'd been fueled by desperation. Desperation that she was also feeling right now.

"I can't break my promise," Benji muttered with plenty of regret in his voice. "I gave my word."

She sighed and kissed his cheek. "Then our best bet is the trust."

However, that was far from a sure thing. Once Benji actually saw the document, he might see it as a way of skirting around that promise. After all, he would still technically be leaving it to her and any future heirs who might or might not be male. But he had to leave the place to someone, and if he didn't stipulate that in a will, the property would automatically go to her after his passing since she was his only next of kin.

In other words, it would break the promise he'd made.

Lana didn't want to worry about that right now, not when it was his health that was her main concern.

"When is your next doctor's appointment?" she asked. "Because I'd like to go with you and talk to the doctor. I want to know more about this bypass and find out what kind of recovery you'll have."

"The appointment's tomorrow to schedule the surgery. And you can come." There was no argument in his voice, but there was some weariness. He rubbed his hand over his face. "I think I'd like a little lie down before dinner." He shifted his attention to Marco. "Would you mind staying around for a while? I'd like to go over some chores you can give that part-time help you hired."

"Of course," Marco readily agreed. He motioned to his shirt again. "But I'll need to grab a shower and wash off the rest of this sweat. I've got a change of clothes in my truck."

"You know where the guest room is," Marco said, heading to his own room at the back of the house. "I won't let this lie down last too long."

Marco and she stood there and watched him walk away. "Crap," Marco muttered. "I was hoping he was bluffing, that this was all just some out-there matchmaking attempt."

"Yes," Lana agreed. She'd hoped the same thing, but it was obvious this health threat was the real deal.

They stood there, their attention on the now empty hall, and the worry so thick that Lana could practically feel it coating her skin.

"Granddad's not going to like the trust when he reads it," she said. "So, please tell me you have some clever idea as to how to get around this. It would lessen his stress if we had a solution."

Judging from the sound of frustration Marco made, he didn't have anything clever to fix this. "I could get you pregnant with the hopes that it'd be a boy," he threw out there. "Sorry," he immediately added. "A really bad joke."

It was. But for just a handful of seconds, her stupid body thought that was a stellar notion. Because it would land them in bed and maybe cool some of this scalding need she had for him.

"I'm really sorry," he said, interrupting her shirtless fantasies of him. "I shouldn't have said anything about a baby."

Because that was a taboo subject. One that he probably figured had reminded her of the miscarriage. Lana felt guilty that it hadn't, that her first thought had gone to sex instead of this loss they had between them.

She wanted to give him a break. Guilt sucked, and they had enough suckage going on right now without adding the old baggage. "Actually, let's put the knocking up as plan C."

He slowly turned to her, and while he wasn't smiling, there was a glimmer in his eye. Or maybe it was just reflecting the glimmer that was in hers.

"I'm guessing the trust idea is plan A," he said. "So, what's plan B?"

"I haven't thought of one yet." Though her grandfather had certainly believed he had the fix. "It won't be marriage. I'm not going to put my family's troubles on you like that."

Marco continued to stare at her, and she thought that maybe he was about to tell her to dump those troubles right on him. There was no way he could actually want marriage.

Was there?

No. Because they weren't in love. There was only the heat, and it was there in spades. Worse, it seemed to be flaming up in leaps and bounds. Marco was well aware of it, too, because his gaze dropped to her mouth, and he gave her a sort of visual kiss. Lana cursed because it seemed to be just as potent as the real thing.

"I'm still sweaty," he pointed out.

She made a show of sniffing at him and didn't get a whiff of any sweat. However, his shirt was still open, and his chest was still damp from the hosing down he'd given himself. And then there was his scent. No sweat, but it was musky and male. He smelled like bottled sex.

"Crap," she muttered under her breath.

"Well, I was working with the horses," he joked. "So, there's possibly some on my boots."

Lana couldn't help it. She smiled.

And then she kissed him.

Her brain was yelling that this was wrong. So wrong. But the rest of her just started clamoring for more and shut out any voice of reason. That was a good thing. She didn't want reason. She wanted Marco's mouth for dinner.

Marco accommodated her. He kissed her right back, along with sliding his arm around her and pulling her to him. She suddenly felt starved for him, as if he were the cure for a long drought. And she knew he was more than capable of *curing* because he was as good in bed as he looked like he would be.

He made a sound of pleasure, one that was mixed with frustration. She totally got that. Kissing, and anything else they did, would feel amazing, but it wouldn't really solve anything. Plus, it would bring this heat right to the surface, where it could muddle the decision that had to be made about the ranch.

That reminder didn't stop her.

In fact, she was the one who deepened the kiss, and it

was her hand that started moving this beyond first base. She slid her hand between them. To his chest. Over all those tight muscles and mat of hair.

That kicked up the heat a significant notch, and this time there was no frustration in the sound he made. It was need, all need, and it quickly got out of hand. Still kissing her, Marco backed her against the wall, pinning her there while he took that magic mouth to her neck. That was the problem with them having been lovers: he knew all her hot spots and knew how to take her from foreplay to the bed.

Which couldn't happen.

Lana mentally repeated that many times before she was finally able to make her exploring hands quit playing with his chest hair. It took several more repeats before she could ease back from him.

When their gazes met, their breaths were gusting, and Lana could feel their hearts thudding against their chests. She could also hear buzzing, and it took her a moment to realize that the sound wasn't only in her head.

"My phone," she managed to say, and Lana pulled it from the side pocket of her dress. She frowned when she saw Matthew's name on the screen. "I should take this."

"You think he forgot another science project?" Marco grumbled, obviously seeing the screen. He was clearly not happy about ending their make-out session. Or maybe he was unhappy that it'd happened in the first place. It wasn't fun to be reminded they were pretty much mindless when it came to each other.

"Matthew," she said, answering the call. "Is something wrong?"

But it wasn't the boy's voice she heard. It was Nolan's. "Sorry about using Matthew's phone," he immediately told her. "But I wanted to make sure you accepted the call."

Lana huffed. She'd had her fill of ploys to get her attention, and she seriously doubted Nolan had anywhere near the justification her grandfather had for using said ploy.

"I'm really busy, Nolan." And, yes, her tone was more than a little chilly. "What do you want?"

"I want to fix your problem with your grandfather's ranch," he said without hesitation.

While she didn't think such a fix could come from Nolan, she was desperate enough to hear any possible suggestions for plan B.

"What fix?" she asked cautiously.

"An easy one," Nolan declared. "You can marry me."

CHAPTER FOUR

YOU CAN MARRY ME.

Those were the words that'd been going through Marco's head for the past two days, and they were continuing to repeat as he rode in from the pasture after checking the fences.

Words that he shouldn't have heard.

But Lana had taken her ex-boyfriend's call while Marco had been standing right in front of her. Hard not to hear when they were standing only inches apart.

Prior to the call, they'd been well on their way to revving up their bodies to the point that they might have dragged each other off to bed. That wouldn't have been a good idea. Even though at the time it'd felt as if they'd had no choice.

There was no choice about this attraction he felt for her, either. Or his feelings. Those were the most troublesome. After all, sexual attraction could happen between plenty of people who didn't even care for each other. It could mean nothing other than just sex.

But feelings meant something.

The trouble was he needed to figure out exactly what that *something* was while dealing with his worries about Benji and the possibility that Lana would accept the marriage proposal from her clown of an ex.

You can marry me.

Lana hadn't given the man an answer while she'd been

standing there, but she had said she would talk to him later before she'd ended the call. She hadn't had that talk while she'd been at Benji's that night, but Marco suspected Lana had contacted the man at some point in the past two days. Maybe she'd even seen him so she could agree to a marriage to fulfill the conditions of Benji's promise.

Marco had never met Nolan, but he was certain about the guy being a clown. And an idiot. Why else would he have let Lana go? Then again, that also made him an idiot clown since he hadn't been able to stop her from leaving, either.

Cursing himself, the situation and everything else he could think of to curse, Marco unsaddled his horse, brushed her down and made his way across the backyard to the house for a shower. Maybe if he made the water cold enough, it would cool down both kinds of heat. The one from the ninety-degree summer temps and the one that Lana had ignited inside him.

Of course, the shower didn't help with the internal heat, but that would have been somewhat of a miracle if it had. Thoughts of Lana stayed with him while the water spewed over him. Pushing into his mind. Taunting him.

Making him ache for her.

That was why he thought he was seeing a mirage of her when he stepped from the shower and she was standing in the doorway of his bathroom. Her back was to him, but if it was a mirage, then it was a darn good one because that was Lana's backside.

"I wasn't gawking at you," she said.

She wasn't. She didn't even turn her head and glance over her shoulder. Though Marco did some glancing of his own once he realized she was the real deal.

Lana was indeed a welcome sight. As much as he could

see of her, that was. She was wearing another of those cotton dresses, a yellow one this time, and it skimmed her butt and hit just above the knee.

"I knocked," she went on, "and the front door wasn't locked. It's hotter than Hades out there, so I thought I'd come inside and wait for you, but then I heard the shower. I came in to shout out that I was here, that I'd wait for you in the living room, but then you stepped out of the shower stall." She paused, muttered some profanity. "Okay, maybe I gawked a little before I turned around."

Marco smiled, and just like that, he felt as if some of the heavy weight had flown right off his shoulders. Lana was here, and just seeing her made him feel better. At least it did until he realized she probably wouldn't have come unless something had gone wrong.

Maybe something with Benji.

Maybe she'd accepted the idiot clown's proposal.

Before those notions could catch and spread like wildfire, Marco grabbed a towel and wrapped it around his waist. That was the best he could do to cover up since all of his clothes were in the bedroom and he didn't own a robe. And besides, he didn't mind being nearly naked around Lana. It also gave him a cheap thrill to know that she had indeed caught a glimpse of his bare ass.

"I just got back from another doctor's appointment with my granddad," she explained. "They scheduled the bypass for Monday."

So, five days from now. Not long at all. Then again, it hadn't been long—only forty-eight hours—since Benji had dropped his health-scare bombshell and told them about his ranch troubles. So much had happened in those hours. Not just adjusting to Benji's medical condition, either. But also the kiss at the police station followed by the make-out session. And her ex's proposal.

"Are you marrying your asshole ex?" he came out and asked.

She whipped around to face him, and he saw the frown on her face. Or maybe it was a scowl. "No. I told Nolan thanks but no thanks."

It was sort of dangerous, feeling as much relief as he did. That relief made Marco want to go to Lana and haul her into his arms. Considering that he was wearing only a towel, that probably wasn't a good idea.

Or maybe it was.

If he took her in his arms now, they'd have sex, and while he was very much looking forward to that, it was obvious that Lana had come here to give him an update. He wanted her to finish that before he started anything else.

He was thinking about starting with her neck.

Then working his way down.

And speaking of down, that was where Lana's gaze drifted. Down to his chest. To the towel.

She swallowed hard and shook her head as if to clear it. Marco wanted to tell her that head shaking wasn't going to fix what was stirring between them, but he decided to give her a few more minutes to come to that conclusion.

"Uh, Granddad nixed the trust idea," she said, her voice a little breathy. "He said it would be like skirting over his promise because he'd essentially be leaving the place to me."

That was exactly the news that Marco had expected, but it did cool him down a little. Clearly, the trust would have been the easiest fix for the ranch, and now they had to move to the yet undetermined plan B. Or maybe even

C, though Marco doubted Lana wanted him to get her pregnant. Saving a ranch wasn't a reason to have a child.

"So, what will you do?" he asked, taking a step toward her. Even though sex wasn't going to solve Benji's situation, it would be satisfying.

And it was inevitable.

Marco knew that when he went closer to Lana and she didn't retreat. She definitely didn't give him any signals to back off. Just the opposite. A silky feminine sigh left her mouth. The sound of arousal. Arousal flushed her cheeks, too, but the clincher was when she licked her lips. He seriously doubted she'd done that because they were dry.

He moved in even more, sliding his hand around the back of her neck and easing her closer. In the same motion, he put his mouth on the very lips she'd just licked. The taste of her jolted through him, making him want her even more, something that Marco hadn't thought possible. Because he already wanted her so much that his body was a hard ache.

Emphasis on the *hard*.

"Should we be doing this?" Lana asked, mumbling around the kiss, but she immediately added, "Don't answer that."

He wouldn't. They both knew it was a stupid idea, with so many things unsettled between them, but it was going to happen anyway. And it was apparently going to happen fast. Lana saw to that when she started touching him. First his chest. Then his stomach.

Then lower.

She grabbed the towel to get it off him, and it dropped to the floor. Now she stepped back just a little, her gaze sliding over him. Drinking him in. Marco did some drinking in of his own and decided that Lana had on way too many clothes.

He did something about that. While grabbing another kiss, he caught onto the bottom of her dress and shucked it off her. It landed near his towel and left her nearly naked.

Her bra was barely there, and with her breath gusting, her breasts were practically spilling out of the cups. Marco helped with that, too, by pushing down the swatch of lace and doing something he hadn't done to her in a decade. He kissed her breasts and took her nipple into his mouth.

She approved.

He could tell from her gasp of pleasure, and when she fisted her hands in his hair to anchor him in place. Not that he was going anywhere. And besides, he could shimmy down her panties while he continued to tongue kiss her breasts.

"You'd better have a condom," she muttered.

He did have some, but there weren't any in the bathroom. That was why he started moving her backward into his bedroom. It wasn't easy to do since he wasn't watching where they were going. Nor was he willing to give up the breast kisses. That was the reason he banged his shoulder and elbow a couple of times, but he finally managed to maneuver them in the direction of the bed. They landed on it in a tumbled heap with him on top of her.

"Condom," she repeated, and she wrapped her legs around him. She also must have decided to increase the urgency and fire because she ground herself against his erection.

Once Marco got his eyes uncrossed, he fumbled around, located the nightstand and took a condom from the drawer. He got it on as fast as he could, which would have been a whole lot faster if Lana hadn't tried to help him. Her help darn near resulted in a hand job before he finally got suited up.

He checked her expression, to see if there were any second thoughts about this. There were none. And clearly she was still in the hurry mode because Lana latched on to his hips and pushed him inside her.

She immediately went still, and their gazes connected. She was tight, wet and perfect. So perfect that his vision blurred a little. He had to focus to see her face. It was perfect, too. And he saw the hungry need in her eyes. A hunger that Marco was sure was in his, as well.

Keeping his gaze on her, he started to move inside her, watching her take him in. Watching the pleasure build. Marco kept the pace as slow as he could. Drawing out the moments. Savoring this.

Savoring Lana.

It'd been a long time since he'd had her in his bed, but it was like coming home. Coming home with intense heat, that was. Heat was definitely going to have a big say in this, and the slow pace had to go. The need drove them faster, faster.

Deeper.

Until he felt the climax slam through Lana. That in turn caused the pleasure to slam through him. He held back as long as he could, savoring every moment of what she was giving him. Before he let himself go.

As soon as he could, Marco adjusted his weight to his elbows so that he wouldn't be crushing her, and they lay there, coming back to earth while their breathing leveled. He finally managed to look down at her and kiss her.

"Did this have anything to do with plan B?" he joked.

He immediately wished he hadn't attempted to go light.

Because he saw something in her eyes. Not the aftereffects of sated passion. But something he didn't want to see there.

Regret.

Hell. He'd figured that wouldn't set in until she'd at least had some thinking time. Apparently, though, Lana was a fast thinker.

"I don't deserve you," she said, her voice thick and void of any trace of the heat that'd just flared between them.

"Is that like a compliment?" he asked, not at all sure what this was. It sounded more like the start of a brush-off.

She stared at him a long time, and despite him still being inside her, the intimacy between them vanished. She moved, his signal to get off her, so that was what Marco did. He landed on the bed next to her.

"It wasn't a compliment," he concluded.

She turned, touching his face and sliding her fingers down his cheek. "You're an amazing man, and I don't deserve you." Lana got up and headed for his bathroom, saying the rest of what she had to say with her back to him. "I can never forgive myself for what I did."

CHAPTER FIVE

LANA GATHERED HER clothes as quickly as she could, and clutching them to her, she hurried to the guest room just up the hall so that Marco would be able to use his own bathroom.

And so that she'd have a minute or two to gather her thoughts.

Of course, she didn't need time to know that having sex with Marco had been a mistake. One that'd felt amazing, but it wasn't fair to him. Not with the past swooping in on her. So many mistakes and regrets, and she didn't want to risk putting Marco through something like that again.

She dressed and freshened up in the guest bath, and taking a deep breath that she was certain she'd need, Lana went into the living room. Marco wasn't there, but she immediately spotted him in the kitchen. He was dressed, mostly, in jeans and an unbuttoned shirt, and he was sipping a beer. He was also eyeing her as if waiting for her to explain what her hasty bedroom exit had been about.

"I don't regret the sex," she told him right off. "I should, but I don't."

The corner of his mouth lifted in a chrome-melting smile. "No regrets on my part, either." He didn't add more, didn't ask her what was wrong. Marco just waited for her to continue.

Lana would, but she went to the fridge and helped herself to a beer. She wasn't much of a drinker, especially when it came to beer, but she thought she might need a few sips of liquid courage to get through this.

"Are you up to a really bad walk down memory lane?" she asked.

He didn't smile this time but nodded without hesitation. "Will it explain why you were in a rush to leave my bed?"

It would. But it wasn't going to fix anything between them. It was the reason she hadn't had this particular heart-to-heart with him sooner. Plus, it was going to bring a lot of pain to the surface.

"When I found out I was pregnant," she started, "it threw me for a loop. I mean, I was on the pill, and we were careful."

"It threw me for a loop, too," Marco replied when she didn't jump in to add anything else.

She nodded because she'd known that it had. He had so much on his plate with the ranch, trying to run it by himself, and the last thing he'd likely wanted to add to that was taking care of a family.

"But you adjusted," Lana pointed out. She took a sip of beer because her throat suddenly felt as dry as dust. "Within a couple of hours, you were making plans." Actually, she believed he'd been over the moon at the prospect of fatherhood.

"Did those plans upset you?" he asked.

"Yes," she admitted. "Because it took me more than a few hours to start to believe we could make it work. During that time, I was wishing that I hadn't gotten pregnant."

He kept his gaze on her face, studying her, and he shook his head. "I think that's a normal response, Lana."

"Maybe." And this part was going to be so hard to say. So hard for him to hear. "But after I miscarried, the guilt and regret came." In fact, it had come like a flash flood.

Marco stayed quiet a few long moments. "You left me because you felt guilty over losing the baby?"

"I left you because I couldn't live with the guilt. I never blamed you for what happened. I blamed myself, and if I'd just taken more precautions, I might not have lost the baby."

"Precautions?" he questioned without hesitating. "Like what?"

"I don't know." She groaned and set the beer aside. It wasn't settling well in her stomach. "Maybe bed rest or figuring out a way to lessen the stress."

Marco put down his beer, too, and took her by the shoulders. "That's BS. Women miscarry babies and not because of anything the mother did wrong. I read about it," he added when she stared at him. "Sometimes, miscarriages just happen."

She didn't know why that surprised her. Of course he would have read about it, because he would have wanted to know what went wrong. He would have tried to figure out how to help her.

Except she hadn't let him even try.

"When I looked at you back then," she went on, "all I could see was the grief." Her eyes stung, but she blinked back the tears. "And even though you never blamed me, being around you was a reminder that I failed. That I couldn't keep our baby safe."

Marco groaned, cursed softly and then gathered her into his arms. He brushed a kiss on the top of her head, but

Lana didn't feel as if she deserved the kiss or the comfort he was trying to give her.

"I was scared spitless when you told me you were pregnant," he said. His voice was as soft and gentle as the strokes he was making on her back. "Maybe I should have let you see just how scared I was, but I was trying to be strong for you."

"You were strong," she admitted. Lana looked up at him. "And you would have forgiven me if I'd asked. I just didn't think I had the right to ask."

"You had the right," he assured her. "It wasn't needed, but the right was yours."

He put his fingers beneath her chin and lifted it, forcing eye contact. She had won the battle with the tears, but she wasn't sure how long that would last. However, Lana was certain of one thing. That being here with Marco like this had helped. Making love with him had helped, too. But it didn't fix their problems with Benji and the ranch.

Marco leaned down to brush a kiss on her mouth, and despite the raw emotion, she felt another flicker of heat. Heat that he would have no doubt stoked into something hotter had there not been a knock at his door.

He scowled, checked the time. "I wasn't expecting anyone, but I'll get rid of whoever it is."

Lana certainly wasn't going to argue with him about that, especially after he kissed her again. Cursing, he finally pulled away from her and went to the front door to throw it open. The gruff "greeting" that he'd likely intended, though, faded because it was Benji on the porch. And he wasn't alone.

Nolan was right behind him.

She snapped back her shoulders in surprise and hurried to join Marco at the door. Lana saw Nolan's car and her grandfather's truck in the driveway. The doctor had said it was okay for Benji to drive, but Lana wished he'd called her so she could have gone back to the ranch to see what this was all about.

"This fella came by looking for you," Benji told her. "Said it was real important, so I brought him over."

Nolan stepped up, extending his hand to Marco. "I'm Nolan Devane. Lana's probably told you about me."

"Yeah, she mentioned you," Marco fired back, and there wasn't even a trace of friendliness in his tone.

Something, maybe annoyance, flickered through Nolan's eyes, and Lana thought this could quickly turn into some kind of pissing contest.

"Why did you want to talk to me?" Lana asked Nolan, and she took her grandfather's arm to move him out of the heat and into the house. Of course, that also meant Nolan coming in, as well.

Nolan attempted a smile before he aimed a dismissive glance at Marco. "We should speak alone. It's personal."

"Uh, I'm thinking it's personal between Marco and Lana," Benji pointed out, and he gave them a once-over.

Lana was almost positive her clothes were askew. Marco's certainly were. Heck, his jeans weren't even fully zipped. And her grandfather didn't seem to have any trouble figuring out what was going on.

Not Nolan, though. He appeared to be oblivious to the vibes in the room.

"Why did you want to talk to me?" Lana repeated, hoping it would spur Nolan to say his piece and then leave.

Nolan hesitated, but he finally nodded. "I guess it's okay if Marco and your granddad know. I mean, they'd find out soon enough. You mentioned the deal with the ranch, that only a male heir can inherit it." He smiled again. "Well, I'm your heir. Or at least I will be if you marry me."

"Marry you?" she repeated, though she wasn't sure how she managed it with her throat clamped shut. "I've already told you no, and I haven't changed my mind."

Nolan's smile widened. "Well, you should definitely re-think it. A yes to my proposal would fix your problem, and it'll give you a ready-made family. I know how much you care for Matthew, and he could officially be your stepson."

She did indeed care for Matthew and had once thought she could be his stepmom. But any notion of that had ended when Nolan and she had broken up.

"You'd be doing me a favor with this marriage," Nolan pressed. "Matthew's already attached to you, and you could step in and help me raise him."

That last part was code for her doing all the stuff for Matthew that Nolan didn't want to do. But her stepping in wasn't the right thing. Matthew had a mother who loved him, and he had a father who shouldn't pawn off father-hood on anyone else.

"You can't marry him," her grandfather and Marco said at the same time.

She would have assured them that she had no inten-tions of that, but Benji continued before she could speak.

"I'd rather break my promise," Benji insisted, "than have you marry a man you didn't love."

Lana stared at him a moment. "Only a couple of days ago you wanted me to marry Marco," she pointed out.

Her grandfather shrugged. "You love Marco. Always have."

She opened her mouth to deny it. But couldn't. Because it was true. And it didn't have anything to do with the great sex they'd just had. Well, not much to do with it, anyway.

Great sex never hurt, but that was only a nice bonus. The real prize here was Marco.

Figuring that Marco would be stunned by what Benji had just said, Lana turned to him to give him an out. She didn't want him to feel trapped into doing something simply because her grandfather had made her see the truth. However, there was no time for an out, either, because Marco hooked his arm around her, dragged her to him and kissed her. This wasn't a reassuring peck, either. This was meant to send the heat inside her soaring.

And it worked.

Despite their audience, it worked just fine.

When Marco finally let go of her, she had lost her breath but not her mind. In fact, everything suddenly seemed crystal clear.

"I love you," she said, but her words were sort of drowned out because at the same time Marco said, "I love you."

Despite her shock over hearing him say that, Lana smiled. It was probably a goofy, giddy grin, but she didn't care. Marco loved her, and she loved him. It didn't matter that it'd taken them so long to get to this point. It didn't matter that being in love didn't fix all their problems. But it was a start.

And that was why Lana kissed him.

The kiss continued until she heard someone clear their throat. A reminder that she needed to deal with Nolan and her grandfather before she could coax Marco back to bed to celebrate. Lana didn't believe much coaxing would be needed, though, because he had a goofy grin, too.

She looked at Nolan, expecting to see some anger on his face. There was a little, but it was minimal. More annoyance at her not fixing things so he wouldn't have to be inconvenienced by his son.

"I won't marry you," Lana said. "But I'll talk to Matthew and tell him that he can still call or visit me whenever he wants. And I'm sure you'll reassure him that you'll be there for him, as well."

A muscle flickered in Nolan's jaw. "I just wanted to do you a favor, and I can see that favor's not needed. Have a good life, Lana." With that crisp farewell, Nolan turned and walked out.

Her grandfather dipped his head but not before she saw his sly smile. Lana wanted to snarl at him for putting this into motion. She didn't like being manipulated. But more than snarling, she wanted to thank him. Without his nudge, she might not have come back to Lone Star Ridge this week.

She brushed a kiss on Benji's cheek and then pulled back to face him. "This doesn't mean you'll get your male heir. I love Marco, but I won't marry him to save the ranch."

Lana expected an argument from him on that. Maybe one from Marco, too, but he simply stepped to her side. "Ditto," he told Benji.

That got the smile off her grandfather's face. "But if you love each other—" He stopped and waved that off. His smile returned when Marco put his arm around her. "All right, being in love is plenty enough. All I want is for the two of you to be happy, and it's obvious you are."

"I am," Lana verified.

"So am I." Marco kissed her again, and when he pulled back, he looked down at her. "I'm hoping you can be around a lot?"

"Plenty. I'm adjusting my schedule so I'll only have to commute once or twice a week to my office. I'll be around so much you'll get sick and tired of me."

"Never," Marco assured her. He snared her gaze and held it. "Never," he repeated.

Benji cleared his throat again. "I'll get out of here so you can...celebrate."

He turned to leave, but Lana pulled herself out of her love trance and stepped in front of him. "I'll drive you back," she insisted. "Then I can come back here for the *celebration*."

"I'll follow you two in my truck so I can bring Lana back with me," Marco quickly offered.

Benji nodded and started for the door again. Once again, Lana stopped him. "You're not upset that you might lose the ranch?"

He immediately shook his head. "Nope. Because I came up with plan B." Benji gave Marco's arm a pat. "I'll adopt Marco."

"Adopt him?" Lana questioned.

Benji nodded. "It's legal. I read about it. An adult can adopt another adult as long as both parties are willing. Then in my will, I'll leave the ranch to both of you. I won't be breaking my promise because Marco will become my male heir, and I won't be asking either of you to keep up that old-fashioned notion of only men inheriting the place. Any objections to any of that?"

"None," Marco and she answered in unison.

All in all, it was an amazing plan. They could merge the two ranches along with merging their families.

"But I gotta warn you," Benji added, "you might have to wait for the deed to the ranch because I plan on living for a long, long time."

She stared at him, the tears filling her eyes. Happy tears. She wanted that long, long time with him, too. And with Marco. Finally, she had it all. The right time, the right place and the right men.

Lana turned to Marco and sealed the deal with a long, long kiss.

* * * * *

"Dawson, I'm going to tell you something that you might not be
ready to hear. You deserve to know the truth." Just saying those
words caused her heart to hammer her rib cage.

He set his coffee cup down on the granite countertop and crossed
his arms over his chest like he was bracing himself for the worst.

"I don't know much about your marriage except that I know you
got married on the last day of January." She held her hand up to
stop him from speaking before he could respond because she could
already see the questions forming in his eyes. "I was honest before.
I haven't been in an accident or had any kind of head trauma."

"Then what?"

Speaking the words out loud was proving to be so much harder
than saying them in her head. She was trying to think of a way to

ease him into the news rather than blurt it out and completely shock him. "There's a really good reason why I don't know anything about this house or the life we shared together other than the fact that I know it was brief."

"Well, then, you need to clue me in because I have no idea how you could forget the fact that you never lived in this house. You looked at Laurel like you've never seen her before and yet the two of you used to work side by side and talk for hours."

"I'm sorry. I'm seeing how difficult all of this is for you—"

"You can spare me your sympathy, Autumn. Just tell me the truth."

"Well, then, let's start right there. My name is not Autumn." She held up the necklace and took a step toward him, noticing how the grooves in his forehead deepened. "My name is Summer."

"You lied to me?" He gripped the edge of the counter like he needed to ground himself.

"No, I didn't. I've never met you before in my life. You were married to my identical twin sister."

Don't miss
Texas Target by Barb Han,
available November 2020 wherever
Harlequin Intrigue books and ebooks are sold.

Harlequin.com

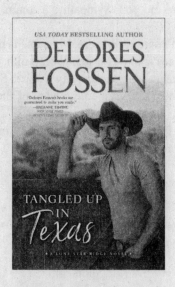

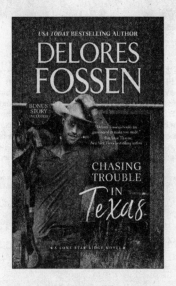

Get 4 FREE REWARDS!

We'll send you 2 FREE Books <u>plus</u> 2 FREE Mystery Gifts.

FREE
Value Over
$20

Both the **Romance** and **Suspense** collections feature compelling novels written by many of today's bestselling authors.

YES! Please send me 2 FREE novels from the Essential Romance or Essential Suspense Collection and my 2 FREE gifts (gifts are worth about $10 retail). After receiving them, if I don't wish to receive any more books, I can return the shipping statement marked "cancel." If I don't cancel, I will receive 4 brand-new novels every month and be billed just $7.24 each in the U.S. or $7.49 each in Canada. That's a savings of up to 28% off the cover price. It's quite a bargain! Shipping and handling is just 50¢ per book in the U.S. and $1.25 per book in Canada.* I understand that accepting the 2 free books and gifts places me under no obligation to buy anything. I can always return a shipment and cancel at any time. The free books and gifts are mine to keep no matter what I decide.

Choose one: ☐ **Essential Romance**
(194/394 MDN GQ6M)

☐ **Essential Suspense**
(191/391 MDN GQ6M)

Name (please print)

Address   Apt. #

City   State/Province   Zip/Postal Code

Email: Please check this box ☐ if you would like to receive newsletters and promotional emails from Harlequin Enterprises ULC and its affiliates. You can unsubscribe anytime.

> Mail to the **Reader Service:**
> **IN U.S.A.:** P.O. Box 1341, Buffalo, NY 14240-8531
> **IN CANADA:** P.O. Box 603, Fort Erie, Ontario L2A 5X3

Want to try 2 free books from another series? Call 1-800-873-8635 or visit www.ReaderService.com.

*Terms and prices subject to change without notice. Prices do not include sales taxes, which will be charged (if applicable) based on your state or country of residence. Canadian residents will be charged applicable taxes. Offer not valid in Quebec. This offer is limited to one order per household. Books received may not be as shown. Not valid for current subscribers to the Essential Romance or Essential Suspense Collection. All orders subject to approval. Credit or debit balances in a customer's account(s) may be offset by any other outstanding balance owed by or to the customer. Please allow 4 to 6 weeks for delivery. Offer available while quantities last.

Your Privacy—Your information is being collected by Harlequin Enterprises ULC, operating as Reader Service. For a complete summary of the information we collect, how we use this information and to whom it is disclosed, please visit our privacy notice located at corporate.harlequin.com/privacy-notice. From time to time we may also exchange your personal information with reputable third parties. If you wish to opt out of this sharing of your personal information, please visit readerservice.com/consumerschoice or call 1-800-873-8635. **Notice to California Residents**—Under California law, you have specific rights to control and access your data. For more information on these rights and how to exercise them, visit corporate.harlequin.com/california-privacy.

STRS20MAX